Wampum Nation

Wampum Nation

John Moynihan

Xlibris Corporation
1-888-795-4274
www.Xlibris.com
Orders@Xlibris.com
98322

To Bill Norton

And you'll never hear the wolf cry to the blue corn moon.
For whether we are white or copper-skinned—
We need to sing with all the voices of the mountain
We need to paint with all the colors of the wind.

—*Pocahontas*
Disney Productions, 1995

Part I

Birth of a Nation

The Lee Side

When he decided to start the Indian tribe, Bill Fletcher was drinking rum punches. He was in the Lee Side in Falmouth, waiting for the 8:15 p.m. ferry to Martha's Vineyard. Divorced for five years, he wasn't what you'd think an Indian chief would look like.

He was a white man who looked like a white man. Good-looking with chiseled features, he had a little swarthiness going for him from the Eastern European genes on his mother's side. It was all he had to help him be an authentic Indian.

"Another Captain and Coke," Fletcher said to the bald young bartender with the tight goatee as he picked up coasters and cash from the heavy oak bar. The bartender nodded back in agreement.

He had his keys and car fob on the bar along with some folded-over bills, mostly ones and fives. He coughed and cleared his throat, then took a sip of his dark Captain Morgan Rum.

He looked up and watched the Red Sox on one of two big flat-screen TVs behind the bar. The color was crisp in HD. The Sox were playing the Tigers and were up 3-2 in the fourth. Halfway through May, it was a beautiful spring night at Fenway. Daisuke Matsuzaka had struck out four by the fourth and was looking strong.

Fletcher looked to his right at the woman on the barstool next to him. She had shoulder-length brown hair and a blue T-shirt on. She had just ordered a glass of white wine and was checking her iPhone as she waited for her drink. She had five or six thin silver bracelets on her left wrist. They were both killing time waiting for the ferry to arrive.

Fletcher watched her check her messages, using her finger to swipe the screen, tapping as she went. She was deeply immersed in the device and didn't notice him looking at her from the side. The soft light from the device highlighted her features. He noticed that she was attractive with a grown-up look. Fletcher was a talker, and he wasted no time.

"How ya doin'?" he said casually as her wine came, and she took a sip.

She put her iPhone down on the bar and looked over at him before she answered. She was used to men talking to her, coming on, and making the first move. She could hold her own in any conversation though.

"I'm doing good," she said. "It's a beautiful night out."

"Yeah, it is. And the Sox are winning. How lucky are we?" Fletcher said.

She smiled and then looked up at the screen to see the score. "It's too early in the season for me to follow them yet. I'm a fair-weather fan."

"We all are. Otherwise, the Sox will break your heart."

She took a sip of her white wine.

"Bill Fletcher."

She looked at him again and decided to engage. She would be leaving in twenty minutes when the ferry came, so she wouldn't be trapped if the conversation didn't go well.

"Carrie Nation."

"Huh?"

"I said Carrie."

Bill Fletcher looked over at her and cocked his head. "Carrie Nation wouldn't be sitting at a bar having a glass of white wine. She'd be busting it up."

She smiled. Few people ever picked up on her name. The Carrie Nation thing. But Bill Fletcher did. And that suddenly made him interesting enough to talk to.

"It's true. That's my name."

"C'mon. Don't bullshit me. Carrie Nation was a temperance freak who went in and destroyed barrooms with a hatchet back in the 1800s. Crazy shit."

"You're right. How'd you know?"

"I like American history."

"So I changed my name to Carrie Nation in college. I just liked the sound of it. It flows right. Some girls got tattoos, some girls got piercings. Some girls screwed the hockey team. I got a name change. It was easier and didn't hurt as much."

Fletcher was intrigued now. He had never met a woman who had a fake name. She seemed confident, though, like she knew what she was doing. Not a crazy fringe type.

Carrie took the offensive.

"So what do you do?"

"I'm a lawyer," Bill Fletcher said.

"Oh shit. Sounds boring already. Is it?" She looked at him.

Fletcher took a sip of his rum drink, tasted the cool sweetness of the Coke with the liquor mixed in. He thought about it before he answered.

"It can be. It often is. It pays the bills, mostly," Fletcher said. "I thought about going to law school at one time but then decided that it wasn't for me. I didn't want to spend the money."

"Yeah, you were smart."

Fletcher nodded. "So what do you do?"

"Retail. I own a store on the Vineyard."

"Oh yeah? What kind of store?"

"A hippie gift shop."

David Ortiz hit a home run with men on first and second, and the bar erupted. Carrie turned back to Fletcher and asked, "So what kind of law do you do?"

Fletcher watched Carrie as she was distracted for a second, standing up in her tight jeans. She was in good shape. He was impressed that she knew enough to ask what kind of law he did. He also knew to be careful or he'd turn her off completely if he said something boring like litigation or some other corporate bullshit.

"Immigration law. And Indians. I do Indian law too." He threw that in to make it sound more interesting. He did, in fact, do immigration law, working from a small shared office on Summer Street in Boston. He could do all the basics like file an H1B visa application or a green card permit. He was very good at the routine residency stuff.

"What's that about?" Carrie Nation asked. She had bright-green eyes and was curious. Fletcher had picked up on her name immediately and maybe did something that was different, not just run-of-the-mill lawyering.

She turned to look at him before he answered. She had a tight T-shirt on that said Black Eyed Peas World Tour that showed off her assets. She gave him a front-on shot so he'd notice. She didn't need to as Fletcher already picked up on it.

"The Indians or the immigration?"

"The Indians."

"Well, I do tribal stuff. Enabling documentation, working with the federal government and state agencies. There's a lot of legal work to be Indian in this state."

"You going over to work with the Indians on the Vineyard? There's a lot of 'em over there, right?" Carrie said as she took another sip of her wine.

"No. I'm going over to fish this weekend, over in Oak Bluffs."

"I keep forgetting what their name is," she said.

"Who?"

"The Indians. On the Island. It's a funny name, you know."

By this time, Fletcher's new drink had come. The bartender wiped the area clean in front of him and put the fresh rum and Coke down. He took a sip.

"The Fluevogs. That's the tribe on the Vineyard."

"Yeah, that's it. How do you say it?"

"Flue-vog." Bill Fletcher pronounced it slowly and phonetically so Carrie could understand it. "Like eggnog. They've been down there forever."

Carrie smiled and drank her wine. "How'd you get interested in Indians anyway?"

Fletcher paused and swirled the swizzle stick in his drink, moving the small square chunks of ice around, getting the drink good and cold.

"Well, I'm part Indian. That's how I got interested." He glanced over at her. "Yeah, that's right. I'm Indian, but just some."

Carrie looked critically this time at Bill Fletcher. She was looking for high cheekbones or some other Indian marker. She didn't see any. She saw a white guy in his early forties with longish dark hair trying to hit on her. And that was it. Nothing at all emanating from the Plains or the Dakotas.

"How much Indian are you?" Carrie asked a little suspiciously. "'Cause you don't look Indian to me, not even a little bit." She looked over his face carefully as she spoke. "Honestly, you look like a white guy."

That was Bill Fletcher's first time telling anybody that he was an Indian, a test run, so he was sailing in unchartered waters. He knew he had to perfect his pitch, get it better.

"Look, I don't need to look like Sitting Bull to be an Indian. It's like being Czech or Hungarian for Chrissake. I just am. It's all a melting pot in America anyway."

Carrie Nation thought about it for a minute. She decided that Bill Fletcher was a bullshitter, bottom line. She let him go with it. She'd heard much more outrageous things anyway by guys wanting to get close to her.

She looked at him again, at his cheekbones this time, and decided that maybe they were higher than normal and bigger, and maybe he did have a strain of Indian in him after all.

"So that's cool if you are. I understand. How much Indian are you anyway?"

Fletcher had to lie on the run. He hadn't fully baked the Indian tale yet, so he didn't know how much lineage sounded right. Too much and he would have to really start looking like an Indian to be believable. Too little, and people would pass him off as a fake, a "wash ashore," as the Islanders called tourists posing as Islanders. He had to bring it in right in the middle somewhere.

"A quarter. I'm a quarter Indian." He took a big pull of his rum and Coke, then put it down on the bar. "Twenty-five percent Injun is what I am." "Injun, huh?" Carrie said skeptically as she listened to him. "Just like Tom Sawyer?"

She decided that Fletcher's eyes, full and big and brown, were maybe Indian looking too. "That's enough. That's almost like the real deal."

Before Fletcher could answer, she got distracted as her iPhone vibrated on the bar and lit up. "Excuse me," she said. She picked it up, thumbed the screen, and began talking on the phone.

Bill turned back to his drink and the Sox on the flatscreen. He checked his Blackberry.

Ten minutes later, the ferry boat arrived at the dock, slipping snug into its berth under a bright canopy of lights. He watched the deckhands position then lock down the car ramp through the window of the Lee Side. His view was perfect. He didn't have to move at all.

In a minute, Toyotas, Subaru Outbacks, and pickup trucks streamed off the big white boat in a long slow line. He watched the cars and people swarm off.

It was time to go. Carrie got up, and Bill Fletcher stood to say good-bye and maybe get her phone number.

"Hey, good luck with the Indians and all. I hope it works out," Carrie said. She picked up her overnight bag from the floor and smiled at Fletcher.

The bar was dark, and he moved back to give her some room to pass by. He was going to try to get her cell number, maybe stop by her store.

As he backed up, he didn't see the golden retriever lying at the foot of the table behind him. People with dogs always came to the Lee Side.

He accidently stepped on the dog's paw as he moved backward. The dog yelped and jumped up in pain. Fletcher was jarred and swung to his left. He couldn't catch his balance in time though and flailed his arms in the air to get stabilized. He fell over backward on an empty chair behind him.

Carrie Nation didn't hang around to help. She thought Bill Fletcher was either drunk or a dork or possibly both. Either way, she didn't like the alternatives. She walked quickly out of the bar toward the boat, met some friends on the ramp, and quickly forgot about the bogus Indian in the Lee Side.

It took Bill Fletcher a minute to get himself up off the floor and regroup. The dog was okay. He convinced the bartender that he was all right too. He paid his bar tab and slunk out into the warm Falmouth night. He composed himself under the cover of darkness behind the floodlit arcs of the Steamship Authority dock as he headed toward the boat.

His coming out as an Indian hadn't gone well.

Bingo

It was Saturday morning on the Vineyard in Oak Bluffs.

Father Peter Mulcahey, a good-looking Irish Catholic priest from County Cork, was nursing a cup of coffee from Kona Koffee. He could have been a politician. Margaret Wellington sat across from him drinking chai tea.

He was the parish priest at Blessed Sacrament Church and from there he covered Oak Bluffs, Vineyard Haven, and Edgartown. Three parishes crammed with Catholics, it was a lot of work. The bishop in Fall River bootstrapped it by keeping one active church along with one rectory to house Father Peter and the two other priests who were there for summer sabbatical.

"So how much did we make on Friday bingo, Margaret?"

Father Mulcahey was dressed in a short-sleeve black shirt and a standard-issue dog collar. He had on clean black pants that he held up with a belt from Menemsha Blues that had small blue-striped bass in outline, swimming around his waist.

He wore a big Timex Triathlon watch that he got from a parishioner whose husband had died from a brain aneurysm. His arms were muscular and covered in dark Irish hair that grew like thatch on his skin. He scratched his right hand as he looked at Margaret Wellington and listened.

"We made over seven hundred and fifty dollars on Saturday night, Father. It was unbelievable. We almost had to turn them away at the door." Margaret Wellington smiled and sat back in her chair. She was a sharp no-nonsense Wellesley educated woman who had immigrated to the Vineyard about seven years ago.

She had come down with her husband, Jed Stevens, the architect. Originally her passion had been oil painting scenes of the Vineyard, routine things like the beach and the ferry dock and the seagulls. She wasn't very good, and her paintings looked like the old paint-by-numbers pictures that were popular fifty years ago.

But Jed had unfortunately died from pancreatic cancer within two years of their arrival, a fast and lethal variety, and she ended up putting away her paints and her easels when she took up hospice care.

She had found the Catholic Church to her liking along the way. It had been there for her when Jed got sick. She had always gone to church early on when they were first married, and now it was a safe haven, a port in a storm for her. She had a daughter named Julie who was off at college, so she had a lot of time on her hands to donate as a new widow.

Margaret Wellington was smart. She had a passion for reading and literature and had a high energy level. She had a head for numbers and helped Father Peter do the books for the parish. She had just dived into it with the bingo.

She was also very attractive in a natural Vineyard sort of way, with a bright smile and auburn hair that she wore shoulder length. Everything was soft and curvaceous about her.

She inhaled, satisfied with the money coming into the parish coffers from the night before, and her breasts swelled with pride against the powder blue cotton of her Lacoste shirt. Peter Mulcahey noticed her chest rise up, and Margaret noticed him noticing.

She felt it, like a flash of lightning on a hot summer night, an electrical storm on the distant horizon with light but no thunder. It was too far away. She kept the pose for a second, then exhaled, her breasts slowly deflating. She shivered with a spark of unholy attraction. They both did. She quickly put it aside, and they got back to business.

"Praise the Lord, Margaret. We need the money." Peter Mulcahey punctuated his thought with a big sip of coffee.

"Is it still that bad?" Margaret asked, looking concerned.

"That bad? The bishop told Father Abutu last week that we had to cut expenses by 30 percent this year or we'd be out of business. How's that? Like we're a fudge store on Main Street."

Father Peter frowned. He was frustrated that the bigwig priests that ran the diocese were all focused on money. That was all they talked about now whenever they got together.

Margaret, always upbeat, dragged the conversation back to the positive. "Father, we're doing great now. The bingo has gone well, really much better than we expected, and we're gaining some momentum. We even had a few Episcopalians there last night." She smiled.

"Really? How did you know?"

"I know some of the ladies from the church in Edgartown, and they knew the women. We lunch together."

Peter Mulcahey looked over at Margaret. She had on khaki slacks and black summer flats with little gold ornaments on the front over her toes. He noticed her, and with his politician's charisma, she was attracted to him. He made things interesting.

"That's good," the priest said. "Keep up your proselytizing for the church, and we'll make you a nun. If we can make inroads into the Episcopalians, we'll increase our take by $500 a week."

"That would help us a lot. We could pay off the oil bill from Smith's pretty soon. Before the winter comes."

"Don't worry about the oil bill, Margaret. The Lord will provide."

Peter Mulcahey knew that Frank Smith's daughter Karen, a junior at Martha's Vineyard Regional Tech, had got knocked up by the star quarterback, who was Phil Wright's son. Filthy Phil. Peter Mulcahey was not surprised. The apple didn't fall far from the tree.

Karen got the abortion quickly, and then she and her mother, good Catholics both, had come to him looking for absolution about a month ago. It was a full-on session loaded with tears and emotion right there in the rectory office. Father Peter let it flow.

In the end, he gave each of them each a penance of five Our Fathers and five Hail Marys. Five for Karen getting knocked up by the football player, and five for her mother trying to hide it. If you can't do the time, don't do the crime, he always said.

He learned early on in the priesthood never to give big penances to parishioners as it turned them off. They shut down after three minutes of saying prayers as it was too much work repeating the words and concentrating on their bad personalities. He understood this fact of human nature and kept prayer penances light as a consequence. The easy priest all the way.

In the end, it was Karen's father's oil company, Smith's Texaco, the big Island oil distributor, that would pay the penance anyway. He made a mental note to call Frank Smith this week to remind him about his daughter's abortion and how the parish needed the winter heating bill of $7,500 heavily discounted. He knew that Frank would find Jesus pretty quick when all was said and done.

"You've done great work, Margaret, as usual," Father Peter said. "Is the hall big enough to hold more bingo players as we grow?"

"It's a good question, Father. We can probably fit about ten more tables in there, but if we get really big, we may need to change the venue. But that would be a good thing if it happens."

"Keep your eyes open for other places along the way." Father Peter nodded.

Peter Mulcahey and Margaret Wellington spent another thirty minutes going over the church finances. They talked about electricity bills and FICA withholding tax that Margaret had to make by Friday or they'd be assessed a penalty by the IRS. They didn't have the cash. Peter was irked because he always seemed to have to deal with the nitty-gritty of the bill paying and the accounting. It always came back to that.

He would make a call to Bishop Guerin later that day to get an additional five thousand dollars transferred into their checking account. Father Peter would tell him that the bingo was ramping up and that it was only a bridge loan until more cash started flowing as the summer went on.

He also knew that the bishop wouldn't forget if he was forced to send cash over to support Blessed Sacrament Parish. Bishop Guerin had a mind like a steel trap when it concerned money.

Provenance

Bill Fletcher was glad to be back in his cheap little office on Summer Street in Boston on Monday. It ended up being a quiet weekend on the Vineyard.

He had caught two striped bass on a surf line at Lobsterville at dawn on Sunday. They were both keepers, each over twenty-nine inches, but he ended up releasing both. He held them gently in the water, moving them back and forth, until their gills worked regularly and they were able to swim back out into the deep. He was a good guy, a natural Indian.

Today he was multitasking, busy juggling three green card applications to help pay the rent and get his Indian thing in gear as well. The immigration cases were a hopeless lot. They were for a husband and wife who were both members of the SEU, the office-cleaning union in Boston. They were employed full-time cleaning big office towers as porters during the day. They thought that they could claim legal status since they had full-time jobs and had started the green card process.

It basically broke down at the economics level for Bill Fletcher doing these wayward cases. He would charge the Martinezes $150 each for the filing of the green card application when the process started. The CBP would take the application and then sit on it for about a year. Nothing happened.

Fletcher couldn't bill his clients any more money unless something happened, like a review or a client meeting or responding to a letter. So there were no more fees coming in. At a buck fifty a head to start, he wasn't getting rich anytime soon.

No matter, he thought as he sat looking out on a rusted brown fire escape and three air-conditioning compressors on the flat roof of the building next door. The aluminum fans turned lazily in the breeze under their grill covers. He wasn't depressed in the least. He had other things, all much more profitable, on his plate at that moment. Starbucks coffee on his desk, he had the phone to his ear, waiting for it to connect.

"New World Genealogy. Can I help you?" The line came alive with an energetic voice.

"Yeah, I need my heritage documented."

Fletcher had done some jailhouse legal research in advance of this call, so he sort of knew what he needed.

"What sort of documentation?" the male voice said. "You want our standard family tree for $150? It's a great value."

"What do I get for it?"

"You get a write-up, a family history, and an extended family tree on a 24 × 24 laminate. Guaranteed six generations of relatives. You'll love it."

Fletcher could tell that the guy was experienced, a real pro. He was slipping little genealogy words into the conversation as they talked.

Fletcher had Googled twenty-five genealogy websites to start so that he could sound like he knew what he was talking about. FindYourUKAncestors. com, Your Canadian Roots, the Family Tree, OneBigFamily.com. There were tons of these genealogy services on the web, and they all seemed the same, real hokey.

Fletcher had the nagging feeling that most of these sites were started by crackpot Brits that loved *Masterpiece Theatre* and Prince Charles. They were all fascinated with their ancestry even if it ended up being lame and watered down.

"What's the family tree?" Fletcher asked as he fondled his paper coffee cup and listened, trying to pick up some nuance from the voice on the other end.

"That's the best part and what separates our genealogy searches from everybody else. Ours is copyrighted right off, so it's the real deal. I'll send it to you in pdf format. You can e-mail it around to all your other family members. People love it."

"That sounds good," Fletcher said, keeping the conversation going.

"Yeah, and we've got a frameable version too. No extra charge when you buy the whole package."

"What's on the frameable version?"

"We print it on heavy stock paper and then put your ancestral symbols along the edge, family heritage-type stuff. Things like leprechauns and clay pipes if you're Irish for example. You know, popular images. Archetypes and so forth. It's great for putting the family tree up on the wall in the man cave."

"That's not going to be necessary for my search," Fletcher said. "I don't have a man cave."

"Then no problem. The cheaper version may do you fine." "Well, my situation is a little more complicated. What do you know about Indians on Cape Cod?"

Fletcher then launched into a deep discussion on what it was that he was looking for.

Sam Aston waited until Fletcher was through then jumped on it like a bird dog. "No problem at all. You'll want our customized search including hidden ancestors. We do it all the time. It's $200 extra for the custom package, but it's definitely worth it. We'll find your past."

Fletcher didn't care because these were all short dollars for the start-up Indian tribe he was building.

"Good. I'll take it. I want the report to be full and thorough. When can you send me something?"

"Forty-eight hours, you'll get a draft report in e-mail format, hard copy in the mail a week later."

Fletcher pulled out his credit card and gave his information right there over the phone. Then he hung up and waited to see what Sam Aston would give him as his treasure map for the future.

Jettison the Old

Fletcher was sitting in Boloco, the burrito place on Boylston Street. He had become addicted to the Mexican food over the past winter and ate there two times a week. The burritos were heavy on his constitution though, and he was always fighting the extra pounds around the middle. He hid it under sweaters and loose button-down shirts.

Today he was with Frank Tamara, another lawyer subletting an office in their space. Frank had a stomach problem, as in he had a huge gut. He was at least thirty pounds overweight. He loved to eat, and Fletcher knew it. Whenever they went out for lunch, Fletcher made sure that they went to burrito and sub sandwich-type places, places with huge calorie counts. Fletcher loved exploiting other people's weaknesses.

Fletcher himself was eating a Cajun chicken burrito. He talked between bites.

"Frank, I'm giving you my notice to quit on my office," he said as he swallowed. Small bits of picante sauce were hanging at the corner of his mouth. Frank Tamara noticed it and silently pointed at his chin. Fletcher nodded and dabbed at his mouth with a napkin.

"Why's that?" Frank said, eyes rose slightly, surprised at the news.

"I'm moving down the Vineyard to become an Indian."

"What?"

"Yeah. I'm part Indian. Didn't I tell you?"

Frank Tamara's eyes got wide as he chewed his burrito. He ignored Fletcher's epiphany and got right to the practical.

"Did you ever sign a lease with us? I don't think so. I think you're just a tenant at will with Carol and me. So oral notice is probably good enough, what you're telling me right here. But send me an e-mail after lunch just for the record. You know, keep it clean and all. Cc Carol too, will you?"

Bill Fletcher was slightly amused. "I just told you that I'm changing my life, and you're worried about my damn notice to quit. Are you missing the point or what?"

"Indian? What are you going to do?"

"I'm going to open a store down on the Vineyard, sell trinkets to the tourists. Shit like that." Fletcher took a sip of his Diet Coke, waiting for a reaction.

"That's a helluva game plan. What about your clients? What are you going to do with them?"

"You mean the five or six clients I have, none of whom ever actually pay me for any work I do? You mean those people?"

"Don't get hostile, Bill," Frank said defensively. "I'm just asking. Everybody needs representation."

Frank raised his burrito to his mouth and took a big bite as a punctuation to his thought. A small smattering of oily beans fell directly onto his tie and then tumbled down onto his crotch. He missed it, and Fletcher decided not to mention it.

"Well, I don't have many clients, but the ones I do have, Frank, I'll give to you."

"Are any paying?"

"Some, a little bit. Do you want 'em? You might be able to squeeze out a few hours here and there. Get the cash up front though, or you're screwed."

"What the hell you know about being an Indian anyway?" Frank asked. "I don't see you as an Indian. You're kidding me, right?"

"I didn't either at first. But the idea grew on me. I just commissioned a genealogy report on my Indian heritage this morning. Four hundred bucks. Should be thorough."

"Save it. I don't need to know. Just capture the high points in an e-mail to me. Maybe I'll come visit this summer, and we'll shoot a deer."

Bill Fletcher frowned. Another nonbeliever. He was ready for it though. None of the attorneys in his office had any real-paying clients anyway. That's why it wasn't a law firm, just a group of itinerant lawyers sharing office space and having their own cards.

Fletcher had argued years ago that they do a firm thing with a respectable-sounding name like Fletcher & Tamara. Nobody wanted to spend the money to buy the stationery and then incorporate. Fletcher was ready as he had just gotten divorced and wanted to plunge into the building of a big new law firm. "Why do it if you don't need to?" was all the feedback he got.

Fletcher knew it was the beginning of the end over three years ago, but he ignored it. And this is what he got. Arguing over deadbeat clients in the Boylston Street Boloco with refried beans on Frank Tamara's tie.

"You want them or not? If not, I'll give them to Carol." "No, I'll take them," Frank said. "And thanks. Now what do you know about retail?"

Frank Tamara adjusted his glasses, getting a small greasy fingerprint on the sidepiece. He thought for a second while he chewed and then took a big sip of diet Dr. Pepper. Before Fletcher could answer, he continued. "I didn't know you were Indian, Bill. You look like the most Caucasian Indian I'm ever seen. What tribe are you joining? The Fluevogs?"

"The Neskeets. They're a small subtribe of the Fluevogs. They lived on the Cape a long time ago, intermarried with the Fluevogs, and got lost over time."

Frank shook his head and laughed. "Good luck with that."

Fletcher paused. "Well, it probably won't be any worse than the law business. What could be worse than this?"

They finished their burritos, threw the paper wrappers and cups in the recycling bins, and headed out.

Frank belched as they pushed their way through the glass entrance door and picked a small bit of bean skin from his teeth. He turned to Fletcher when they were on Boylston Street.

"Don't forget to send me that e-mail with your notice. I'm gonna put your office on Craigslist this afternoon. Pronto. You know Carol will shit if we don't rent it quick. The overhead."

Indian Office

Bill Fletcher got up early the next day and took the 8:00 a.m. ferry over to the Vineyard for a reconnaissance mission.

He was standing in an empty office on the second floor of a tired building on Main Street in Oak Bluffs. Main Street had all the honky-tonk retail in the town, from fudge shops to African clothes. It was a fitting place for a tribal office.

Fletcher had ditched his khaki pants and Docksiders. He had on faded jeans and a broken-in black leather jacket, biker style, with short zippers at the wrists. They were up, giving him some room to check his watch and put his hands in his pockets to jiggle his car keys if he needed to.

He was starting to put his plan into action. The first thing was to shed all the vestiges of the old lawyer life in Boston. That meant chucking the whale belts, the khaki pants, and the blue button-down shirts that he owned. He had to change his wardrobe to Indian and live the part.

Fletcher moved the miniblinds in the window with his finger and looked down at all the activity on the street below. The locals and early season tourists were having breakfast at Carol Ann's across the street. It was one weekend away from Memorial Day, the start of the summer season, and the buzz was in the air.

"How much for the space?" Fletcher turned and asked the real estate broker standing over at the electrical panel, fiddling with the lights. Marty Schatz looked up just as he hit the right breaker, and the fluorescent lights came on, bathing the room in bright white light. "Twelve hundred a month, plus utilities," Marty said, no hesitation.

He had his hands resting easy in his tan barn coat. It was a clean new one, the kind that a hip real estate broker would wear to look like a local. But Fletcher could tell that Marty wasn't an outdoorsman, just a broker trying to make a living.

Bill Fletcher thought about the price before he answered. "How long's it been empty?"

The agent thought for a second, doing mental arithmetic. "Eighteen months, maybe two years."

"Why so long ? It seems like good space," Fletcher said.

"Everybody's working out of their house now, saving money. They bring in a cable for the Internet, there's no need for an office, and right off the bat, they save all that rent money."

Fletcher sized up the real estate agent. He was probably forty with shortish hair and clean-cut looks, trying to make a buck.

"Yeah, I hear you. Saving money is definitely the way."

"What are you going to do with the space?" Marty needed to qualify his prospect, and he had to do it now. He had another showing in thirty minutes, at 11:30 a.m., over in Vineyard Haven. Time was short.

"I'm going to open an office. I'm Indian, and this is going to be our tribal office. Administration, Indian affairs, all the management stuff." Bill Fletcher was getting more comfortable saying it now.

The rental agent's antenna went up immediately. He was suspicious. Fletcher could tell.

"What kind of Indian? Fluevog? They've got their offices up in Aquinnah. Why aren't you up there with them?"

"No, Neskeet. We were originally part of the Fluevogs in Mashpee on the Cape but split from 'em a long time ago. Moved to Truro." Fletcher was just making it up as he went.

Marty Schatz paused for a second, looking at Bill Fletcher, not sure if Bill was being straight with him or not. "Don't take this the wrong way, but you don't look much like an Indian. No offense intended. And I don't want an Indian office where a bunch of kids all drugged up on pot and speed hang out on the stairs. All longhairs. That's not going to work for this landlord."

"I'm about 25 percent Indian. Papers and everything to prove it." Fletcher walked around the office, looking it over, visualizing how he'd set it up with desks and workstations to run the business. "How about a thousand a month, and I pay the utilities?" Fletcher finally countered. "It's all I have for now."

"That's cheap," Marty said. "Real cheap."

"You haven't rented it in over two years, remember?"

Marty turned it over in his head. "The owner's not going to take a bogus LLC, Indian or otherwise, on the lease."

Fletcher knew where he was headed. "I'll sign personally on the lease. But it'll be in the tribe's name. I need to be able to deduct the lease payments." Fletcher looked over at the agent.

"Bill, I don't know what kind of scam you're running. But you keep it clean and quiet, and the office is yours for a thousand a month."

"Done deal. I want a twenty-four-month lease with an option to extend for two more years. Once this thing starts up, the Neskeets need a home."

Marty Shatz laughed. "Then home it is. The owner will be happy that I finally rented the space. We haven't had any traction for a long while." Marty Schatz looked out the window then added, "You also get the view of Main Street, up and down."

"One more thing," Fletcher said after they finished talking about the details and were headed down the narrow stairs out into the bright sun. He looked up at the front of the building. "I'm going to need a sign on the front out here."

"The sunglass shop has the main signage rights on the front," Marty said. "It's in their lease."

"No, I just wanna put a blade sign up. Something small and discrete that says this is the Indian office. Probably two feet square, that's all."

Marty didn't hesitate. "You got it. Keep it small and simple, and I'll help you get it through. You'll have to get a permit though."

And that was it. Fletcher had just negotiated the new home of the Neskeets, the long-lost Indian tribe of Cape Cod. He walked back to the ferry, happy with his accomplishment. He had put the first piece of the puzzle into place.

First Draft

The report from NewWorldGenealogy.com came back in three business days, just like Sam Aston had promised.

Bill Fletcher was sitting on the couch in his living room reading it with an irritated feeling in his bowel. He was a lawyer, so his first instinct was to mark up the document, to give comment. He pulled out his pencil and start underlining sections of the text, circling and putting boxes around paragraphs that he didn't like and were questionable.

He took a sip of coffee from an Indian mug that he had in the kitchen. It was an old Disney one. It was faded blue with a tepee on one side and an Indian brave with a horse on the other. The original white on the inside was now coffee-stained brown from countless workings. Chipped in places, it was the coffee mug of a warrior. Fletcher sipped slowly as he read.

He put the report down and looked around for his Bluetooth earpiece. He found it on the table under a pile of bills and put the soft flexible rubber bud into his ear. He picked up his BlackBerry and keyed in the NewWorldGenealogy.com number and waited. He watched the blinking blue light on the phone as the call connected.

"New World Genealogy. May I help you?"

"Sam?"

"Speaking."

"This is Bill Fletcher over on Martha's Vineyard. The Indian? You just sent me your draft report a couple days ago."

"Which one? I've got a lot of reports working right now." Sam Aston paused, sitting in his office in New Hope, Pennsylvania, trying to remember off the top of his head who the hell Bill Fletcher was.

Fletcher was irritated. He had to be the only Indian that Aston was researching, and he still didn't remember him. But Fletcher couldn't lose his cool because he had to work with Aston to get the report right.

It was like dealing with a prickly immigration judge or a squirrelly client that didn't want to pay. On the good side, Fletcher knew that Aston would be very pliable, almost like Silly Putty, and that he could move him around the field of genealogy as he needed to.

"You remember. I'm the Indian from Martha's Vineyard."

Silence on the phone. "Let me pull up the report on my screen and see who you are," Aston said. Bill Fletcher could hear the keys click quickly on the keyboard in Aston's office in New Hope.

"Okay. Now I got your report up on my screen. Of course I remember you. You're the Neskeet. What do you think of the draft?" Aston scrolled through the report and got to the gist of it quickly as he waited for Fletcher to answer.

"The report sucks. That's what I think. It doesn't have my lineage right. You missed all of my Indian heritage. Starting with Binky Fletcher. Third generation down on the tree. See him there?"

"I do. But he's not Indian. I researched him to be a clam digger and a local hunter in Mashpee in the 1860s, around that time." Sam Aston sounded confident.

"Nope. You missed it. You've got it all wrong. Binky and his brood were Indian, pure and simple. They sprang from the Fluevog. They were an offshoot and started their own tribe right around that period. They intermixed the seed. You know?" Bill Fletcher waited.

"I don't think so."

"You've got to look harder and find that Indian connection that I'm talking about."

Sam Aston immediately sensed that he could charge Bill Fletcher another five or six hours of additional research time to root out the connection and see if it even existed. This happened all the time, people expanding their search to try and find a long-lost duke or a prince in their lineage and ending up with their forgotten dyslexic Uncle Luke.

This was all gravy for Sam Aston. He already had the report completed in draft form. Digging deeper wasn't that hard on a marginal cost basis. Sam was all about the profit margin. But he wasn't quite ready for where Bill Fletcher wanted to go.

"Bill, I can do the additional research at $125 dollars an hour, but it'll be a two-hour minimum. I'll do a second draft report with a revised family tree, plus backup, in two days' time. I'll e-mail the supplement to you in advance for discussion."

Fletcher liked where Aston was heading. He knew now that he could get what he wanted. He cut to the chase and hit Aston with his knockout punch.

"How about $2,000 extra for your time to do the work? I know it's a complicated search and the Indian records are thin around that time in Mashpee. Everything is murky. I tried doing it myself but got caught up in my underwear. That's why I hired you."

Aston was flabbergasted. Two thousand bucks was a whole week's work. "You sure you want to pay me that much?"

Now Bill Fletcher paused for effect before he spoke. "I'm sure. And I'm sure that I need you to find that elusive Indian connection for me starting with Binky and going forward from there. A real, clear Indian connection that I can show to people on a family tree, solidly researched, complete with tons of backup. Beer-tray quality. You get my drift?"

The light went on slowly with Sam Aston, but it went on. "So you really want me to find your Indian heritage, huh?"

"Bingo. You got it," Fletcher answered, smiling. "There's probably another thousand bucks on top of the first two thousand if you manage to find that Indian connection clearly and lay it all out in good detail. You with me?"

Fletcher fiddled with his coffee mug on the couch arm and turned it so that the tepee faced him while he waited for that piece of information to sink in with Sam Aston. He waited in the silence, but not for long.

Sam Aston was back on track now. "Now I got it, Bill. The Indian records really are all murky on Cape Cod, just like you said. I might have missed some obvious things doing my initial work, rushing to get the first draft done. I'll go back in and have a closer look, and we'll see what I can find."

"I'm confident, Sam." Fletcher drained the rest of the coffee from his mug.

"The Fluevogs, huh? Who are they again?"

"It means People of the Light," Fletcher said. "But I need you to find an offshoot tribe from the light people, a smaller tribe that did their own thing on the Cape, my tribe. The Neskeets."

"Can I bang your credit card for the first two thousand now before I start the extra research?" Aston asked. Business was a bit slow.

"Absolutely, Sam. And you can hit it for the bonus thousand if the report is good when you send the second draft to me. Am I being clear?"

"Clear like the people of the light. Your Indian ancestors, the Neskeets, and all that shit. I'll look more closely today and see what I find. I bet there's a lot of stuff that I missed. You know?"

"Send me something as soon as you find it. I'm feeling Indian, and I need to be validated with a written provenance. And you're just the guy to do it."

Fletcher rang off and pulled the Bluetooth out of his ear. As he put the earpiece down, he bumped the coffee mug off the couch arm with his elbow, and it fell onto the floor, shattering into a jumble of coffee-stained pieces.

Revised Edition

Bill Fletcher was in his new office on Main Street, leaning back in his Aeron chair and talking on the phone, his black cowboy boots up on the shiny oak desk. They were big, size twelve. He had purchased them last year on an impulse when he was in Boston at Rodeo Outfitters on Boylston Street. He had found them under his desk when he moved the last of his stuff from his office before Frank Tamara started charging him holdover rent.

He had his glasses on and the revised genealogy report in his lap. Sam Aston had overnighted a hard copy to him at no extra cost.

"Yeah. Now this is what I'm talking about," Fletcher said manically into the phone. "You looked a little closer, didn't you? You've got real Indian everywhere in my family tree now." He reached down, put his hand in his crotch, scratched his balls, and waited patiently for Sam Aston's answer.

Sam didn't hesitate. "Yeah. I think I was a little off base on the first family search I did for you. This time I focused on Mashnee and found a truckload of Indian heritage stuff there pertaining to you and your kin. It was surprising how much I found."

"That's Mashpee."

"Right. That's what I meant. Most of the stuff was Fluevog, though. But then I did a little more digging, and I found that little clamdigger cousin of yours, and no shit, he was solid Indian through and through, just like you said. I had missed him on the first pass. Just missed him. What can I say?" Sam Aston sounded pleased with his research.

"But once I found your seed-spewing relative down there in Mashpee, I was able to put the pieces together, real easy, going forward. You're Indian, there's no doubt about it. Textbook Indian, you might say."

"You caught it on the second pass, just like I knew you would. Good man," Bill Fletcher said. He was pleased. He moved his hand down to the lever on the right side of his Aeron chair as he talked to unlock it and began rocking slowly back and forth. He looked up at the ceiling. It was in rough shape like everything else in the office. "So what does that make me?"

"Huh?"

"What does that make me from an Indian perspective?"

Sam Aston caught where Fletcher was going.

"Why, that makes you one lucky Indian is what that makes you."

"How much Indian am I?"

"I think I concluded 35 percent or more, didn't I?"

Fletcher thumbed through the 110-page report. He stopped on the section that Aston had titled "Indian Heritage" and quickly skimmed through it. "Yeah, that's what it says."

"Is that enough?"

"I think I need about 55 or 60 percent Indian to be legit."

"How so?" Aston asked. He immediately got a little nervous in the pit of his bowel. All these questions by Bill Fletcher pushing, pushing, pushing him to find his Indian heritage when there really wasn't any were a little over the top.

"I'm forming a tribe. No. That's a miscommunication," Fletcher said. "I'm actually reclaiming my family tribe, the one that's always existed that's been long lost on Cape Cod. The Neskeets."

Sam Aston, family genealogist from Pennsylvania, went quiet. "Jesus Christ. I had enough trouble making up this individual Indian connection for you. Now you want me to find a whole tribe? What the hell's their name again?" He was exasperated. "Neskeet. The Neskeets of Cape Cod." Fletcher had had time to create the fake provenance in his head about the Indian tribe and his heritage. "Like parakeet. Those little birds? Only this is Neskeet. Sounds exactly the same."

Sam Aston did some figuring, running through the report, and then responded, "It'll cost you."

"How much?"

"Another thousand."

"It's a deal," Fletcher said. "But I need it in the next two days."

"You got it. But understand that I'm going to have to footnote the report. Put a disclaimer in it."

Fletcher wrinkled his brow." You better put it in small letters, way in the back like a financial footnote. And it better be weak."

"Yeah, I will. All it's going to say is that the report is based on the best available information available at the time. I don't want to get my license pulled here in Pennsylvania."

"Those records are so screwed up down in Mashpee on Indian heritage that you could find ten tribes down there, and nobody could say otherwise," Fletcher said.

Sam Aston was back on firm ground now. "Maybe so, but it's my ass in the sling, not yours."

Bill Fletcher agreed to let his credit card be banged one more time once the final report was in his hands and he approved it. Before he rang off and let Aston get back to looking for bogus Indian records, he gave him one more piece of direction.

"I'm going to need the report and then a two-by-three family tree, laminated, that I can frame, showing my heritage."

"You got it. You want icons around the edge or not?" Aston said.

"What've you got?"

"I can do shellfish, fishing nets, bow and arrows, a tepee, and maybe beads and wampum. I'll bookmark some samples, and you can pick."

Bill Fletcher smiled. "That's a deal. Gimme your best stuff."

He knew that with the extra cash as an incentive, Sam Aston would not disappoint in the provenance area.

Bingo

"B-53. G-20. O-36."

"Bingo!" sang out the little old lady with gray hair in a bun, with the cat-eye glasses looped around her neck on a bright purple lanyard. Her thin age-marked hand shot up in the air without hesitation. She was clearly a pro.

Fr. Peter Mulcahey stood at the front on the dais holding the microphone with the thick black cord and looking around the room, trying to pick the woman out. He eventually found her in the back to the right. It was Mrs. Kingston. She was a pain in his ass. He had already spent two useless sessions planning out her granddaughter's wedding in the fall.

"We have a winner. Right over there." Fr. Peter raised his long arm and pointed out Mrs. Kingston in the back. "Here we go. A lucky hundred-dollar winner. What a night!"

He needed a drink badly. This was one of his toughest assignments. Calling numbers for the weekly bingo game at the parish hall. Two hundred golden agers stuck on Martha's Vineyard with nothing to do but pray on Sundays and play bingo during the week. They had the energy of a pack of Huns.

He always had to stay late, eat banana bread with nuts, and drink stale decaf coffee with them making small talk until almost 11:00 p.m. He hated the banana bread, and Christ, it was boring.

But Peter Mulcahey didn't have much to complain about. The bingo games were really bringing in the cash. The church made about $750 a night on the games when he ran them, and that was good money in the current state of the economy.

They only had to heat up the hall for one night a week. The system was gas-fired hot air, so Father Mulcahey could keep the room cold until an hour before bingo then crank the heat on at the last minute. It was always warm as a sauna in the parish hall by the time the game started. With all the people, he could set the thermostat back to 60 degrees by 9:00 p.m., and the body heat kept the room warm the rest of the night. So his variable costs were down next to nothing. He hadn't put a pencil to paper to do the calculation, but he figured it cost him no more than fifty bucks to heat the hall for bingo.

Fr. Mulcahey didn't ruminate on the fact that the bingo was basically legalized gambling. He could care less as none of it pulled on his ethical heartstrings. No, what bothered him most was the fact that he had to circulate with the parishioners for the whole night and make small talk. Particularly with the older women. Christ, they were getting to be an irritation. He gave up his microphone duty soon enough and went to the back of the church to mingle.

"And how are you tonight, Mrs. Stanley?" Father Peter asked the woman to his right with short gray hair cut in a bob and a pink sweatshirt on that said Ask Me About My Cats. She was short and squat, like a wrestler, and she appeared to be in good shape. Peter Mulcahey knew that she walked along the beach every day for forty-five minutes. She'd kick his ass in a fight.

"Oh, wonderful, Father." Patricia Stanley immediately brightened with the attention from the priest. "Did I tell you that my sister has colon cancer by the way?"

"No. Mother of God, that's horrible, Pat. When did it happen?" Fr. Mulcahey reached for a sugar cookie and bit into it, waiting for Mrs. Stanley's response.

"It's awful. They found it during her colonoscopy last week. It was routine, they said. She'd had one before, over at Cape Cod Hospital. Thought it was a polyp, but it turned out to be something else. We're broken up about it."

Fr. Mulcahey took a sip of lukewarm decaf coffee from a small Styrofoam cup. It was either that or Hawaiian Punch. He let Pat Stanley ramble on for a while and describe her sister's nightmare in considerable detail. But then he cut her off, he had had enough.

"Pat, I'll say three Hail Marys tonight for you sister. And I'll offer up a prayer at Sunday Mass for her quick recovery."

Patricia Stanley beamed and was grateful, but Peter Mulcahey didn't linger. He was already off and mingling with the other women at the end of the food table. He searched for a chocolate chip cookie before he was ready to get back to number calling.

At ten o'clock that night, Father Mulcahey was walking around the empty room with a black plastic trash barrel with a liner. He was tossing in empty coffee cups and napkins, straightening up the room. He had two helpers wandering around too, helping clean up the mess.

He'd wanted to start selling alcohol at the bingo sessions, but just the light stuff. If he could sell white wine and Budweiser, he figured he could double his gross every night. The parishioners would play more cards and stay longer. He figured he could lengthen the game time, and they'd make a few bucks on the markup on the booze. He thought he could double his net to $1,500 a night. It was easily more lucrative than trying to run additional Masses on Sunday. And less boring too.

Late that night, long after the bingo tables were stowed away and the colored plastic chips put in their containers, Father Peter Mulcahey sat back in his leather easy chair in the rectory, feet up on the hassock, shoes off. He was drinking three fingers of Dewar's neat. Straight-up scotch in room temperature to take away the pain of the bingo.

He picked up the clicker that Joanne Proctor had conveniently left on the side table, perfectly positioned, for him. On came the Catholic channel with a young priest talking about the trials and tribulations of the African outback. He frowned and fingered the channel selector a few times. Up popped an old rerun of Jane Fonda in *Barbarella*, running around in a lion-skin bikini. He settled back in his chair and took a sip from his tumbler of scotch.

He made a mental note to ask Joanne to get another half gallon of booze when she went shopping later in the week. He seemed to be going through the brown liquor quickly. He started to relax as the scotch took hold.

He was grateful that the bingo generated enough cash to provide for necessities for the parish and to provision the rectory. Half gallons of Dewar's scotch were essential. Praise the Lord for the little things for they lined the path to heaven.

Final Report

"Jesus, this report is beautiful, Sam. You did good work." Bill Fletcher smiled as he flipped through the pages of the Fletcher Family Genealogy Report, all rights reserved by New World Genealogy Inc. "You nailed it."

He dog-eared one of the pages, an important one, and then put the report down on his desk. He picked a zit on his nose as he rocked back and forth in his Aeron chair, talking to Sam Aston down in Pennsylvania.

"Well, it turns out you're as Indian as Sitting Bull, Bill. I missed it the first time."

Sam Aston was confident this time in speaking his words. He felt good about the revised report he created for Bill Fletcher. "I picked up all your rich Indian heritage on closer inspection."

"I knew you'd find it," Fletcher said. "My great-uncle was a scoundrel of an Indian. Sowing his wild, promiscuous seed all through the Mashpee women."

"Yeah, there's Indians everywhere in the Mashpee records. It's hard to keep 'em straight, even for a trained researcher like myself. Everybody screwin' their cousins like rabbits."

"Yeah, but they gotta be Neskeets, not Fluevogs. I don't want to be fighting those guys for every dollar on the Cape. I needed my own sovereignty."

"Right. Neskeet it is," Aston said. "Any number of your people can claim their heritage as a Neskeet, and I'll find the connection. By the way, I charged your card for $3,500 this morning."

"That's fine. I'm satisfied with your work," Fletcher said. "It was well worth it to me, finding my heritage and all. I'll finally be able to sleep at night." Fletcher paused. "Now, if I need you to testify as to my authenticity or state under oath that I'm a real Indian, are you okay to do that?" That was the critical question, and it hung in the air.

Sam Aston didn't miss a beat. In for a penny, in for a pound, he always said.

"No problem at all, Bill. I'll travel up for depositions, testimony, anything else you want. That shit is so murky, everybody's part Indian by my way of thinking down on the Cape. All at my research rate of $250 an hour plus travel costs, and I'm there."

"So be it, Indian researcher. Your work is quality. Go forth. The provenance you built for me is rich and full."

"And pretty believable too. I really spun it pretty well," Aston said.

"That you did."

Sam Aston almost didn't want to ask the next question, but he did anyway. "So what are you going to do with my report, anyway?"

"I'm forming an Indian tribe on Martha's Vineyard, and I'm the chief. We'll create some rip-off businesses, rape and pillage, do all the usual stuff, you know." Fletcher rocked forward in his chair. It was time to end the conversation with his hayseed family researcher.

"The Neskeets on the Vineyard? That's the tribe you're creating?"

"One and the same."

"Jesus Christ," was all Sam Aston could say. "You know that I put a disclaimer in the footnotes of the report."

"It's not important. Nobody reads footnotes. All those Indian records are murky at best anyway. You've done enough good things for me for one day in this report, and I'm grateful," Fletcher said. "Now go spend my money."

"Tell me how it turns out, will you?" Sam Aston said. "And good luck with it."

After he hung up the phone, Aston made a vow to stick to the Canadians going forward who were looking for their French and British ancestors. It was much less money, but at least he didn't have to fabricate whole swatches of family history like he did for Bill Fletcher's Indian tribe.

Less stress, and in the end, it just wasn't worth it to go out on a limb like he did for Fletcher.

Arranging the Merchandise

Carrie Nation was in the Equinox, arranging scented candles at the front of her store. She was working at a big flat pine table made with barn boards, each one about twelve inches wide and polyurethaned with a bright gloss. She was putting squat colored candles in a straight line across the tabletop. She was building a candle pyramid.

First she had a group of cranberry candles, then some lemon verbena, and lastly a row of chamomile ones. Then on top of all those, stacked about eighteen inches high, she put the pièce de résistance, the vanillaroma-scented candles. They were a little more slender, about the thickness of a baseball bat, with little wicks bent over at the top. She loved the vanilla smell, and by putting them on the top of the pyramid, the candles acted like little room air fresheners giving out their scent to everybody walking by in the store.

She lit one vanilla candle and put it flat on the table in front of the design stack, like an offering at a Buddhist shrine. The light flickered gently, and the vanilla scent infused the room with a sweet-smelling overhang.

Carrie had on a long hippie skirt and sterling hoop earrings. She had a nice figure and filled out the skirt in just the right places. She wore a tight T-shirt with sleeves cut at the shoulder that had a Jasper Johns flag painting on the front with a distressed look. On the back it said Arlo Guthrie World Tour and had a bunch of dates. The shirt kept her breasts high and tight. She was dressed as a sexy hippie, wearing wedge clogs to finish it off.

It was 10:00 a.m., and she unlocked the front door to the store, but it was too early for customers during the first week of June. So she kept working, rearranging items on the shelves, stocking inventory, bringing things up from the basement, dusting the goods.

The store was a mix of tourist souvenirs, head shop, and natural products for healthy living all in one. The tourists generally loved the items she sold, and she priced everything low enough to make for a lot of impulse purchases as people drifted in after a long day at the beach. She had a separate island of suntan lotions from Banana Boat to Coppertone to custom Vineyard stuff made by the locals.

The store was her pride and joy. She had been a schoolteacher in Melrose for ten years teaching art and English literature, but she burned out from trying to teach spoiled, bratty kids.

So she took a flyer and started the Equinox on the Island five years ago, and she was able to make it into a modest success. It turned out that she loved retail and the artistic expression of setting up the store and deciding what products to carry and sell. She had a real knack for it. Plus, it gave her winters off.

Bill Fletcher walked in the door ten minutes later. He was up in the front of the store looking at the incense display, picking out individual sticks and bringing them up to his nose, smelling each scent: frangipani, desert sky, summer rose.

Carrie recognized him immediately. She walked up behind him and stood there, hands on her hips, as she looked him over. He was dressed more island now, like one of the local contractors who came in to buy Zig-Zag papers in the store. She noticed that he had started to lose the preppy look since she had last seen him.

"You make it over to the Island all right that night?" Carrie said as she moved in front of him so he could get a good look. He had to think for a second to place her.

"Where do I know you from?" Fletcher said. He put down the joss sticks for a minute, now looking closely at Carrie Nation, taking her in.

He was impressed with what he saw. He thought that she looked like a New Age version of Gracie Slick or maybe Stevie Nicks. He liked them both, so he paid attention.

"The Lee Side last month, remember? We were talking before you tripped on that dog on the floor. You were trying to make room for me to get out. You made an ass of yourself."

Now Bill Fletcher remembered her. She had dropped her mainland clothes and went native on the Island, and pretty radically. But he liked the hippie-dippy look on her.

"I did, didn't I?" he said, nodding, just accepting the naked truth as Carrie said it. "Thanks for stopping and helping me out that night. I was flat on my ass and not moving too well."

Carrie started laughing. "I know, and I'm sorry! I couldn't stay around to help you. I was mortified when you fell over the golden retriever. I figured that there was a little alcohol involved. I was shocked it happened so fast. The karma just wasn't right that night."

Fletcher smiled, looked at Carrie, and changed the subject. "I like your new look. Kind of earth mother, huh? You're keeping it real."

"It's faux hippie. I like to play dress up in the store when I'm here."

"You work here?"

"I own the place," Carrie said. "This is what I do."

"You like it?" Fletcher asked, looking back at the incense sticks. He was clearly impressed.

"Love it. It's a lot of fun. It's a people business, basically."

Fletcher grunted. "How much are these joss sticks? The frangipani ones. I want about ten of them."

Carrie Nation went around Bill Fletcher and walked to the front counter. She shook the mouse on the Apple Mac Pro, waiting for the pricing screen to come to life. She glanced up at him. She decided that she liked Bill Fletcher's new look and that she'd play it out a bit. She needed a little excitement anyway. She was a people person, a salesperson.

"What're you going to do with them?" she said as she scrolled down the inventory screen. "A dollar each. If you buy the box, I can give it to you for $8.50." She looked up at Fletcher and fingered her big hoop earring.

"It's for my office. I want it to smell a little funky."

"Have you thought about a vanilla candle or something like that? Or maybe a cranberry one?"

"I'm not a big candle guy. This will do fine," Fletcher said.

"Too bad, 'cause we're having a sale on 'em."

Carrie Nation was no believer in fate, but it was pretty coincidental that Bill Fletcher walked into her store that morning. Kismet. She wasn't going to let it pass. She pushed out her breasts in the Jasper Johns T-shirt and waited as Bill Fletcher rummaged through his wallet for a bill.

"So we never finished that conversation about you being Indian and all and what you were going to do down here."

Fletcher smiled, impressed. "You've got a good memory."

"For some things," she said.

He handed her a credit card instead, and she noticed that it was an American Express Slate card. One of those with a high credit limit. She swiped it through the reader and waited for Fletcher to say something as the transaction was processed.

Fletcher took his card back and didn't miss his cue. "So how about we try it again over dinner, and I give you the rest of my story. But no dogs involved."

"Your story?"

"My Indian story," Fletcher said calmly. "It's kinda fun."

So they agreed on dinner later in the week. Bill Fletcher left the store with a box of frangipani incense sticks and a whole new appreciation for the artwork of Jasper Johns.

The Application

Armed with the report from New World Genealogy, Bill Fletcher went straight to work. He was renting a small bungalow across the street from the water at the Inkwell in Oak Bluffs. It was once a ramshackle garage that the owner had converted into a tiny apartment with views onto the Sound from the front and to Sengekontacket Pond from the rear deck. It had two rooms, shotgun style.

He began working off his laptop on the couch, eating Cheese Nips by the boxload and drinking Chardonnay wine while doing the basic research. He had come a long way from his busted marriage and dead-end law job in the city. Sitting on the Vineyard with a new future, this was his chance to break out, drop his conformity, and do something fun for a change.

He Googled *Indian tribe formation* for starters and got about forty references for Indians and Indian tribes and all kinds of other extraneous bullshit. He quickly hit into the main vein, which was the path into the federal government.

It was straightforward enough with a filing package that was addressed to the Department of the Interior. There was a form, Form 25B, and a process that all Indian tribes went through to get certified. If you got the certification, you were golden.

Then you could get a grant for federal funds to do holistic things like plant corn and vegetables, educate the youth, erect a tribal hall, or build a fifty-thousand-square-foot casino with a 766-room hotel attached to it. Just to be able to do all the basic Indian pursuits, the sky was the limit.

Bill Fletcher was actually quite good at doing paperwork and filings as part of his old day-to-day law practice. His experience in immigration law was also helpful as it was essentially an administrative practice that consisted of filing a lot of forms with people that loved rejecting them for the slightest error or omission. It was careful, detailed work, and that was just what filing for Indian tribal recognition was all about too.

The first thing Fletcher did was review the filings of several other Indian tribes at the Bureau of Indian Affairs, the BIA, within the Department of the Interior. It was all there and all available online, ripe for the picking. He was excellent at what he called reverse engineering, which was nothing more than looking at previous filings by smart lawyers from white-shoe law firms who were all well versed in Indian law and administrative processes. They were also paid a shitload of money by Indian tribes to get the paperwork right. Fletcher drafted right off it, copying, paraphrasing, and editing as necessary.

He was good at it and had been cribbing pleadings for years in the Massachusetts state court system. Every lawyer in Boston did it. He often thought that there was just one attorney who did primary research and work on a topic and then five hundred other Boston lawyers just ripped it off and plagiarized it. The sacred trust of the law as he knew it.

Fair enough. Bill Fletcher didn't care. He was just reading to copy the shit out of previous filings and learn the essentials of what a federal Indian tribal application had to contain.

He planned on doing a giant cut-and-paste job, tailoring it all as needed for his tribe, the Neskeets, the lost Indians of Cape Cod.

Martha Stewart Redux

Around his research and the 25B tribal application work, Fletcher set about decorating his office. The space he rented was essentially one big room, a bull pen, with a conference room attached. He put his desk in the corner where he could get the view down Main Street, the money shot, and still be able to watch over all the activity in the room. He could manage the fledgling tribe right from the corner at his big oak desk.

He nailed up a wool blanket behind the receptionist's desk that had a lot of earth tones in it, blues and browns and greens. It looked like a horse blanket with color. He picked it up, secondhand, at the Salvation Army. It was just an old hippie blanket, but he decided he'd make up a history for it and say that it was from his Indian uncle's old stallion on the Cape.

Next up was the American flag. He found a print of the flag that Carrie had on her T-shirt, the one that held her nice breasts in place the first day he saw her in the Equinox, in a local frame shop in Vineyard Haven. It was in a stack of used prints, 50 percent off.

It was a rare find, and he was lucky to get it. It was two feet by three feet and was mounted on a piece of thin foam board. The edges were all beat up and crinkled, so the whole effect was just what he was looking for—a little Americana thing, but with an Indian twist, distressed and beaten up. He nailed it up with two roofing nails, aluminum ones with big round heads, right in the middle of the wall over the leather couch that was there for relaxing. Easy Rider meets Neskeet Bill.

Last but not least, he got the boyfriend of the girl downstairs who ran the sunglasses shop to help him install a deer head on the wall above his desk. He picked it up on Craigslist from a guy in New Bedford who was a hunter. He had a $1,000 lottery hit and got pressure from his wife to buy a fifty-one-inch flat-screen TV for the family in the living room. Enough was enough, she said. That was it for the deer head. He had moved it into the garage, and Fletcher looked it over as it sat on the floor over by the snowblower. He bought it immediately.

It was a big buck with a six-point rack and two little black glass eyes. It was a little dusty from sitting out in the garage, but it was the ultimate Indian tribal artifact. It was a nice touch for the office keeping with the distressed Indian theme. The buck's head was majestic looking out over the room. You couldn't miss it.

Fletcher soon realized that home decorating was not that hard, and he had a bit of a knack for it. He found the box of frangipani incense sticks he bought at the Equinox and lit one up, laying it in an empty quahog shell ashtray he bought for seventy-five cents. The smoke swirled up to the ceiling in little wisps, giving off its musky aroma. Soon enough, the room had a smell from the sixties.

So there it was, simply done. He had spent about three hundred dollars decorating the place, including the buck's head, which had cost a hundred fifty. It was a steal. The office of the Neskeet Nation was now complete and open for business.

Here we go, Fletcher thought.

Dinner

Bill Fletcher and Carrie Nation went out to dinner at the Sweet Season Café. Fletcher was wearing his Sunday-go-to-meeting Indian outfit, clean jeans and a blue-striped shirt that he bought online at Lord & Taylor. He got rid of his old L.L.Bean button-down shirts and went to pointy open collars. They gave him a hip musician's look, and that fit just fine. The jeans were lightly faux distressed. He stayed away from the jeans with the big holes in the knees and thighs with strings hanging down that gave off the derelict look.

Carrie had on jeans too, but nice ones with black boots. She had on a plain-red pullover top that she accented with a big blue beaded necklace. No T-shirts tonight.

They were drinking light, Bill having a beer and Carrie sipping a white wine. The place had a mix of tourists and locals looking for good food. Plates of seafood and black mussels over linguine were coming out from the back.

"Imagine us meeting up on the Island like this. It's a little amazing, huh?" Fletcher said. "Kismet."

Carrie, with her youth and attractiveness, was clearly in a class above him on the dating circuit. Bill hadn't done much dating since his divorce, and he was out of shape and not that good at it. He was a little oafish.

He sipped his Bud slowly, keeping in control. He was trying to decide how much he liked Carrie Nation and how to play it.

"More like two degrees of separation," Carrie responded. "It's a small island when you get right down to it. We'd have met at some point."

Carrie drank her wine slowly, fingering the glass, looking at the light-amber liquid. She was deciding whether she was going to sleep with Bill Fletcher later that night or not. Make the big decisions early on, and then relax and enjoy the night either way.

"So what's with the store? How'd you get into retail?" Fletcher asked, drilling down.

"I taught school for a while, years ago. I was doing art and English in grade school in Melrose. It was a beautiful town, but I wasn't making enough money, really any money at all. And honestly, I hated the kids. All they wanted to do was give me shit. The whole thing was negative. I lived for the vacations."

Fletcher could picture it, the young boys causing trouble, and all of them wanting to jump on her bones, the same as him. It was a basic male instinct. He remembered high school and sex being all he thought about. They probably gave Carrie Nation a run for her money.

"So, yeah. I started the store three years ago for something different to do. It's been fun. Retail is good, and T-shirts are big-profit items if you do them right. You know how?"

"I've got no idea," Fletcher said, slightly piqued.

"You've got to go high quality. Top end. Two hundred, three-hundred-stitch cotton with good strong collars. The T-shirt has to be thick and have a good hand feel to it. That's the problem with most of the T-shirts down here on the Island. The merchants want to cheap out. They use a synthetic mix with mostly polyester, not heavyweight cotton, and the shirts come out feeling thin and cheap. Bad quality. The collars are tight around the neck, and they're not comfortable. The parents and the kids that buy them don't even get back home to New Jersey, and the shirts have shrunk up so much by the second wash that they have to be tossed."

Fletcher laughed and looked over at Carrie and decided to try her out. He couldn't believe that she was so into T-shirts. It boggled his mind. But it was cool; it showed she was passionate for her craft, her art form. Just like he was passionate about the bullshit Indian thing.

"Good hand feel, huh? That's what we're all looking for, I guess."

Carrie Nation blushed slightly. "Don't mock me. Don't laugh. T-shirts are a business on one level, but they're an art form too. A popular art form. Done right, they tell a story. Walking art, I call it. You know it when you see it."

Bill Fletcher could see Carrie Nation was tough and smart and had an attitude. He liked her for that. He figured that she could probably hold her own real well in a fight. She seemed like a good businesswoman. She had a tight body and sharp, discerning eyes. She didn't miss a trick. He wondered how she could help him if they could do anything together going forward.

Big cuts of haddock and swordfish came, grilled with crisscross patterns on the skin and lemon wedges on the side. The waiter also put down a plate of angel-hair pasta with marinara sauce. Fletcher and Carrie were drinking a bottle of Pinot Grigio. The conversation traveled from his old law practice and marriage to her undergraduate degree in art history from Villanova in 1996. Bill Fletcher did the arithmetic in his head as he sipped his wine, thin beads of sweat on the glass, and figured out that she was thirty-two years old. No wonder she was in such good shape.

Dessert came over Carrie's protests. It was rice pudding.

"I'm stuffed. I can't eat anymore. I just want a taste. One spoonful," Carrie said as she took one of the two teaspoons on the white paper tablecloth and broke into the rice pudding. She took a small piece that had plenty of raisins. If she was only having one bite, it was going to be a decadent one.

"So you mocked my T-shirts," she said after tasting the rice pudding and then putting the spoon down. "At least it's an art form. What are you really about with this Indian thing, this fake crap?" She swirled the remnants of the white wine in her glass and waited for Bill Fletcher to respond. The wine had loosened her up.

"What do you mean?"

"The Indian bullshit. You can't possibly think that you're Indian. You're Caucasian, a white man. Pure and simple."

"You can still be part white man and have some Indian in you. It happens."

Fletcher looked over at Carrie looking at him. After the bottle of wine, she was looking like she was movie-star quality very quickly. Her bright eyes sparkled.

"Basically, Shakespeare said it best," Fletcher said. "Nothing is ever right or wrong, but thinking makes it so. And that's what being an Indian is for me."

"When did he say that?"

"I don't know. One of his goddamn plays I think. Doesn't matter, the point is still there." Fletcher put his spoon down with finality. "Anyway, being an Indian chief is a helluva lot better than being a shitty immigration lawyer. That much I know."

"Or at least pretending to be." Carrie said.

"Whatever. Maybe I'll just be a curiosity, a bust, a weirdo. We'll see. Maybe the tribe'll grow on the Vineyard. It can't be any worse than the Fluevogs."

Carrie cut to the chase. "So how do we work together? There's got to be ways that I can help you sell something, make some money. Maybe even, God forbid, T-shirts."

Fletcher was surprised. "You'd help me?"

"It's not all altruistic. I need new stuff for the Equinox. My merchandise is getting boring and kinda stale. I need a new product line, and you may be it."

They got up and left the restaurant. It was a beautiful June night. They headed back to Carrie's place for a nightcap. She had already decided by the time the entrée came that she would sleep with Bill Fletcher that night. She was decisive if nothing else. She liked his eyes.

Back at her apartment, in her big four-poster bed, she conquered her first Indian chief.

Cranking Up the Machine

Once the phone lines got installed and the office was operational, the first thing Fletcher did was get a sign made for the front door. An Indian sign.

He needed visibility and presence for the fledgling operation. So he went to JD Ullson, the Swedish sign maker over on Barnes Road. Ullson was a wash ashore from Minneapolis years ago.

"What kind of sign you looking for? I've got hundreds. I can make anything you want." Ullson watched Fletcher finger the sample signs on the workbench.

"I need something with an icon, an iconic image."

"You want something about the Vineyard?'

"Yeah, That or the Cape. Something that connects to Indians," Fletcher said.

"You Indian? Or having this done for a friend?" Ullson looked at Fletcher with his large watery Minnesota eyes, sizing him up.

"It's for me." Fletcher put his hand in his pocket, looking for his glasses to see the sign types.

"How you paying?"

"Cash on the barrel, in advance. How's that?" Fletcher got right to the point.

"I think I got some icons for you, then," Ullson said. "Come on with me into the back."

So Fletcher paid JD Ullson, Swedish sign maker to the Vineyard elite, fifteen hundred dollars for a 24 × 24 inch sign that had a gilt-edged scallop shell on it with the words *Neskeet Nation* below in small red letters. It was understated and iconic. It was a beauty. He gave old JD an extra $100 to move the job to the top of the pile. It would be done in a week.

Fletcher liked the idea of the scallop shell. It was brilliant. It was a clean and recognizable part of the summertime Cape experience. It was distinctly

Indian. The Indians used wampum, pieces of clamshells, for currency way back when, so it was a perfect icon.

*   *   *

A week later, Fletcher was in Kona Koffee getting a cup of strong coffee, fortification for the day, around ten o'clock. He was talking to Blinkey, the barista with the lazy eye and Mets baseball cap. Blinkey had on an old Entrain T-shirt, the Vineyard funk band from the nineties. They were still playing in gigs on the Island. They never left—the Island or the nineties.

"Large dark roast, no sugar," Fletcher said.

Blinkey smiled. "Hey, man. How's the tribe coming?" He thought it was a gas, Bill Fletcher starting an Indian tribe just a couple of doors down the street.

"Good. You got a minute?"

"Yeah, what's up?"

Fletcher convinced Blinkey for twenty bucks to leave his coffee station for a few minutes and help him out on the street. Sara, the sexy little high school girl cleaning the back and doing prep work, said she'd take over the counter for a while. It was slow anyway after the early morning rush.

So there they were out on the street, Bill Fletcher up on the aluminum ladder drilling in the angle-iron support piece. Blinkey had the square scallop shell sign under his arm, steadying the ladder.

"Hell, this is cool, man." He held the sign out to take it in. "Neskeet Nation. You are kickin' it." Blinkey had turned his Mets cap backward so he could see Fletcher better as he steadied the ladder and passed up tools. He lit up a cigarette while Fletcher worked and he watched.

"Yeah. It'll look pretty nice. This'll cause a little stir around here, I expect," Fletcher said, talking like a Maine lobsterman as he pulled a pair of bull-nose pliers out of his jeans. "Pass me those two rings, will ya?"

He looped them onto the black-iron support jutting out from the side of the building. He put his shoulder weight on the bracket, testing it. It was sturdy as hell. He had shot two big lag bolts into the side of the building to make sure the bracket and the sign wouldn't come down on someone's head in a high wind or a nor'easter.

"Okay, pass me up the sign."

Ten minutes later, the Neskeet Nation went public. The sign was up, swinging gently in the breeze. Fletcher pulled on the rig one more time. It felt solid. He climbed down and admired JD Ullson's handiwork.

"The clamshell's bitching, man," Blinkey said as he puffed on his Marlboro and exhaled. "It's a nice touch."

"Scallop. It's a scallop shell," Fletcher corrected.

"Whatever," Blinkey said. He grinned with his crooked nicotine-stained teeth and two-day island beard.

The two of them stood on the street, looking up at the sign. It hung majestically.

"It looks authentic, doesn't it?" Fletcher said.

"It looks dynamite. Shit, even better than our sign." Blinkey looked over at the Kona Koffee sign in comparison then took one more drag from his cigarette and dropped it on the sidewalk. He crushed the lit head with his black Converse basketball sneaker. "I gotta get back. Sara will have a bird."

"Yeah. Thanks for the help."

Bill Fletcher put the aluminum ladder back in his car. He looked at the sign from a different angle, now standing across the street. It still looked bitching. People would be talking.

He had begun the branding process in a big way.

Provisions

Fr. Peter Mulcahey drove his blue Chevrolet Impala slowly up Main Street, looking for a place to park. The car was a gift from the Shanahan Family when old Mrs. Shanahan died in bed two years ago at the ripe old age of ninety-two. The car had ferried her grandchildren around the Island in summer when they arrived for vacation from Short Hills, New Jersey. She had kept the car in her garage most of the time. It was ten years old and in mint condition.

Peter Mulcahey just needed to strap a longboard on top, and he'd be the surfing priest from Los Angeles, stepping right out of a sitcom from the seventies. He fantasized that he'd have his board shorts on with a dog collar and would spend his time counseling teenage girls not to get pregnant and the boys to stop smoking weed. Spreading the good word among the delinquents.

He hated the car because it was too goddamn big to drive around, even for the Island. The power steering kept crapping out as well. On the good side, the parish got it for free, and Bishop Guerin told him to accept it gratefully as the diocese had no money for a new Honda Civic like he wanted.

He finally found a spot in front of Superior Market and angled the car in slowly, swinging the wheel, trying not to hit the green Town of Oak Bluffs trash truck parked to his right. He barely made it. He got out and slammed the big door shut, leaving the window down. No need to lock it; this was the Island, the safest place on earth. All he had was an old foldable umbrella, a worn copy of the Bible, and a box of Kleenex in the backseat anyway.

He headed down the sidewalk toward the market to buy some dry kibble for Jackson, the little Irish terrier that he inherited when he took over the parish three years ago. Jackson was the rectory dog. Joanne Proctor, the rectory manager and majordomo, had forgot to get more dry food when she did the big shop during the week, and now the little growler was hungry.

The new Neskeet Nation sign just caught his eye as he walked, the bottom edge gently swaying in the sunlight. He stopped and looked at it for second. It had a big clamshell carved on the front, covered in gold leaf. Very upscale and understated. He thought it might have been for a new interior decorator on the Island. Lord knows, you never could have too many.

He looked over at the door on the building where the sign was. It was a ratty old one painted bright red. On the door was a hand-lettered sign that said Indian Office Upstairs with a limp arrow pointing up. He wondered.

He went into Reliable Market and looked for dry kibble and more Kleenex for himself. He loaded Purina Dog Chow in the big thirty-pound bag into the carriage. It was the cheapest on the shelf. Maybe not the best tasting for the dog, but he knew the Lord would want him to economize.

He splurged on himself, though, and got the expensive Kleenex, the ones with aloe for the rectory. He was always sniffling and blowing with his big Irish nose, and Joanne usually bought the cheap discount kind for him to use. This box cost a dollar more than the generic ones, but the creature comfort was well worth the difference.

He got to the front of the checkout line and knew the girls ringing and bagging.

"Good morning, Father." The priest was an Island rock star in his own right.

"Morning, girls." He hefted the big bag of dog food onto the black belt. "Now tell me, what's that Indian sign next door all about?"

The high school girls laughed.

"We've got some more Indians on the Island now. This is a new group. I forget their name, but the guy who runs it comes in here all the time."

"More Fluevogs? I thought they were all up in Aquinnah?" he asked.

"No, this group isn't them," the other girl said.

Peter Mulcahey noticed that she was attractive, her dark hair pulled back, dressed in tight jeans.

"They call themselves a tribe though, Father. The guy's name is Bill. I forget his last name. He seems nice enough."

"An Indian named Bill? What does he buy?"

"Junk food mostly. Gatorade and Cheetos. Pints of Häagen Dazs Vanilla Bean ice cream. All the expensive stuff."

"I see," Father Mulcahey said as he pondered that thought for a moment.

The girl pulled out a box of cards, looking for the Blessed Sacrament one. It was Superior's old-school accounts receivable system, cards in a box. She finally found the dog-eared relic and noticed that the church was up to date in its payments. She smiled. She put it on the counter and gave Father Peter a pen. He noticed her looking at the card.

"Joanne made a payment last week. We should have plenty of credit."

"You do, Father. You're all set," the girl doing the checking said.

He signed his name with a flourish.

"Paper or plastic, Father?" the cute girl in tight jeans doing the bagging asked. He looked at her and then down at her breasts for a second in an ultratight T-shirt. He couldn't help himself. He quickly looked up again.

The girl caught his look and felt a rush inside. She put the Kleenex in a plastic bag and handed it to him.

"Indians, huh?" he said. "Tell the man to come and say hi some day. We can have lunch. Maybe I'll convert him."

He winked at the girls as he hefted the dog food under his arm and walked out.

Peter Mulcahey back on the street started walking and thinking. A new tribe of Indians on the Vineyard. What a curious thing. He'd put his feelers out and find out what the hell was going on. They didn't need any more crazy Indians on the Island. They had enough. That much the Irish priest knew.

The Application

Everything seemed to explode all at once, like a thousand bottle rockets.

Bill Fletcher was busy. He was up in his office putting in long hours on his desktop, working on the Tribal Recognition Package for the Bureau of Indian Affairs, completing Form 25B along with its many supplements. The BIA didn't make it easy.

It was a critical piece of the puzzle though. In fact, it was the most important. If the tribal package went through and he got federal recognition for the Neskeets, he'd have legitimacy. Then he could apply for grant monies. He knew that there was seed money, start-up funds, that he might be able to tap into with a few well-written applications to gin up the machine. From there, it was open hunting season for long-term funding. Few people were as good as him at writing bullshit and making it sound meaningful.

So he spent many hours Googling *Bureau of Indian Affairs +Applications* to find out how to craft a tribal recognition package correctly.

He went online to the BIA itself and reviewed TRPs that were submitted over the last ten years by fledging tribes using big, high-powered law firms. He didn't waste any time though. He downloaded the application quickly with Adobe Acrobat, converted it to Word, and started filling it in with Neskeet information. He wanted to get the forms into the system. He could always amend them on the fly.

*   *   *

Later that afternoon, he was on the phone to New Mexico Indian Traders, talking turquoise.

"What do you have in a men's bracelet with a big chunky turquoise piece?" He cradled the phone to his ear and fingered the long cord that draped down to the floor. He had bought the twenty-six-foot version from Radio Shack and clipped it into his desk handset. Now he could stand up and walk around while he talked to dissipate his extra energy.

"Yeah, I need something nice, but not gaudy. It's got to be thin enough so I can get my shirt sleeve over it too."

"How much do you want to spend?" the saleswoman on the other end immediately asked. Qualify the prospect was the first rule in the jewelry sales business.

"Enough to look good. I'm an Indian chief, believe it or not." Fletcher let that one hang in the air for a second.

"Ha. No big deal. Everybody's an Indian chief down here in New Mexico. The place is full of 'em. They all come down here, buy some turquoise jewelry and blue jeans, and bingo, they're transformed. A thousand turquoise bracelets, a thousand Indian chiefs," she said. "You want sterling or gold?"

"No shit." Bill Fletcher grunted into the phone as he thought about it. It rang true. Everybody wanted to be an Indian, it seemed. The competition was fierce.

She described about ten pieces that weren't on the website yet and then sent him an e-mail with JPEG photos so he could decide then and there. He called her back in three minutes.

He also splurged and bought a big turquoise necklace, nothing gaudy, just something that he could wear to town meetings or other public events if called upon to speak and show off his Indianhood. He was building his wardrobe and his credibility at the same time. And nothing said it stronger in the Indian business than turquoise.

"I'll take the one in sterling with the big round opal on the top."

"That's a nice one. You've got good taste. I think it'll be close to fitting over your sleeve too. If not, just let it dangle on the end of your arm. It looks sexier that way anyway when you're in a casino playing cards."

"I said I'm an Indian chief."

"Uh-huh. And that's why I said *casino*," the saleswoman said. "How you paying for this?"

"MasterCard."

"Go ahead."

Bill Fletcher quickly finalized his purchase, ordered next-day air shipping, and made a mental note to check his credit card balance online after the call. He was spending money like shit through a goose, and he needed to keep some capacity on his card. It was expensive starting up an

Indian tribe. He needed more cash quickly, or he'd crash and burn. He made a mental note to get back to working on the applications.

As he put the phone down onto its cradle, he thought about the conversation he just had with the salesclerk at the jewelry store in New Mexico. Gambling indeed.

The casino thing was something worth looking into. He had never thought in that direction, but he had to be open to money-making opportunities—all of them and from wherever they came.

He'd check it out more when he had time.

The First Opportunity

Bill Fletcher and Carrie Nation were in the Purple Onion having lunch. It was his treat. It was a warm June day; everybody was getting ready for summer. The place wasn't crowded, and they had a table all to themselves at the front of the restaurant with the windows open, looking out on Main Street.

A big spider plant was hanging down right off Fletcher's left shoulder, between the windows, with giant bursts of baby tendrils and long stringy vines.

They ordered burgers and draft beers, and the waitress brought the two beers over in big frosted mugs with wide handles and heavy bottoms, old-school style. Carrie could barely lift hers up.

"I like the turquoise bracelet," Carrie said as she put her mug down on a coaster after she took her first sip. "Where'd you get it?"

Fletcher smiled. "I wasn't sure you'd notice."

He had his sleeves on his checked shirt rolled up a quarter turn, so it was hard not to notice. It looked like he had a blue rock strapped to his wrist.

"Not notice?" Carrie smiled. "That thing is the size of a Chevrolet. You could have asked me to help you order something a little more subtle, you know."

She fingered the piece of jewelry on his wrist. "I would have picked something for you that was a little smaller, slightly more discreet." She smiled and looked up. "But I gotta hand it to you, you're getting the hang of being an Indian real quick. I'm surprised, actually."

Fletcher's ears perked up, and his brow wrinkled a bit. This was valuable feedback. Carrie was very perceptive to all totems of popular culture.

"How do you mean? Don't pull my chain, okay?"

She looked at him with a flash of her blue eyes. "I'm watching you change, right before my eyes. I thought it was a joke at first, you saying you were Indian and all, cheap Boston lawyer. But you're slowly doing it, converting and all that. Course correcting. You're definitely getting the look down all of a sudden, I'll give you that."

"Yeah?" Fletcher rubbed the turquoise bracelet as they spoke. "Is it too big?"

"No, it's fine. It's actually very tasteful. I'm surprised that you picked it out. None of the men down here wear jewelry like that, so it's a good way to stand out. It's very Indian is all I mean. It's a nice touch for a chief."

Carrie sat back and looked at Fletcher.

"I think it's the hair too. You look good with it longer. It's dark, so it looks Indian too."

She reached out and touched a clump of it, moving it around the part a little. "Let it grow out some more, even longer. But you've got to stay clean shaven 'cause that's what Indians do. No facial hair, okay? I'll help you with your look if you want."

Never one to pass up free help, Fletcher jumped on it. "Yeah, I can use the help. You've got that good eye for detail."

Carrie Nation looked at Bill Fletcher. He was attractive, maybe even good-looking, for an Indian. Who knew? It was all a lark, she figured. She could do dress up with the best of them and have some fun with it. They were just dating anyway, casual, so she'd let the summer play out and see what developed.

"This place is full of bullshitters anyway," she said. "The whole island is one big con game. Most of the Indians I see down here have never been any closer to a horse or a buffalo than you or me. It's a joke."

Fletcher looked at her. "That may change, just wait."

"Huh?" Carrie looked around the restaurant. She had on jeans, pink sneakers, and an Indian batik cotton top with colored thread woven in. Not American Indian, but India Indian. The real dark-skinned guys. She looked good, filling out her clothes in all the right places, Fletcher noticed. Very hip and modern.

The burgers came, and Fletcher pulled off the lettuce and tomato first thing and threw them to the side. He grabbed the ketchup bottle and made a big puddle of the red goop on the plate for his fries.

They tucked into first bites.

"So I have an idea," Carrie said, "to start getting your brand out there and make it known. It'll help me out too. Synergistic. You know what I mean?"

"I love synergy," Fletcher said between a mouthful of fries.

She put her burger down and picked up her handbag from the floor. It was light blue with beach imprints on the side and big plastic handles. The thing was the size of a suitcase, but it was what all the girls were using that summer to haul stuff around. Big clunky bags, all throwbacks to Elizabeth Taylor in the sixties.

"My brand?" Fletcher said as he took another big bite.

"Yeah, you're brand. I'm thinking T-shirts. Quality ones with your logo and all. All two-hundred thread count cotton for sure. What are you calling your tribe again?" She pulled out a stack of sheets from the bag and put them on the edge of the table. "Let's take a look."

They waitress came and took the plates away, and Carrie Nation and Bill Fletcher spent the next half hour going over her T-shirt designs for the tribe.

"What are you calling yourself again? The Neskeets? I keep forgetting that name. It sounds funny," Carrie said, arranging the pieces of paper with the images she had drawn freehand on the tabletop.

"Yep, the Neskeets," Fletcher annunciated precisely.

"Yeah, whatever. Parakeet, Neskeet, we'll work with it," Carrie said.

She was into her pitch now, talking and arranging her designs. "We'll only do high quality, like the Black Dog ones. We'll have the image of the clamshell and the word *Neskeet* below it. Then on the back, we'll do something like The New Indian Nation 2010."

"I like it," Bill Fletcher said. "It has a ring to it, and it'll stand out. Differentiate us."

"Yeah, I think so. But only high-quality shirts, and not a ton of styles. Two for men and maybe three for women. And a bunch for kids. The hipsters from New York will all want their kids to have an Indian T-shirt. It'll be cool, you watch."

Fletcher liked the idea. It was a great kickoff for his reach-out campaign. "How much will you sell them for?"

"I'm thinking twenty-five bucks, and it'll be a great high-quality shirt. People will pay that if it's durable and it lasts. But they've got to see the quality right away. They've got to feel it. I can probably do them for twenty each, so we'll make five bucks a shirt."

"As long as we're not losing money, that's all."

"No." Carrie shook her head. "I'm going to make it a profit center. It'll be front-window stuff in the Equinox. Plus, it'll help sell my other hippie inventory."

They sat for thirty more minutes and talked ideas and details. It was cool. Fletcher looked around and saw that there were plenty of empty tables at this point in the season, so they weren't taking up space for tourists spending money.

Fletcher picked up the check and put it on his new company credit card. He had gotten three or four credit cards in the name of the Neskeet Nation, LLC so that he could charge things like that lunch as a business expense.

He was going to create a nice auditable trail for the accountants. He knew that the feds had got Al Capone, the old-school Chicago gangster, for tax evasion. It was a little-known fact, but they got him for basically bad records and not all the murders he committed.

Fletcher wasn't going to be sloppy on the bullshit details. He'd give the feds and the tax cops all his receipts if they asked for them and be buttoned down. Human nature and small minds always missed the big picture and focused in on the details. He could certainly arrange that.

He paid the bill and left a good tip. He and Carrie walked out of the restaurant.

Carrie's T-shirt idea was a game changer, and they both were energized for different reasons going out the door and back to work.

Real Indians

Carl Sunapee drove along Beach Road in his brand-new Cadillac Seville STS. It was a deep-maroon red, and it gleamed in the sunlight.

He got a new one every three years, on lease, as befitted the chief of the Aquinnah Fluevog Indians. He had some old seventies Philly Sound music on, a greatest hits CD playing Harold Melvin & the Blue Notes. Teddy Pendergrass was singing deep and low in the background with Carl's fingers tapping out the beat on the wood-effect steering wheel.

He had added custom alloy rims off-Island for the Caddy when he got it at French Motors in Newton in the spring. They weren't gang banger rims, but they were custom, and they tricked out his ride a bit.

It was just the kind of car that someone important on Martha's Vineyard would drive, almost verging on tacky, like Spike Lee or Vernon Jordan when they weren't playing golf or drinking at the bar at Farm Neck.

He had vanity plates on the STS, paid the extra money at the Registry of Motor Vehicles every year for them. The plates said FLUEVOG1 in big red letters that nearly matched the paint job. He had just made it with the letters, thank Christ. The Massachusetts RMV only allowed eight letters maximum on a vanity plate, and FLUEVOG1 fit perfectly. Otherwise, his second pick was INDIAN.

He had to admit, it was a nice touch.

Carl got to the end of Beach Road near the ferry terminal and turned left going past the police station. He had his window down and his arm out, resting it on top of the door. His big gold Rolex shone like a healing crystal on his wrist. People knew who he was.

He looked at the town police cars, all new Dodge Challengers, as he drove past. The black-and-whites were sitting in the sun, angle parked. He nodded in appreciation. Give it to the cops; they had nice rides, almost as nice as his.

He did a California stop in front of the bank, meaning he slowed way down and tapped his brake lights, never coming to a full stop, then he rolled through the corner. He headed left up Main Street. Manny Fernandez had said that the place was halfway up on the left, just past the Kona Koffee shop.

He turned the music off so he could think clearly as he moved slowly up the street in the line of traffic. Sure enough, just like Manny had said, he saw the clamshell sign, swinging on its davits, next to the sunglass shop, saying Neskeet Indians and the hand-lettered sign on the red door, stuck there with Scotch Tape and the big black arrow pointing up the stairs.

There was a space right in front of the building, so he swung in and parked the STS. He got out, stretched, and closed his door slowly. He crossed the street to get a better perspective as he looked up into the Neskeet offices.

He had to hand it to whoever was doing this shit; the sign looked good, nice, and professional. Like a pro had done it. He shook his head as he compared it mentally to the Fluevog office up in Aquinnah. They didn't have any sign over their door. It had fallen off in a hurricane three years ago. And even when they had one, it was a piece of shit.

Carl was incredulous. He couldn't believe that there was another Indian tribe on the Vineyard that he didn't know about. He took a deep breath, shrugged his shoulders, and headed into Carol Ann's Diner right in front of him. Damn. He needed to run his trap lines and get some recon on what was happening with these so-called Neskeets.

Everyone knew him inside. The place was full of locals and a lot of tourists too. Carl Sunapee was a minor celebrity on the Island being the chief of the Fluevog Indians, the real Indians of Martha's Vineyard. He sat on an open stool at the counter and got a cup of coffee.

"Hey, Carl," Cheryl, the counter waitress said, dropping a white ceramic cup and saucer in front of him and filling it with black coffee. "What do you think about those new Indians across the street?" She didn't waste any time getting right to it.

Carl was going to take it easy at first, be friendly, signal to everybody that he wasn't ticked off in the least that someone else was trying to hijack his franchise about being Indian on Martha's Vineyard. He was too cool for that.

"Who you talking about?" Carl laughed as he sipped his coffee with cream and one sugar.

"The Neskeets," Cheryl said from down the counter.

"Goddamn news to me."

"Yeah, they've been here since April. The sign went up two weeks ago. I haven't been in there yet, but they seem nice enough."

She came over and wiped the counter down next to Carl. "The guy's good-looking, I'll give him that." She smiled.

"Who? The guy that's running that place?"

"Yeah. Kind of a Don Draper type."

"He better looking than me?" Carl asked.

"Nobody's better looking than you, Carl," Cheryl said as she adjusted the coffee machine without looking back.

Carl sipped his coffee quietly. "What's his name?" Carl asked, not wanting to appear too interested.

"Bill Fletcher. He comes in all the time. Nice guy." Cheryl stood in front of Carl Sunapee. "He sure doesn't look like he has any Indian in him, though. He looks like a wash ashore."

They both laughed. Nothing was more derogatory than being called a wash ashore by an Islander.

Carl was an Islander and a Fluevog Indian. So he had the double mojo, the street cred, the real deal, and everybody knew it.

"Shit. It's fine with me," Carl said, sipping his coffee, not getting upset. "It's just that I'm Indian, and I never heard of them before, if you know what I mean."

"It's crazy, isn't it? Two Indian tribes on this little island," Cheryl said as she moved over to take another customer's order.

Carl talked to some of the locals for a bit, drank his coffee, and paid his bill. He left a good tip, as always. That was one of the things that Indian chiefs did. The real ones at least. They took care of their constituents.

"I'm curious, is all," Carl said as he got up to leave the restaurant, taking a toothpick from the plastic dispenser next to the cash register. He waited for his change.

"Find out what you can for me, Cheryl, will you? There's plenty of space for all of us Indians on the Island, but I'd jut like to know who the hell my relatives are. Who I'm dealin' with. That's all."

And that was it. Carl stayed cool about the new Indians on the block. He didn't telegraph any bad vibe to the people in the diner. But he wasn't happy, not by a long shot.

He put his black alligator wallet back in his pocket and walked out the door to get another look at the Neskeet sign. He had to hand it to Bill Fletcher. It sure looked cool and official.

Shirt Shop

Carrie Nation had what they called a soft opening in the retail world for the new Indian T-shirts in the Equinox.

Her store sales had been picking up with the summer coming on and the tourists returning. She had some nice clothing, stylish things for the beach crowd and then a little hippie section where she sold incense and rolling papers and jewelry. She sold a lot of rolling paper and pot pipes. They still smoked plenty of weed on the Island, no doubt.

She had worked hard over the last month putting the shirts into production. She'd hunker down over the countertop in the store when it was slow and do draft after draft on tracing paper of men's and women's tees, sketching the designs. The clamshell in the center, in blue, in green, all kinds of variations.

Bill came over frequently in the afternoons, seeing her there in jeans and black clogs, leaning over the counter working away, her brown hair hanging over the paper, focused and intent.

Coming in from outside, Fletcher knew how he wanted it to play out and how it sometimes did, him putting up the Back in Ten Minutes clock sign on the door and then taking Carrie into the women's changing room in back.

Jeans pulled down with one leg up on the wooden bench, Carrie showed Bill creativity that he'd never experienced before. Bill Fletcher, Indian chief, would have his squaw up against the changing room wall, both of them flushed with the excitement of the adventure.

Carrie finished the T-shirt design soon enough and quickly had about a hundred made for men and women in stonewashed colors of blue, red, and green. The clamshell was big and iconic on the front of the shirt with the words *Neskeet Nation* below it. On the back in small letters in a square box, it said The Real Indians of Cape Cod. And underneath, Summer of 2010. It turned out to be an instant collector's item.

She put the shirts in the front of her store, on the big wooden table with wide pine boards polyurethaned within an inch of their life, facing out at an angle for people to immediately see coming in the door. She had one T-shirt, her best design, hanging on a pine pole above the display. It turned out to be a perfect hook for customers on the street.

Bill Fletcher came in on Thursday looking for some back room nooky and maybe a few more incense sticks for the office. He saw the T-shirts and was impressed.

"Hey, the display's pretty cool. The T-shirts look awesome."

"Do you like it?" Carrie went over to the display, looked at it, and fingered the shirt on the pole. She unconsciously refolded the top T-shirt in the stack and then squared off the piles as they talked. She could have worked at the Gap.

"Are you selling any yet?" Fletcher asked.

"Believe it or not, they're flying off the shelves. Like shit through a goose, as you'd say. But I don't want to be vulgar." Carrie winked at Fletcher as she finished arranging the shirts.

"The Summer of 2010 thing on the back is a nice hook. Like a rock concert. It's a souvenir for the tourists, a remembrance. Everybody's buying 'em. I've sold out twice."

"Huh?" Bill Fletcher asked, more than a little surprised.

"Yeah. Business is great."

Carrie walked back over to the front counter. She was wearing one of her long skirts and wedge clogs. Sexy faux hippie again. "I'm all of a sudden doing well. This is my best start for a summer season, ever. People come in, buy a Neskeet T-shirt, usually two, and then see all my other stuff. I'm upselling like crazy. It's incredible."

And so it went. Carrie started selling a lot of the Indian T-shirts, and the whole virtuous cycle was spawned. The Neskeet Nation rose up on the back of two hundred weight-cotton shirts from Indonesia.

Federal Government

It was a warm June day in Washington, DC. The trees and bushes had turned green, and the city had a lush feel as the stifling summer heat started to roll in. The tour buses were littered all over Capitol Hill and the Mall. Everybody was flocking to see the two big slabs of black granite in the *V* at the Vietnam memorial and then strolling over to the World War II display area.

Over at the Bureau of Indian Affairs at 150 K Street, things were cooking. The big squat office building at the corner of K and Eighteenth housed the headquarters for the Bureau of Indian Affairs, the BIA, where all the important decisions were made. While there were certainly other Indian administrative offices scattered around the city, including important departments like history and artifacts, the administration of the Indian tribes was all done right there at 150 K.

Harold Schumer, senior project manager in the Indian Tribal Unit, sat in a big-window conference room, half listening to the meeting going on around him and scratching his hairy arm.

He looked out the window at the street people sitting on benches in the park below, across from the building on Eighteenth Street. Filthy bastards. Each took up their own part of a park bench with their own shopping cart and cardboard boxes sitting on the bench next to them.

One guy with a straggly beard was standing behind an azalea bush, legs spread, pissing into the bushes. *God damn homeless people*, Harold thought to himself. After all the programs in place to help them in the district, including free housing and food, they still liked to pee in the bushes and sit on the benches all day. It made all the parks stink like the zoo. It was criminal, them taking up all the space in the public areas everywhere, nowhere for the office workers and tourists to sit and eat lunch. Just irresponsible was what it was. Harold shook his head in disgust.

Harold Schumer, BIA project manager with a law degree from Georgetown and five years in the department, turned his attention to Mindy Sanchez sitting at the head of the table. She was a staffer, another attorney actually, who was below him in the pecking order and who went through all the tribal applications and dealt with the paperwork when it initially came in.

Harold spent a long minute looking at Mindy and pretending to listen. She had a killer body. Large breasts that were beautifully formed that she showed off in a Victoria's Secret uplift bra, tight against her white cotton blouse. They were straining against the fabric of the shirt, softly pushing out in exactly the right places. She knew how to showcase her assets.

Mindy also wore tight skirts slightly above the knee and high heels. She was the fashion plate of the office. She was Harold's sexy chica fulfilling all his Hispanic fantasies, and she kept him from spending time surfing porn in the office. He didn't need to—he had the real thing right down the hall. It made for fun meetings.

"So the good news is that this tribal application looks complete. The 25B is filled out correctly, and all the supporting schedules are in as well. I think we may have a winner here," Mindy said.

"De novo or a reconstitution?" Harold asked. He jumped right to the technical specifications.

"Brand new, de novo, believe it or not," Mindy said. "The group is called the Neskeets, and they're from Cape Cod."

"How come we haven't heard about them before?" Harold was quick to ask. "I thought that was Fluevog country and tight as a tick. That's Carl Sunapee's area, isn't it? I'm surprised that there's a new tribe down there with everything being so mature." Harold looked at Mindy and then waited.

"That was my take at first too. But this tribe actually has roots from a different part of the Cape, farther down, near Chatham. It all looks legitimate, believe it or not."

"How's the ancestry supported?"

"He has a solid report backing up his tribal claim," Mindy answered. "I even talked to the researcher."

"Did Justice review the file? What do they think?" Harold knew that everybody had to be on board, particularly the Department of Justice, before a new tribe could be processed.

"Yeah, they did. They cleared it. I have the letter here," Mindy said. "And the Bureau's reviewed them last week. There were no priors or any federal problems at all."

Harold and Mindy continued the Neskeet Nation file review.

"So who's the principal?" Harold asked.

"A guy named Bill Fletcher. Boston guy. Came up from out of nowhere. Not so unusual. At least he's not from a flophouse in the South End." Mindy knew her Boston geography and was testing Harold now. Harold had his undergraduate degree from Boston University, so he knew Boston cold.

"Mindy, there are no flophouses in the South End. It's all yuppie condos and restaurants."

"I know, it's just like Georgetown. It's criminal."

They both laughed.

Harold Schumer nodded his head and looked through the paperwork lightly. It was thick, probably an inch in height, held together nice and orderly with a big two-inch alligator clip. The biggest-size alligator clip they had in the office to be able to hold it all together.

He didn't have the time to read through the Neskeet Nation Indian application in detail though. He knew that it was all mostly bullshit anyway. They all were. He wanted to get the meeting over so he could call the Parks Police and have that homeless fucker rousted out of the park, the one that was pissing on the azaleas. The pee smelt like hell once the hot weather set in and the acid in the urine hurt the plants' growth. Harold Schumer turned back to Mindy, glanced at her tits, and was back to the matter at hand.

"Well, it looks like this is Bill Fletcher and the Neskeet Nation's lucky day," he said. "Believe it or not, Frank Simpson mentioned to me in the section heads meeting that we needed to get more money out or we'd lose it. That tribal grants were at their lowest in over thirty-six months. He joked that we'd lose our jobs if we didn't bring in some new business. This app will certainly help."

Mindy Sanchez took a big breath in. It was exciting to possibly be in on a new tribe formation. Her blouse tightened even further over her breasts, if that was at all possible. She could feel her chest pushing out against the cotton. She turned them full on to Harold, getting his attention in a point-and-shoot maneuver.

"What were you doing in section heads?" she asked.

"Carol was away, and I filled in. Nothing important."

"Nice," she said.

He threw the alligator-clipped file back across the table toward Mindy. "This all looks good. Draft the authorization letter, and I'll sign it today.

Let's get a package out this week. Qualify them for a start-up grant, subject to verification of course, for initial costs and expenses."

Mindy looked over at Harold. She pushed her hair off her face, waiting. "For how much?"

Harold didn't hesitate. "Go for ten million, the minimum. With start-up costs, a new tribal office, and all the other bullshit, they'll piss through that like lightning. Maybe they'll start a casino while they're at it."

"Bill Fletcher is going to be one happy man come Friday," Mindy said.

"So be it," Harold said. "Good for him. But schedule quarterly audits so we can be sure that they don't spend the funding on bullshit. I don't want it to look bad, or we'll be screwed. It was whiskey in the old days, and now it's money. It can't reflect poorly on us."

Mindy couldn't believe that Harold Schumer would say something that racist in the office, particularly the Indian Affairs office. But the inner workings of the BIA had never failed to blow her mind.

Whatever, she thought. She could see that the meeting was over anyway.

But Mindy knew that Harold was right about having to keep track of the federal money once it went out. She would have to check up on the Neskeets regularly because ready cash was dangerous stuff for anybody. It was amazing what the tribes spent money on in the past and called legitimate. If the public found out in these tough economic times, they'd freak out and put their BIA heads on a post.

"Thanks," Harold mumbled as he walked out of the room. "Good summary."

He headed toward the smaller conference room down the corridor. It had a better view of the park and, therefore, the homeless people. He'd call the Parks Police from there. He was determined to get that guy who peed in the azalea bushes today. The fucker.

The Golden Letter

Bill Fletcher sat fiddling at his desk on that bright sunny day in June. He'd always remember it. It was like wandering around in the Egyptian desert for twenty years in the hot sun, looking for important archaeological stuff, not finding any, and then stumbling into King Tut's tomb.

The air-conditioning was on, and the office was cool. He liked his creature comforts. There was no need to be an uncomfortable sweaty Indian chief.

He was starting to go through his mail that he just retrieved from the post office. He had a pile of junk mail along with a lot of bills and letters. Fletcher was amazed at how many bills he quickly accumulated on behalf of the Neskeet Nation.

He'd have to taper back soon enough on expenses if he couldn't bring some of his money-making ideas to fruition quickly. He was burning through his $25,000 seed money quickly that he had in his checking account.

A thick letter arrived from the Bureau of Indian Affairs. Fletcher saw the return address immediately and saw his name listed as "Principal, Neskeet Nation" in the little cellophane address pane. He flushed red immediately, and a jolt of electricity coursed through his veins.

Screw it, he thought. *Go for it*. He ripped the top of the envelope open with his pen cap, and he pulled the letter out from inside. He quickly scanned it. The first sentence said it all.

> The Bureau of Indian Affairs, after careful consideration, hereby validates the claim of the Neskeet Nation for recognition and sovereignty under US Code Section 572 (1)f-g.

Bill Fletcher knew he was a made man from that point forward.

It had worked. His bogus Indian application, swaddled in the best legal jargon and wordsmithing that he was capable of, had won the day.

It was a joyous event for Fletcher. He read the letter again slowly, word by word. The text was all good. It referenced the genealogy report and how the tribe was a legitimate group that had habituated on Cape Cod over 150 years ago. He couldn't believe that the bullshit he had thrown against the wall had stuck. In fact, it had stuck and hardened like cement.

The last paragraph on page 1 was the culmination. It said that the Neskeets qualified for a grant of funds from the Bureau of Indian Affairs to "establish the administration and structure" of the tribe. He could tap into a grant for an office and community center, for computer equipment and hardware, and even to fund Indian-related business ventures to allow the tribe to become self-sustaining.

It was all a heady brew. And the amount of the grant to get the Neskeet Nation up and running to fund his start-up tribe?

Bill Fletchers's eyes moved slowly down the second page to the next to the last paragraph. He scratched his nose slowly as he read the antiseptic words on the page. The United States federal government was in a generous mood with plenty of funds for the Neskeets.

The letter stated that the tribe was allocated a grant for ten million dollars. That it was available to Bill Fletcher as soon as a qualified bank account was set up and wiring instructions were delivered to the BIA Accounting and Cash Management Department.

Bill Fletcher was caught off guard and astonished. He blurted out "Yes! Yes! Yes!" He threw his fist into the air.

He read the letter again. "Ten million dollars! Unbelievable!" he said under his breath. He had hit the Indian lottery. What to do? He put his black cowboy boots up on the desk and got comfortable. He looked out the window of the Neskeet Nation offices and smiled. It was a big, broad genuine smile, a heartfelt one.

He nodded his head in appreciation of the unlikely events that were suddenly happening to him: meeting Carrie, the T-shirt business, and now the federal grant materializing.

Here we go, he thought.

Part II

Houston, We Have Ignition

All Business

Father Peter Mulcahey was having lunch with Margaret Wellington on the harbor in Oak Bluffs.

They were at Susan's Snack Bar, sitting on the top deck under a Corona Beer umbrella and faux fishing nets draped over the railings. Margaret was eating a Caesar salad with grilled chicken, and Father Peter had a tuna pocket on pita with fries. They both had glasses of Pinot Grigio. Peter Mulcahey decided a long time ago that living well was the best revenge.

He looked over at Margaret. She had on a bright scarf that picked up her soft complexion. They were both excited from the success of the bingo games in the parish. It was a little wellspring of money that was paying off a lot of overdue bills sitting on the rectory table.

"It's all good, Margaret, isn't it?" Father Peter said as he looked at her across the table.

"Yes, Father. We're grossing over $1,500 a night now. It's helping our finances big time."

"Do we have to pay tax on it?"

"Not according to Bill Peters."

Margaret Wellington took a bite of her salad before continuing, "He said that it was charitable and essential to the purpose of the church. We have to be careful and not have it classified as unrelated business taxable income. He called it UBTI. If that happened, he said we'd be in trouble with the IRS. That we'd be screwed, as he put it."

She laughed and looked over at Father Peter. He had a sparkle in his eyes.

"What does that mean? I'm just a simple man of the cloth." He gave her a big stage wink.

"What it means, Father, is that Bill Peters said that you should say a prayer before the start of every bingo game if you can, and that would cleanse the game and make it holy, make it a part of the Catholic faith, so to speak. That way he'd be able to classify it as church related so there'd be no UBTI, and he could keep it off the tax return. You'd be protecting his CPA license and all."

They talked more business as they ate and enjoyed the early summer sun. It was a spectacular day on the deck, and they had called it right to eat outside.

If had certainly been a long time ago for her, but if she didn't know better and if this wasn't the pastor of her parish, Margaret Wellington swore to herself that it felt like she was on a date. She had the same excitement and sexual tension that she had meeting men after college.

But now, she no longer had any inhibitions in her life. The pain and suffering from the loss of her husband, Jed, from pancreatic cancer, had washed all that shyness and self-consciousness away.

Now she was free. She decided to put her trust and faith in the Lord. She caught the eye of their waitress and ordered two more glasses of wine as they ate and talked.

"Can I have a coffee cup if you don't mind, please?" Peter Mulcahey asked the waitress, who had her hair pulled back in a ponytail when she brought the two refills. The girl brought one over, and he poured the second wine into the ceramic cup. He handed the empty wineglass back to the waitress.

"Here, you can take this now." The two women couldn't believe his chicanery.

"It looks better, you know," he said as he laughed. "It's a small island, and I've got to keep up appearances."

He winked at the college girl waitress who caught on to his bullshit immediately. She took the wineglass and left the couple alone.

"You're too much, Father," Margaret said as they ate and drank.

"Call me Peter."

"Well, you're still too much Peter. Hiding wine in a coffee cup. It feels like a cheap movie."

Peter Mulcahey sipped the cold white wine and looked at Margaret Wellington.

"It is a cheap movie, Margaret. It's called Martha's Vineyard, remember? It's a seaside version of Peyton Place, with beach sand and suntan lotion."

They finished their food and continued to talk about money.

"We've got to increase the games to twice a week," Peter Mulcahey said. He was bold now with the two wines in him, fermenting in his stomach in the warm sun.

"That's easy to do, Peter. We have the rec hall on Tuesdays and Thursdays reserved for parish outreach."

"You need to move one game to Friday night. I think we'll get more people to come if it's a weekend night. Something to do for the parishioners. Dinner and bingo. And white wine. They all go good together."

Peter Mulcahey was a good Irish businessman at his core.

Margaret thought about it for a minute." I think you might be right. I bet we'd do great if we have bingo Tuesday and Friday nights. It might work."

"Just have faith in the Lord, and we'll get all our bills taken care of."

They got the check, and Margaret Wellington paid. "It's on me, Peter. I thoroughly enjoyed this. I'll treat today."

The priest made no pretense of paying for the meal. It was one of the perks of priesthood.

"Just run it through the bingo expenses, Margaret. This is business, you know. It's deductible." He winked again.

"You can call me Margie, Father, if you want," she said.

She had a slight buzz herself from the two wines and the summer sun. She couldn't believe she had just said that to Peter Mulcahey, her parish priest.

She looked over at him as they got up and decided that he was handsome with that rugged Irish look. And she knew that he was gentle at his core. She wondered for an instant what it would be like having sex with him. She blushed deep red as they started to walk across the deck to the stairs to leave.

The cute college waitress stood over at the service station filling plastic ketchup bottles, killing time. She noticed that the handsome priest put his hand in the small of the attractive woman's back as they left the table, and they headed toward the stairs. It was probably his sister, she thought, over to the island for a visit.

Why else would he make such an intimate gesture like that? He was a priest, for God's sake.

New Money

The first thing that Bill Fletcher did after he came down from his adrenaline high the next day was go to the Martha's Vineyard Bank and set up a tribal savings and checking account.

He was dressed Indian: jeans, checked dress shirt with pointy collars, the turquoise bracelet on one wrist, and his big Timex Ironman watch on the other. He wore his black cowboy boots with the two-inch heels, polished up nicely now that he had money. He also had on his Indian chief persona, leader of the tribe, Big Balls Bill today.

The only problem was that he didn't have any tribal members to lead. That part, getting new acolytes into the fold, would be next on the to-do list. He just hadn't had time lately with all the other stuff happening. He figured that getting the money in the house was job number one, so he focused on that, like any good start-up entrepreneur would do.

So there he sat in a small spare conference room at the bank with an attractive bank manager, a Vineyard mother, with her fresh-scrubbed good looks and earnestness. She had on her best "eager to please" attitude. She smelled good, and her hair was still slightly damp from her morning shower. She probably had two kids and a carpenter for a husband, Fletcher figured.

The room had two pictures of Vineyard ferries on the wall, with little brass plaques underneath each. They sat in wooden barrel chairs, the ones with the upholstered arms and backs that had small little rivets outlining the padded parts. The conference room was all glass, and the two of them were looking at bank customers doing their business right in front of them.

"So here's your paperwork for both the commercial checking and savings accounts combined, Mr. Fletcher," Donna Stevens said as she looked Fletcher over. She was all business as she pushed the papers over to him, each marked with little red "Sign Here" arrows.

"Call me Bill," he said as he quickly looked over the forms. "Are we going to be able to make wire transfers into this account?"

"Absolutely, Bill." She was a fast learner.

He looked at the name on the account. "I need this to be in the tribe's name and my own name individually. It needs to be a joint account."

"What's the tribal name again?"

"The Neskeet Nation."

Donna Stevens tried not to laugh. She looked a little more closely now at Bill Fletcher. His dark hair had grown out onto his collar, and he seemed to have a bit of a protruding jaw. Maybe Indian, maybe not. She really couldn't tell if he was just bullshitting her or telling the truth.

"We'll need identification, Mr. Fletcher. KYC type information. All the basics."

"What the hell is that?" Fletcher said.

By this time, Donna Stevens's morning scent had overtaken the small glass conference room. Fletcher realized that he could be horny in a minute for this Vineyard MILF, but he didn't have time to flirt this morning. Without the money in his account, he was nowhere.

"KYC. Know your customer. It's a new group of federal banking regulations. We'll have to do a brief background check on your organization." She made a little smile as a punctuation, telling Fletcher that it had to be done. "It's basic. I just need to run your account names through our anti-money laundering software for a check. It's all pretty routine."

"Look, I need to be able to wire money into this account today. Federal funds type stuff, with wiring instructions and all the setup." He looked over at her, pushing the signed papers back across the table.

"Donna, I'll get you all that other stuff as we go. I promise."

Donna Stevens cocked her head a bit as she thought. "It's a little unusual for wiring capability to be put on an individual account so quickly. Usually that takes a week to set up, that's all."

"I need it today." Fletcher put the pressure on her immediately.

She looked back at Bill Fletcher, her first Indian chief customer.

"How much do you want to wire into the account, Bill?"

"How about ten million dollars?"

"I'm sorry?"

"Ten million. Today." He let that sink in for a few seconds." Can you do that, Donna? 'Cause otherwise, I think the bank down the street said they could if you can't." Bill was being an asshole all of a sudden.

"I'll be right back." Donna Stevens said as she got up and stepped out of the room.

Fletcher watched her walk out. She was full of energy and determination. She walked quickly across the bank to the closed offices on the other side. He could see that she was a real go-getter.

When she came back a minute later, no more, she had a middle-aged white guy with a small paunch in tow.

Jack Fraker, president of the bank, happened to be in his office that morning, working. He had on a white button-down oxford shirt with a red rep tie. Classic and conservative. He also happened to be available to do a little battlefield KYC right there in the conference room. Donna and Jack Fraker were both smiling big at Bill Fletcher.

Fletcher didn't waste any time. He quickly explained the Indian thing and the formation of the Neskeet Nation. Jack Fraker was looking at him, smiling and assessing, as he listened. He had been conned by a lot of customers in his time, but he didn't know how to read Fletcher. With the longish hair and the square jaw, hell, he could be an Indian. Who the hell knew nowadays?

He did know, though, that he needed big new customers and that a ten million dollar depository account would blow through all his performance plan hurdles for the next three years. He was thinking about the bonus he'd get from the board and being able to finally buy that new Grady-White fishing boat.

Fletcher himself was good at playacting. He had his rap down. He finished his quick synopsis of the Neskeet Nation and pushed forward to seal the deal. He put his left hand on the tabletop, relaxed like, and lightly drummed his fingers.

Jack Fraker noticed the giant chunky turquoise bracelet on his wrist sitting there like a talisman. The turquoise jewelry did it. It sealed the deal. The bank president knew an Indian when he saw one.

He sighed and spoke. "Bill, we'd love to have you as a customer. I think Donna and myself can expedite the paperwork here today and have your wiring capability active by noon. We can move heaven and earth for our best customers, even new ones. Will that work?"

Fletcher smiled, satisfied with where it was headed. He had accomplished his biggest task for the day already, and it was only 10 a.m.

"That's great, Jack. I knew that you could help expedite things. It'll be good for the bank, working with a local Native-American organization like mine, helping us grow roots in the business community. It's going to be the start of a beautiful relationship. Trust me."

"Exactly," Jack Fraker said.

"There might even be some good PR for the bank along the way here. The local angle and all."

"Who knows?" Fraker nodded, throwing his hands open in a "we'll see what happens" gesture.

The three of them bullshitted for another fifteen minutes in the bank conference room while Jack Fraker and Donna Stevens sold Fletcher a bunch of monthly add-on account services that he didn't need.

Fletcher didn't care; he was happy to be charged some hefty monthly fees as long as he had the basics in place, and fast. He knew the bank needed to make money on the account any way it could.

They finally finished and shook hands all around, and Jack Fraker escorted Fletcher right to the front door. He gave Fletcher a subtle homey little pat on the shoulder as he was ready to walk out.

"You're going to like our service, I guarantee it."

"I know I will," Fletcher said as he walked out onto the sidewalk and headed up Main Street.

Jack Fraker walked back through the bank and into the conference room where Donna Stevens was reviewing the application papers for Fletcher's account. He cut to the chase.

"You have a copy of that letter from the feds, right, for our file? Call that guy who signed it right now and find out what the story is with this guy. Do some due diligence. The last thing we need is to get caught with our pants down on this one. The ten million is nice for our depository funds, but we've got to make sure the money's clean. The guy looks like a drug dealer, and that's the last thing we need. Make sure you put a copy of the AML database search in the file too for backup in case we get audited."

Jack Fraker walked out of the conference room scratching his head. He continued to be amazed at the crazy customers who came in the door, even after all these years.

Executive Wheels

Bill Fletcher was on the 8:00 a.m. ferry steaming toward Woods Hole. The boat was the *Island Home* and was the newest addition to the Martha's Vineyard Steamship Authority fleet. She was big, holding over 150 cars and seating for 435 people. The design was still old-school, a double-ender, with wheelhouses at both the bow and the stern.

It lay squat in the water as the cars and passengers were loaded. Once they were underway, the boat pushed the water rather than cutting through it as it ploughed forward, creating a trim little *V* wave at the bow. It was a flat calm day, high summer, and the seagulls followed the boat out across Falmouth Sound.

Fletcher had walked on and was sitting upstairs in the canteen, drinking coffee. The coffee was miserable, as was the rest of the food on the ferry line, but it was all that was available. There were no Starbucks kiosks on the MVSSA. It was mostly steam table stuff: coffee in big urns, hamburgers on beds of lettuce wrapped in plastic, and hot dogs on rollers. All bullshit. Fletcher was nursing a large dark roast and a honey-dipped doughnut. He was watching the news on the big flat-screen TV mounted on the far wall of one of the seating areas.

He strategized about the Neskeets. Fletcher didn't want to end up like most of the other Indian tribes out there. The Fluevogs went glacially slow and did all the traditional things like craftwork, native history telling, and having small-time gift shops loaded with Disneyland trinkets.

The big Indian tribes out west, including the Dakota, the Sioux, and the Navajo, did pretty much the same thing, but they were based in the Plains states. They bought small businesses like 7-Elevens, gas stations, and Subways at intersections in the middle of nowhere and ran them. They were all a bunch of small-time thinkers.

The more risk-taking Indians went forth and built casinos across the land, mostly in Mississippi and Connecticut. Tribes like the Mashantucket Pequots. They had brass balls for sure, and the money flowed like manna when the Mohegan Sun Casino they built was first opened. It was the second-largest casino in the world after the Venetian in Macao.

Now, though, in the Obama era of lean times, the customers had deserted the casinos. That left the Indians with a shitload of debt on a bunch of worthless buildings with fiberglass tepees and giant waterfalls out front. That wasn't where the Neskeets were headed.

Fletcher knew that the key to success was to establish multiple business ventures quickly that would start to turn cash and, at the same time, serendipitously showcase the Neskeet name and build the brand.

He continued to daydream while he watched the news and drank his coffee. He found that he always worked best when he multitasked, never focusing on just one thing, flitting instead from topic to topic. His grade school teachers diagnosed it as ADD, but it worked for him. He went a mile wide and an inch deep.

The boat arrived on time and gave the big rubber bumpers a soft nudge as the nose of the *Island Home* slid into its berth. In minutes, Fletcher was in a beat-up red cab, one of Falmouth Taxi's finest, talking about the Red Sox with the driver and headed to the Hyannis Jeep Chrysler dealership.

"So what kind of vehicle are you looking for?" the tall salesman with the buzz cut and the pressed dark pants asked. It was still early, and Bill Fletcher was the only one in the big car lot with bright plastic flags tied and fluttering from the light poles. The Cape retirees typically didn't arrive until after eleven.

"I'm looking for a Jeep Grand Cherokee. One that's loaded."

The salesman immediately perked up. It was their best-selling model, and the dealership made a lot of money selling them. He focused on Fletcher, sizing him up for the likelihood of a sale.

"We've got some basic ones over here with a single CD player and Quadratrac for the snow."

Fletcher looked at the sad-sack salesman. "I'm not looking for anything with a single CD player. That's old-school. I'm looking for something fully loaded. Every option you've got. I want an iPod hookup too. What've you got?"

Fletcher squinted in the sun as he looked at the salesman. He knew that the guy was going to have a good day by the time it was over, selling him an expensive SUV.

The salesman scrambled on the fly, going over the inventory in his head as they walked and talked.

"Okay, I got you. I've got a couple over here both loaded. Take a look." Now he started selling Fletcher big time.

The two men walked across the front of the dealership lot. A string of balloons were tied to the pylon entrance sign. It was a beautiful day to buy a car.

They arrived at two big Jeep SUVS, one green, one white.

"Let's take the white one for a drive," Fletcher said immediately.

Ten minutes later, the salesman popped on a magnetic dealer plate, and the two of them were off, Fletcher at the wheel, riding down Main Street in Hyannis in the big Grand Cherokee.

"This one's top of the line. It's got everything," the salesman said.

"It smells great. I love that new-car smell, huh?" Fletcher said as he put the stereo on, checking out the bass line, cranking up the volume for a few seconds. The car reverberated with the sound of a Cape hip-hop station.

"Yeah, it's totally new," the salesman said. "The white's a nice color for you too. Clean and crisp."

Fletcher winced a bit and turned onto Oceanview Drive for the ride back.

"No. White's a girl's color. I'd rather it was red, bright red. Like a damn fire truck. You know what I mean?"

The salesman laughed. "Yeah, I do. We can look for one like that if you want. It'll take a week or so to find one in the regional inventory."

"No, I don't have the time," Fletcher said. "Besides, you're right. This one makes a statement. It's crisp, just like you said."

The salesman started to think that Bill Fletcher might actually buy the big rig, so he started in with the flimflam and the sales pitch. Fletcher stopped him cold.

"Whoa, buddy. You don't have to sell me. I've already decided this car's the one." He smiled. The car salesman glowed.

They headed back toward the dealership on a good vibe.

"What'd you say you do again?" the salesman said as he needed to qualify Fletcher now. They rolled down the street slowly.

"I'm an Indian chief. Head of the Neskeet Nation over on the Vineyard. Ever heard of them?"

"Nope. But I've heard of the Fluevogs over there. You related to them?" The salesman ran with it, not getting thrown with the Indian thing.

Fletcher pulled back into the lot in front of the sales office. He fiddled with the electric seat controls as they talked.

"They're the competition actually. We're the new guys on the block." Fletcher winked at the car salesman, who didn't know what to think. He didn't want to lose the car sale though, so he kept the conversation going.

"Kind of funny, you saying you're an Indian chief and buying a Grand Cherokee, huh? It's ironic, all that Indian stuff, you know what I mean?" He laughed at his own bullshit, flowing freely.

Fletcher looked back. The kid got it.

"That's why I picked this rig. The Grand Cherokee shouts out Indian, real authentic like. No kidding. Now you're catching on."

Fletcher moved the heating controls. "How's the AC work?"

"It'll freeze your ass off in five minutes. Trust me." The salesman paused. "How you paying for this vehicle, mind if I ask?"

Bill Fletcher looked at the young guy sitting across from him. "MasterCard, the whole thing. I want to take this friggin' rig off the lot today, right now." He said it with no hesitation.

"This is a fifty-thousand-dollar vehicle loaded up like this. Your card have that kind of limit?" The salesman wasn't rattled in the least. It was put up or shut up time for this yahoo Indian, he figured.

"Let's go check it out and see," Fletcher said. "But I'm in a hurry, so do it quick."

They headed into the dealership office with the keys and the cardboard number from the mirror.

An hour later, Bill Fletcher waved to his car salesman as he headed off the lot in his brand-new white Jeep Grand Cherokee, washed and waxed, compliments of the dealership. He tapped the brakes for a second, rolled left onto Main Street, and headed back toward the ferry terminal. He tooted his horn twice but didn't look back. He had a noon reservation to make.

The salesman kept waving as Fletcher rode out of sight. He had just made a $3,500 commission on that one sale. His day was made. Hell, his whole week was goddamn made, and it was basically easy as shit. The guy didn't haggle with him at all on the price. Nothing. He paid almost full sticker. He was going to celebrate and head to Red Lobster for dinner.

The salesman was blown away when he ran Fletcher's credit card through. Fletcher had a $100,000 limit on the card. The first time he ever saw that. The $53,265.27 for the Grand Cherokee sailed right through. *Fucking amazing*, he thought.

There really were some heavy hitters living on the Cape.

A Lucky Find

Bill Fletcher drove down Main Street in Vineyard Haven slowly, looking for a parking space in his new Jeep Grand Cherokee. Carrie was along for the ride. The rig was eye-catching, no doubt, with the big tires and alloy rims. Carrie had told him to go for a vanity plate, make a statement.

She had suggested NESKEET for the plate. That way he could showcase the tribe. He liked that idea but decided to take it in a different direction, to go more radical. So the plate said INJUN in big red letters on its white background. It was in your face for sure. Carrie shook her head when he installed the plates last week.

She had her window open, the AC was cranked up high, and she had some Fela Kuti on the CD player. It was African drumming music with a rhythmic, insistent beat to it. She brought it along for the ride.

"Good stuff, huh?" she said as they snaked slowly down the street, looking for a parking space. The car smelled brand-new. Fletcher had hung a green Little Tree air freshener from the heater controls for effect. He got it at the Gulf Mini Mart.

"Huh?" Fletcher was distracted.

"You like this music?" She adjusted the volume down a little so that it wasn't overpowering, just flowing right there in the moment. "It's African beat music. Different, huh?"

She was sitting back in the seat; she had on jeans with big oval Brigitte Bardot sunglasses on. Her head bobbed slightly to the beat, following it.

"It's not bad. It's kind of like Indian music a little, I guess," Fletcher said.

"It's nothing like Indian music. That's all tom-toms and shells. This is smooth and flowing."

"You're right about that. The Indian music I've heard is mostly discordant, a lot of yells and rattles and claps. I can't stand it."

Fletcher found a space ahead on the left. He let a blond mother, hair pulled back with her three kids in a black Land Rover, back out in front of them so he could take her spot.

"Where's this guy from?"

"Fela Kuti? He's Nigerian. A political statement kind of guy."

"I need some new music for the office, something mellow and relaxing. Bring this over next week, and I'll try it out."

Carrie jumped out of the Jeep, her clogs clomping on the pavement. He decided that he had to take her counsel more often, particularly for the Indian brand-building thing. He was too scattered with all the tasks he was trying to work on all at once. He needed to bounce more stuff off her, get her opinion. She was focused.

They went into the Martha's Vineyard Goodwill and Thrift Store next to the bookstore. Carrie loved to go to the thrift shop and look for bargains and hip pre-owned clothes. It was her favorite place to shop.

Fletcher liked going there occasionally, and he was able to come up with a few nice additions to his Indian wardrobe, like expensive dress shirts with wide pointed collars. They gave him that North Dakota, Indian-gone-to-Vegas-type look. The rich people on the island always dropped stuff off at the thrift store, so there was always a good assortment of new things coming in.

"Bill, come over here," Carrie said. She was standing at a rack of jackets and coats. "What do you think?"

Carrie had pulled a jacket out of the tightly packed rack bursting with clothes and laid it on top. It was a light-brown suede jacket with fringe down both sleeves and across the shoulders on the back. It was a hippie coat, suede with fringe, the prototypical sixties vintage icon.

She stroked the suede. It was like brand new.

"Here try it on."

"This looks like what hippies wore in San Francisco in 1967," Fletcher said. "In Golden Gate Park."

"I know. Isn't it cool?" She pulled at the little pieces of suede fringe hanging down. "You'll look like Dennis Hopper in *Easy Rider* in this. It's beautiful."

"Maybe. This is a Woodstock jacket."

Carrie stepped back, hands on hips, and looked critically. "It's perfect on you. You've got to get it." She smiled. "I'll buy it as a gift, a special Indian coming-out jacket. It's neat."

Fletcher walked to the mirror in the back of the store, shrugged his shoulders, and looked at himself. He had to admit that he looked good in it.

Carrie nodded. "It's you. It's pure Indian too. That coat says more about your Indian heritage than anything else you've got. It's as good as your turquoise bracelet. Better. It's like a deer pelt on your back." She looked and nodded again. "Yeah. This is a must-have Indian item for your wardrobe."

Fletcher dawdled for a minute preening in the mirror, but finally agreed with her that the coat was a great Indian prop. He'd wear it when he really wanted to go native and wow the crowd. The fringe was cut medium short, so it didn't look like a total druggie heirloom. He finally went with it.

"This is perfect for you," she said as she twirled the suede fringe in her fingers, waiting to check out. "It is so Indian. And you look great in it. Right out of central casting."

Carrie paid for the jacket with her credit card, saying that she'd deduct the cost as a marketing expense for the Equinox. Fletcher wore it out of the store, looking Indian as hell. It was all coming together.

Bill Fletcher and Carrie Nation went back to his beachfront apartment riding a good shopping vibe, having bagged the coat. They ended up having sex on the couch, under the deer head, the six-point buck, mounted on the wall. A light breeze ruffled the curtain on the open slider.

Afterward, they opened a bottle of cold chardonnay that Fletcher had in the fridge. He decided at that point, with Carrie naked and curled up next to him on the sofa sipping wine, that his life had taken a hard right turn for the better. His new suede coat lay on the chair in the corner like a talisman, a good luck charm.

He should have turned Indian a long time ago.

Ramping Up the Business

Father Peter Mulcahey stood behind Margaret Wellington, dressed in his full uniform, waiting for his lead-in. Tonight, he was a classic sixties priest walking right out of the set of *Father Knows Best*. He had on a pressed black short-sleeve shirt, a clean dog collar, black slacks, and black L.L.Bean loafers polished bright and shiny. He looked like a pro.

This was a "show the colors" night, and he was ready. The Blessed Sacrament Parish Hall was full of people and rocking with a bingo vibe. There was a sea of heads sitting at the tables that were set up in every available space. Each table had eight people, four seats to a side. There were thirty tables, so 240 people. They all paid $10 for admission.

Margaret looked over at Peter Mulcahey. He was a handsome man in good shape and with good arms. He cut a striking figure in his priest garb and short dark hair. He was Black Irish through and through, and very sexy at that. She decided that he could use some nurturing, some love though.

Margaret herself looked attractive tonight, representing as the head of the Ladies Sodality. She wore her hair up in a chignon and had on a blue silk scarf with little anchors in a repeating pattern. She finished the look with shiny black kitten heels with a little toe cleavage. She looked like a ripe geisha ready to be plucked.

"All right, everybody." Margaret stood right in front of Peter Mulcahey, tapping the microphone with her finger to get the crowd to quiet down. "Can I have your attention for a moment?" She took a deep breath. "Father Peter is now going to lead us in an invocation prayer."

With that she handed the six-inch old-school microphone with the silver golf ball head to Peter Mulcahey. He grabbed it like a pro athlete in a relay race, sweeping the soft black rubber cord off to the side in a smooth motion so he didn't trip over it stepping forward. He raised the microphone to his lips and invoked.

"Father, God of mercy and might, bless this house on this, our appointed bingo night. Let everyone gathered here be afforded good luck and your beneficence."

He didn't know exactly what words to use to sanctify a bingo night, so he just free formed, letting the words spill out onto the crowd. He was an Irish priest, and public speaking, the impromptu saying of prayers, was second nature to him.

"May God have mercy on us all and bring peace to his people gathered here tonight. A-men." He left the inflection on the *A* in *amen* to give the ending a little Amish tilt. He knew how to work it.

He also knew, like all the best priests knew, to keep the homilies short and sweet. He ended it quickly and gave the mike back to Margaret.

"That's it, everybody, let's play bingo!" Margaret said.

She and Father Peter stepped off the stage and left the microphone to the numbers caller, who quickly started the action. Peter Mulcahey picked up his coffee cup that he had filled with white wine before going up on stage and drained it.

They walked over to the side of the table that was set up as the cash bar. The wine and beer were flowing freely. $3.50 for a glass of wine or $3.00 for a bottle of beer. Father Peter had shrewdly priced it slightly above breakeven to build up business. He took one of the big bottles and filled a plastic glass with white wine for Margaret Wellington. He also refreshed his coffee cup right up to the brim with wine.

"Margaret, you've done a spectacular job with the bingo. These nights are a big hit with the parish."

"It's more than just our parish though, Father. These people are coming from all over the Island."

"Call me Peter, Margaret, will you? You don't have to stand on formality with me. I told you that."

The wine was starting to go to his head. He brushed up close to her and could feel the warmth in her body. "Jesus, we must be minting money with the wine bar here," he said.

"It's like a gold mine, Peter." She looked out over the heads." We're doing really well. And it was all your idea—having the second night and serving alcohol too."

Father Peter smiled. "Saint or sinner, Margaret, we all need an occasional drink to take the edge off at the end of the day and a spot to get together for some camaraderie. It's basic human nature."

They stayed for an hour, drinking and mingling with the bingo players. Around 11:00 p.m., they counted up the receipts. They had made over $2,000 for the night. *Not bad business for a sideline*, the priest thought.

As Peter Mulcahey walked home alone from the parish hall, he realized that he liked running bingo games with Margaret Wellington a helluva lot more than saying Mass and passing the collection basket for a take of no more than $75 a service. At least the bingo games felt like joyful life.

He suppressed that thought as he put the key in the rectory door and headed up to bed. The dog collar was chafing his neck. He took it off and dropped it on the hall table.

Ah, Margaret, what to do about her, he wondered as he poured himself two fingers of Dewar's scotch and rubbed his neck. He couldn't decide whether she was put on this earth as his protector, St. Margaret of the Bingo Chips, or as a dark angel dedicated to his physical temptation and downfall. He shrugged and decided to let it play out.

* * *

Bill Fletcher was in line at Kona Koffee for a cup of tall dark roast. It was 7:00 a.m., and he needed his fix. The coffee shop was right up the street from the Neskeet Nation offices, and he liked going there a couple of times a day. Not so much for the coffee as the interaction with the locals and the tourists. He could get a pulse of the Island action in there in thirty minutes.

He moved through the line and finally came up to Blinkey, the barista. He had worked there for over four years, which was a lifetime in barista lives. People moved in and out of working at Kona Koffee continually. To get someone to stay there beyond a summer season, even stay a winter on the Island, was off the charts.

Blinkey had a lazy eye, his left one, that wandered around at will. It was straight out of a Mel Brooks movie. He wore a Mets hat backward to comply with the health code while he worked. It looked old and punished.

"Yo, Bill." Blinkey nodded his head to Fletcher to show his respect for him. "How's the Indian thing going?"

"Not bad." Fletcher was impressed that an important trendsetter, a local like Blinkey, actually recognized him. Of course he should have since Fletcher was in there buying coffee two times a day. He nodded back.

"Tall dark coffee, cream, no sugar."

"You got it." Blinkey went to work. When he came back, he was about to pass the cup of coffee to Fletcher. Fletcher stopped him.

"Double cup that, will you? That stuff's too hot for me," Fletcher said.

"No problem."

Blinkey handed the large coffee in two cups over to Fletcher. "You got your card?"

"Credit card? I'm just paying cash."

"No. Your Kona Koffee punch card, man. Ten cups and you get a free one. It's cool. You come here a lot, so you'd use it."

Bill Fletcher thought about the Kona Koffee card for a second. It all of a sudden gave him an idea for the Neskeet Nation. It clicked.

Blinkey could see that Fletcher didn't have a card. No problem. He whipped out a new one from under the counter and used a beat-up ticket punch tethered to a long piece of string to put a hole in it before handing it over to Fletcher.

"Here you go, man. You'll get a free cup in no time with all the coffee you drink around here."

"Yeah, thanks a lot, Blinkey. You're the man."

Fletcher got his coffee, took a sip, then headed out the door and back to work.

Good Business

Carrie Nation was standing at the front table in the Equinox, folding and arranging Neskeet Nation T-shirts. They had suddenly become a hot item in town for tourist kids and the locals. Everybody was wearing one, looking hip.

She was dressed as Island Girl today in cutoff jean shorts with some threads hanging down and a pink Neskeet Nation T-shirt on top. She had sterling bangles on her right wrist and a pink rubber Breast Cancer Awareness wristband on her left. The cancer wristband was hip, but more importantly it was pink, so it matched her T-shirt. Carrie knew how to mix hip and relevant.

She finished it off with pink-painted toes and flip-flops with little flowers on them. It looked like she had just washed in from the Anthropologie store in Santa Monica.

The Neskeet clothing line had suddenly become her best seller overnight. She had to set up two tables for the T-shirts alone. They were in all kinds of styles for both men and women. She had stacks of them folded neatly in bright summer colors. On a third table she had canvas belts, tote bags, and coffee mugs.

She was putting all her retail skills to work in a hurry. Carrie had run the Equinox for three years, and it had always done okay as a hip beachwear and funky summer stuff place. She had managed to make a profit every year.

But this year, right now, was different. It was like the retailing doors were blown off. The Neskeet Nation T-shirts hit a vein, and that was all it took. It had gone viral. The shirts had a simple design in a lot of basic pastel colors. With the clamshell logo in a circle on the front, they had become a necessity for all the hipsters on the island. They were this summer's totem. And once the hipsters had them, then the tourists all jumped on board too.

She created a teaser in the front window of the store. Buy a T-Shirt and Join the Neskeet Nation Free. She had brainstormed the idea with Fletcher one morning when he walked in with a cup of Kona coffee. He showed her his Kona Koffee punch card and asked her why they couldn't do membership cards in the tribe just like that. She paused for a minute. *Why not indeed*, she thought, and the idea suddenly clicked.

Carrie Nation took Fletcher's punch card idea and transformed it into a Neskeet Nation membership card complete with all kinds of perks. She made it into a plastic swipe card for the Neskeet Nation with a picture of Bill Fletcher on the front. He looked like Hunter S. Thompson with his Ray-Ban Aviators on looking out to the future. It was just like one of those casino courtesy cards that they did in Vegas.

She would give out the card to any customer that purchased a T-shirt, mug, or belt. All they had to do was go online and register at the Neskeet Nation website. Once they did that, they were officially a member of the Neskeet Nation. The registration allowed them to qualify for raffles for free T-shirts with new designs, concert promotions, and other junk that Carrie gave out almost daily. It was a huge hit.

Bill Fletcher started counting all the people who signed up and registered as "members" of the tribe as real Neskeet Indians. All of a sudden, he had a tribal membership in the hundreds and swelling daily. An Indian chief needed a tribe to lead, and now he had one. It was an online tribe, but a tribe nonetheless.

It also allowed Fletcher to do reports to the Bureau of Indian Affairs with big membership counts that included the new tribal members. Instant tribe that he could sort in his big database by age, sex, income level, and sexual orientation. The federal bureaucrats loved the granularity.

He told Carrie as he sat in his office one morning that he had to pinch himself every day. He had fallen out of a burning plane and landed in a patch of soft, fluffy daisies. It was a big virtuous cycle occurring in Bill Fletcher's life just then. Good things really did happen to good people, he concluded. But you had to believe.

Two girls came into the Equinox. One was a lanky blonde and the other a brunette, two obvious high schoolers with small shoulder bags. They wandered around for a bit and then headed straight over to the Neskeet Nation T-shirt table. It was like gravitational pull: two flecks of iron being drawn to a large junkyard magnet. Carrie picked them out as hip kids looking for the next big thing, and they had suddenly found it.

The tall brunette put her bag down on the floor and started to look at the T-shirts.

"These shirts are kind of cool," she said to her friend as she held a pink Neskeet Nation shirt up in the air, checking out the design. It was a woman's tee, cut narrow and sleeveless. Carrie noticed the single strand of Indian love beads on the girl's wrist.

She wandered over and joined the conversation.

"You like them? They're our newest thing." She put her hands on her hips and gave the girls a front shot of her own Neskeet Nation shirt.

The girls looked at Carrie. "You're wearing one!" the blond girl said. "It looks good on you."

"Yeah, thanks. They're our hot tee this summer. A lot of cool designs."

Carrie let that sit in the air to see what kind of response she'd get. The two girls looked Carrie over with her jean shorts and flowered flip-flops. They liked what they saw, an older hip woman.

Now the brunette picked up a shirt to look at it as well, getting into it. "So what's the Neskeet Nation?"

Carrie used her stock response. She had practiced it to get it right. "They're a long-lost Indian tribe right here on the Cape. They just got recognized by the federal government this year. Part of the proceeds of each T-shirt sale goes to a college scholarship fund for Indian youth. It's cool and responsible at the same time." That usually got it.

The girls looked impressed. Neskeet Indians were something they could get behind. An underprivileged and oppressed class in the midst of white American society.

"For real?"

"Absolutely." Carrie had their interest and laid it on thick now. "But they're not a crappy Indian tribe with overweight rich guys pimping casinos and steak dinners. This group is legitimate."

"That's so cool."

"Yeah. It's real," Carrie said. She refolded two shirts on one of the tables that weren't perfectly straight. "These shirts are made partly from recycled Egyptian cotton too." She looked directly at the girls with her earnest look. "The Neskeets are big into the environment. And into probiotics, besides." Carrie threw that in as an afterthought because it sounded cool.

"Isn't that digestive stuff?" the tall brunette asked.

"Absolutely. This tribe eats a lot of nuts and berries." Carrie winked. "They're good for you in a natural, regular way, if you know what I mean."

The girls laughed. Carrie laughed. She knew that she'd made the sale.

The only question now was how many T-shirts each would buy and what else as well. The girls moved slowly through the display. "I've got them in a dressy tee like I'm wearing, but there's also a nice beach pullover over here."

Carrie moved to the second table and unfolded a big blue shirt. "I wear it around the house all the time as a sleeping tee or for hanging around. It's comfortable and a lot cheaper than anything from Victoria's Secret."

That did the trick. Like all good summer consumers, the girls bought two T-shirts each, one for dress and one for lounging. How could you not? The bill totaled $79.58. As the girls checked out, Carrie gave them each a plastic Neskeet membership card with Bill Fletcher's picture on it.

"He's kind of cute. A good-looking Indian, almost like Brad Pitt."

Carrie nodded. "I know him. He's for real." She left off the fact that she was sleeping with the chief in her spare time.

The girls left happy. Carrie thought that it was almost too easy.

She knew that she and Fletcher were sitting on a retail gold mine. It had the summer buzz for real. They had caught lightning in a bottle.

But like all good summer buzzes, it wouldn't last forever. So she had to capitalize on it while she could. Otherwise, she'd be at Kona Koffee this winter working next to Blinkey, slinging coffee to the locals, and being cold.

Storm Clouds

Carl Sunapee sat in the tribal meeting room at the Fluevog offices in Aquinnah with a frown on his face. The Fluevog offices were in the same building as the US Post Office. It was a plain wood-shingled building built about fifteen years ago.

Carl's cousin Felix had put the deal together. The building was on Fluevog land. Felix had been able to hold up the GSA development by dragging his feet in granting the ground lease to the post office. In return for the lease, Felix made the post office build the shell of the entire building and the entranceways for both units.

The post office was to the right and the Fluevog offices were to the left. The federal government had to build one big, wide handicap ramp to access both entrances so lame post office patrons or old Indians could walk their walker or wheel their chair up the shallow ramp and turn left or right, suit yourself. The Fluevogs had saved about $50,000 and the hassle of having to build a separate ramp for their own entrance. Felix had created value for the tribe from the get-go.

Carl, Michael Nunes, and Sandra Watson were sitting in the tribal meeting room. Carl had been in a bad mood for days. His wife, Louise, had told him so and yelled at him for it. He ignored her for the time being. He had too much on his mind.

It wasn't much of a meeting room, to Carl's way of thinking, where they sat. Just two heavy brown folding tables pushed together, the ones with the metal swing-down legs and a little hinged piece you locked in place to keep them stable.

They were made out of melamine, that heavy pressboard material that had gone out of style twenty years ago. The local churches had hundreds of 'em hanging around in basements and rec halls. Carl knew that new tables were made out of molded plastic and were light as shit. They were easy to move around so you didn't have to break your balls lifting them.

There were five or six metal folding chairs scattered around the table in no particular order, with about twenty more leaning against the wall. There were plastic throw-away saltshakers and pepper shakers on the table in the center along with a few leftover paper napkins. The place looked ready for a Sunday night bean supper instead of the important Indian tribal meeting that Carl was trying to hold.

"I don't like it, not one goddamn bit." Carl drummed his fingers on the brown table and licked his lips as he thought. "These guys have come in and taken over our franchise."

"They've stolen it is what they did."

"Who are they anyway?" Sandra, the tribal elder, asked.

Carl sat up. "I've done a little reconnaissance. It's not 'they' at all. It's one guy, a single fucker, goes by the name of Bill Fletcher. He's a goddamn hustler is what he is. And a good one at that."

"They also got a bunch of people claiming they're Indians now, and not Fluevogs either. They're saying they're part of that Nonantum Nation, whatever the hell that is." Sandra said.

"That's *Neskeet*, honey," Michael Nunes said. "If you're going to dis the enemy, at least get their fucking name right."

"No need to swear, Michael, I don't like that kind of talk, and you know it."

"You don't mind when Carl swears when he says fuck this or that."

Sandra adjusted her glasses and looked over at Michael Nunes through thick plastic lenses that made her eyes look huge, like a big watery striped bass. What a fucking idiot he was, she thought.

"Carl's the chief. He can say what he wants."

"But you never let me say the same kind of things."

"You're not the chief, that's all. You're a rank-and-file Fluevog and therefore a bag carrier, when it's all said and done."

Sandra dismissed Michael Nunes just like that. She was an elder and was not about to take any shit from a guy that did auto bodywork. And bad bodywork at that.

Carl brought the group back to order. "Now wait a minute here, people." He banged his half-empty Belmont Springs water bottle on the table for attention. "We've got to get our shit together on this. I'm going to watch Fletcher closely and figure out what he's up to." Carl looked at both of his tribal mates for support. "We need to see what he's doing in

Oak Bluffs. He's working a bunch of businesses over there, and they're all probably making money."

Sandra Watson pushed her glasses up before she spoke. "Well, there's probably enough money on the island for all of us to share it, if it comes to that."

Carl Sunapee looked up. It wasn't easy being the chief sometimes. He shook his head.

"Sandra, you're missing the point. It's our franchise he's going after. The Indian one, here on the Island. We've had a legal monopoly here for a long time. That's why we've been able to sell the crappy bow and arrows and beads and modeling clay over in the gift shop in Aquinnah. We've never had to compete in the real world. It's been easy, that's why it's worked for so long."

"Well, maybe now we do, is all," Michael Nunes said. "How bad can it be if he gets to stick around?"

Carl was quiet before he spoke. "If Bill Fletcher hangs around, pretty soon we'll all be pumping gas for tips over at the CITGO in Vineyard Haven wearing headdresses and making war whoops. And we'll be filling up his Cadillac with gas, not mine. Not on my watch, if I can help it."

With that, Carl adjourned the meeting. He'd have to get the group more organized than they were now. Maybe even take things into his own hands if it got bad enough. He knew that Bill Fletcher would whip their asses in a fair commercial fight if given the chance. He'd siphon the tourist money right out of their Fluevog buckskin wallets quicker than shit.

He couldn't let that happen.

The Sweat Lodge

Bill Fletcher was in Muscle Development at 6:30 a.m. with a cup of Kona Koffee dark roast wrapped in its cozy in his right hand. He was tired. He usually didn't get up this early, but he was on a mission. He was dressed in gray sweatpants, Nike running shoes, and a big red cotton hoodie that said South Beach across the back.

Mike Jackson, the owner, was a thick gym rat, a refugee from the mainland many years ago. With big shoulders and a short neck, Mike was the perfect ex-marine except for the fact that he never got into the Marine Corps. He got rejected on medical grounds. He was classified 4F, psychologically unstable. At that point, he took up exercising with a manic determination and never looked back.

The gym was a medium-sized place on Billings Avenue, the service street that ran parallel to Main in Oak Bluffs. There was a weight room, a spinning room, an exercise room, and a place for a steam bath and a sauna. It was two notches down from a big health club in the city. The place was fairly crowded at 6:30 a.m. with exercisers everywhere lifting weights or working the treadmill, everybody looking at themselves in the floor-to-ceiling mirrors. Narcissism never went out of style on the Island in summer.

"I looked at your numbers. Not bad overall," Fletcher said as the two men strolled through the club. "There's been a little softness over the past twelve months though." Fletcher decided to lead with a solid punch.

"Hey, you contacted me about buying this place, not the other way around." Jackson had a clipboard with a pen on a string in his right hand. It was the check-in log.

"Look, we've had an uptick here the last two months with summer coming on. It's our best season."

He scanned the list of names on the paper.

"Most of these people I don't know, which means they're tourists, people who are visiting and want to get a workout in. This place has great name recognition for visiting off Islanders. You can check it out."

"I'll give you that," Fletcher said. They walked through the club, Mike Jackson pointing out all the shiny equipment. Fletcher sipped his coffee as they strolled, trying to wake up.

"That Smith machine alone cost us $10,000 last year. It's the only one on the Cape that I know of. It's for serious weight lifters, and we get our share of them. Plus, we're strong on the cardio stuff too. I've got a woman that teaches three spinning classes a day here. She's built like a whippet. Unbelievable body." Mike Jackson winked at Fletcher. "The hardcore types love her."

"You do any yoga?"

"Yeah, you bet," Mike said. We do basic hatha in the morning and then bikram hot yoga in the evening. Take a look at this."

The two men walked into another room. It was gleaming with overhead track lighting and hardwood floors. It was pristine. Over in the corner were a few mats. Fletcher tried to sound like he knew what he was talking about.

"That's not enough mats, is it?" Fletcher pointed with his coffee cup.

Jackson shook his head. He knew that Fletcher didn't know jack shit about the business. He began to think he was wasting his time. "Those are just extras for drop-ins who pay the day rate and want to get a quick session in while they're on vacation."

They stopped at the middle of the floor, and Jackson continued. "Mats are personal. Everybody brings their own. Women go nuts at the idea of doing yoga on a mat that somebody else sweated on. They sciva it. It's like wearing someone else's thong." Mike shook his head. "It just doesn't happen."

"Gotcha," Fletcher said, now understanding. They continued walking.

"Yoga in this room is a big draw. We do hot yoga two times a day, at six and eight p.m. I had a special heating system installed last winter. We can get the temperature up to 104 degrees in here in twenty minutes. The women love it. We get $15 a session for drop-ins and also run a special six-session package. We call it the six-pack."

Bill Fletcher smiled. "Catchy. How's that work?"

"Like a friggin' magnet. We get a ton of business from it."

Mike Jackson smiled. "I hired two knockout women from off Island who wanted to be here for the summer, real yoga instructors, and they're an unbelievable draw. They're all-stars for sure."

The two men paused. "I know that we can increase net by 20 percent this summer alone with more yoga classes. Yoga is where the action is. It's not in the heavy weights and spinning. That's old school. There's still a market for it, but a little less right now."

Bill Fletcher had seen enough. "Okay, let's talk," he said. "You got an office?"

"Nope. Not separate at least. All my space is productive. We can sit at the closing table."

"Closing table?"

"Yeah. That's where my two salespeople close their sales to new customers. It's next to the entrance."

"How's that work?" Fletcher asked.

"I hire two hard bodies in the summer on commission to get new memberships."

So the two men went to the closing table to talk turkey. Mike Jackson, strong and big as a bull, spoke first.

"So what's the deal? You said you wanted to buy the place. How much?"

"I'll pay you three hundred thousand for the business and pick up the lease payments. Right now, this week."

Mike Jackson sat up. The price was about double what the business was worth. He was shocked.

"You know anything about the health club business?"

"Not a damn thing," Bill Fletcher said without missing a beat. He figured it was better to lay it out there on the table and not piss the guy off. He sipped his coffee, which was now starting to get cold. "Is that going to be a problem?"

"Not if you're committed to losing another hundred thousand operating this place," Jackson said." There's a learning curve."

Bill Fletcher knew exactly what he was talking about. "So how about an exclusive management contract for two years until I learn the business? You run the place for me for $100,000 a year. Manage it and teach me the ropes."

Mike Jackson thought about it for about three seconds. "You're on."

"But I'm going to be making some changes. And you're going to have to go with them, no bullshit."

"I'm all about change," Jackson said. "What are you thinking about doing?"

"This place is going to go a little more Indian," Bill Fletcher said. "We're going to keep the core of the exercise program but change the theme a little bit. Make it more ethnic."

"Ethnic, huh? How do I get paid?" Jackson asked.

"You'll get a weekly paycheck like everybody else here on staff," Fletcher said.

"No, I mean the $300K large. I want that now if you want the keys to this place."

"You got a checking account?" Fletcher said.

"Two of 'em."

"Then go talk to Donna Stevens over at Martha's Vineyard Bank and give her your wiring instructions. She'll set you up for electronic transfers." Fletcher looked over at Mike Jackson. "You can even have the funds this week. It's still early."

Jackson's eyes widened.

The two men talked over the details, but Mike Jackson kept drifting over to the thought of a big payday coming his way. He had trouble concentrating and kept thinking about the new Harley-Davidson Fat Boy he was going to buy as soon as the money cleared. He'd have it by next week.

"This is going to be fun," Bill Fletcher said as they shook hands, and he got up to leave. Mike Jackson almost broke Fletcher's hand; his grip was so tight and powerful and full of adrenaline.

"No shit. Whatever you say, boss," Mike Jackson said. He was committed. "You just got yourself a new Indian warrior."

Fletcher walked out thinking that the old adage had once again proved true. Just get 'em by the balls, and their hearts and minds will follow.

Lights, Camera, Action

Bill Fletcher and Carrie Nation were sitting in Carol Ann's Diner having breakfast. He ordered the eggs Benedict with a side of home fries and a bagel with cream cheese. She got the half grapefruit and homemade yogurt with berries along with an orange juice chaser.

"My business is on fire right now. I've never had a year like this," Carrie said as she moved the yogurt around in her bowl, mixing the red and blue berries in with her spoon. "The T-shirts are flying off the shelf. Honestly, I can't keep them stocked. It's crazy."

Carrie looked up from her food at Bill. "You know what else? You're starting to look more Indian every day. Letting your hair grow longer was a big plus. You've got that chief thing going on much better now."

Fletcher took a big bite of his eggs Benedict. He had shoveled the goopy cream sauce all over the poached eggs. "You think so?"

"Yeah. It's a little bit scary. You're becoming more Indian every day. Either that or I'm falling for your bullshit." She smiled. "Either way, I'm going to have plenty of money this winter for once."

"I'm growing into the role, that's all. This place always had room for a second Indian tribe. There just wasn't the demand. Now we've created it."

Carrie moved over to the grapefruit. First she cut through all the individual little triangles of fruit methodically as Fletcher talked about some Neskeet money-making ideas. Then she ripped open a pink packet of Splenda and sprinkled the thin white power over the cut pieces of fruit.

"I just bought Muscle Discipline." Fletcher just threw it on the table, hitting her like that.

"What?"

"Yeah, yesterday."

Carrie swallowed a piece of grapefruit.

"What do you mean you bought Muscle Discipline? That's a health club, for chrissakes."

"I know. I think it'll fit in nicely with our Indian tribal thing."

"But that's an exercise place. What do you know about running it?"

"Not a goddamn thing," Fletcher said. "But you do. You can run it."

Carrie ate a few pieces of her ultrasweet grapefruit. "Hmmm. Maybe I can." She thought about the prospect. "I can sure run the yoga part at least. I go there three times a week as it is. Now I can work out for free." She smiled at Fletcher.

"I kept the muscle man on as manager, Mike Jackson. So he'll help you run it. At least the exercise part." Fletcher sipped his coffee and finished his eggs.

"I need you to pump it up some and bring some Indian energy to the place. I'm thinking about some tie-ins to the Neskeet Nation. Maybe even a name change for the club."

"Yeah, maybe." Carrie said. "But if we do, it's got to be something that's catchy that has a hook." She poked at the grapefruit as she put her marketing mind to work. "This may be a fun challenge."

Bill Fletcher motioned for the check. "I don't know much about marketing challenges, but I'm thinking the sauna and the hot yoga room ought to lure them in once you upscale it. The potential is definitely there."

The perky waitress with her hair pulled up with a scrunchie left the bill on the table. Fletcher picked it up and pulled out his wallet, fishing for bills.

"Lure who in? The tourists?" Carrie asked.

"No. The tribespeople. The Neskeets."

"Are you signing people up?" she asked.

"I'm talking about all those people that are signing up on the website that you're giving cards to over at the Equinox. The ones looking for free T-shirts and concert tickets. They're officially Neskeet Nation tribal members now. You gave 'em all a swipe card to prove it."

Carrie finished her grapefruit and pushed it away from her. "Are you serious? That's just a marketing thing I'm doing to get some crossover for the store and our other products."

Bill Fletcher shook his head. "Not anymore. Those people are now my people. I'm counting every one of them as official Neskeet Nation Indians. It gives us instant credibility."

Carrie thought about it for a minute. "Whatever you think. The website is getting a lot of hits. I don't have enough time to manage it with all the other things going on. I'm overwhelmed, honestly."

Bill Fletcher nodded. "I know you're busy. I'm hiring a girl to run the office, and she'll be our webmaster and do all the online things for the Neskeets. We need to have a real strong web presence for this thing to really take off."

"You're absolutely right. We need strong web marketing if we want to grow. I'll get on it today."

The two fledgling Indian entrepreneurs got up to leave. Fletcher paid the bill at the cash register in front. He looked at Carrie on the way out. She had on a Neskeet T-shirt that said The Nation on the front with an Indian warrior, head down, in silhouette on the back. She finished it off with a short jean skirt and chunky mules. She looked like a hip Vineyard tourist. She was just starting to surf her big wave in the retailing world, compliments of Bill Fletcher.

They headed back to the Neskeet offices, the walk-up on the second floor.

"I've got some ideas for the gym right off," Fletcher said. "Let's talk."

"I can only stay a few minutes," Carrie said. "I only have one girl at the store right now, and we're busy."

*   *   *

Carl Sunapee was in the Cooked Goose bar talking to Hank Flowers who owned the place. Hank was a crusty Islander and a businessman. He was always on the make, running the bar, doing concert promotions, and grabbing money however he could.

He and Carl had gone to school together in Martha's Vineyard Regional High School, class of 1972. They had smoked a lot of weed in Hank's Chevy Nova in the high school parking lot. They were Island blood brothers.

Carl was drinking a Diet Coke with a lime. They were sitting in the front by the street as the morning staff poured ketchup and set the tables for lunch. The sun shone in through the window at a slant onto their table. It was so bright that Carl wanted to keep his sunglasses on but decided that he needed to look into Hank's eyes to see what was going on.

"So who the hell is this guy?" Carl said as he aggressively poked his lime down into his soda with the straw.

"I don't know, some wash ashore, as far as I can see. He's selling some T-shirts though." Hank looked up. "Every goddamn kid in here at night has got one on. Some of the girls wear 'em real well, if you know what I mean." He laughed.

Carl frowned. "I know what you mean, and that's just goddamn it right there. How the hell can this guy say he's an Indian and sell so many T-shirts like that?" Carl shook his head. "It's like he blew into town on the ferry and took over."

"You should have been doing this shit a long time ago, Carl. It serves you right. You never exploited that Indian franchise you had all to yourself. Ever. I've never seen one damn T-shirt out of the Fluevogs in twenty years. What the hell is wrong with you? You sit up there in Aquinnah selling bracelets and wampum shells. Young people don't want that goddamn shit. They want fresh stuff."

Carl Sunapee was pissed. He took a sip of his Diet Coke and glanced outside. He saw a kid with a Neskeet Nation T-shirt walk by on the street. They were everywhere.

Hank Flowers continued. "Let me tell you something else. His girlfriend, the one that owns the Equinox, is doing a cross promotion with Entrain here Friday night. They got the DJ giving out T-shirts to the best Indian dancers in a dance concert. In fact, Fletcher had me run a wet T-shirt contest here last Thursday. Thirsty Thursday Indian night, I called it. Every girl that came up on stage had on a cutoff Neskeet Nation T-shirt. That was the rule. I had one of the bartenders wet 'em down with a garden sprayer. We blew the doors off the place that night."

Carl Sunapee's jaw dropped as he listened.

"You never saw so many beautiful young wet Indian tits in your life. All pokin' through the Neskeet T-shirts." Hank smiled.

"Those girls aren't fucking Indian," Carl said.

"Nobody in the bar was asking for proof, I'll say that. I'm only telling you so you know what you're competing against. That guy is slick, is all."

Carl Sunapee went quiet. He had clearly underestimated Bill Fletcher again and the things he was capable of doing. He looked up at Hank Flowers.

"Hank, I'm not looking for a lecture now from you. I can see that we're losing the fort here. I just need you to keep your eye on him for me. Find out what he's up to. Give me some recon. Bill Fletcher is no goddamn Indian, I can tell you that much."

Hank Flowers put his lips together and nodded at Carl. "You're probably right on that one. I'll give you that. But I'll tell you one thing. He's a hell of a good businessman. That Neskeet shit is all over the place like wildfire, and it's helpin' my business too. You could learn a lesson there if you hung around some."

Carl finished off his Coke. He wasn't interested in learning any lessons. He had already learned what he needed to know.

"I'm looking to mount my own attack on him. This island's not big enough for two Indian chiefs. The Fluevogs are the real deal. You ever hear of Little Big Horn and Custer?"

"Yeah, I did," the bar owner said as he fingered the saltshaker on the table. "Just make sure you're Crazy Horse and not General Custer is all I can tell you," Hank said. "You've sure as shit met your match."

Summer Romance

Margaret Wellington decided to go for it. She added an extra drop of Allure perfume behind her ears and rubbed it into the small soft hair on her neck. She unbuttoned her blouse to just above her bra with the easy-open front clasp. She was headed to an accounting meeting with Father Peter Mulcahey. She decided that she'd answer for her sins later.

Peter Mulcahey met her at the door of the rectory. He was dressed in khaki pants and a blue Polo shirt with a little yellow horse on the left breast. He left his priestly uniform up in his closet for today's meeting with Margaret Wellington.

He was feeling flush with all the money coming into the church from the bingo operation.

"Hey, Margaret," he said as he stopped and looked her over. "You look great, as usual. How did I get so lucky to have such a bright and charming woman running our finances in the parish? You're like Moses leading us through the financial desert."

He threw a little scripture into the conversation. That never hurt, he knew.

Margaret got right to it. "Call me Margie, Father, please. We know each other too well." She smiled, taking it slowly, no rush, seeing what developed. "You left your collar off today, Father. You look like you're straight off the pages of *GQ.*"

She looked him over. She could keep the repartee going with the best of them.

"*GQ?*"

"*Gentlemen's Quarterly.* Where all those handsome young men wear the nice clothes. You'd fit right in."

Peter Mulcahey brightened. His vanity was easy to buff up.

"You make me laugh, Margaret. Particularly as I'm not so young or good-looking." He quickly changed topics. "We're in the black financially today because of what you've done for us. I can't thank you enough."

"Father, I do this out of love and respect for the church. You know that."

"Call me Peter."

They walked through the rectory and went toward the office on the first floor. They stopped by the kitchen en route. Margaret fished in her bag and pulled out her present.

"Well, Peter, I brought a bottle of wine for us to celebrate the parish's newfound wealth."

Father Peter looked impressed as he took the bottle. "Solvency, Margaret, only. We'll never be wealthy here in Oak Bluffs."

She laughed as she watched him read the label on the wine bottle, figuring out the vintage and the type.

"It's a simple Pinot Grigio, Peter, just right for the summer. We can have some now or you can save it for later. Whatever suits you."

Peter Mulcahey thought a moment. "Let's have some now. The church won't mind," he said. He had sealed his fate.

Margaret kept it going. "Well, Peter, the church has been here for me ever since Jed passed in 2008, and it's filled a tremendous void in my life. I'm grateful."

"That's what the church is for, Margaret. To fill a void in people's lives." He left her to go and get a bottle opener.

Peter Mulcahey came back with clean wineglasses and the open bottle of Pinot Grigio. He poured two glasses, and they headed to the couch in the business office to talk about the good luck they were having in the parish with the bingo games.

Before long, the first glass had turned into the second and then the remnants of a third.

"You know, Margie, I decided a while ago that you were put on this earth to test me."

Margaret Wellington blushed deeply as she turned to Father Peter on the couch, putting down her accounting spreadsheet. "Why is that, Peter?" The wine was going to her head now in the warm quiet rectory.

"I'm terribly attracted to you in the flesh, I have to admit, and I'm ashamed about it. A priest can't do that, you know." The wine had loosened him up as well.

She smiled over her glass at him. Her moment had come. "But I noticed you left your priestly clothes upstairs, probably in your closet. Today, you're just Peter Mulcahey to me, a handsome single man, like anyone on the Island."

Margaret moved closer to give Peter Mulcahey a full-on shot of her cleavage along with her Allure scent. It was quiet and still in the rectory. She heaved a small sigh. Peter Mulcahey put a hand on her knee and gently rubbed her warm flesh.

"Joanne is gone for the afternoon, if you're wondering."

"Where is she?" Margaret had forgotten about the rectory manager.

"She left at noon to go shopping off-Island with her son at Target in Falmouth. No one else is around for the rest of the day. I checked the schedule."

Margaret smiled. Of course he had checked the schedule. She weighed her options in that split second when Peter Mulcahey put his hand on her. It felt warm and inviting, very sexual. She took it as a sign from God.

"Peter, in that case, I'm here to give you your worldly communion. I bet you've waited a long time for this."

Margaret Wellington turned and unbuttoned the remaining buttons on her blouse and then undid the front clasp of her bra, freeing her breasts. She brought Peter Mulcahey's head over to the promised land, and that's all it took. The randy Black Irish in him took over.

They got into a clutch right there on the couch in the rectory study. As they pulled each other's clothes off, Margaret had the presence of mind to ask if the door was locked.

"Yeah, it is," Peter Mulcahey answered hoarsely.

In the end, Peter Mulcahey came quickly, right there in the study. She did too, twice. After they recovered, Peter explored Margaret's body, from her suntanned legs to her soft streaked hair. Relaxed and stretched out on the sofa, she held Peter's head in her hands.

That summer afternoon, Margaret Wellington attained her own manner of salvation right there in the Blessed Sacrament rectory.

She was surprised that the sex was so good.

*   *   *

Bill Fletcher, the chief of the Neskeet Nation, was outside the health club watching the new sign go up. He sipped a cup of coffee as he supervised.

A gigantic truck was parked on the street with a hydraulic arm and two big stabilizers that swung out from the side. The driver had put a big orange cone on top of the right arm that jutted out into the road. A line of cars were backed up, snaking around the big truck.

"That's it. Put her right up there," Fletcher said as he watched the new sign swing up into place. He was happy as shit.

Iron-head Mike Jackson with the big arms came out of the health club, curious to see what all the commotion was about. He looked at the old Muscle Development sign on the ground over by the sidewalk.

"What the fuck is going on?" he said.

He had a blue bottle of G2 Gatorade, half-empty, in his hand. He used it to point at the old sign. "What's wrong with this?"

Fletcher looked over. "We just changed the name of the club, that's all."

"What did you change the name to?"

"The Sweat Lodge. Take a look." Bill Fletcher pointed to the new sign.

Iron Mike looked up.

"Are you shitting me?" he said. "There's a lot of goodwill in the Muscle Development name. I built it up. It took years."

"Doesn't matter," Fletcher said dismissively. "The Sweat Lodge works on two levels. One, it's a hip name for an exercise studio, which this now is." He looked over at Iron Mike for emphasis. "And two, it works on the Indian level, as in a real sweat lodge with an oversized sauna and hot yoga room. You get it?" Fletcher winked at Iron Mike. "An Indian sweat lodge. It all ties in."

"I think it's stupid is what I think," Mike said without waiting.

"Get over it." Fletcher said. "You'll be amazed at all the new business that will come, just watch."

Mike Jackson shook his head. He wondered why the hell he ended up selling the gym to an asshole like Bill Fletcher, a guy saying he's an Indian and just making wholesale changes to his life's work.

Then he remembered that he had hemorrhaged cash for three years running the club and losing money, and that he was on the verge of declaring personal bankruptcy when Fletcher walked into his life. Signing personally for all that gym equipment and the Smith machine probably wasn't the smartest thing he ever did.

Maybe the sign isn't so bad after all, he thought.

Office Help

Fletcher had placed an ad on Craigslist for admin help for the Neskeet Nation offices. Now he had a sexed-up twenty-one-year-old sitting across from him in the office. Her name was Carol Ault, and she was wearing a short jean skirt with pink flip-flops. She crossed her legs and dangled one flip-flop off her foot as she spoke. He was having trouble concentrating.

Fletcher was wearing his big turquoise bracelet on his left wrist, as usual. It was his talisman, his Indian signature piece. He had polished the shit out of it the night before with Aunt Nelly's Silver Cleaner so it would look impressive.

"So, Carol, do you know how to type, answer the phone, pay bills, that kind of stuff?" Fletcher moved the bracelet around on his wrist unconsciously. "Just be able to handle a lot of Indian administrative-type things? It's not rocket science for sure, but that's where we need some help."

"Yeah. I can do all those things. I'm real good at them. I used to work at Island Insurance up the street. You can call them if you want." She popped her gum. "I organized the whole office, did the admin, built their website, and made it interactive. All kinds of things." She gave Fletcher a nod.

Bill Fletcher wasn't sure whether she meant that he'd be surprised that she worked at Island Insurance or that she could do all the tasks. Not that it mattered. He was fantasizing about having sex with her in a faraway tropical place, just the two of them, alone and naked.

"I like your bracelet," she said.

The compliment jarred Bill Fletcher back to reality. He liked that Carol was comfortable enough with him to go personal.

"Thanks. I got it in New Mexico. It was a gift from another Indian. A tribal chief from the Sioux that I met when I was out there. We were meditating on a rock."

The girl laughed. She could smell bullshit a mile away. "Funny, I don't see you meditating on a rock, ever. I see you maybe drinking something on the rocks."

She tugged her skirt down a little unconsciously as it rode up on her thigh. She could see Fletcher glance over. "Are you a real Indian?"

"Don't I look like one?" he asked.

The girl paused and studied Bill Fletcher. He was kinda good-looking for an old guy with his dark complexion and longish hair. A little over the hill for her tastes, but she decided that she'd have sex with him if it came to it.

"Yeah, kind of. You sort of look like an Indian, I guess."

"So when can you start?" Fletcher got to the point.

"How about tomorrow?" the girl said.

"That works. You working now?"

"I'm working part-time at Kona Koffee right down the street."

It clicked for Fletcher. "I thought you looked familiar. I go in there all the time. You don't want to stay and be a barista?"

"No, I need to get on with my life." She rearranged herself on the seat, sensing that she was going to get the job. She spread her legs a bit so that Fletcher could see her red thong. She knew that would seal the deal. "I don't drink coffee anyway."

Bill Fletcher liked her. She had gumption and was a bit of a smart-ass. He decided that she'd be able to handle all the shit heads that crossed his path every day, the ones that he no longer had time for now that he was an Indian on the make.

"Well, Carol, you've got the job. Show up for work tomorrow, and we'll make you a member of the Neskeet Nation."

"But I'm not Indian," she said.

"The requirements to join the tribe aren't that stringent. You'll get in. Trust me."

With that, Bill Fletcher just hired his first full-time staffer for the Neskeet Nation.

*   *   *

Carrie Nation was inside the Sweat Lodge accessorizing the place. She and Bill had talked about it a few nights ago over at his place. Really her place now too, as she had been sleeping over there a lot this summer.

They'd get a bottle of chardonnay, a box of Triscuits, some cheap Brie cheese, and bingo, instant strategy session. It was always talking about the Indians with Bill. He got excited at the empire they were creating. Carrie smiled to herself, knowing it was a Hollywood set built on bullshit.

She was enjoying it though and was determined to ride it out for however long it lasted. Living with Bill Fletcher, she had no living expenses. They'd do takeout or go to restaurants every night of the week. Her store had never been so busy selling the Neskeet T-shirts and other stuff. She was raking it in. *God bless the Neskeet Nation*, she thought.

Carrie, with her confidence and funky outfits, had taken a lot of Bill's ideas and just ramped them up. It was Carrie who created the initial Neskeet Nation website and then built the T-shirt promotions into it. It was her idea to create the plastic membership cards for discounts and free gifts, but it was Fletcher who decided to count the people who signed up as actual tribal members. That was genius. Their relationship was symbiotic.

Carrie embellished the website by constantly putting in new promotions, keeping it fresh. Customers that signed up for the free membership in the tribe with a T-shirt purchase were automatically registered to win free gifts like massages and dinners out. That promo alone pumped up the membership to 1,500 people. Bill said that he needed a big tribal-member count to be able to qualify for even more federal Indian grants and ancillary bullshit like that.

Carrie managed his wardrobe, saying yes to that Indian accessory or no to another. It was her fashion sense that propelled big Bill Fletcher into the Indian tribal elite. He looked dead-on for a modern-day Indian with his jewelry, jeans, and suede fringed jacket, all the funky Indian stuff that Carrie had picked out for him.

Once the grant came through, Bill Fletcher funneled a good chunk of cash her way to help develop complimentary businesses. She bought new inventory for the store and spent a lot of money on their online presence. Fletcher was painting in the bigger picture now, and he didn't sweat her spending habits. He was focused on building the tribe as quickly as he could. He knew it wouldn't last forever, and they had to get while the getting was good.

The sex came naturally too. Carrie had a good body, knew how to use it, and lavished her pleasures on Bill with enthusiasm when the mood was right. Fletcher started going regularly to the Sweat Lodge and slowly tightened up a lot of his loose stuff from his sedentary lifestyle. They started out slowly at first, but once Fletcher got a good taste of it, he dove in headlong.

That was fine with Carrie as she had a healthy libido. They ended up most nights doing it out on the beach near the high grass in the dunes. Or on the leather couch or the queen bed in Fletcher's small apartment, under the picture of Sitting Bull on one wall and the deer antlers on the other. It was a beautiful six-point rack.

Carrie was on a roll today in the Sweat Lodge making some basic design changes. She was in a short suede Indian skirt with a tie-dyed T-shirt tied in a knot at her waist. She wore a beaded Indian bracelet on her wrist. She dressed the part to get inspired.

She was bringing an Indian theme to much of the inside of the club. She had hired a local artist to paint an Indian landscape of the sparse Dakota Black Hills on the back wall in the exercise room. Then she had him draw in a pod of three women in the foreground riding racing bikes through a buffalo herd on the plain. They all had buckskin cycling uniforms on.

"Move those raccoon tails more to the left," Carrie said as she directed one of the decorators in the gym. "And put the tom-toms right over there next to that big exercise machine, that Smith thing." Fletcher had given her carte blanche to make over the interior of the club into a Neskeet Nation Indian showplace. She decided to take it in a sixties Indian direction, à la Disney productions.

Carrie directed the workers around, holding her arms, trying things out. She had focused particularly on the sauna and steam bath areas, calling them sacred Indian purification spots. She put a big dream catcher outside the steam bath entrance for special effect. It worked. The place looked like a theme restaurant on steroids.

"Yeah, that's it," Carrie said as she watched one of the installers hang a bow and arrow with a deerskin quiver over the door to the steam bath. "It looks perfect right there." She wiggled her tangerine toes in her flip-flops and smiled.

Calling in a Marker

Carl Sunapee was sitting in the small conference room of the Oak Bluffs Police Department. It was early afternoon, and he had a muted red Hawaiian shirt on with his big gold Rolex watch, the sports model with the oyster bezel. It was the kind that James Bond wore. Carl had a natural style about him, always cool. He was no pretend Indian. He was the best put-together real Indian on the East Coast, and he pretty much knew it.

He had the thick arms of a bricklayer, which he was in a previous life on Cape Cod until his back gave out, and he quickly realized that it might be easier to make a living as the head of the Fluevogs than hauling hods of S&H bricks up rickety ladders, making chimneys for rich white folks in Yarmouth.

He was a presence sitting there in the office—red shirt, thick back, nice watch, muscled forearms on the table. He scratched at his arm hairs distractedly as he listened to Mike Francesca, the Oak Bluffs police chief. Mike himself was big and stocky, but soft and thick around the middle. He could barely fit into his police uniform. Too many doughnuts and sitting for hours in the squad car on the side of the road with the radar gun had done him in.

"Carl, we've got nothing on him to date. In fact, he's been a model citizen. Christ, he even made a $1,500 donation to the Police Athletic Association last week. It was out of the blue. Someone told him that we needed money, and bingo, there it was. He made the gift in the name of the Neskeet Nation."

Carl shook his head." Fuck the Neskeet Nation. I can't believe this guy. He's making donations to the police, and he hasn't even been here a year. Who does he think he is?" Carl looked over at Mike and nodded. "He's setting you up, Mike. Taking advantage. He's gotta be pulling some shit. We both know it."

Mike Francesca smiled. "All I know is that you declined to support the PAA this year when we came looking for a contribution. Remember?" He tapped his fingers on the brim of his police hat, which was sitting on the edge of the table.

Carl frowned and made up a cockamamy excuse on the fly. "We didn't have enough money in the cash account that day. Send me an invoice now. We'll send something over for sure."

Mike continued. "Look, the guy blows into town and is clean as a whistle. He's got an occupancy permit for his office, and they're quiet. He's an attorney, for Chrissakes, a straight arrow."

Carl shook his head. "You've got to be able to get him for something. Check his sign, will you? Have Frank check his sign and see if it's the right size. That thing looks too damn big on the street."

"You mean that little blade sign that's hanging over his entry door with the clamshell?"

"Yeah. That's the one."

Mike Francesca was exasperated. "C'mon, Carl, you're shitting me, aren't you? I can't run him out of town 'cause of his sign."

"Just check it for me, will ya? I gotta rock him back a bit for something."

"Jesus H. Christ." Francesca ran a hand through his hair. "You're going about this the wrong way. You need to build your goddamn brand and compete with the asshole, not sabotage him. He's a white guy for shit's sake, a fake Indian, and he's whipping your ass."

"I know what he is. But he's created buzz around here faster than shit running through a goose. I told my guys that we weren't marketing ourselves aggressively enough last year. Nobody listened, the lazy bastards. Now we've got our backs to the wall," Carl said and sat back in his chair and folded his arms. "Mike, I'm calling in my marker with you. Do some database searches on Fletcher and see if you can find any dirt on him. If he has any criminal history, prior arrests, anything like that. Do some deep background on him and his band of misfit Indians, for Chrissakes."

Mike Francesca looked out the window and saw a good-looking blond girl walking by with a tight Neskeet Nation T-shirt holding in her breasts firm and high. He pointed her out to Carl.

"Now that's what I call Indian. A good-looking Indian squaw, part of the Neskeets, Carl. Why can't you do something like that?" Francesca said. "Shape the hell up, will ya? Give us more college-girl Indians. They're fake but easy on the eyes. You know what I mean?"

Carl Sunapee didn't say a word. He shook his head. "I don't know. We may have missed the boat on this one. It may be too late."

Mike Francesca laughed and slapped the table. "You're right about that."

Carl looked over at Mike Francesca darkly. "I'll tell you one thing. We are not going down quietly on this. If big Bill Fletcher wants a fight, he's got one. He's going to quickly find out who the real Indian chief of the Island is, pronto."

Carl got up, ending the meeting. He checked the time on his big Rolex and then headed back out to the street in a thoroughly pissed-off mood.

Hearing Confession

Father Peter Mulcahey sat in the confessional booth, waiting for his next penitent. It was warm and quiet in the back of the church, just right for a nap.

He had his iPhone in his lap, and he was watching an episode of *Glee* that he had downloaded from iTunes for $1.99. He had one earbud in his right ear, and the other one dangled down on his black short-sleeve shirt.

But he was always ready to spring into action if someone entered the booth. He had the volume down low, but loud enough to hear. He drifted between the video on the small screen and thinking about Margaret Wellington. The road to hell was paved with good intentions.

There was a gauzy fabric-covered window in the door to the booth where he sat as well as in both of the kneeling stations for the sinners. When he came to the Island five years ago, the priest's booth was dark, and he couldn't see the people in the church or, more importantly, the people coming in to confess their sins.

So he took his BIC pen and ripped a hole in the cloth window that looked out onto the church pews from his perch inside the booth. Then he called Harry the maintenance man over and pointed out the ripped confessional window covering.

"Let's replace all of them while we're at it so the window covers match."

Harry was all over it, wanting to get it just right for the newly installed Fr. Mulcahey so that he could perform his sacred sacrament of confession in just the right atmosphere. It was important shit.

So Father Peter directed Harry to get a nice light gauze covering—the lightest of light, transparent almost—so that he could see who the hell was out there in the pews and, more importantly, who were coming into the confessional booth.

It took them several times to get the right level of see-through cloth, but Harry nailed it on the third try. Now it was like a two-way mirror; Father Mulcahey could see who was in the church or who was coming into the confessional, but they couldn't see him because of the low light in the booth. It was perfect. He now had an edge on every one of the sinners, not that he wanted one.

In came Mrs. Whitten, widowed for five years now and thick as a brick shit house. *She could start for the Pittsburg Steelers at right tackle*, Father Peter decided. She waddled into the booth, knelt, and confessed her sins.

As usual, she had nothing—not one real, honest-to-God sin. *How could she?* Father Peter thought. She came to confession every week. She didn't have time to get a running start on doing bad stuff.

She had coveted the new car that her neighbors, the Flahertys, bought last week, a Toyota Highlander. Big friggin' deal. He gave her five Our Fathers and five Hail Marys for her penance. It was a lot for such a minor sin, he knew, but he also knew the old woman had nothing else to do in her life and needed the psychological boost she'd get once she said all the prayers.

"By the way," Father Peter added as she struggled to get up off the tiny little kneeler in leaving, "the Highlander got a bad rating in consumer reports. No gas mileage. Think about that."

Finally, in came a good-looking blond high school girl. The attractive Catholic girls all wanted to purify their souls every thirty days and erase their sins to be able to start the month off clean. He was lucky as he had had a string of them come in recently, confessing summer sex and similar high jinks.

The girl came in, kneeling down soft and quiet. He could smell her sweet sexy perfume through the screen immediately. The high school girls always wore too much.

"Bless me, Father, for I have sinned."

"Get on with it, child," Peter Mulcahey said as he listened.

"Father, I've had sex with my boyfriend twice this week."

"Oh? What is the nature of your sins, my child?"

"Oral sex, Father."

"Go ahead."

"My friend Cindy says that a blow job isn't really considered sex at all. It's just friends with benefits, FWB. What do you think, Father?"

"Friends with benefits indeed. It's all frowned upon in the eyes of the church, unfortunately, my dear."

"Well, I'm truly sorry for my sins, Father." "Don't go so fast, my child. Tell me the particulars if you want the Lord's forgiveness."

"Yes, Father."

And so it went. Peter Mulcahey got all the details. He worked them out of her like a good police detective. In the end, he wasn't sure who was getting turned on more, the girl telling him all about her sex acts or him listening. Confessional sex. It didn't matter; it was all good.

Finally in a hoarse voice, he gave her penance—two Our Fathers and two Hail Marys. It was a light load considering her sins.

But he was always careful with good-looking girls and MILF mothers who confessed extracurricular sex acts to give them very light penances so they'd come back often for more forgiveness. He liked the stories, so he kept it easy and light. It was like he was running a sex therapy session right out of the confessional with a string of good-looking women looking for salvation. Dr. Drew Pincus in priest's garb working the sin circuit.

The church got quiet again. Father Peter checked his watch. It was 3:45 p.m., quitting time. The rest of the parish's sins would have to wait until next week. He shut his iPhone off and pocketed it along with the headphones.

He left the booth and went immediately to the front pew. Father Peter always made sure he sat in the front when he said his own prayers. He made a big production out of it to be sure that any parishioners lurking in the back of the church would see him doing his thing. He was always buffing up his image. It was part of the job.

He knelt on the kneeler and said his own penance for his transgressions with Margaret Wellington, for his weak soul, for succumbing to the temptations of the flesh. One Our Father and one Hail Mary. Not a lot, as he didn't want to break out into a sweat praying. Plus, the goddamn kneelers were uncomfortable as hell.

He threw in a Glory Be to the Father, a transitional prayer, for good measure at the end. *What the hell*, he thought. It was a short filler and served as icing on the cake. He wanted to cover all his bases with the Lord.

He didn't linger. He saw on his iPhone that Margaret Wellington had called while he was doing confessions earlier. Working on Saturday afternoon was always a pain in the ass because he was out of communication for a couple of hours. He quickly finished his prayers and headed back to the rectory to take her call in private.

Here we go, he thought.

* * *

Carl Sunapee's cell phone rang while he was in the Vineyard Haven ferry terminal. It was the theme from *Rocky*, and he had it set to loud. He was waiting to pick up his sister from New Bedford on the 3:15 p.m. boat. She was staying over for a few days to hang out with his wife and see the kids. It was another pain in the ass.

A few tourists looked over at him, hearing the hokey ring tone. They were irritated. They heard loud ring tones back in the city, and they didn't need it following them to the bucolic Vineyard. Carl ignored the phone for a second, standing there and letting it ring. He was dressed in a nice summer shirt, madras shorts, and his porkpie hat. With his gold Rolex watch, he looked like an island version of Shaft. Can you dig it?

Carl didn't care about the tourists around him. He was irritated too, but for different reasons. It was his island. The wash ashores and the day-trippers could all go to hell and swim back across to Falmouth for all he cared. He had bigger fish to fry.

He pulled the phone out of his pocket and saw that it was Mike Francesca calling. He answered it just before it went to voice mail. He brightened because Mike never called him unless he needed to tell him something important.

"What's up?" Carl said into the phone.

"I'm following up from our conversation last week in my office. Remember?"

"Yeah, you find out anything? What you got?"

Mike Francesca let the question hang in the air for a second before he answered. He knew how to build drama. He could have been a TV cop on *Law and Order*; he was that good.

"I hate to burst your bubble."

"Yeah?" Carl said. But Mike had already just burst Carl's bubble.

"I didn't find a damn thing. Fletcher's clean as a whistle. Even his bar membership is up to date."

"Bar membership?" Carl was puzzled. "What's that about?"

"Remember I told you? The guy's a lawyer in addition to being an Indian chief. How's that for a hot shit? You got any lawyers in the Fluevogs? You could probably use a few right now."

"Lawyer my ass," Carl said as he ignored Mike's comments.

"Yeah, well, I ran all the state and federal databases on him and came up dry. Bone-dry, in fact. I even ran a CORI on him. Nothing. He hasn't molested any kids or buried any women under his porch either that I could find." Mike Francesca paused and let it sink in. "So there's that."

Carl took the information and frowned. He thought for sure that Bill Fletcher would have all kinds of murky fraud charges outstanding. He oozed fraud. He was no Indian chief for damn sure.

"Look, I gotta go," Mike Francesca said. "I'm workin' a traffic detail at the agricultural hall."

"What about the sign?"

The cop was one step ahead of Carl. "Oh yeah, I forgot. It's all legal. He even got a variance for it because it was a little over the size limit for blade signs. He knew it. He got Joe Nunes, the building inspector, to sign the variance. It's all right in the file. I checked."

"No shit." Carl said. He was flummoxed. He shook his head and frowned.

"We'll talk later," Mike said. He had no time to handhold Carl Sunapee today. "We'll find something."

Mike rang off before Carl could answer and got out of his cruiser. He donned his fluorescent-green police vest and walked out into the intersection. He started to direct traffic like a symphony conductor directing the Boston Pops.

"I'll get that God damn fake Indian chief, variance or no variance," Carl said softly to no one in particular in the ferry terminal as he closed his phone. He put his cell back in his pocket. Then he saw his sister walking down the gangplank.

Sweat It Out

Bill Fletcher walked into the Sweat Lodge at eight in the morning with a big lemon-and-lime Gatorade. He was there to work out and get a steam bath.

Mike Jackson was sitting at the front desk, checking IDs and handing out towels. His biceps were huge, and his arms popped out of his T-shirt. He was wearing an old Muscle Development shirt to be obstinate. Fletcher was irked.

Mike needed to get on board with the new branding, and greeting people with one of his old T-shirts was not the way to do it. Fletcher wasn't going to let on to him that he was pissed. That would be tactical error number one of the morning.

"Morning, chief."

"Morning. I need to get you some new Neskeet Nation T-shirts to wear while you're working here. Didn't Carrie drop any off?"

"I haven't seen any," Jackson said, straight-faced, as he let three girls in for yoga while he and Fletcher talked around them.

"What are you doing this morning?" Mike asked. He could see Fletcher's gym bag.

"A little stretching, a little steam. Work out the kinks." As they talked, he watched a fat German guy head toward the locker room.

"Who's he?"

"Tourist from Berlin. He and his wife got the weekend special. They're staying at the Island Inn. We offer a special there for early exercisers. Ten bucks for a workout. The wife is doing the yoga class."

Bill Fletcher smiled. "See, the promotions are working already."

Fletcher went in and exercised for about twenty minutes. Light stuff, nothing more. He was really there to check out the customers, the women really, and see who was coming in.

Mike Jackson had said that he was getting a lot more walk-in traffic with the name change. Everybody wanted to be part of the Indian thing, and the gym got sucked into the buzz.

Fletcher hung out on one of the spinning bikes, which were situated in a line, eight of them, over by the entrance door. He pedaled aimlessly, pretending to exercise with the resistance set to zero, while he watched people coming in. He was also distracted from watching the small flat-screen TV tuned into the *Today Show*.

He noticed that there were two types of women coming in. The hard-body exercisers that were there to do a real workout, and then the yoga types who were there to get into Hindi positions on the mats.

The yoga women had softer bodies with more curves, and Bill Fletcher naturally gravitated toward them. The hardcore exercisers were like whippets and could easily have beaten the shit out of him. They frightened him.

He finished "exercising" and went to the men's locker room and stripped down. He picked up the *Globe* sports page and his Gatorade and headed into the steam room, the Indian sweat lodge, for a quick steam bath.

He decided at that point that life was rich and full and that he had fallen off the shit wagon onto a pile of roses. He never amounted to much in the Boston legal world, and look at what happened.

He didn't deserve it. But he was a go-getter, and America sometimes rewarded those that took a flier. He drank his Gatorade and wondered if he could convince Carrie to come over with him some night after the gym closed, after 10:00 p.m., to have sex in the sauna. It was a possibility.

Buffalo Bill

Fletcher was in his office on the phone with black cowboy boots, pressed jeans, and his chunky turquoise bracelet. He paced back and forth along the windows.

"Yeah, that's right. No. No, I don't want to buy buffalo meat. I want the real deal. Yeah. Big giant buffalo. On the hoof, live ones. A herd of them, actually."

Bill Barrows, head of national sales at New Era Buffalo, Inc., in Monfort, Colorado, couldn't believe what he was hearing. The guy on the line was talking about a huge order. It would make his quarter.

"I want twenty-five buffalo, the real live ones."

"You sure you don't want buffalo meat, sir? I can transfer you to our fresh meat division. You said you're a chef."

Bill Fletcher smiled into the phone. "I'm not a chef. I'm a chief. An Indian chief. And I want a buffalo herd. A big beautiful buffalo herd. Are you not listenin'?"

"Well, we've got live buffalo. We've got plenty, matter of fact. Just not too many people order them live, that's all," the salesman said. "Unless, of course, you're Ted Turner."

Fletcher didn't miss a beat. "Think of me as a mini Ted Turner down here on the Cape. You know where Cape Cod is? The land of the cod and the buffalo?"

"Yes, sir, I do. My wife and I went out to Cape Cod for a vacation a few years back. It's a beautiful place. I didn't see too many buffalo down there though. Just a lot of sand dunes and beach grass."

"You're right about that."

So Bill Fletcher stopped pulling the buffalo salesman's willy soon enough, and they got down to business. He went through the types of buffalo that the Neskeet Nation could buy and the kind of buffalo that hobby farmers usually ordered. Now that's what he was talking about, live hobby buffalo.

"I want the kind of buffalo that roamed the plains when General Custer was alive and the Sioux were chasing him. That's the kind of beast that I want down here on the Cape."

"You want the buffalo-steer mix we've got? We breed the classics with high-grade Texas steer, and you'll get a hell of an animal. Great tasting but with most of the buffalo look. We sell a lot of them. The buffalo meat is a little tough on its own otherwise."

"Not interested," Fletcher said. "These buffalo are for looking at only, so I don't care about how gamey they are. We're not eatin' them. This is for visuals only, you understand?"

"I do know. A lot of people buy 'em that way. American Classic is the type you want then."

"I want the good lookers, the kind with the massive heads and the little chin beards. You know the kind?"

"Yeah, I got it." The buffalo salesmen knew exactly what Bill Fletcher needed. "They're $5,000 a head, FOB Denver."

"FOB?" Fletcher asked into the phone.

"That's freight on board. At Denver. Means I put them on the truck at Denver, and you pay to transport them all the way to Boston."

"Cape Cod."

"Yeah, wherever the hell it is that you're at. The terms are all standard. How you paying?" The buffalo salesman brought it right down to brass tacks.

"Wire transfer," Fletcher said." You accept that?"

"I don't see why not."

Fletcher got the wiring instructions from Bill Barrows in an e-mail while they finished talking about the details on the phone. He ordered twenty-five buffalo, a small herd no doubt, but just the right size to roam the grassy plains of Martha's Vineyard.

With taxes, vet certificates, and truck transport to the Island, the total came to $132,571.

"Bill, I've got to tell you, you've just made my quarter. No, my whole goddamn year. I've never had a sale like this, this quick, do it all in one call, in all my time here at the ranch. This was awesome."

"Well, I've got no time to waste. I'm making up for one hundred years of neglect. The Indian hunting grounds are fallow."

"Not anymore they're not."

"When are you going to ship 'em?" Fletcher asked.

"As soon as that wire transfer clears. Tomorrow probably at the latest. I'm getting the trailer lined up today."

"I can't wait."

"Better watch it when they come. They'll be a little ornery from the ride. You can bet on it," Barrows said.

Fletcher hung up the phone and let out a satisfied sigh. Buying the buffalo herd would be a game changer for the Neskeets. Nobody could touch him after that. Nobody. It would put the Neskeet Nation on the map. Indians and buffalo—it was as good as peanut butter and chocolate.

He walked over to Carol Ault in the other room. She was wearing pink flip-flops and had matching toenails. She was surfing websites and shopping when she wasn't doing Indian business. She had a big grin on for Fletcher.

"We're getting buffalo?"

"You heard."

"Yeah, well, it was hard to miss it. You were almost yelling into the phone, you were so excited."

Fletcher nodded his head." You're right. But you've got to keep it a secret for now. I don't want anyone else knowing about the buffalo until they're on the boat coming over. Capish?"

"I get it. It'll be a big surprise."

"Now you've got work to do. Here are the wiring instructions for the money. Call Donna at the bank and get her to start a wire this afternoon to New Era Buffalo. The amount's on the sheet. We have until 3 p.m."

Cute Carol nodded her head. She had never done a federal wire transfer in her life. In fact, she didn't even know what one was. But she was resourceful, if nothing else, and could fake her way through the instructions and learn it the first time. She was a quick study.

"Something else you've got to do today," Fletcher added.

"What's that?" Carol looked up at the Indian chief with her blue eyes and dark hair. He wilted. It worked every time, she knew.

"You need to call Ken Richards at town hall and tell him that the Neskeet Nation wants to rent Island Park for the month of August or at least part of it. Tell him we'll pay good for it."

"We putting the buffalo there? Cool."

"We're going to put most of 'em up at Sam Morse's place on Middle Road in Tisbury. I rented one of his fields up there for a year. He thinks that we're raising cows, though. He's gonna be a little surprised when he sees what's coming. He'll shit."

"No kidding," Carol said.

"Then we're going to put two or three of them right there in Island Park, close to the ferry terminal. They'll be a tourist attraction and a huge curiosity. Like a giant petting zoo. Everybody will love 'em."

Carol frowned. "That's going to be kind of tough, isn't it? It's a little crowded over there."

"We'll make it work," Fletcher said and dismissed her comments as negativity. "Call him and set up a meeting for me. I'll go over and talk him into it."

Carol got on it quickly. It was much better to be busy than not. By close of the day, the Neskeet buffalo had a home on Martha's Vineyard. It wasn't home on the range, but it was a good alternative.

*   *   *

Carrie Nation was working in the Equinox selling T-shirts and Indian shit. She was wearing her long jean skirt and a low-cut Neskeet T-shirt, complete with a big stone necklace, a blue headband, and a ton of bangles on her arms. The necklace settled in perfectly between her breasts.

Her business had taken off, and she was euphoric. She was ringing up so many sales and making so much money that she thought the jolt of it all was better than sex. She paused a second, thought about it, and then quickly backtracked. It was a close second to good sex, but way better than being poor like she'd been for the last four years. Retailing was certainly fickle. She was determined to ride the wave as long as she could.

She ordered about ten thousand more T-shirts in a variety of styles and colors. Her biggest seller was a simple one with the clamshell image and Neskeet Nation printed below it. The cotton was prewashed, slightly faded, very soft and pliable. Everybody loved them. The shirt was a throwback to the first generation of Black Dog T-shirts that took the Island by storm over forty years ago. *Synchronicity*, she thought.

Bill Fletcher walked into the store. It was cool outside, and he had on his suede jacket with the fringe, the one that he got at the thrift store. The little waves of fringe moved left and right as he walked.

"That's a nice touch, wearing the jacket," Carrie said as she looked him over. "The fringe looks good on you. My instincts were right."

"I look like goddamn Neil Young," Fletcher said. "Harvest and all."

"He's too old. You need someone younger to channel. Like Sherman Alexie."

"Who's he?"

"That Indian writer. He's hip."

Fletcher ignored her reference. He didn't have time to read right now. "How are sales going?"

"I'm crazy busy. I grossed more last weekend than I did in all of July last year. It's fantastic. I'll take you away on a vacation to the islands this winter to celebrate. It's on me, I promise."

Fletcher smiled as he walked through the store, looking at the merchandise, running his fingers over the neat stacks of Neskeet T-shirts in pastel colors.

"Be careful what you wish for, sweet pea, 'cause it may come true."

"I hope it does come true. Are you kidding?" she said.

"We need a T-shirt with my picture on it. I'm the tribal chief, and I've got nothing."

"You want one? I'll do it." Carrie thought for a second. "I'll do a silk screen of your face and make you into a Bob Marley figure. An icon. What do you think?"

"I think that you should only do it if we can make money on it. Otherwise, stick with your popular stuff. Don't mess up the formula."

Carrie thought about it and answered noncommittally. "Let me work on it."

Fletcher liked what Carrie had done with the store. It was basically a company store now for the Neskeet Nation. Most of her other tchotchkes were gone.

"What happened to the scented candles?" he asked.

"I got rid of them. I needed the room for more Neskeet products, more Indian stuff."

Fletcher nodded.

"I basically sell around the Neskeet T-shirt display. I built up the clothing accessories and Indian paraphernalia as supplements. The flip-flops, belts, and canvas bags are all moving well. All the other stuff wasn't selling, so out it went."

Fletcher nodded. He knew that they had caught lightning in a bottle.

He was sleeping with the hippest retailer on the Island who was helping him capitalize on the fifteen minutes of fame that the Neskeet Nation was enjoying that very summer. She also happened to be good-looking. The romance was serendipitous.

"You go, girl," he said to no one in particular as he headed back to the office, enjoying the Neskeet vibe.

Money from Heaven

Father Peter Mulcahey was engaged in a shakedown. It was a little distasteful, but he had no choice. So he held his nose and dove in.

He had Frank Fitzgerald sitting across from him in his office in the rectory. The door was closed so Joanne Proctor couldn't hear them talking. Father Peter suspected her of always listening in on his conversations, lurking around, with a bad habit of dusting the furniture or mopping the floors near his office whenever something juicy was going on within.

At first, Father Peter thought it might be Father Zaremba, the tall distinguished African priest over for a summer sabbatical from Zimbabwe, who was the information leak. Father Peter loved looking at him. He was tall and very black with a shaved head and wire-rim glasses. He was slow and thoughtful. It was like looking at a gazelle on the African veld.

But soon enough, he realized that Father Zaremba was out of it most of the time, probably from being malnourished since childhood. He told the cook to give Father Zaremba an extra scoop of rice most nights to make up for lost meals. But he decided that he wasn't the information leaker, that it was Joanne all along.

Frank Callahan was a big burly man, a roofer by trade. He did the expensive roofs on the Island for the wealthy clientele, the ones with copper downspouts and sheathing around the drip line. It was expensive work. He specialized in copper and slate.

Slate roofs were for the old sea-captain homes over in Edgartown. They increased the value of the house by double their installation cost. Most buyers never understood that while the roofs looked nice, they were a black hole of money to maintain. They found out soon enough once Frank Callahan and his men got to working up there on their scaffolding and high ladders.

Frank was dressed in a blue Polo shirt and clean jeans with his Nextel on his belt in a holster. He was wearing big yellow Timberland boots with Vibram soles. They were his Sunday-go-to-meeting boots, the ones he wore out on bids and when he met customers.

Peter Mulcahey had on his blacks and his dog collar. He wasn't about to shake someone down without being in full uniform, having the power of the Lord palpable right there in the room. He felt good, having just run two miles earlier in the morning and then doing some light weights at the Sweat Lodge. *What a bogus name*, he thought. *Some kind of fake Indian thing going on.*

"So we need a new roof, Frank," Peter Mulcahey said with no smile or subterfuge.

"You want me to do it? I'll give you a great price, Father. All my labor and materials at cost. No markup. For the church and all, you know? You've done a lot for me and my family."

"That won't be necessary, Frank," Father Peter said as he lightly drummed his fingers on the big mahogany desk.

"So what kind of roof do you want, Father? Straight black shingle or textured?" Frank jumped right into the conversation, happy to help out. He was always on the hunt for new business.

Frank's Nextel chirped with conversation from one of his supervisors on a job site. He reflexively reached down to his holster and turned the volume to zero as he focused on the potential new job at hand. New business was always the most important.

So there they were, Frank Callahan and Peter Mulcahey, two strong-willed Irishmen, sitting in the rectory office, talking. There was a big cross of Jesus being crucified on one wall with dried palm fronds draped across the top of the wood. On the other wall was a picture of Cardinal Patrick O'Malley, leader of the Boston Catholics, smiling and looking down in his Franciscan robe. There was also a new Dell computer on the desk with a big flat-panel monitor.

Peter Mulcahey finally dove in. "You see, Frank, we really don't need a roof."

"You just said you did, Father." Frank was puzzled. He rested his hand on his phone holster, leaning back in the nice chair, getting comfortable, listening.

"It's just an expression. A cover, if you know what I'm saying, in the priest business." He looked straight at Frank Callahan. "It means that we need money, Frank. We need money for repairs and the other things that keep the parish going." He paused. "It's not a real roof that we need, just an expression. It's a figure of speech."

The light clicked on immediately with Frank Callahan. He frowned. "So why don't you pass the plate for an extra collection, Father, for capital costs and all."

"No can do, Frank. The parishioners are broke here. This is a poor parish."

"How much you need?"

"Ten thousand dollars."

Father Peter let that sit for a minute. He looked sideways out the window at a cardinal sitting in the spruce tree outside.

"Are you shitting me, Father? Pardon me, but you want me to fund that amount?"

"You look prosperous, Frank. I hear the roofing business is good."

"It is good. Very good. But I can't swing all that."

Peter Mulcahey finally played his ace card and got to the point. There was no sense in prolonging this dicking around.

"Frank, remember when your oldest daughter was pregnant and had the abortion but still wanted to receive communion? She got knocked up by that rough football player there, Ed Chandler's son. Remember that?"

"Yeah. I do, Father."

"And you remember who went to the bishop in Fall River and got the special absolution for her so that she could still receive the sacrament in church, head held high?"

Frank nodded. "That would be you, Father."

"And do you remember when your other daughter, Jennifer, was seven months pregnant and wanted to be married in the church in Oak Bluffs, how I made that happen as well?" Father Peter paused for effect. "The sex is supposed to happen after the wedding, Frank, not before. Your daughter, lovely young woman, was waddling down the aisle, if I remember correctly."

He looked at Frank Callahan to finish up. "So your wife and daughters, all good Catholic women, got what they wanted. A piece of the flesh and the sacraments too. Their souls are saved. Things worked out for you. I'm truly happy."

Frank Callahan paused. "Father, it feels like things are about to work out pretty well for you too." He looked stone-cold at the priest.

"I hope so, Frank. You know I find this distasteful, but the Lord's will be done. Both Bishop Guerin and I appreciate anything you can do." Father Peter was done. "Just send me the check this week."

The business at hand completed, they talked for a little while longer. After Frank Callahan left, Father Peter Mulcahey felt frisky. He called up Margaret to see if she was available for dinner that night.

*   *   *

"How about some ice cream, something sweet? French vanilla with fudge sauce," Carrie Nation said.

She was lying spread-eagled on the big double bed in Bill Fletcher's small house, facedown, her head on the pillow. She wiggled her toes. "That was the best sex we've had all summer. It was awesome."

Fletcher smiled. "You're right. It was good. We're certainly getting along, that's for sure."

He got up and looked for his pants. "You really want ice cream?" He threw on a purple Neskeet Nation T-shirt that was badly wrinkled as he looked for his car keys.

"Indulge me. I just indulged you, didn't I?"

It was cool out. He put on his fringe suede jacket and loafers with no socks and headed for the door. "I'm going to get some fudge sauce too."

He walked outside in the warm night air toward the big white Grand Cherokee, his head down. He was looking for his car keys in his pocket as he walked. He pulled them out and then looked up.

There on the windshield was a broken arrow with a rubber suction cup tip stuck to the glass right in front of the driver's seat. It was from a child's bow-and-arrow set. You couldn't miss it.

Fletcher scratched his head and saw a little scrap of paper taped to the arrow's shaft. He picked it up and read it.

"INJUN GO HOME!" it said in big black rough letters.

It was a message, no doubt. One that Bill Fletcher promptly ignored.

He wasn't surprised either. He had actually been waiting for some petty vandalism to come his way. He knew that he'd never bring the Neskeets to the promised land without stepping on a few toes along the way. He was ready. These tin horns on the Island didn't know who they were dealing with.

Fletcher pulled the broken arrow off the windshield and threw it in the bushes. He got in and started up the big SUV, put it in Drive, and headed to the island minimart for Carrie's ice cream.

He hadn't noticed, but someone had also smashed dog shit onto his rear license plate. You could barely read the word *injun* in the running lights with all the dog crap smeared on the surface.

Advance Work

Bill Fletcher and Carrie Nation were in the bingo hall at St. Mary's parish off County Road. They were seated at a brown eight-foot folding table with six other people, mostly old farts. Everyone was happy.

The table had a white paper tablecloth on it and, on top of that, a covering of bingo cards and multicolored chips everywhere. Each old person played at least three cards, and the seventy-five-year-old pixie with the short-cropped gray hair and sweatshirt that said ASK ME ABOUT MY CAT at the opposite end from Fletcher played six cards.

"Tell me again, why are we here?" Carrie asked. She was sitting, watching the action, sipping white wine from a short clear plastic cup. She had a bingo card in front of her and a stack of colored plastic chips.

"We're here for recon. Reconnaissance. To learn how the operation's run. This is the biggest social event of the week in Oak Bluffs, and I want to find out why." Bill Fletcher was observing, taking it all in.

Father Peter Mulcahey got his introduction from Margie Wellington, waved to the crowd like a rock star, and then said his benediction. He didn't linger or waste time.

"In the name of the Father and the Son and the Holy Spirit." He finished the prayer quickly, almost like a legality, making sure that he did what the accountant told him to keep the bingo session outside the grasp of the taxmen at the Massachusetts Department of Revenue. *What a racket,* he thought as he left the stage and went back to work the wine bar.

Bill Fletcher listened and watched Father Peter finish his prayer in about thirty seconds, wish everyone good luck, and then depart the stage. He could see that the guy was a pro, an experienced money raiser.

The bingo caller, another golden ager, started in, right on cue. "B-29. G-17. H-23."

Carrie looked at her card. "Yeah," she murmured as she moved a red chip over the number H-23. She winked at Fletcher and sipped her wine.

"H-34." And on it went.

Fletcher went up to the cash bar to get himself another beer and a second white wine for Carrie. Peter Mulcahey was working the crowd next to the bar, chatting up the Islanders as they came over like the host at a giant cocktail party.

"Father, this is great fun, makes me want to convert," Fletcher said.

Peter Mulcahey shook Bill Fletcher's hand and noticed the turquoise bracelet immediately. Fletcher noticed him noticing.

"Bill Fletcher. I'm the chief of the Neskeet Nation." He held the priest's firm grip. "We're reclaiming the Island."

Peter Mulcahey's eyes lit up. "The Indian tribe? That's you?"

"That's me, indeed."

"Well, I'm impressed. And honored that you've come to our little social event here. But I was expecting someone more traditional, like Sitting Bull, with long black hair and eagle feathers on a string. You know." Peter Mulcahey winked at Fletcher, like a little leprechaun.

"No, Father. I'm all that's left after all the inbreeding with the white man for 150 years. A pasty half-Caucasian Indian. Pathetic, isn't it?"

Bill Fletcher could talk the ear off a brass monkey. He quickly engaged Father Peter in a long-winded sidebar on the Neskeets and their peripatetic journey to the island of Martha's Vineyard. Father Peter was impressed with Bill Fletcher and could see that he was as sharp as a tack. This wasn't another slacker Fluevog trying to steal a free ride and a full-time job with benefits.

He decided on the spot to stay close to Fletcher going forward. Maybe he could convert him and his Indian tribe to Catholicism. It'd mean a whole lot more people to play bingo or drop a bill in the collection basket on Sunday.

Fletcher brought the wine back to Carrie and sat down.

"I'm bored. How much longer?" she said.

"Not much. I just wanted to get a feel for the operation. It looks like a moneymaker. They charge ten bucks a head to get in, five bucks a card, and they have a cash bar. I bet they pull out two thousand bucks a night here. All cash and under the table."

Carrie was impressed with Fletcher's arithmetic. "Yeah, but you have to play this stupid game to make any money."

"C-16."

Carrie put another chit down on her card and completed the row. "Bingo!" she yelled and raised her hand. The checker came over and looked at her card then dropped two twenties and a ten dollar bill on her table.

"Congratulations. Another lucky winner!"

They left soon after. Carrie was hungry after the lame excitement of the bingo game. They went to Carol's Snack Bar on the harbor and mingled with the tourists.

"So what did you think?" she asked as they shared a big heap of fried clams sitting in a red-checked paper container.

"I think the bingo thing is a gold mine."

"Nothing but old farts, if you ask me," Carrie said as she sipped her beer and pulled out a clam from the stack. "I love the bellies."

Bill Fletcher grabbed the saltshaker from the table next to them and shook it lightly onto the pile of fried clams.

"I think it's a lot cheaper than slot machines. There's no capital cost. And there's zero start-up time. I'd need to check the licensing statute though."

"Huh?" Carrie said. "What are you talking about?"

"You'll find out soon enough," Fletcher said.

*   *   *

Carl Sunapee was in a meeting that night with the executive committee of the Aquinah Fluevogs. They were sitting in the tribal offices in the same conference room, the big four-bulb fluorescent fixture throwing harsh light down onto the table. It matched the mood of the group.

It was Carl, Joe Nunes, and Manny Fernandez. Carl was drinking a Diet Coke, trying to watch his weight and being good.

"So what the hell are we going to do with this asshole?" Manny said, jumping right into the meeting.

Carl shook his head. "It may be too late. The horse is already out of the barn. The guy's got action going everywhere."

"Don't gimme that Indian bullshit, Carl, about the horses and the barn. Just tell it like it is. You called the meeting."

"Whoa. Carl's right," Joe Nunes said. "The guy's got a lot of traction out there. He's created buzz. Something we haven't been able to do with our Indian thing for twenty years here."

"We've got the gift shop at Gay Head that's been losing money for the last five years. That is *not* working."

"People don't give a shit about the clay cliffs at Aquinnah anymore and Indian trinkets in the gift store."

"Manny's right. That's all old school. The dream catchers are lame and outdated. It's embarrassing."

Manny Fernandez let it fly. "We need some apps, some Apple iPhone apps, is what we need. Bring us into the modern world. Apps to find restaurants and shit."

Carl Sunapee was quiet while the men bickered. Porkpie hat on the empty chair beside him, he slowly stroked his tight goatee as he thought. Finally he spoke.

"I tell you one thing. This guy is not taking over our shit so easily."

"Absolutely not. This is our island and our birthright. If it takes a little violence to fix this guy, then that's what it takes," Joe said.

Carl put his hands up, gesturing as if to stop. "Now I'm a peaceable man as you all know. But dangerous times require dangerous solutions. That's all I'm saying."

Carl and the rest of the committee continued in executive session. An hour later, after blowing off a lot of steam and coming to no firm conclusions, they ordered cheesesteak subs and beers.

Even executives got hungry once in a while.

Prospectin' for Gold

Ralph Sampson and Bill Fletcher were standing in the old A&P store in Vineyard Haven. They were over by the cash registers and the checkout lines that were still there in the otherwise mostly empty place. Ralph had just opened the electrical panel in the corner and pushed up all the breakers for the interior lights. The old grocery store lit up in bright fluorescent light.

Ralph was the leasing agent for Cape Properties who had the listing for the vacant storefront. He was dressed in his Cape Cod business uniform of khaki pants, black L.L.Bean loafers, button-down shirt, and blazer with the little gold buttons. He could have passed for a sailboat owner over in Edgartown.

Fletcher was equally conservative for the meeting. He wanted the space, so he didn't wear anything to spook the guy, like his fringed suede jacket or the turquoise bracelet. He had on a conservative shirt with a BIC Soft Touch pen in his pocket, clean jeans, and his polished black cowboy boots. He was the model of an East Coast Indian chief.

"Why'd they leave?"

"They need a bigger store to make it work. This location was too small and inefficient. Nine thousand five hundred square feet is just not the right size for a grocery store today. Too small really for food, and too big for a clothing retailer. Plus, the store was outdated. It needed a full upgrade including electrical and HVAC, and the owner didn't want to put in the money. So they left. They're before the Board of Appeals in Tisbury now for a Jones Road location."

"Yeah?" Fletcher said, interested.

"I think it'll be tough. People on the Island don't like chain stores, and they think A&P is a chain store. They never should have left this location. I told 'em that."

"It looks pretty visible."

"It is. It's amazing. You're right across the street from the ferry terminal, so you get tons of walk-ins and day-trippers every single day. And they're all looking to spend money. It's unbelievable."

"You have much interest in the space?"

"Some. Like I said, it's an awkward size. It's too big for T-shirts, but I got a lot of interest for that. I've got a guy coming this week from the Cape with a knock-off Pottery Barn concept that might work here. He's got ten locations. There's plenty of money on the Island to buy upscale kitchen equipment, I'll tell you that."

"I bet."

Ralph handed a flyer to Fletcher as they walked slowly through the space. It had all the key features of the store in bullet points: twelve-foot ceiling height, full AC with an updated eight-ton compressor, 440V electrical service with step-down transformers, four walk-in coolers, twelve refrigerated cases with glass doors—everything for a budding grocery store magnate like Bill Fletcher.

Ralph Sampson looked Fletcher over as they walked and talked. The empty store was pristine. All the aisle racks were gone, the ceiling was intact, and the floor holes were patched over. There were structural support poles every fifteen feet, but they were painted bright red and gave the place a busy uniform feel.

"Well, what do you think?" Ralph asked as they walked slowly through the space. He pointed out features as they strolled. "Two secondary circuit breaker panels over there."

"I'm thinking that I'd use the space for a meeting hall for the Neskeet Indians. No build out for the time being, I'd use it just as it is. Maybe throw up a Sheetrock wall in the back and build one or two offices. That's all."

Ralph Sampson brightened. "You could do that easily. Meeting space is within code for general commercial. You wouldn't need zoning approval or anything. With no TIs, you could start tomorrow." He laughed. "The owner doesn't want to spend anything much on build out for the next tenant."

Fletcher nodded. "Yeah. That's what I thought. Can I really start tomorrow?"

"You serious?"

"As a heart attack."

Sampson paused. "Look, the owner is looking for a long-term, credit retail tenant for the space. No doubt about it. I don't think an Indian tribe with an office use will fit the bill."

But Fletcher was on to something and was not to be thwarted. "Look, let's do this on a month-to-month tenancy thing for now. Totally at will. That way, the owner can pick up some rental income in the interim and boot me out when he has a real tenant. There's no cost to put me in, and he can keep fishing for the trophy tenant. Thirty-day notice, that's it. How about it?"

"I think he's looking for seven thousand a month."

"I can swing that," Fletcher said without pausing.

"Plus utilities, but that shouldn't be much. These lights are all T11s, so they run pretty cheaply," Ralph Sampson said.

"You bet," Bill Fletcher responded, already thinking about the space for the Neskeets.

So they went to the Black Dog for a cup of coffee and hammered out the details. Ralph Sampson promised to e-mail a completed form lease, ready for Fletcher's signature, later that afternoon. Fletcher wrote a fourteen-thousand-dollar check for the first month's rent and a security deposit right there on the spot.

The cash sealed the deal. After their coffee, they went to Tisbury Hardware, and Ralph Sampson gave Fletcher a duplicate key and the pass code to the security system. He was in.

Suddenly, Bill Fletcher had his casino, just like that.

Here we go, he thought.

*   *   *

Later that day, Fletcher met with Jim Barry, the town selectman that he was friends with. This time he was dressed in full Neskeet regalia with the turquoise bracelet, scruffy cowboy boots, and fringe jacket.

"Jim. Good to see you again."

"You bet, Bill."

The two men were sitting in Barry's office in the back of town hall. It was cramped in the small space. There was just enough room for the big oak desk and two chairs in front that Barry had put there for visitors.

"How do I do a charitable deed for the town with the resources of the Neskeet Nation?" Fletcher wasted no time in getting down to it. "You have any Little League fields that need updating?"

"We might have some that need a little shot of cash somewhere, I expect. That landscaping gets expensive," Jim Barry said. He was being cagey.

"How about I donate $10,000 to the town recreation department, and you do with it what you want. No strings attached."

Barry's eyebrows went up.

That was just the kind of donation that Jim Barry liked the most, the no-strings-attached kind. But over the years, he had learned that in Oak Bluffs politics, there were no such thing as no strings attached. The bigger the donation, the bigger the string. But it was cool. He could finagle with the best of them. He was third term with no serious competition in sight.

"That's fine. Make it out to Cash, and I'm sure the boys in the rec department will be thrilled. They'll put it to good use. I'll take it to them personally."

Fletcher pulled out his checkbook and wrote the check out in quick, swift strokes before Jim Barry could change his mind and go defensive on him.

"Sure enough. The town has been good to the Neskeets since we arrived. I always like to share the wealth a little, you know?"

"They'll probably name a basketball court after you," the selectman said.

"Whatever," Fletcher replied as he finished his signature with a flourish and handed the $10K check over to Jim Barry.

They finished their meeting, and Fletcher was happy. He knew that setting up a good foundation with the local political establishment was critical for a lot of Neskeet initiatives.

He wasn't exactly sure what they were at that point, but he'd likely step on some toes along the way and need political help. There was no better icebreaker than money, that great facilitator of genuine goodwill.

The Buffalo Herd

The Steamship Authority deckhand couldn't believe his eyes, which were bugging out of his head at that point. So the first thing he did was whip out his smartphone and snap a picture of what he saw in front of him, and then he sent it to his girlfriend.

There on the hot asphalt tarmac in Woods Hole was a tractor trailer as big as he had ever seen, probably bigger. The tractor was one of those over-the-road rigs with the big long snout and the sleeper cab behind the driver. It was bright blue with thin white pinstripes all around. The paint job looked perfect.

On the door in block letters, it said Monfort Livestock, Denver, CO. Under the driver's window, there was small hand-lettered script that said Bill Jones, Owner-Operator.

The other nice touch was the steer horns. There was a big set of them, yellowish and ugly, mounted on the chrome radiator grille, which itself was as big as a refrigerator door, at the front of the truck. The horns were bolted onto the grille, leading the way, showing everyone what the hell was coming at 'em.

The whole rig was polished up to within an inch of its life. It looked immense.

But behind the tractor was where the real action was taking place. It was pulling a monstrous cattle trailer that was over forty feet long and twelve feet high. Inside the trailer were twenty-five heads of buffalo, chewing hay and braying like hell. Twenty-five sets of eyes were calmly looking out at the action in Woods Hole.

"Am I gonna fit this thing all right on the goddamn boat?" Bill Jones asked, a little concerned.

"Shouldn't be a problem," the deckhand said. We'll have to snug one car line over to the side, though, 'cause your trailer wheels are wider than most of the ones we get. It's cool though."

"I got an over-the-road permit for it."

The deckhand shook his head." I don't need a permit, I believe you. I just got to fit you on the boat." He looked back and forth, sniffing. "Man, the smell is unbelievable. How'd you stand it?"

Bill Jones swung out of the cab and climbed down the ladder on the two side steps, then jumped to the ground. "That there is the smell of twenty-five nervous buffalo being in a truck for two days. Warm buffalo urine. Good stuff, huh? It's okay because I'm in front of it travelling seventy-five down the interstate mostly, so I don't smell it that much. It's another story, though, when I stop. It's the smell of the ranch."

"You got that right."

"It's been building all the way from Colorado."

The truck caused a small uproar on the dock. There were over thirty people, mostly waiting boat passengers, walking around, trying to get a look at the giant beasts in the back. You could just barely see the big dark eyes, the giant heads, and the little beards looking out; the buffalo were chewing hay slowly, masticating, and peeing. Cell phone cameras clicked everywhere.

The deckhand stood in front of the big tractor trailer and slowly guided it along the dock. The Steamship operations people decided to put the truck on the *Menemsha*, a big muscular freight boat, because the car and truck area was out in the open, not enclosed. If the buffalo went into the regular ferry, the place would have stank to high hell for a week.

With a big hiss of the air brakes releasing, Bill Jones swung the giant tractor trailer around perpendicular to the dock and then backed the rig slowly down the ramp onto the boat using his two big side mirrors. The guy was a pro. The buffalo were jittery as they sensed the backward motion, which was not at all like travelling seventy-five in a straight line forward.

Once the truck was on, the deckhands filled in around it with tourist cars and other vehicles. In about fifteen minutes, the deck was full, and the freight boat pulled out in the Sound with the sun glinting off the white paint on its hull. Lucky for the buffalo, the water was flat calm. It was a pristine Vineyard day.

Bill Jones went inside the wheelhouse and bought a cup of coffee in a big Styrofoam cup, put cream and two sugars, and chatted up the other passengers. He even treated himself to a doughnut. He was a rock star that day. Plus the fact that this was his first ferry boat ride made the boat trip special. He mostly moved livestock from one ranch to another back home in Colorado. There wasn't much demand for ferries back in Missouri and Oklahoma and the rest of the Plains states. Jones was determined to enjoy every minute of the trip.

*   *   *

Carrie Nation had been busy herself. She had the job of building out the old A&P store into a giant Indian bingo hall, and she had to do it in three days.

"We're already paying rent on the store," Fletcher said. "We need to get it producing revenue as quick as we can." When Carrie asked him how he wanted the interior done up, all he said was "Think Halloween," which she did.

She didn't waste any time. She found a local artist friend who she commissioned for $500 to paint a giant mural on the inside wall of the empty store.

It was a Thanksgiving scene, and it had turkeys and pumpkins and corn painted everywhere for atmosphere. Half of the painting was Indians in traditional headress and loincloths. On the other side were Pilgrims with buckle shoes and hats holding big blunderbusses.

In the middle was an Indian chief alongside the head of the pilgrim village, the lead elder, with a big black hat and cape. They were shaking hands and smiling, exchanging bingo cards for a stack of bills. There was a pile of bingo chips on the ground around the turkeys.

Leave it to Carrie to tell a history lesson like she wanted it to be told. It was revisionist history, pure and simple. In big letters at the bottom, it said NESKEET NATION in case anybody forgot.

Carrie got some green cornstalks and baskets of squash and tied the stalks to the red columns that were sticking out all over the place. It had the effect of being in a giant cornfield designed by Tim Burton. When Bill Fletcher saw it, all he said was, "You've got to move the baskets of squash or the old people will trip over them getting to the tables. We'll have a lawsuit the first week."

So Carrie moved the squash baskets to the front and bought about a hundred orange crepe paper pumpkins from iParty online and used those instead. She hung bunting down from the fluorescent lights and tied little pods of balloons to the ceiling to give the place a festive look. For five hundred dollars, the place looked great. Or at least good enough to stack in thirty tables and 240 folding chairs along with a podium for the numbers caller and a place for a big cash bar over to the left side up front that was easily accessible and right next to the entrance when you came in. You couldn't miss it.

Fletcher finished off the effort by putting up a big plastic sign on the front of the store. It had an ocean-blue background with big yellow block letters advertising Indian bingo, no mistake about it. They fastened it with clothesline and ten penny nails to the front of the facade where the old Atlantic & Pacific sign had been. It looked good. Instant Indian gaming without the capital expense, the five-hundred-room hotel, or the three years to get a permit.

Carrie had wanted to do a real sign professionally done and permanently mounted on the front of the store, and all Bill Fletcher said was "No goddamn time for that. Let's go with the plastic."

And that was that; the signage was up in forty-eight hours.

* * *

Fletcher himself had been plenty busy over the last week pushing paper as Carrie, his de facto girlfriend now and head squaw of the Neskeet tribe, was doing the interior decorating at the Indian bingo palace.

He was in closed-door session a lot of the time with Jim Barry, king of the selectman and his new-found asshole-buddy. Fletcher quickly found out that old Jim liked being a decision maker and the center of attention for what was going on in town. Who didn't? Fletcher was happy to oblige.

"Tell me again why the full board doesn't have to vote on this?" Barry asked Fletcher as they sat in his office, the two of them locked in executive session.

Bill Fletcher was more attorney today than Indian chief. He had on a nice blue pressed button-down shirt and was working off a pad of yellow legal paper with a Montblanc pen. There was no turquoise bracelet in sight, nothing rinky-dink about him. He was in his element, taking federal law. He even wore a suit coat.

"Because under federal law, recognized Indian tribes can sell beer and wine at tribal meetings. It's a given. Federal law, as you know, clearly supersedes any state and local statutes. It's basic," Fletcher said. He put his pen down.

Jim Barry winced a little and then went quiet as he thought about it for a bit. "And tell me again why the bingo thing isn't considered gambling?"

Fletcher had already prepared for this question and was on firm ground in giving his answer. "Because it's an exempt use for a nonprofit organization. The Neskeets are a federally recognized tribe. We're a bona fide 501(c)3 organization, no messing around. I already sent you a copy of our federal charter last week."

"Did I get that e-mail?"

"I sent it two days ago along with a pdf of our federal approval and permits."

Barry shrugged. "I'm sure it's in my inbox. I'm a little behind."

"Not a problem," Fletcher said. "I'll send it again today. Just so you'll have an extra copy. Easy. And I'd encourage you to send it to the rest of the board to head off the discussion from going the wrong way."

Jim Barry nodded his head. "That I'll do tonight, right after you send me the stuff again. I'll forward it to everybody with a little note. Saying how it's all legal and such. It'll be easier than writing a whole new memo from scratch. I hate that shit. Writing memos."

Fletcher smiled and nodded, himself in total agreement. "So do I. Doing all that bullshit like writing memos from scratch. Let's keep the work to a minimum. Anyway, the key to it all is the word *federal*. That trumps any local statute by a long shot. Particularly the Oak Bluffs rules and regulations."

"I'm sure it does," Jim Barry said. He looked at his watch; he was playing golf at four at Farm Neck and didn't want to be late.

Fletcher hammered it home just to be sure. "It's like a full house. It beats three jacks every time."

"Huh?" Jim Barry nodded his head absentmindedly. He was wandering now, wondering if he had enough fresh golf balls to play eighteen holes, or if he needed to buy a couple sleeves before he teed off. Or if he was hungry, should he have a quick sandwich and a beer first. A lot of things to decide when you went golfing. It wasn't as relaxing as most people thought. Jim Barry finally came back around and focused. "Just give me the ammo, Uncle Bill, that's all I need."

"If anybody asks, tell them we're just like Father Mulcahey's bingo parties over at the Catholic church on Thursdays," Fletcher said with finality. "They've been doing that bingo for a year now, and everybody loves it. We're just like them."

Jim Barry scowled and pulled out his handkerchief." You can be sure that people will ask about it, a whole lot of 'em too. But I'm persuasive, you know that." He wiped the bottom of his nose and sat back. "Now what about that donation to my campaign fund?"

Fletcher didn't miss a beat. "Yeah. Your campaign fund. Every campaign's got to have some money. I'm wiring over ten thousand tomorrow on behalf of the Neskeets to show our support for all the great things you're doing here in the town and for your reelection. Right straight into your account. No strings attached."

Jim Barry held up his hand in protest. "Whoa. No wires here. Just a bag of cash. Bring the money over to my office tomorrow in a sub sandwich bag along with a Coke and chips. Just like an Italian with everything on it. Know what I mean? That way you can say you brought me lunch."

"Yeah, I do," Bill Fletcher said. "I know exactly what you mean. You'll be eating well tomorrow, then."

Jim Barry looked more closely at Bill Fletcher. "And with a little luck, you'll have your operating permit this week, quick as greased lighting."

"Like shit through a goose," Fletcher said as he winked.

"Amen to that."

The meeting was over.

Clouds on the Horizon

"Christ save us," Father Peter Mulcahey said when he saw the scene in front of him.

He was inside the Neskeet Nation bingo hall for his own personal reconnaissance mission on Thursday night. He was solo, deciding to leave his new concubine, Margaret, at home. He told her earlier in the day that he was going to the hospital after dinner to deliver the sacrament of Holy Communion to the sick folks laid in. She had wondered why he didn't do it earlier in the day but didn't push him on it.

The place had been open about three weeks, and Bill Fletcher and Carrie Nation hadn't wasted any time. It was chock-a-block full of people. A lot of the gray hairs from Blessed Sacrament had magically migrated over here. It was now obvious why Father Peter's bingo was dead as a wake for an old person.

The place was also packed with rowdy sunburned tourists. All of them were in Neskeet Nation T-shirts and flip-flops, had sunglasses on top of their heads, and were drinking white wine in little plastic cups and Budweiser in bottles by the carload. They all looked like they had come straight off the beach.

Fletcher had a bunch of cute young waitresses dressed up like Hooters girls with extra tight T-shirts, the Neskeet logo on the front and DRINK SQUAW on the back. They finished off the look with ultrashort jean shorts and crisp new sneakers. They were sexy and busy as hell with trays full of drinks going everywhere.

He wondered why so many people were wearing Neskeet Nation T-shirts, and then he saw the sign on the wall. ADMISSION FREE IF YOU WEAR THE TEE. No wonder. The lure of free admission was the catalyst. They were like a crowd of Romans in the Colosseum getting loud and crazy together.

So that answered it for Father Peter Mulcahey. This was why attendance at the Blessed Sacrament bingo games had dropped off to a trickle. All his customers were here instead. It wasn't too hard to understand why either.

Bill Fletcher had put four big flat-screen TVs around the room that showed the numbers being called up front. The screens also scrolled over to the prize money available every minute as well. It felt like an off-track betting parlor in New York. A single game win was worth $125, and winning on two cards was worth $300. *No bloody wonder*, Father Peter thought, *why the place was so packed.*

The players could make double, almost triple, the prize money here than over at Blessed Sacrament. With admission being just five bucks if you didn't have your T-shirt on, it was a bargain.

Peter Mulcahey was pissed off. He realized now that Fletcher was suddenly formidable competition, and it was maybe too late. Christ fucking save us indeed. He saw Fletcher over at the bar, and he headed that way. He needed to assess the situation firsthand with the master of ceremonies.

"Bill, you've done an amazing job here so quickly. How did you put it together so fast?"

Fletcher was happy to see the priest in the hall. He figured that having the head of the Catholic church there was like having Sitting Bull come to a meeting. It was a good sign.

"It wasn't that hard, Father. There's an exemption for bingo for charitable organizations, as you probably know." He stacked up plastic cups as he talked.

Father Peter did know it and well. It was why he said a prayer before the start of every bingo session—trying to keep the activity beyond the reach of the auditors.

"But your Indians—are they charitable?" Peter Mulcahey asked innocently. He could have been a law professor.

"Ah, good question, Father." Fletcher nodded. "I just set up a 501(c) 3 subsidiary last week to keep it all kosher. I was a lawyer in my past life, did you know? So I did all the paperwork myself. Dotted all the i's and crossed the t's." He winked at the priest.

It was at that moment that Father Peter realized he had badly misjudged Bill Fletcher as a lightweight Indian carpetbagger who had parachuted into the Island for the summer alongside the tourists. He badly regretted it now. Carl Sunapee had made the same mistake.

Fletcher was now competition in the fiercest way, fighting for the bucks of the local people. It would be a steel-cage match for the two of them from here on out, Father Peter thought. But he didn't dwell on the negative. It wasn't in his nature. He decided to switch gears and get down to brass tacks.

"So how do you make money at this operation? You can't possibly be profitable with your payouts so big."

Bill Fletcher nodded. "You're right, Father. You're a good businessman. We make it all on the bar pretty much."

He turned around and made a sweeping gesture with his arm at the big bar behind him." We're selling ten cases of wine and beer every night. And it's all legal. We price it cheap, and we do a ton of volume. That's the secret."

"At two dollars a glass of wine?"

"They're small glasses, Father."

"And why don't you need a liquor license to do the volume you're doing?"

"Because it's all ancillary to the nonprofit activity. So it retains its character and isn't subject to any local regulation. Plus, we're Indian, so federal law prevails. Pretty neat, huh?"

Small glasses and no regulation. That was enough for Father Peter Mulcahey to hear. His stomach rolled over. This was going to be tough. It was redistribution of wealth from the Catholics to the Native Americans in a big way.

Bill Fletcher paused from his work of stacking the glasses and pointed to the wall. "Plus, Father, we keep all the booze right there in the coolers from the old A&P. It's perfect. They're all working fine too. We had zero capital costs to start up. Just had to turn 'em on and use some Windex."

Father Peter Mulcahey turned and strode out of the Indian bingo hall five minutes later. He had seen enough. He was as blue as the liquid in the Windex container that Bill Fletcher had used to clean his beer coolers earlier that night. He was surprised that it was unraveling so fast.

*　　*　　*

Carl Sunapee was just as direct in his assessment when he went on Friday night to see the Neskeet bingo palace. Fletcher was working the front door and recognized the head of the Fluevogs immediately when he walked up.

Fletcher had set up a small velvet rope to keep people orderly and in line as the bouncer he hired checked IDs for drinking and fastened on little blue bracelets. The operation had grown considerably over the past few weeks. He waved Carl forward.

"You're in for free, chief." He patted Carl on the back. "Professional courtesy. We've got an Indian reciprocity thing going on here." Carl laughed as he showed his ID, got his bracelet, and headed inside.

Carl stayed all night to get the lay of the land. He played bingo, had a few white wines, even won $150 on a bingo card. Net out the booze he drank, at the end of the night he was still up a hundred bucks when he left the bingo hall late. He could see why people would go there.

The next day, Carl went over to the police chief, Mike Francesca, for a full and frank discussion.

"What the fuck is going on there?" Carl asked.

"What do you mean?" Mike said. He started out slow, wary of Carl to say the least. He continued. "Fletcher's got a valid permit for the bingo. He got it from the board of selectmen. Jim Barry led the charge. Like his ass was on fire, he moved so quick to push the permit through. But I'm duty bound to recognize it though. You know that. It's all official."

Carl was pissed off and showing it. "Permit, shit. The guy's got a goddamn casino going on in the old A&P space. It's incredible."

"It's just bingo," Mike said defensively.

"Just bingo? He's got zero overhead is what he's got and cash coming in like a waterfall. Maybe I should do the same thing for the Fluevogs, huh?"

"You're too late, Carl. Fletcher's already gone ahead and done it," the police chief said.

Carl frowned and held his tongue because, in a horrible basic way, he knew Mike Francesca was dead-on right. Bill Fletcher, Boston lawyer turned Indian, had out-Indianed a real Indian chief. He couldn't believe it.

Carl kept his composure though.

"There must be something you can do, isn't there, Mike? The crowds and the kids and all the bullshit are causing a traffic jam at the Five Corners. And the trash and the noise. I've never seen so goddamn much trash in my life. How about that?"

Mike Francesca went quiet, thinking, turning it over in his head. Finally he spoke. "Look, I hear you, Carl. I suppose I can bust his balls on a couple of little things if you want me too. Small stuff."

"Yeah. I want you to," Carl Sunapee said. He pulled out his wallet and gave Mike Francesca five new one hundred dollar bills.

"Here. This is for the Police Athletic League. Sorry I didn't give it to you last week. Go buy some new bats. Maybe your Escalade needs a couple new tires."

Mike Francesca nodded and silently pocketed the money.

"Thanks, Carl. This is a fair down payment. A show of good faith." He looked over at his friend. "'Cause I'm sure you know that tires for my Cadillac cost a whole lot more than that."

Warriors Massing on the Plains

Carl Sunapee had called an emergency meeting with the Fluevog tribal council the next day back in Aquinnah. He drove his maroon Cadillac Seville STS over from his house in Edgartown.

The sky was bright blue. It was a Cape Cod August day. One of the ten best days of the year, if you were counting. There were big cumulus clouds on the horizon, hanging over the water. Carl looked at them for a few seconds as he drove, left arm out the window, the soundtrack from *Shaft* playing on his six-CD changer in the trunk.

Who's the cat that won't cop out when there's danger all about? Shaft. Can you dig it? It didn't sooth him though. He shook his head as he drove, distracted with his thoughts, tapping his fingers on the polished car door.

He decided the clouds were the kind you'd see in those expansive shots of Indians on the Great Plains. The kind that Ansel Adams used to photograph. The ones where the Sioux massed on one side of the plain and the US Cavalry formed up on the other. Then they ran at each other, guns blazing, and all damn hell broke loose.

That's what was happening here on the Vineyard, he decided as he drove along Beach Road to Aquinnah. He was Sitting Bull, and Bill Fletcher was General George Custer. Only he didn't know it yet.

Carl pulled into the parking lot and nosed in to his reserved parking spot. It didn't really matter because there were empty spaces all around, but it still felt nice pulling into the one marked FLUEVOG CHIEF just to the left of the big blue handicapped space. Both spaces were right in front of the stairs. He was a sucker for the perks of the office.

He wasted no time when he got inside. It was nuclear war. The other three members of the council were there already, talking up a storm.

"What the hell is going on over there?" Manny Fernandez jumped right into the fray, no introduction.

Carl sat down. He was so agitated that he didn't even take off his porkpie hat. It was a nice one with a snap brim in a brown check and a small decorative feather on the side. Real cool.

"I'll tell you what's going on," Carl said. "Fletcher has opened up a damn casino on the Island, that's what's going on. He's ignored about a million regulations and set up shop, just like that."

"We've been trying to get gambling on the Island here for ten years, and nothing's happened. How's that dude done it?" Manny said.

"Simple," Carl said. "All he has going on is bingo. Ratty-ass, old-time bingo to start. But now he's got his foot in the door. And that's all he needs."

Clarence Sykes, the tribal elder who was a shellfisherman over in Menemsha, piped in. "Look, what do we care? We don't want shitty little bingo. We want slot machines and a big hall for blackjack. We need a hotel too for all the tourists from Connecticut and Boston."

"Yeah, bro. You're right on with that thought," Manny Fernandez said as he seconded the fantasy. "Git us some of those hotels. Big buildings. I'll get myself a suite for the weekend too. Do it up right." He smiled.

Carl shook his head. "All that shit is exactly what we don't need. Fletcher's got no overhead, see? He just put up a goddamn plastic banner that said Indian Bingo, and away he went. He picked our pockets clean. He doesn't have the cost of one slot machine, and he's raking in the cash. Who needs the hotels and the costs and the infrastructure when you can get the cash instead? He's a genius."

"Sounds like he's done beat us at our own game," Lionel said.

Clarence Saunders added, "And that chick of his? That sexy little bitch? She's good. She does the Indian thing just right, puttin' an edgy twist on everything. People love it, the T-shirts and all that clothing. Why can't we do that shit? I've been telling us to do T-shirts for five years now. We'll just steal her designs, that's all."

"Yeah, it's simple as that."

Carl ignored the brawling. He drew in a big sigh, held it for three seconds like the yoga book said to do to get to that calm place, then he let it out slowly through his nostrils, saying his mantra as he exhaled.

It was supposed to put him in control. He scratched his goatee. Except that he had forgotten his special word already. So he used the word *peace* to get control; he did it again. It started to work finally, and it brought his anger down a notch.

"Look, we've gotta put this guy in his place, no doubt. He's stolen the franchise. This is all out war."

"No shit," Manny agreed. "We need to whomp on this guy but good."

Carl shook his head. "We've got to be a little more subtle than that though. I'll make some phone calls and pull in some chits that people owe us. We've got to use leverage to make the story end right."

"Do you think you can do it?" Clarence asked. The mood was dark.

Carl Sunapee smiled slowly. He exhaled deeply again. "That's why I'm the chief of this here great Fluevog nation. Don't worry about it, boys. I'll fix the situation."

The meeting rambled on for two more hours.

Fling

Father Peter was sitting at the bar of the Oyster House, having a Coke and chatting up the tourists and locals. He was dressed in his civvies today, no dog collar, in a blue Polo shirt and dark slacks. He had on black pecan kilties with no socks. With his tanned arms and his TAG Heuer watch with the stainless bracelet, he looked like a Polo player on break on the Island.

He was mad at Bill Fletcher who had quickly become a pain in his ass, stealing all his bingo players away. It put a definite crimp in the parish cash flow.

Screw it, he thought as he lightly poked at the ice in the bottom of his glass with a cocktail straw. He was just going to go with the flow, see where it went, have a nice lunch with Margaret. The negativity would drag him down otherwise, and he wasn't a negative person by nature.

He was an evangelist, an upbeat man of the word. And today he was a happy and horny proselytizer, waiting to meet with a sheep in his flock. A good-looking female ewe.

The bartender brought over another Coke with lime and placed it in front of the priest on a fresh cocktail napkin with a sailboat pattern.

"How's it going in the parish this summer, Father? Making any money?" he asked with a wink, just showing that he knew the priest among the locals, that his eye was good, even with Peter Mulcahey dressed in his civvies.

"It's been a great year so far," Peter Mulcahey answered automatically. "The tourists have been generous on the weekends. It's all good." He smiled.

It was a stock answer, and it rolled off his lips with practiced ease. If the bartender asked more questions, he had a whole host of answers to throw out to keep the conversation going but not say anything. Happy-priest speak. He was a pro.

Just then, Margaret Wellington came in. She was smiling, wearing capris and black kitten heels. She had on a blue scoop-neck top with short sleeves, an uplift bra, and a single big ceramic bangle on her right arm. She looked like Audrey Hepburn from the sixties.

She came over to Peter Mulcahey, and they shook hands lightly. Peter moved off the barstool. The hostess seated them at a nice table in the center of the restaurant. Father Peter liked it there in the middle. It made him comfortable. *See and be seen*, he thought, *hiding under the cover of daylight.*

Margaret's scent of Allure perfume and freshly washed skin soon drifted over him, and he inhaled deeply. He immediately knew then he was a goner. The spirit was willing, but the flesh was weak.

She ordered a white wine, and he stayed with Coke. He was going to fight it as best he could. The wine came as they talked.

"How are things, Margaret?" Peter asked. "You look fantastic, by the way."

"Call me Margie, Peter, if you'd like. We don't have any formalities anymore." She winked at him over her glass.

"Well, Margie, give me an update so I can say this is a business lunch."

"Honestly, things were better on the finance front last month. But I don't want to ruin it on this beautiful summer day."

"Why, what's happened?"

"I think you know what's happened. Our newcomer friend, that Indian gentleman, has taken out our oomph."

"But our bills are paid," Peter said as he jabbed at his ice again, his tell. She noticed it.

"Don't be upset, Peter. All the bills *are* paid. I checked just before I came here. I knew you'd ask. We're a hundred percent current for the first time."

She took a sip of her wine and enjoyed the headiness of the early afternoon. Margaret put her finger on it immediately. It was the feeling of excitement and romance, like what a high school girl felt on a first date. Margaret wasn't going to resist; she was going to nurture it on its own, see where it went.

"We were doing so good there too for a while," Peter said.

Margaret brightened and quickly changed the subject. "I've got some good news, Peter."

He waited.

"Frank Callahan, the roofer, sent in a check for $10,000 two days ago as a donation. Straight out of the blue. Can you believe it?"

"You're kidding. For what?"

"He didn't say. It was strange though. He had a yellow stickie on the check, and it said 'I hope this stops the roof leak, Father. May God bless you. Frank.' What was he talking about? Do we have a roof leak in the church?" Margaret asked.

Peter smiled. "It's just an old Irish expression. It means the donation is there for a rainy day. Frank Callahan is a good man, that's for sure."

* * *

After lunch, Father Peter walked back to the rectory with Margaret. It was a big rambling Victorian house two blocks up from Main Street. They went in the front door, and Joanne Proctor was there in the kitchen cutting up a pan of brownies.

"Oh, Father. Hello, you're just in time. I'm letting these brownies cool and heading over to Reliable for some groceries and then to Edgartown for a few errands."

She looked at Father Peter and Margaret Wellington coming in together. Margaret blushed as she said hi too cheerily.

A flash of realization washed over Joanne Proctor, but she beat it down like any good single Catholic woman would do.

Father Peter naturally defused the situation. "I'm giving Margaret the collection plate money, and then I'm going over to the hospital to see Mrs. Moffat. Give her communion." Father Peter didn't miss a beat.

Joanne Proctor covered her bases herself though. "I'll be gone for a couple hours, at least. Is there anything you need while I'm out, Father?"

She had no desire to come back and see anything that she didn't want to see. Her Catholic faith was too pure and strong. "Do you want any more of those Kleenex Puffs then, Father?" she asked.

"What?"

"The Puffs. The ones with aloe. I saw that you bought a box last week. They're easier on the nose, I know. Just tell me if you want some more, Father, and I'll get them."

Joanne smiled as she grabbed her keys and headed out the door. She didn't miss a trick.

Where the Buffalo Roam

The buffalo found a home, a very nice one, up Island.

They rolled off the ferry in Vineyard Haven that hot day in July, the stench of buffalo shit almost overwhelming, and went directly to a farm lot that Bill Fletcher had found for them by dialing around from the Neskeet offices.

He had convinced the Morses, one of the oldest families on the Island who themselves had a big working farm, to lease the Neskeets thirty acres on a six-month lease for the buffalo to roam up on Middle Road.

And what a spectacle it was. The Middle Road tract opened up onto a majestic vista to the water. The twenty-five buffalo quickly acclimated and were walking around, grazing on native grasses and buckets of corn. Traffic was backed up to Menemsha from Middle Road because so many people were coming to gawk at the giant beasts.

Fletcher immediately put Carrie on the case as the project manager for the buffalo. He was stretched too thin with everything else he was working on to add any value, as he liked to call it.

But Carrie was a value adder, big-time. So she got smart real quick about the buffalo.

"Is it all right if I sell some tees up there by the entrance?" she asked. "We can market them out of the back of Carol's pickup truck. I'll make a nice display in the bed and everything."

Fletcher had no problem with it. In fact, he encouraged it. "Yeah, go ahead and sell what you can. Opportunity knocks only once."

Carrie thought about it all for a few days and came back to Fletcher with more ideas. "I want to do some natural ecological things up there at the entrance too," she said. "Watch what I come up with."

Fletcher was ecstatic.

A week later, there it was, a little farm stand at the entrance to the grazing fields. BUFFALO TOURS AND INDIAN HISTORY. THE WAY THEY DID IT. It was big as life on a sign on two pressure-treated fence posts planted firmly in the soil. It was done on a four-by-eight sheet of exterior-grade plywood painted beautifully that Carrie had commissioned. It looked homey and natural, which was exactly the look she was shooting for.

Fletcher had cut a deal with the Morse kid, Billy, who needed some summertime money for his tuition at Brown. He paid him twenty bucks an hour plus diesel fuel for taking the tourists and locals through the field in a hay trailer attached to his big green and yellow John Deere 450 tractor.

Son of a bitch if the whole thing didn't look good and feel farmy right from the get-go, Fletcher thought. The Morse kid, no stranger to the hype machine himself, put bales of hay in the trailer for the tourists to sit on then practiced the slow ride through the field. He put a sign on the back of the tractor in medium script that said Tips Accepted with a little smiley face. Underneath, he printed even smaller the sign: Have a Nice Vineyard Day!

Carrie bought ten bags of molasses feed at the Agway Store in Edgartown and had Carol Ault put a handful of the food into little quart Baggies. They sold it to the visitors for $2 a bag and labeled it Natural Buffalo Feed, Certified Organic. The tourist kids loved it.

The buffalo thought they'd died and gone to heaven. There was no grazing for hours on a hot, barren field foraging for dried shoots of grass. Instead, there was corn and molasses meal flattened out everywhere from the big John Deere tractor tires. And if they wanted big handfuls of it directly, they only had to saunter up close to the big rig as it wound its way through the field and nibble it from the tourists.

It was crazy. A month ago, the beasts had to saunter over miles of prairie just to get enough grass to survive on. Here, they were getting fat, dumb, and happy just eating, walking around the field, and looking statuesque. Their giant heads nodded, they chewed away, and the little beards on their chins moved up and down. It was straight out of a Winslow Homer painting.

Somebody had done something right, the buffalo figured. And that somebody was Bill Fletcher.

It all made for great photo opportunities, but like the sign said NO GETTING OUT OF THE WAGON. KEEP YOUR HANDS AND ARMS INSIDE PLEASE!

Speaking of photo opportunities, the people over at the *Vineyard Gazette* damn near wet their pants over the story. New indian tribe brings buffalo to the island, the great beasts stroll the plain again.

The paper sent a writer and photographer to interview Bill Fletcher over at his Oak Bluffs office. Fletcher then drove both of them along with Carrie up to the field in his Grand Cherokee to seal the deal.

Billy Morse took them on a slow tour with the John Deere 450 and stopped in the middle of the field. The buffalo herd crowded around, waiting to be fed. They were not disappointed.

The photos were spectacular. The editor at the *Gazette* decided to devote the whole front page of the Friday edition to the Neskeet Nation. The giant beasts, the buffalo, were there above the fold under the headline looking as if they were on the Great Plains of Minnesota.

There were articles on Fletcher and Carrie, the tribe, the T-shirts, the Equinox, and the bingo parlor. It was all fawning and incredibly complimentary.

Carrie was pulling fifteen hundred a day out of the enterprise from the admission charge at $5 a head, the sale of the organic buffalo feed, and of course, more T-shirts. The markup on the feed was staggering by the time you broke it down and put it in the little Baggies. The T-shirts practically flew off the truck at twenty-five each, stonewashed and all-natural cotton.

Fletcher quickly hired a Tisbury cop to work the traffic detail up at the Middle Road intersection because of the congestion, all paid for by the Neskeets. The police loved it because it meant someone was getting seventy-five bucks an hour for a four-hour shift. Fletcher had them do three shifts a day, making sure the road was covered 8:00 a.m. to 6:00 p.m.

The police cruiser parked on the side of the road also helped to create more buzz around the buffalo. There were no complaints from the police as the overtime money flowed like manna from heaven. It was all the harmonious business cycle one more time.

Carrie decided soon into it to design some new T-shirts with a buffalo theme. She sketched them out quickly one afternoon while she sat at the Equinox. She knew immediately that they'd be huge sellers. Buffalo and oppressed Indians. *What's not to like for hip college kids and wannabe tourists?* she figured.

Carrie herself also became a mini celebrity on the summer-job circuit for the local youth. She was hiring all kinds of kids to haul hay, break down buffalo feed, work in the Equinox, sell T-shirts out at the farm stand, and drive to Falmouth to pick up new ones as they were produced. There were over ten kids on the payroll at fifteen dollars an hour, all under the table so they didn't have to pay taxes. She knew how to do it.

It was all a virtuous cycle of money.

Bill Fletcher and Carrie Nation knew instinctively that they couldn't pay for publicity like they were getting at that point. They were celebrities that Friday when the *Gazette* came out with the Neskeet Nation edition. That night, they celebrated with a fried seafood dinner and a bottle of sauvignon blanc over at the Blue Dory.

Later that night, full of wine and fried clams, they made love out on the deck at Fletcher's house past the Inkwell under a full moon. They were sated, and the world was wonderful. They had landed in clover, no doubt.

*   *   *

When Carl Sunapee saw the article in the Friday *Gazette*, really the whole front page of the paper about the Neskeet Indians, he damn near shit a brick.

He wasn't much of a reader, but all he had to do was look at the front page and realize that something had to be done, and fast.

Police Lunch

Mike Francesca was out working among the people. He was parked in his Tisbury police cruiser at the corner of Main and Water in the 7-Eleven parking lot. The cruiser was nose out, facing the traffic that was snaking through the Five Corners intersection.

The line of cars were slowly making their way up the slight grade to turn right onto Commercial Street. Mike sat in his car with the computer screen up and open so it looked like he was checking vehicles or searching for criminals with outstanding arrest warrants.

He was really eating lunch. He had a Pepsi Big Gulp in the coffee holder. It barely fit. With a little bit of work, he was able to wedge in the bottom of the cup into the plastic holder. As long as he wasn't moving, it was stable. The thing was huge. It was a great soda value.

He had a pile of napkins in his lap, right on the crotch of his stretchy blue police pants, so he would be able to grab some quickly if he needed to. On the keyboard, he had two bean burritos wrapped in paper resting on the 7-Eleven plastic bag. That way, none of the drippy bean sauce would get onto the laptop keys and wreck his machine. It was all neat and orderly, there for easy access. He was a pro at lunchtime logistics in the police cruiser from years of practice.

Carl Sunapee walked out of the store with an orange Gatorade and a pack of Listerine breath mints in a plastic bag. He saw Mike sitting in the police car and came right up beside him on the driver's side. Mike saw him coming though, always checking his mirrors.

"What's up, Carl?"

Carl didn't waste any time. He got right to the point, no pussyfooting around. "Where you at with those Indians?"

"What Indians?" Mike tried to slow Carl down a little.

"What Indians?" Carl repeated. "The Neskeets. Those fake fuckers running the bar out of the A&P. Those ones."

Mike nodded his head, put his bean burrito down on the laptop, and carefully wiped his fingers before he spoke. "Well, I talked to the selectmen, and I think I can move on them pretty soon now. They've got too many people in there at night. We counted 175 on Thursday night alone."

Carl heard the number and shook his head. "A hundred and seventy-five? Jesus Christ. We don't have that many Fluevogs in the tribe on the whole Island. No wonder they're getting rich. What the fuck, Mike?"

"Don't get your underwear all knotted up, Carl. That's not just Neskeet Indians, that's everybody coming and going. And it doesn't matter who it is, Indians or otherwise. It's just too many people. We'll deal with it, believe me. The other shop owners are complaining now as well, so it's not just you. Carol's Creamery says it's draining away their ice cream business on the nights they play bingo. The trash crew's pissed 'cause all the barrels are full outside." He looked up at Carl. "Now they gotta work and actually pick up the trash." He snickered at his joke.

"So what are you going to do?"

Mike nodded and took a big sip of soda. "The selectmen are bringing an order to the building inspector to review the occupancy permit and require Fletcher to get a bigger one for that many people."

"How's that?"

"The old A&P had a permit for 125 people maximum at any one time. For people shopping for groceries and stuff. General commercial."

"You gotta fix that then. And pronto," Carl said. "You can't leave us honest citizens in the lurch with a flagrant violation of the law like that."

Mike took another bite of his bean burrito and finished it off. He wiped his lips and then balled up the wrapper on the keyboard and handed it to Carl. "Here, take that, will you? The trash can's right behind you."

Mike pointed to the side of the building. Then he got back to business.

"Look, Carl, I hear you. We're gonna deal with Fletcher this week or next. It's gonna happen soon, trust me."

Carl wrinkled his brow. "Soon? Why not now? As in drive your patrol car right over there pronto and put a sticker on his window that says NO MORE FUCKING BINGO. All caps, just like that. I'll write it up for you."

Mike smiled. "It's not that easy, pardner."

"Why not?"

Mike nodded, then looked up at Carl for effect. "Because old Bill Fletcher has been making a lot of contributions to the selectman and police officers' retirement accounts, if you know what I mean. Big contributions. We're all planning for our retirement down in Florida. You catch my drift, Carl?"

The light snapped on for Carl Sunapee. Bill Fletcher had become the godfather.

"So what are you telling me, that you need to get his permission, to ask him, before you shut him down?"

"No, not at all, Carl. I know I owe you this one," Mike said. "You've got that marker out with me from that weekend in Vegas before. All I'm saying is that it's going to take a little while longer is all. Stay cool."

Carl knew that he had pushed Mike as far as he could. He took a breath in deep into his lungs and held it for a three count to calm down before he spoke.

"All right then. Just do what you can. I'd sure appreciate it though, speaking for all the Fluevogs on the Island."

Carl patted the top of the driver's door on the cruiser for emphasis as he walked away. He was almost desperate.

Investment Lesson

Bill Fletcher was sitting in the same front office as before with Jack Fraker at the Martha's Vineyard Bank. Donna Stevens wasn't present. In fact, there wasn't anybody else present. Just Fletcher and Jack, hashing it out.

Jack was dressed in his high-summer bank president's uniform. Pressed khaki pants, L.L.Bean loafers polished to a high shine, and a blue oxford button-down shirt with long sleeves. He always bought his shirts oversized, 17.5 × 34, so that the collars and sleeves would fit comfortably around his neck wattles and heavy arms. He was falling apart astonishingly quick, and comfort was key for those longs days at the bank.

He finished it off with a conservative blue tie with little sailboats in a pattern. A bank president on the Island needed a tie to let the people know that their money was safe with him. He hated the damn things.

Fletcher had on his turquoise bracelet with a blue short-sleeve Polo shirt and dark pressed slacks. More casual businessman than Indian today, talking about important investment stuff.

"Jack, we've got a good relationship, maybe great, don't you think?"

"The absolute best as I see it, Bill," Jack Fraker said without even thinking.

He had answered the question in a microsecond. Those kinds of questions were really a test, and he was good at passing tests. That's why he was president of the bank. He only had a degree from UMass Dartmouth, but he was a good street fighter.

He also knew a shakedown was coming. He could smell it, like rotting bluefish on a dock, from a mile away. He blinked, sat back, and waited, his hands intertwined on his stomach. He had to hand it to Fletcher though. He wasn't heavy-handed in his approach. He was subtle. Fraker liked that.

"I need help, Jack," Bill Fletcher said. He let the words drift out and hover in the cool air-conditioned room.

"How can we help, Bill?" Jack said, putting the whole heft of the bank behind him in his answer.

"Well, I'm no finance guy, but my calculations show that the Neskeets have over eleven million dollars in the bank right now."

"That's right, Bill. I checked on the account before you came in. It started out with the wire transfer for ten, and it's grown from all the deposits along the way. You're pretty successful with all your Indian businesses. You have the knack, for sure."

"Yeah, thanks. The people seem to have an insatiable appetite for all things Indian. They're intrigued by history and folklore. It's a renaissance period in Native American history for us."

"The T-shirts help a lot too," Jack Fraker said as he smiled. "So how can we help?" He tried getting to the point to put the bad news out on the table.

Fletcher paused and rubbed his turquoise bracelet for effect. Then he looked up at Jack and launched. "I think that the Neskeets need a cultural icon, a totem, to be able to identify with. Public art. Something for the community to connect with."

"What are you thinking about?"

"Well, you know that big statue over by the ferry dock in Ocean Park of the Civil War soldier?"

"Indeed I do. Will Ferrets. That statue has a plaque commemorating both the Union and Confederate troops for valor. It's unique, celebrating both sides of the Civil War on one statue. Leave it to the Islanders, never able to choose sides in a battle. Nothing like it anywhere in the country."

Fletcher sat back. "I was thinking about moving it. I'd like to place it over at Sunset Lake, with its own pavilion, something bigger and more dignified as befits a significant war memorial. You know?"

"Huh?" Jack Fraker said. "That statue's been at Ocean Park a hundred years."

"We'd pay for it, of course. The Neskeets would pay the freight, so to speak, for the move and all." Fletcher laughed at his joke, keeping the mood light. "We'd make it more grand and heroic for a war memorial. Spend the money to do it right."

Jack Fraker worked his lips trying to avoid a frown, not knowing where the hell this was going.

"And what would go in its place, Bill?"

"A Neskeet statute, a symbol of modern-day Native Indian culture. You can't deny that Indians have played a major role in the development of the Island's history. They're fundamental to all of it. The wellspring."

"Yeah, that's true. But that's the Fluevog history you're talking about. Not your tribe. Not the Neskeets."

"Indians are Indians."

Jack Fraker ignored the comment. "What kind of statue are you thinking about?"

"A statue of me, that's what I'm thinking. Looking out at the ocean, towards the horizon. Like Columbus."

Jack Fraker couldn't keep his composure. He let out a snort and smiled at Fletcher.

"You're goddamn kidding me right, Bill? They'll never let a statue of you go up at Ocean Park. It'll never happen."

Fletcher nodded his head in agreement.

"I think you're right about that, Jack. Dead-on right. It would never happen. But don't the kids need a new Boys and Girls Club on the Island? Or how about full scholarships for two students in Oak Bluffs to go to whatever private college they want? Funding for four years, a full boat, no costs to the parents whatsoever. Nada. Would that do it?"

Jack frowned now and drummed his fingers on the table, agitated and thinking. Fletcher was working him good.

"You know how much political capital that would take to get a statue of you in the park? And to have to move that Civil War monstrosity? All the history do-gooders would have my balls in a sack. You can imagine."

"I can imagine, Jack, I really can." He paused for a second. "But in exchange, I'm also willing to keep the Neskeet money right here in your bank, all of it, in a noninterest bearing account, just like it is now. Probably forever. That's a lot of spread you'd be making using my cash at no cost and lending it out to Islanders for truck loans at 8 percent. Eight hundred basis points on eleven million dollars adds up."

Fletcher played his trump card real smoothly.

Jack Fraker looked at Bill Fletcher. He had misjudged the man and his skills. Fletcher was right. It was a lot of money for the bank. A huge pile of income.

"I can't promise you anything on this one," Fraker said. "It's not my decision. It would be up to the selectmen, really the town. Jesus Christ."

Fletcher knew he had Jack Fraker committed at this point, hook, line, and sinker. Having that much cash flow for a little bank like his was too much to pass up.

"I know it's not your decision to make, Jack. But you're a pillar of the Island community. I see you in action every day. If the bank puts its weight behind this initiative quietly, the thing'll gather momentum and move forward. I can feel it."

The two men talked for another thirty minutes about town opposition and how much the Neskeets would have to do to make the statue happen. Fraker mentioned Jim Barry and the other selectmen needing to weigh in and all the necessary town hearings. The public process and all. He was backpedaling like a motherfucker so as not to get jammed up by Fletcher.

But as soon as Fletcher heard Jim Barry's name mentioned, he relaxed. He knew pretty well how the public process worked with Jim.

"No promises, Bill," Jack Fraker said as he ended the conversation. "This is a tough one." He put his hand up in mock protest.

"That's why I came to you, Jack." Fletcher smiled. "You're the best mover and shaker in town. Help me out here."

"Do you have a design for the statue?"

"As a matter of fact, yeah. I do have something sketched up."

"Send it over to me, and I'll take a look."

"No problem," Fletcher said. "Just give me a bit, and I'll forward some sketches, see what you think for starters."

The meeting ended on a positive note. Jack Fraker made sure of that, leaving no bruised feelings or ambiguous thoughts. He was behind Fletcher's plan 100 percent.

He said good-bye to Fletcher and walked him to the door. Then he watched him go across the street in the crosswalk. "You crazy bastard" was all he could mutter under his breath.

Jack Fraker went back to his office and pondered the situation. He didn't know what to think about Bill Fletcher at this point, his biggest customer, the so-called Indian chief.

*　*　*

Father Peter Mulcahey was on high alert. Bishop Guerin was coming to the Island for a visit. Both men weren't happy about it.

Father Peter hated the visits because he had to get the parish in tip-top shape. It was like an inspection by an army general. Joanne would have to clean the rectory within an inch of her life, and then the Brazilian cleaners would have to put a spit shine on the church as well. He also had to call Madeiros Landscaping in to do an extra grass cut at both places and a shrub trim. It was easily an extra $300 of money that they didn't have. He wondered why he put up with this shit.

Bishop Guerin hated the visits too because his gout always acted up on the trip, and he wasn't sure why.

He always came over in his black Lincoln Town Car. The diocese had to spring for the car reservation and two round-trip tickets, one for the bishop and one for his driver. Tour the parish, tour the church, give a benediction, and then have dinner with Father Mulcahey. The basic routine every time.

Peter Mulcahey didn't know why the bishop was coming over as the only times he ever visited was when the parish kept asking for money. The church could save a thousand bucks, Father Peter calculated, if the bishop didn't come, and they just had a quick conference call instead. They could call it even. *WTF*, he thought.

Father Peter hadn't asked for money in over six months with the bingo going full swing. Blessed Sacrament was current on their bills too. He had even made a prepayment on the winter oil bill. *How about that for good fiscal management?* he thought to himself.

"Did you hear that Bishop Guerin's coming over next week?" Joanne Proctor said as she was on her way out of the rectory on Monday at 6:00 p.m.

"Yes, I did," Father Peter said flatly. "I saw the e-mail on my iPhone this morning. It's a pain in the ass," he added under his breath as he walked into the coatroom, hanging up his jacket on a wooden hanger.

"I'm sorry, Father, I couldn't hear you. Something about your gas?" Joanne's ears were sharp.

Peter Mulcahey retreated quickly. "I said that I'm looking forward to it."

"Indeed. We both are, Father."

Joanne Proctor left the rectory, quietly closing the door behind her.

Father Peter headed up to his room, fishing in his pocket for his iPhone as he climbed the stairs. He was planning on having what informed members of the laity called phone sex with his new girlfriend, Margaret.

The Virtuous Cycle

Carrie Nation was in the Sweat Lodge at 5:00 p.m. for the early evening hot yoga class. She had convinced Fletcher that they needed much more yoga and specifically hot yoga if they were going to attract a decent following of women and hipsters. She told him that the basic sauna and steam room were not going to cut it with the affluent tourists and locals. She was spot on.

So she hired a twenty-five-year-old brunette named Rachel, who was a certified bikram hot yoga instructor, to run the yoga program at the Sweat Lodge. She was a refugee from Manhattan for the summer and had the three-hundred-dollar blond coloring and hair-straightening job to prove it. She was lithe and earnest and sexy in her little LuLulemon yoga uniform. Carrie had picked right hiring Rachel as she was the heart and soul of the program.

The tie-in was direct and obvious for the Sweat Lodge and hot yoga. But it worked—the Indians, the hot rooms, the yoga. It was a little campy, but the women loved it. Carrie always worked it with a wink and a nod, keeping the marketing light and lively.

Carrie was dressed in a pale-blue Athleta unitard today, stretching and sweating her way to holistic happiness along with twenty other women in the room. She looked around to get a feel for the group. As a retailer, nothing substituted for the basic gumshoe detective work of interacting with your customer. The people in the class were a mix—some young, some in their thirties or forties—but all were summer trendsetters with expensive mats and yoga clothes just like her. She sensed that she had hit the right crowd.

"Now let's go to the upward facing dog," Rachel said. The class all moved as one into the incredibly difficult position. After that, they did the lotus position and then the seated forward bend. That one was a crusher for Carrie as it bent her vertebrae and disks right over almost in half.

The class finished up, as an optional last position, with the headstand. Carrie did it just to prove that she could, but it felt like she was ready to burst a blood vessel in her head balanced upside down with the blood rushing to her brain. *Who needed drugs for a rush like that?* she thought.

Carrie had killed two birds with one stone—she got the tough yoga session in under her belt to stay in shape, and she also checked out how the course was going with Rachel instructing. Multitasking was the key.

The class ended, and Carrie went over to Mad Mike at the front desk. "What do you think?"

Mike looked her over first in her tank top and sweating breasts. Her hair was pulled up with a scrunchie off her neck. He liked what he saw.

"I think that we're hitting it out of the park. Incredible."

"What do you mean?" She took a sip of her purple G2, the low-calorie Gatorade drink.

"I mean that traffic has gone up 30 percent since you and your old man Indian chief have taken over. The workout T-shirts and the Indian junk really pulls them in. Plus, the additional yoga sessions were a stroke of genius. I never thought to tap into that crowd that much. They come a lot and spend freely. Our net is up 25 percent this month alone. I'm glad Bill forced me to do an earn out on the sale price over twelve months. I'm into the percentage splits already. It's great."

Carrie knew that Mike was right. He had run the health club for years with the same exercisers and muscle heads as his core group. It was a workout place. That could only take the gym so far.

And it just felt different now too. She knew the Indian stuff was hokey, but she was able to market the hell out of it to all the young hipsters who just wanted a cool yoga studio. Less weights and more mats. That was her canvas.

Carrie went over the books with Mike for about thirty minutes to show him that she was watching the details.

Then she pulled out her iPhone and sent out a tweet. "Over at the Sweat Lodge for hot yoga, what a great workout! You gotta try it! So cool!" Carrie was a master marketer with 147 characters, you betcha.

She sent out tweets three or four times a day. It was free, and it was good exposure for the various Neskeet marketing campaigns. Nearly everyone who was a Neskeet tribal member tweeted or visited the Neskeet Facebook page fairly regularly. Carrie had over 1,756 followers on Twitter and 800 friends on Facebook. The social media outreach kept it fresh, and the Fluevogs couldn't touch it. It was like they were all Luddites, she decided.

Then she showered and headed out to dinner with the chief himself, Bill Fletcher.

*   *   *

Before he went out, Bill Fletcher was on the phone with Guy Phillips, the director of the Friends of Vineyard Farm Animals Foundation. "Yeah, Phil, it's going well. What I'm calling for is to ask you what you thought about us moving two buffalo over to Waban Park for a couple days so the tourists can get a closer look at 'em easily. You know not everybody can get up to Middle Road to see the thundering herd during the day. The logistics are tough."

Fletcher listened to the Phil's concerns then got impatient.

"No, no. We'd have them there for just a few days, during the Ag Fair dates, to advertise farming and all. We'd let the kids come up close and touch the buffalo and feed them some molasses mix and hay. They're pretty docile really. We'll donate all the proceeds to your foundation, of course."

Bingo, that did it. The magic words *donate the proceeds to your foundation* did the trick. Phil quickly agreed to a kiddie display with the buffalo right there on the spot.

"Yep, we have insurance and everything," Fletcher said. "We'll name the foundation as an additional named insured. I'm sure. Great."

They finished the conversation. Bill Fletcher had just got another touch point for the Neskeets into the local community with the mini buffalo herd up close and personal downtown for a few days.

He was pretty good at marketing himself.

Iconic Images

Jack Fraker, bank president, was sitting in his other office in the Vineyard Haven branch. The nice one with the second-floor view of the harbor and the ferry dock. It was the kind of office that a bank president was supposed to sit in and make decisions about investments and other important bullshit. He played with his magnetic filings executive desk toy as he thought.

Not like that little fishbowl office that he had over in Oak Bluffs where every tinhorn Islander could come in and see him doing his thing running the bank. No privacy at all to read the paper, scratch his ass, or look at new Boston Whalers on the web.

And that asshole Bill Fletcher was always cornering him in the glass-walled conference room, asking him to do crazy things like approve a freakin' statue of himself for Ocean Park.

He laughed to himself when he thought of it. He knew that the crazy white guy turned Indian, Bill Fletcher, would never follow through on his half-baked idea anyway. He didn't have the balls. He had nothing to worry about.

Sally Karas, the head teller, came in with two pieces of paper for him. "You've got a fax, Jack."

"Yeah, what is it?" he asked.

"She smiled slightly as she handed the sheets of paper to him. She stepped back and put her hands on her hips, looking at Fraker. She had worked at the bank for over twenty years. Sexy, in an old-fashioned way.

"You didn't tell me that you were sponsoring a new statue for the Neskeet Indians over in Oak Bluffs," she said. "You've very secretive in your old age." Sally winked, having some fun with her boss.

The first one said in big bold handwriting WHAT DO YOU THINK, JACK?!! BILL. Jack Fraker immediately frowned and shook his head, flipping over to the second sheet.

It was a line drawing of Bill Fletcher standing on a pedestal in tight jeans, cowboy boots, and a check shirt. His left hand, with the chunky turquoise bracelet, was on his hip, and his right hand was holding a Blackberry smartphone up to his ear. It looked like he was talking on it. He had on Ray-Ban Aviator sunglasses. It was all done in a dark bronze.

Jack lost his composure; he couldn't help it. "Is he goddamn serious?" he said out loud.

Sally blushed a deep red then ran her hand through her hair, pushing back the same pesky piece that kept falling across her face. She watched as the tips of her boss's ears turned bright red.

Sally got a little scared. She didn't want Jack to have a myocardial infarction or a little ministroke right there in the office. That would be real inconvenient as she had a hair appointment at eleven o'clock. She tried to calm him down instead.

"I think he is, Jack," she said. "It's sort of camp. I like it. It's the depiction of an Indian chief in modern warrior garb with the cell phone and all. Tongue in cheek, you know?"

Jack snapped out of his momentary trance. "Modern warrior garb, Sally?"

"Cowboy boots and a Blackberry, Jack. What else do you need?"

Jack Fraker shook his head in vehement disagreement. "I'll handle this myself," he said, shooing her out of his office and back toward the teller counter. He closed his office door and called Fletcher as fast as his autodialer would allow.

Bill Fletcher was ready for him. "Well, do you like it? I think it's very realistic in a pop iconic sort of way," Fletcher said, underselling it, coming in light at first.

Jack Fraker was not going to be messed with. "Are you kidding me? This will never go up in Ocean Park. Never."

Fletcher was wondering if he had showed the statue to old Jack Fraker too quickly. Maybe. "Now calm down, Jack. There's a lot of good in that statue."

"Yeah, like what?"

"Well, I'm not wearing a kilt, and my penis isn't hanging down below my knees."

Fraker burst out laughing. "Well, that's true at least."

"It's also art."

"How so?"

"The sculpture is done by Piers Staadt. He's a famous artist. You know him?" Fletcher said.

"I never heard of him. Who is he?"

"He's an interpretive sculptor. He has a piece in MOMA in New York. That's as good as you can get."

"What's MOMA, for chrissakes?"

"The Museum of Modern Art, Jack. You know what I'm talking about? It's the most recognized art museum in the world. It's on Fifth Avenue." Fletcher laid it on thick, thinking the address alone would sway him.

Jack Fraker stopped him. "Bill, isn't there some place over in Paris called the Louvre that's pretty good too? I'm a hick from the Island, but don't try to bullshit a bullshitter about museums."

Fletcher paused to let that sink in. "You're right. Look, all I'm saying is that this is art. Don't think of it as me selling a statue of myself. You need to think of it as popular art. As a cultural thing. Like the LOVE sculpture in Philadelphia."

"I'll see what I can do," Jack said, "but no promises. It's going to be an uphill battle. Why don't you ever make things easy?"

"That's why they pay you the big bucks, Jack. To solve the big-client problems."

Jack Fraker frowned. He could barely afford his daughter's tuition at UMass Dartmouth as it was. He had to take a line of credit out on his already fully mortgaged house that he got from the bank—his own bank. He never would have qualified for a line of credit otherwise. He was too overextended. Thank God he worked there and could participate in the employee loan program. They couldn't say no to him.

The two men talked for a while longer, and Bill Fletcher used his lawyerly background to press his case.

"And in the end, Jack, I'll take my eleven million dollars out of the bank and go right on over to Vineyard Savings and Hank Phillips. They're waiting for me over there. Hank calls me all the time to see how I'm doing. He likes the statue, by the way."

Those were the magic words that got Jack Fraker's attention. The removal of the Neskeet deposit account, all eleven million worth.

They finished up ten minutes later with Jack promising to take the rendering over to the selectmen's offices and Jim Barry with the bank's full backing in a few days. The statute was the best thing to come down the art pike in a long while. The accounts would stay at the bank. It was a done deal.

As they rang off, Fletcher said to Jack Fraker, "Remember, Jack. Never say never. Maintain that positive attitude. It'll pay dividends for you in the long run."

*   *   *

Carl Sunapee was at the CITGO station over on Front Street. It was ninety degrees out. He was filling up a red plastic jerrican with gasoline in the back of his wife's big black SUV. He borrowed it for the day.

The attendant, Frank Griggs, came over, wiping his hands on a rag. "That's a big container you got there, Carl. You're boat run out of gas?" He laughed while saying it. They were old friends, and he knew Carl didn't own any boat.

"No, Frank. It's for my lawn mower. I got a big yard to mow." He smiled back, and the two men, asshole buddies from back in high school, shot the shit.

"Don't fill it up too much 'cause it'll expand in this heat and run all over the place. And don't work too hard now, Carl. It's hot out here today. I don't want to see you get sick and get airlifted to the city."

"Don't worry about me, Frank. I'm Indian. You know that. I'll take it good and slow and sit on my ass for half the day before I get around to doing any kind of work anyway. It's in my blood."

"I'm counting on you, Carl," Frank said as he lifted his stained Red Sox hat and scratched his head. "Be sensible."

"Don't worry about me."

Carl paid for the gas, put the small black cap back on the plastic jug, and bungee corded it in the back of the Chevy Tahoe so it wouldn't bounce around and leak.

He made one more stop at Phillips Hardware over in Edgartown where he bought a portable plumbing torch and a lighter before heading home.

"Sensible, shit." Carl said to himself with the window open as he drove along Beach Road.

Love Eternal

Margaret Wellington was looking at herself in the mirror. She decided that she hadn't looked this good in ten years. The stress lines on her face had vanished.

She'd lost fifteen pounds eating veggies and giving up white carbohydrates. Her stomach was getting firmer. The blond highlights that she got at Vineyard Images did wonders in highlighting her strong nose and high cheekbones. Julie, the young color stylist, had been right on the money.

She looked like a Nordic beauty with a middle-aged twist. She also noticed that men would occasionally take a second glance at her now when she went into Vineyard Haven to shop. She knew that stuff was usually reserved for the twenty-five-year-olds.

She also knew that she had a beautiful set of breasts, and she showed them off to maximum effect. Nothing tacky or overtly sexual, just the expert use of uplift bras, undone buttons on her summer blouses, and sheer, gauzy material. She worked it well.

Margaret Wellington also knew what the real secret of her newfound beauty and confidence was. She put her finger on it immediately. She was falling in love, pure and simple. It was a deep, passionate, sexual love too.

The only problem was that she was falling in love with Father Peter Mulcahey, who happened to be an ordained Roman Catholic priest, a celibate, a man of the cloth, and the pastor of the Blessed Sacrament parish on the Island.

She didn't care. The priest thing didn't bother her a bit. After her husband, Jed, had died from that horrible cancer, she looked at life differently. She decided that she had to go for it now because things you wanted or loved in life were so ephemeral, they could vanish in an instant. It was no joke; it had happened to her.

She also justified it on the basis of just good old physical sex, that most wholesome human activity. Peter Mulcahey was a handsome randy Irishman descended from the bogs of County Cork. The Catholic Church was never going to stomp down his sexual drive and his love of life into a celibate, monastic existence.

If it wasn't her, Margaret knew that Peter Mulcahey would be having sex with some other woman in the parish. She just happened to be the lucky one, the right girl at the right time.

Besides, it was a thousand times better than him having sex with young boys in the church basement, messing them up psychologically for life, she decided. So she convinced herself that she was doing the Catholic Church a favor, really a public service, by keeping Father Peter in the heterosexual mainstream.

Father Peter was falling for her too. It was obvious. He was resisting her charms and trying to stay a good celibate priest, but she had a power over him that was much stronger than religion. It was called sex.

Whenever she brought the bingo receipts over in her summer shorts, Victoria's Secret push-up underbra, and a small hint of Allure behind her ears and on the soft hair on her neck, he was gone.

"Where are you now, Margaret?" Father Peter said into his iPhone. He always called her Margaret, her formal name, when they started a conversation. It made him feel better that the relationship wasn't intimate, that it was on the up and up. That she was just another single woman helping around the parish.

"I'm bringing the bingo receipts over now, Peter." Margaret gave him a heads-up. Time to get ready.

She was driving in her convertible VW Bug, robin's-egg blue with the top down, talking on her cell. The wind gently threw her hair back. She looked like she was cruising around Rome in 1965, la dolce vita. She downshifted into second as she approached the Four Corners intersection. She could hear Peter better as the car slowed and the wind died down.

Peter Mulcahey's mouth went dry. Bringing the bingo receipts over. He was powerless in the face of temptation. He also knew how the afternoon was going to end.

"We can use the money." He swallowed and thought quickly. "Bring the donations over now, and we'll make a deposit."

"Should I stop and get something for Joanne on the way, a muffin or some iced tea?" she asked. The question hung in the summer air.

"No need to, Margaret. She's gone off-Island for the day to visit her sister in Hyannis."

Margaret Wellington's heart jumped. *Off-Island* were the magic words. That meant there were no time constraints. There'd be no rushing this afternoon if she had her way. She was in the mood too.

"Park behind the church in the lot so your car won't get any of the sap droppings on it from the tree in front of the rectory."

"Yes, Father, I will," Margaret teased.

"Call me Peter, will you?"

"Yes, Father, I will."

She knew immediately that he didn't want people seeing her car parked in front of the rectory all afternoon.

Peter Mulcahey opened the back door of the rectory with a fresh hint of Burberry cologne and let Margaret Wellington in. He had on a black Polo shirt with a little purple Polo logo on his chest, barely visible. The muscles in his arms were taut. He had worked out at the Sweat Lodge in the morning with the free pass that Bill Fletcher had given him last week. Margaret thought that he looked like an older model, a middle-aged stud with black hair.

They sat in the backyard in the private fenced-in area with the umbrella and expensive lawn furniture that one of the parishioners had donated to the church the year before when they sold their house.

Father Peter had made a pitcher of sangria with slices of orange and lemon floating on top with the ice. It was very European. He left a wooden spoon in the pitcher to mix the wine and the fruit around. It tasted sweet and washed away the edges of the heat as they sipped. They had two glasses each and laughed and flirted.

Father Peter finally said, "Let's go over the books, Margaret, and see how the numbers are." He put his wineglass down and stood up. "C'mon in. You've always been good with figures."

Margaret rose and headed toward the back entrance first. As she climbed the steps, she turned and looked at Peter Mulcahey. "Be sure to lock the back door so we don't have any uninvited guests."

Father Peter's fate was sealed.

* * *

Bill Fletcher was over in his office ruminating. A second follow-on grant had come through from the Bureau of Indian Affairs. It was for tribal outreach and was for another two million dollars. He was surprised as he hadn't even applied for it. It just materialized out of thin air. The Neskeets now had over twelve million in grants. He didn't complain.

In the beginning, he had just wanted the federal license to be an Indian tribe so that he could sell small goods and services like T-shirts and do tours and related stuff. He figured that it would've been a good platform to hack out a summer living.

The getting of the grant money was just a windfall. With all cylinders now firing, there was over thirteen million dollars in the cash account as of yesterday, the last time he had checked. The total included the grant money as well as the cash flowing in from the gym and the Equinox. He couldn't believe his good luck. For a small-time lawyer like himself previously shagging visa applications, he had finally hit the big time. He felt like he was in Bill Gates territory.

He called Carol Ault into his office. She was turning out to be one helluva good administrative assistant and easy on the eyes. She had a short suede skirt on today with medium heels and had her black hair done in a braid. Authentic Indian.

"What are you working on?" he asked.

"I just updated our Facebook page and then answered a lot of posts on it. It takes a lot of time, but it's good PR for us. It's fun."

"Great. Keep it up."

"I'm also going to send some tweets out to keep people engaged. Carrie is working with me to do a daily Groupon special coupon for Neskeet merchandise to help develop our traffic and drive people to the Equinox. It's a free giveaway thingie. A promotion."

Carol sat in the seat to the side of Fletcher's desk, crossed her legs, and gave him her best vampy pose.

"We're going to try crowdsourcing next for fun."

"Whatever that is," Fletcher said.

Fletcher was not a Facebook, Twitter, or a crowdsourcing kind of guy, but Carrie and Carol were, and it showed. It helped get the word out quickly. He was grateful for all their social media skills. It wasn't his bag though, and he left it to the women to develop.

Carol was no dummy. She liked to go camp when the opportunity arose. Today she had a small Indian seagull feather right in the middle of her braid. It stuck straight up, like a rocket ship. It was performance art. Bill Fletcher liked his Indians a little tongue-in-cheek, so it was all good. He approved.

"I like the feather."

"Thanks."

"How's the website coming?" he asked.

"Check it out and see what you think. Carrie and I have been through three rounds of changes so far."

Fletcher nodded.

"How about the boiler room?"

"Huh? What's that?"

"Sorry. I meant the phone bank. How's that coming?"

"Oh, that. It's coming along good. The Verizon guy came last week. He says that he has to upgrade the lines coming in outside on the pole and that he can do it next Thursday."

Fletcher's plan was to have a phone bank, a small one to start, to troll the Internet and make cold calls for donations to the Neskeets. It would be a cross between QVC and Joel Osteen, the evangelical guy out of Houston. It would be Neskeet phone bankers selling stuff or asking for money.

He knew that they'd be good at it, and he was planning on making it a regular part of his *Indian Studio Hour* when he finally got a low-frequency TV license. He had sent in the application to the FCC last month. He was thinking Conan O'Brien with a spicy Indian twist.

"Well, keep humping it, Carol. We need all the media help we can get. We're just a struggling little Indian tribe trying to get our name out there."

"Humping it, Bill? That's something I'd be okay at, huh?"

Carol Ault smiled, stretched, and then adjusted her braid. She knew Fletcher liked looking at her, and she was happy to oblige. He paid her well, and she like showing off her body. Performance art is all that it was, nothing more.

Summer Bonfire

Carrie and Bill Fletcher were sitting outside on the back deck of their rented house. It was a cool night with the breeze blowing in from the east. They had just grilled shrimp on the Weber, along with summer squash and eggplant.

Carrie had made some rice pilaf from a box on the stove. They were finishing off the bottle of Pinot Grigio, their feet up on the blistered deck rail close to one another. Fletcher had his arm resting across Carrie's lap. It was a peaceful night in Indianville all the way around.

"We're doing great at the Equinox," Carrie said. "Never in my wildest dreams did I think I'd be this successful in that store. This could all be a fawning write-up in the Thursday Styles section of the *New York Times*. Really it could."

She sipped her wine, amazed and a little surprised. She wiggled her toes in her flip-flops and listened to the rhythms of the summer night.

"New moon's out," Bill said, using his wineglass to point to the west. He was wearing a deep-blue Polo shirt hanging out over his stonewashed jeans. His size 12 New Balance 990s, the sneaker of old hipsters, were propped up on the rail too. "We've got nice weather coming in for the next two or three days," he said.

Carrie poured more wine into her glass. "Where are we going with this?"

"What?"

"This whole Indian thing, this craziness." She opened her arms in a wide gesture. Carrie looked over at Bill. He was ten years older at forty-two, but she could stay with him if he asked her to, she decided. He had a good head, was ambitious, and he didn't want kids, so it could probably work out between them.

It had so far. They were good businesspeople, they got along, and the sex wasn't bad either. No, she corrected herself, the sex was actually very good, and that was important.

"You know what I mean. We can't keep doing all these different things forever—the buffalo, the T-shirts, the bingo. It's a hoax, plain and simple." She smiled and rimmed her wineglass with her finger.

"I know. But we're good at what we're doing."

"What are we doing, Bill?"

"Having fun. We—you and I—are creating this mini empire from whole cloth. From nothing, really. It's all rank bullshit, but it's working. I'm lucky I found you, Carrie. I just had this crazy idea of starting the Indian tribe mostly for fun, but you've fleshed it out, given it texture and substance. It wouldn't work otherwise."

Carrie nodded her head and sipped her wine. "Let's just slow down a little and focus on the T-shirts and the clothing line, okay?" she said. "We're making great margins on the shirts, and we can scale the product up on to the web and sell the clothing worldwide. We'll hire an SEO guru and sell the hell out of the stuff. Bring it to a different level."

"SEO guru?" Fletcher asked.

"Search engine optimization. I told you before. They're the guys that use Internet black magic to make sure that the Neskeet website gets thousands of hits when people Google the right keywords. It gets us out into the fast lane of Internet traffic." Carrie smiled.

"That sounds important," Fletcher said.

"It is. We haven't even scratched the surface on our website yet, but I'm figuring this winter when it slows down a little is when I can work on it all. When we're down in Antigua." Carrie winked at Fletcher and adjusted her wrap skirt.

Just then, a flame lit up the night beyond the marsh in the back and Great Kettle Pond. They were looking out toward the bright patch in the night sky. It was obscured by a small stand of pine trees and hedges close by.

"Wow! It looks like a bonfire," Carrie said. "It's so pretty. It went right up!"

"Yeah. I like the way the flames lick and shoot up. I wonder what they're celebrating. They'd need a permit for a fire that big," Fletcher offered.

"I like the orange color under the moon," Carrie said. "It's beautiful."

She finished her wine and put the glass down on the redwood deck. "I'm going to take a shower, I'm beat."

"Yeah, me too," Fletcher answered.

He lingered a bit and watched the bonfire light up the night sky as he sipped his wine. He didn't notice the sirens that were faint in the distance heading around Great Kettle Pond from the other direction.

* * *

"What do we have?" Bill Norton said as he pulled up in his blue pickup truck. He had a red light stuck on his roof with a coiled extension cord to his lighter outlet.

"Car fire, chief. It's a big one too. The thing went right off. It looks like someone doused the car with gasoline first, it flared up so quickly. Everything's burning real fast."

A fireman in a yellow jacket sprayed white foam retardant from a narrow gauge hose all over the vehicle. It didn't do a thing to slow down the flames.

"What make is it?" the chief called out.

"It's a new Grand Cherokee. I can tell by the taillights, or what's left of them."

"Can you read the plates?"

"The front one's melted down from the engine burning up. The rear one's still readable. It says INJUN," the fireman said.

"That should be pretty easy to figure out then. Go call the Fluevogs." He smiled as he said it, knowing there'd be a good story somewhere in the background. "Ask Mike Francesca to run the plates. He's right over there," the chief said.

A second fire truck and then a third one responded in the meantime, and there were over ten firemen now trying to put out the flames from the car fire. A small crowd had gathered to watch the excitement of the car burning.

The night sky did look like a bonfire, just as Carrie had said.

There under the summer moon, Bill Fletcher's Jeep Grand Cherokee burned bright and melted away, right next to the rose hips on the side of the pristine kettle pond. The heat felt good against the cool summer night. The season was quickly changing.

Part III

Denouement

Burnt Offerings

Mike Francesca was sitting back in the Neskeet Nation offices interviewing Bill Fletcher about his burnt-up vehicle. He had his legs crossed, relaxed, drinking a cup of Kona Koffee. He was in no hurry. Mike was really just getting a feel for the Indian operation that Fletcher was running out of his little office there. He took a sip of his dark coffee, put it down gently, then clicked his pen to write in his notebook that was sitting open on the conference table.

"So you didn't notice your car was missing at all last night, Mr. Fletcher?"

"No, not a clue, officer." Fletcher was playing it straight and formal with Mike Francesca. He needed a good police report to file with his insurance company so he was committed to the minimum of sarcasm and his usual flip talk. It was hard for him.

"In fact, I was sitting with my girlfriend on our back deck drinking wine when the fire started."

"What were you doing?"

"We were actually watching my car burn on the other side of Kettle Pond but didn't know it at the time. It made a pretty fireball when the gas tank exploded. *Poof.* If I knew that it was my car, I might have been more interested." Fletcher tapped the table in slight irritation with his finger. The interview was tedious.

"Then what did you do?"

"After I watched my car burn?"

"Yeah."

"Went to bed."

Francesca scratched his eyebrow. "Anything else?"

Bill Fletcher wasn't sure whether to tell him about the doggie sex he and Carrie had to finish the night off with, but he thought the better of it and passed on the details. Nobody liked a wise guy, and he didn't want to alienate Chief Mike Francesca and the Oak Bluffs Police Department.

Speaking of wise guys, Mike Francesca knew a wise guy when he saw one, and he figured Bill Fletcher fit the bill. He also decided that Fletcher was no Indian chief either. He looked more like a used-car salesman who washed ashore on the Island.

Mike paused, trying to build some drama around the arson. Then he asked his last question. "Do you have any idea who'd want to steal your car and then torch it, Mr. Fletcher? Seems pretty violent, don't you think, setting it on fire like that?"

Fletcher thought Mike was too heavy-handed, no subtlety, reaching too much. He paused and pretended to think for a second before he answered.

"No, officer, I don't have a clue as to who'd want to do this to my car. I'm going to chalk it up to alcohol and college high jinks. The summer crowd rich kids and all."

Mike pursed his lips like he was sucking on something sour. "Maybe. But I doubt it, Mr. Fletcher. Feels like someone doesn't like you or the Neskeet Indians on the Island. The rich kids don't do this kind of stuff too often. They could get burnt, or worse, rip their Abercrombie jackets. No, I'm thinking this wasn't a random act of destruction." He shook his head and frowned.

"No harm, no foul, officer."

"But they burned up your car."

"I've got insurance. I can't sweat the small stuff, officer. I've got bigger fish to fry."

Mike Francesca wrapped it up about ten minutes later. He closed his notebook ceremoniously like he had just solved a big case and clicked his pen closed.

He put the pen and the notebook back in the side leg pocket of his police pants. He loved those pants, pockets everywhere. Before he left, he hung around Carol Ault's desk for a few minutes, checking her out and asking a few questions. She had beautiful breasts, and he locked on to them immediately.

When things settled down, Bill Fletcher reflected on the events of the night before. He had a good idea who had sent him the message. He figured that it was the guy who wore a porkpie hat and drove a maroon Cadillac STS. The Neskeets must have been stepping on Fluevog toes a little too hard.

Later that day, Fletcher was standing in a driveway in Vineyard Haven talking to an old coot in a gray T-shirt.

"How much for it?"

"She runs real well. I don't really want to sell her, but I have to, ya know?" The man smiled, ignoring Fletcher's question about the price.

There in front of them on the broken asphalt driveway was a green 1990 Oldsmobile Vista Cruiser. It looked like a beached aircraft carrier. It was one of the first-generation late model giant station wagons. It had a big wheelbase with fat tires and sat squat on the pavement. It had a For Sale sign on the windshield.

Best of all, it had fake wooden door panels. So it was a nineties woody, a nod back in time to the golden age of California woodies and surfing dudes and driving the Pacific Coast Highway.

All good stuff, as far as Bill Fletcher was concerned. He could channel Jan & Dean and the Beach Boys as good as anybody.

"This car leak anything?" Fletcher asked. He had driven old cars in Boston before and knew their weak spots straight away.

The owner was ready for the question, and answered it deftly. "Nope, not a leak of any kind. Oil pan's just about perfect with a new gasket and all. Like she just rolled off the assembly line in Flint."

Fletcher smiled. "Flint, Michigan?"

"That's right. That's where she came from. First generation of Vista Cruisers. This one's been babied. I've even got the production papers from when she rolled off the assembly line in the glove box."

"Any big repairs along the way?"

"Nothing. Not a thing wrong with this baby. She's in vintage shape, ready to be shown at car shows on the Cape or drive it over to the A&W root beer stand. But you don't have to baby her. You can use her as your everyday car, no problem. She's tough."

"Uh-huh."

Fletcher ignored the codger's bullshit and looked inside. The interior had a huge front bench seat with a big wood-grained steering wheel. You could have sex with two people on the seat and still have room to drive and be comfortable, he figured.

The owner watched Fletcher looking at the car and falling in love. He figured he had hooked him by this point. So he played his ace card. "She's got a cassette deck that still plays too. I put it in later, after the fact, but it's good quality, after-market stuff."

Fletcher got in and sat behind the wheel. It was like driving your living room couch. The dashboard was wide and gleamed with all kinds of Detroit chrome and plastic instrumentation. Fletcher stuck his head out. "Does the heat work?" He fiddled with the dials. "Winter's coming."

"You betcha. She heats like a bear. With the big V8, your balls will be toasty in about ten minutes. Trust me."

"How does she ride?"

"Smooth as silk. You kidding me? Just look at her. Like a whale on wheels. She's solid and steers nice too. It's like driving a house. You only need to use one finger once you point her in the right direction and start moving forward. They put an oversize hydraulic pump on the power steering mechanism the first year. Those engineers did it right."

That sealed the deal for Fletcher, one-finger steering. He bought the car on the spot for five thousand dollars. He wrote a check right out of the Neskeet cash account. The owner signed over the title on the roof of the car and handed the big, beefy keys to Fletcher right after. They were done in twenty minutes.

"How 'bout a sticker?" Fletcher asked, looking to see when the car was last officially inspected.

"That's the beauty of this rig. She don't need one. She's over twenty years old, so she qualifies as an antique. So there's no emissions testing, only safety stuff once every five years. You're good for two more."

"Beautiful."

The owner pocketed the check. "Forgot to tell you. There's an Earth, Wind, and Fire cassette in the tape player. You can have it, complimentary. It's on me." The gray-hair man smiled and tipped his Red Sox hat.

Fletcher put the keys in the ignition and turned over the big block Olds engine. It started right up and purred in idle. He put the big station wagon in Drive and went down the driveway, made a left at the end, and headed back toward town.

Earth, Wind, and Fire was playing low on the speakers. He had the driver's window down and his left arm dangling out of the door, and he was humming along to the music. He decided the Vista Cruiser was much cooler than the Jeep Grand Cherokee, no doubt about it.

Once again, he ended up making lemonade out of lemons. The Vista Cruiser was a car perfectly fit for an Indian chief.

And Fletcher knew it.

His Holiness

Father Peter stood on the dock, waiting for the black Lincoln Town Car to roll off the ferry. He saw it soon enough with the high polish and dark smoked windows.

He waited at the curb in his most priestly pose. He had on a starched white dog collar, a clean shirt, pressed slacks, and slip-ons. All in black, it matched his mood perfectly.

The saving grace was that it turned out to be a day trip for the bishop. He had to be back to do a funeral the next morning in New Bedford. Father Peter had helped with getting the reservations the night before, so he knew how long the bishop was staying. Amen. He knew that he had the stamina to suck it up for just one day.

The Lincoln stopped at the curb, the door opened, and he got in. The bishop was there in the backseat, reclining and thin in a pressed black sportcoat.

"Good morning, Father Mulcahey. Nice of you to have me over for a visit. I do love coming. I'm hearing that things are going well, yes?"

"They are, Bishop," Father Peter answered. "We've got a full day too. I think you'll like what you see. We've finally become self-sustaining. We pay our own bills now."

"I know, Father Mulcahey. You haven't asked us for money in over twelve months. We notice the little things like that in the archdiocese. Tell me, how have you done it, Father?"

"Bingo, Bishop. That's how. It's been God's best answer to our prayers."

That started the conversation for the day. Father Peter knew that he'd get much more traction with the bishop if they started with money matters and got that stuff out of the way first.

So they went to the rectory and sat in his office for an hour, going over the books. Joanne had brought in tea and finger sandwiches. They ate, talking about the Vatican and the sex scandals, and then got back to business.

"Do you want to see the church and the grounds quickly, Bishop? We've got new carpet for the confessionals."

"Show me the bingo hall first and how it works, Father Peter."

Father Peter's eyebrows shot up. Bishop Guerin was focused this trip.

"I want to see how you set up for the games. The logistics and all."

So off they went to the Blessed Sacrament Parish Hall where Father Peter walked the bishop through the details of the bingo tournament. How much they grossed on the cards, the liquor they sold, the entrance fees. He brought it right down to the net. He even showed the bishop where the numbers caller sat with the microphone.

"We start off each session with a blessing, Bishop," Peter Mulcahey told the holy man, trying to slip a little Catholic religion into the monetary discussion to soften it up a little bit.

"Asking the Lord for good luck for the parishioners?"

Father Peter smiled. "Always that, Bishop. But it also maintains our tax exemption so we don't get hit for UBTI."

Bishop Guerin turned to face his priest." So tell me about that."

"Our accountant says that as long as we fold some Catholicism in at the beginning of the bingo session, the money we make is exempt from the unrelated business taxable income rules. UBTI."

"And what do you think?"

Father Peter looked over at the bishop. "I don't have a clue, honestly. I'm a shepherd of the flock, Bishop. I like tending souls."

Father Peter laid it on thick, like an Irish plasterer with a trowel. Bishop Guerin nodded. He had given the right answer. Souls before profits, but don't screw up the money part either.

"Let's go have dinner, Father," the bishop said. He had talked enough details for one day and needed a drink badly.

So off they went to the Oyster Bar for dinner. Father Peter had made reservations for a discreet table in the back. He ordered a bottle of sauvignon blanc for the two of them, the bishop's favorite. They ate shrimp cocktails and drank wine. Over dinner, Bishop Guerin got to the heart of the matter.

"Father Peter. I want you to be our new bingo coordinator for all of the diocese. Come over to New Bedford once a week and teach the priests how to run an operation just like yours, from soup to nuts. It'll put us on a whole new financial footing."

Peter Mulcahey nodded as he listened. Now he knew why the bishop had come. Father Peter was good at the money raising, and the bishop was tapping into it. He was relieved. He was terrified of a missionary posting to Third-World Africa. This was much more interesting than hearing confession or saying Mass too. He agreed to the job on the spot.

"I'll gladly do it, Bishop Guerin. No problem. When do we start?"

"In the fall, Peter. After the kids are all back in school. We'll have tuition payments coming in, and we can buy the equipment we need for the bingo sessions in bulk." Father Peter thought that Bishop Guerin should have been a managing director at General Electric.

The two priests finished dinner, Father Peter keeping his eye on the clock the whole time. He didn't want Bishop Guerin to miss his boat. NFW.

They shook hands and parted ways outside the restaurant.

"We'll be in touch, Father Peter. You're doing the Lord's work here, no doubt. Keep it up."

Peter Mulcahey shut the rear car door for the bishop and followed the red taillights of the big Lincoln as it headed down Main Street toward the boat wharf. It was foggy in the early evening darkness, and he watched until the lights were out of sight.

Then he pulled out his iPhone and called Margaret Wellington. It had been a long day.

*   *   *

The nighttime was the right time for bingo for Bill Fletcher and his Neskeet Nation. He was over at the A&P storefront supervising the nightly game, now run four nights a week. It was becoming one hell of an operation.

There was a good crowd tonight. Fletcher hovered over by the bar, watching the bartender pour out white and red wine into clear plastic cups. They only charged $2.50 for a glass of wine, and they were selling like gangbusters. The money flowed.

Fletcher watched the young woman bartender with the tight T-shirt put out ten little plastic glasses and then pour white wine from a jug into all of them. Her shirt said NESKEET NATION in big block letters across her chest. She was well endowed, and there was no missing the connection between the bingo, the tribe, and her breasts.

"Make sure you pour an honest glass, Melissa. These bingo people are thirsty." Fletcher winked at her breasts.

Melissa nodded without looking up.

"I gotcha, Bill," she said.

It was a fine line that Fletcher was treading with the liquor sales. He didn't want to be accused of getting people drunk when they were there, but he wanted the bingo crowd liquored and loose, spending money and hanging around.

He was in bed later that night reading about Sitting Bull and the battle at Little Bighorn in Montana. He was fascinated with that beautiful big piece of American hubris. He had a little pocket light clipped to his book that he had purchased at the Good Grape Bookstore.

Carrie was beside him, breathing softly in her sleep. She was curled up in the fetal position with her back pushed into him. Domestic bliss. He didn't know what the hell he did to deserve all this tranquility, but he'd take it.

Before he turned off the light, his Blackberry buzzed on the nightstand with a new message. It was Melissa, closing up the bingo parlor and making the night deposit at the bank. They had pulled in $3,561. It was a new record for one night of bingo. "Pretty cool, huh?" she texted.

He typed back. UNBELIEVABLE!!!!

Fletcher switched off the light and spooned in behind Carrie. She stirred lightly. He adjusted his pillow and ruminated in the glow of the Indian moon streaming in through the bedroom window. Other than his car being torched the week before, it had been a good week.

Cruising

Bill Fletcher drove slowly up Main Street in his big green Vista Cruiser with the fake wood panels. He had just washed the car, and it shone brightly in the sun. Fletcher had his Ray-Bans on. He had the driver's window down, left arm resting on the door. He had one hand on the wheel with his seat pushed way back. Earth, Wind, and Fire was playing on the cassette deck again, a little loud, the music pulsing through the big interior. He didn't know how to get the tape out of the player in the glove box.

He looked like a Latino lowrider from LA plucked right off Figueroa, cruising the neighborhood looking for chicks or a gun battle. His dark complexion sealed the deal.

He found a spot up on the left. He gunned the car, took his foot off the gas, and glided the big rig smoothly into the space. He put it in Park, pulled the key, and got out. He had on his deerskin fringe jacket.

"What happened to your car?" Carl Sunapee said. He was like an apparition standing right there with his porkpie hat on, appearing out of nowhere. He had his hands on his hips, talking to Fletcher.

Carl had been walking along Main Street when Fletcher drove up. He saw him and came over, flashing a big wide smile. A cat with a canary kind of grin.

"Nice jacket," Carl added for icing before Fletcher could answer his first question.

Fletcher was smooth, though, and unflappable. He never let on about the Grand Cherokee and thinking that Carl had torched it.

"Thanks, Carl. It's a throwback, old-school Indian style. It's not as cool as your hat, but it's a close second, you know?"

"I been wearing this hat a long while. You've got some catching up to do," Carl said as he nodded.

Fletcher stood next to Carl on the sidewalk and looked back at his car. "You like it, huh? I had a little accident with my Grand Cherokee and made the move to this old cruiser. It's an Olds '88. It's more my style anyway."

"What kind of accident?"

"Gas line broke, and fuel spilled all over the engine. Poof, the whole thing went up like a grease fire in a Weber grill. Can you believe it?"

Carl shook his head as he walked around the car, never looking up at Fletcher. "Too bad for you."

Fletcher smiled. "What'd you hear? Anything else?"

"Nothing. I don't listen to that street talk." Carl moved closer. "I hope your insurance was paid up, maybe they'll just tag you for the deductible."

"I've got plenty of insurance and plenty of money." Bill Fletcher knew how to poke the Fluevog chief.

Carl leaned down underneath the Vista Cruiser's front end. "You got something leaking down here." He put his fingers on the ground to steady himself, like a lineman in a three-point stance. He bent over and looked around underneath. "It looks like tranny fluid to me. It's thick. Definitely the transmission."

Fletcher was irritated. "I've got more at home in the garage. It's no big deal."

"You ain't gonna get a sticker with that stuff coming out, I'll tell you that," Carl said. "Plus, you're going to ruin your gears."

"I'll get it fixed next week."

Fletcher didn't wait for any more of Carl's critique as he pushed through the front door of the Neskeet offices and bounded up the stairs. He had work to do.

"Next time you might want to check your fluids" was all Carl could say to himself on the sidewalk.

MV Hospital

Dr. Frank Borman was the physician on call in the emergency room on Tuesday afternoon at the gleaming-new Martha's Vineyard Hospital. It was a sunny day in early September, and the Island was still humming with a lot of tourists day-tripping from Falmouth.

He had spent the afternoon so far bandaging up a woman who had fallen off her moped on a sand patch at the little bridge on Beach Road.

Then there was the roofer who had shot a nail into his right hand with an automatic nail gun, the stupid bastard. He had thrown the gun down with the safety off, and the trigger hit a copper pipe that was stubbed for a plumbing vent. It fired the nail out at 150-foot pounds of torque right into his hand, sitting flat on the asphalt roof. He winced coming in.

Luckily, the nail shot almost all the way through and ripped a clean, precise hole, like a bullet from a Glock. The guy looked like Jesus Christ with his stigmata—the nail went through dead center of his palm.

"Six penny, nice clean opening" was all Dr. Borman could say as he carefully inspected the hand after his nurse injected a big shot of novocaine right above the wound. He took the nail out using surgical grips and a no. 6 scalpel, dropping the bloody piece of iron in a stainless steel pan with a soft *ping*.

As he cleaned up, the roofer gingerly flexed his hand and spoke. "It feels pretty good, doc. Am I gonna need more surgery?"

"Probably not. Just keep it clean and try to set the safety on the nail gun next time, please." And that was it.

The commotion came later in the afternoon.

An Oak Bluffs ambulance came screeching up to the emergency entrance and quickly braked to a stop outside. Out jumped two paramedics and a little girl with a woman trailing close by. It was definitely the mother,

Dr. Borman decided as he headed out through the automatic doors to meet the entourage along with two nurses.

"What happened?" he said. "Large animal bite" was all the paramedic said as they pushed inside.

He saw that the girl had her hand wrapped in a white terrycloth towel and was wailing as she was led into the emergency room. Her mother held the hand with the towel above the girl's chest.

The group went into one of the new trauma rooms. The girl sat on the examining table, and the towel was unwrapped. There was blood, but it wasn't overwhelming. It wasn't a ruptured artery or anything that severe.

Dr. Borman instantly breathed a big sigh of relief. He hated working on spurting veins and deep wounds of hysterical kids with their parents hovering right next to them. It made him too nervous.

"She was bit on the arm by a goddamn buffalo," the mother said, now a little more composed in the hospital ER with a doctor at hand. "Can you believe it?" Her anger flashed.

Everybody looked at the girl's arm with a thin trickle of blood coming out. Dr Borman clicked on the overhead surgical light and pulled down his magnifying halo.

He quietly inspected the girl's arm. It was a good-sized nip that the animal had taken, but there was no ripped flesh or cartilage. The skin was punctured, but he had already made the decision that the girl didn't need stitches. A simple cauterization would suffice.

"What happened? What do you mean buffalo?" Dr Borman said. He worked the dirt out of the wound with some antiseptic on a cotton gauze pad as they talked.

The girl howled as the green liquid stung like hell. The ER nurse held the girl's arm steady as the doctor cleaned the wound.

"It was that goddamn Indian display over at Waban Park that we took her to," the mother said, getting her anger focused now that she realized her daughter was going to be all right.

"You mean 1,200-pound buffalo like you see on the plains in Colorado?" Dr. Borman asked again as he worked, trying to keep the mood a little light, diffuse the situation some.

"Yeah, that kind. The real ones," the mother said. "I couldn't believe that the keepers were letting the children get close enough to feed them. It was totally stupid. What were they thinking?"

Dr. Borman stayed quiet and focused. *What were you goddamn thinking as a mother*, he thought to himself as he applied a compression bandage, *who let their children pet buffalo?*

"They shouldn't let adult buffalo near children. They're big unstable animals. You're lucky it's just a nip," he said as he made progress with the wound.

Frank Borman pulled up his magnifying lens and looked at the girl's mother. "Be careful next time. Luckily, it's just a minor break. We don't need to do stitches." The mother breathed a deep sigh of relief.

An attractive nurse handed Dr. Borman a syringe then cleaned the little girl's arm. She started crying again.

"It's okay, honey. This is only going to pinch a second. It won't hurt. It's a tetanus shot." He looked at her mother. "She needs a tetanus booster regardless. There's no knowing where that buffalo's been."

The shot was administered, and the case was closed as far as Dr. Borman was concerned. He'd be a son of a bitch though. Buffalo on Martha's Vineyard. Who'd have thought? But he seemed to remember something about the whole thing with the Indians from the *Gazette* a few weeks ago. He had just glanced at the pictures and didn't have time to read the story.

The mother lingered for a second and talked to the emergency room nurse while she processed the discharge paperwork.

"I can't believe that I was so stupid that I let Anne feed that buffalo. I knew that creature was too big. I could tell. He looked so docile though, so beautiful."

"You never can tell," the young nurse said. "These kinds of accidents happen all the time."

The mother nodded then shook her head before speaking. "Those assholes should be sued for having those buffalo so close to the children. It's dangerous is what it is."

*   *   *

"Look," Jack Fraker told Jim Barry the selectman as they sat in his office in Oak Bluffs. "I never liked that frickin' Civil War statue anyway at the edge of Ocean Park. It doesn't belong there, and you know it." He paused for emphasis. "Who the hell cares about the Civil War anyway? It happened a hundred and fifty years ago."

"You're right. Fletcher's going to pay to have it moved over to Sunset Lake and rebuild it with a bigger pedestal and monument anyway," Jim Barry replied, getting into it.

"Something big and grand. We'll do a big ceremony, and everybody will be happy. It's a win-win."

"It's gonna cost him," Jim Barry said. He had a fingernail clipper in his hand, and he was snipping off a nettlesome nail on his right ring finger.

"How much?"

"We need the Neskeets to fund a maintenance contract for five years for the landscaping of all of Ocean Park as part of the deal. The budget's busted right now. We have absolutely no money. Plus, all the costs of erection for the new statue and moving the old one are his too. Do they have that kind of money?"

The bank president didn't even blink. "Money they've got, Jim. These guys aren't like the Fluevogs. They're rolling in dough. I think Fletcher's printing it in the basement or something." Fraker laughed at his joke.

"Then we need to have him print us some," Jim Barry said. "I know Fletcher. If he wants it, he'll spend his money."

The bank president nodded his head. "You're right. He's a businessman, bottom line. My kind of Indian. This'll be a done deal tomorrow."

Government Retraction

Harold Schumer was in his boss's office, which was piled high with case files and documents. He had to hand it to the Bureau of Indian Affairs. They had nice offices for a federal agency. They had solid maple office furniture and good quality HP desktops and printers. Not any hand-me-down federal bullshit like so many other agencies had.

It was clearly an overreaction by Congress. The Indians had been shit on from the 1850s or so, and the federal government was trying to make up for all its bad behavior. It was a lot of work.

There were real Indian artifacts on the wall at the reception area that were cool looking. Several framed land treaties hung along the interior corridors as well. Harold, being a nerdy, intellectual lawyer, had actually read them. One of them, a land grant, dated back to 1863 and was signed by Abraham Lincoln. It hung right there on the wall outside his office, no laser security or high-tech fasteners protecting it. It was amazing stuff.

Jim Sampson was a busy man. He was a high-level career bureaucrat in an appointed role making $225K a year for keeping busy doing nothing except attending a shitload of meetings and pontificates. He kept his office piled high with case files and thick documents. You could tell he was busy. He and Harold Schumer had cleared off the side table in his office, the one for meetings with his staff, and were sitting talking about the Neskeets.

Harold brought his gaze in from outside where he had been looking out at the pigeons on the ledge.

"God, those damn birds are filthy," Harold said.

"I know it," Sampson agreed. "They shit everywhere. They put the mesh up there last month with the little barbs to stop them from nesting on the ledge, but it doesn't work for shit. Their asses have so many feathers that it looks like they're comfortable sitting on the barbs." He shook his head. "Goddamn property management company is worthless."

"There's more now than ever out there," Harold said.

"You're right, the little bastards." Sampson had had enough small talk. "So, did you fill out the 504 for the Neskeets when they came through?"

Harold was ready for him on this case. He had all his paperwork in order and had reviewed it early that morning and brushed up on all the details so he wouldn't be caught flatfooted.

"Yeah, it was the first thing we reviewed."

"And the bureau ran the ID checks?"

"Yeah. They were all clean as a whistle. I've got them here if you want to look."

Jim Sampson came right to the point. "Well, Houston, we've got a problem. Senator Pullman called yesterday complaining about the funding for the tribe."

"Why? What for?" Harold's radar was now instantly on, and he flushed slightly red as a small current of electricity lit up his system.

Senators were always dangerous predators and usually a pain in the ass when they started snooping around. They were like velociraptors. You could lose your head easily. They were too important to be ignored.

"The Fluevogs are all in his district. They're all over the Cape and the Islands."

"So?"

"So they're all totally pissed off. Carl Sunapee talked directly with Pullman twice so far. The Neskeets have come in and stepped on a lot of toes and dicks down there, and the old Indians are pissed off. Apparently, this guy Bill Fletcher is a real cracker, an Indian go-getter. He's shaking them up."

Jim Sampson looked up at Harold Schumer for effect after he flipped a few pages of the file on his desk, lightly scanning the material. "Look, I don't want to sugarcoat it, Harold. Pullman wants the grants pulled back that we gave them for start-up operations."

"The seed money grants? You signed off on those yourself. Everybody did."

Jim Sampson went quiet.

Harold was a little incredulous at this point. He fidgeted a little. This would be a shit storm to go down there and take back the money from the Neskeets. Definitely bad press, he figured. And it was never done. The BIA never took money back. It had too much more to put out.

"I know," Sampson said. "It's not pretty."

"The whole thing?"

"How much did we give 'em?"

"If we add both the formation and the follow-on maintenance grants, it's a total of eleven million."

"Jesus Christ. I didn't realize that we gave them that much. They're first timers." Jim Sampson frowned then looked at Harold Schumer again. "Pullman wants us to take it all back and make it subject to a regional Cape and Islands tribal management plan."

"Why?"

"Because he knows that will tie the money up for five years easily. The Fluevogs, his big voting constituency, will be happy, and it'll look like he's orchestrating a big regional tribal plan where all the tribes can coexist and live in peace and harmony."

"That's not gonna happen," Harold said flat out. "They'll be taking Winchester rifles out against one another if this happens."

"We both know that, but I don't give a shit about the Neskeets. They're nobody. Start by just telling them that we're gonna review their operations. Standard audit stuff. We do it all the time. Send Mindy down to review the books. Find some stuff wrong and then yank the money back. Say it's provisional until they fix the things you write-up."

"Then what, send the money back to them?"

Jim Sampson shook his head, looking at Harold like he was a dummy, which he thought he was.

"Hell no, the opposite. Make sure that it'll take about three years for them to fix the stuff you cite them for."

"That's effectively never, then," Harold said. "They'll never see the money again."

Sampson smiled. "Then everybody's happy. Pullman and the Fluevogs are happy because their rivals just took a torpedo in the side of the ship. The Neskeets are pissed but happy because you're not telling them they can't ever get the money back, just that it'll take a little more time and a review. Give 'em some hope, you know?"

Sampson nodded and then finished. "And you and I are happy because we keep our jobs and don't get an internal Congressional review up our asses. It's a great story all the way around."

Harold Schumer was still surprised that they were going to pull the money back. That was rare. It wasn't like eleven million dollars was a lot of money either for the federal government. Pigeon feed, really. Pullman must have been pissed off enough for him to apply enough pressure to get this to happen, Harold figured. He shook his head. He'd have to finesse the whole thing very carefully with the troops.

Jim Sampson pushed the Neskeet file back over the polished mahogany desk to Harold Schumer. They were finished.

"Get Mindy on the case today. Have her head the audit review. I want her down there next week. She'll like the Vineyard in the fall. She can walk on the beach barefoot. She'll have to take off her high heels with the red soles first though." They both laughed.

*   *   *

Bill Fletcher backed his station wagon out of the parking space and headed over to see Guy Phillips about the buffalo. He threw the Vista Cruiser in Drive and headed forward. He noticed the little pool of shiny fluid on the asphalt where he'd just parked. It was about the size of a small pizza and was a darkish red.

Son of a bitch, he thought to himself. Carl Sunapee had been right about the tranny fluid leaking. He didn't say it just to bust his balls. Fletcher was surprised.

It was a minor problem, no doubt. He'd stop at the Texaco garage and leave the car during the day tomorrow. They'd get one of their grease monkeys to throw a wrench on it and tighten the transmission seal. That would probably do the trick.

He loved the car though, leak and all. It was a big wide cruiser with plenty of room to spread out inside. It had a huge passenger area with two full seats and the back area for storage to boot. He could fit a marching band inside. It was pure cool.

He pulled up to Waban Park a minute later and parked the car on the grass over by the high fence and the buffalo.

"We can't leave the buffalo here anymore, Guy," Fletcher said the second he got out of the car. No small talk.

Guy Phillips looked at Fletcher, who was restating the obvious. *What an asshole*, he thought.

"You mean 'cause of the arm nip yesterday on that little girl from Boston? She was feeding the momma from up too close. I told her to be careful. She moved and spooked the buffalo."

"Spook, schmook," Fletcher said. "We're lucky it was just a flesh wound." He shook his head. "You were clairvoyant though, asking about our liability insurance coverage the first thing before we did this, Guy. You knew about these beasts?"

Guy Phillips laughed. "No. I just know a shit pile when I see one forming. These are big animals, and we're not on the plains of Colorado. Stuff like this happens all the time. Don't worry. I'll move 'em back to the big field up-Island tomorrow with all the others. They'll be happier there anyway."

Bill Fletcher didn't hang around making small talk with the animal husbandry guy. Buffaloes were big dirty beasts. He shook hands then parted company. He had a bingo game to prepare for that night.

Wampum Nation

It was gray and overcast, a perfect day for an Indian statue dedication. The wind whipped onshore from the west from Cuttyhunk. The flags were straight out on the houses around Ocean Park, and Mike Francesca knew that meant the breeze was blowing at least eighteen knots hard and full.

He pulled the brim down on his Oak Bluffs officer's dress hat a little more to make sure it wouldn't get blown off and he'd look like a crazy asshole chasing it all over the grass. The thing cost eighty bucks at police supply, and he only had one. He was in his dress uniform today owing to the dedication and all. Oak Bluffs' finest, two of them, were there to make a ceremonial showing.

The eight-foot statue was covered in a white cotton shroud that was tied down with blue ribbon. The cotton cover billowed loosely as it filled with wind and tugged at its tie. It was all supposed to come off with one tug when someone pulled the ribbon at the bottom. *We'll see*, Mike thought to himself. He had his Swiss Army knife in his pocket at the ready, just in case. He wasn't climbing up any statue in this weather though to help if there was a problem.

Mike Francesca looked out at the people in front of the statue as he reached down and adjusted the volume on his two-way radio sitting in its nylon holster on his belt. He adjusted the round rubber nipple like a pro, never looking down once. It was a good crowd for the event; he figured over a hundred people had showed up for the dedication.

The dignitaries all sat on folding chairs on the grass right in front of the statue. Bill Fletcher was there right in front, wearing his suede jacket with the fringe. The little pieces were whipped around everywhere by the wind. His black hair was tied in a short ponytail. He looked like a happy hippy Indian.

Jim Barry, the selectman, spoke first. Then Jack Fraker took the microphone and said a few words. Mike could see that it pained the chubby banker to get up there and say good things about Bill Fletcher and the Neskeet Nation, but you had to do what you had to do, he knew. Fraker was mercifully short.

Then came Bill Fletcher, who was also very brief. He knew attention spans were short, and people needed a drink and a place to warm up out of the cold and straighten their hair.

The wind whipped around as Fletcher went to the podium. The suede fringe on his coat was blowing left and right. He kept his Ray-Bans on, though, as the bright gray sky was full of glare and it hurt his eyes.

Mike Francesca stood off to the side of the important people and looked up at the podium. He thought that Fletcher looked like one of the characters from *Easy Rider*, that biker flick he watched on Spike TV the other night. Peter Hopper, maybe.

Fletcher got right to it and laid the razzmatazz on real thick.

"This statue represents the face of Native America: one man overcoming old Indian vices of gambling, liquor, and guns. It signifies the spirit of all Indians. The Neskeets are part of a new American culture that emphasizes truth, justice, and the American way." He threw that in from the old Superman TV show that he remembered.

That was it. He stepped aside and pulled like a bastard on the ribbon. It came off in one swoop, and then the wind got under the white cotton cover and blew it straight up and across the park into a big fast-moving ball of cloth. It looked like a giant tumbleweed as two people chased after it.

And there it was. An eight-foot statue of Bill Fletcher, chief of the Neskeets, in a leather jacket and dungarees. He wore his Ray-Bans, and he had the BlackBerry up to his ear. In his other hand he held a traditional Indian peace pipe. He was wearing cowboy boots. At his feet, he stepped on a pile of poker chips, an empty whiskey bottle, and three broken arrows. The symbolism would hit you over the head. In medium lettering on the pedestal, it said WAMPUM NATION. It was a nice touch.

Fletcher had paid $50,000 to Piers Staadt, the famous out-of-work alcoholic Swedish sculptor, to design and create the statue. He got his money's worth. Fletcher thought that he looked good up there, talking on his smartphone, looking toward the ferry landing like he had someplace to get to.

The crowd oohed and aahed and clapped at the end after Fletcher had said his thank-you's and had finished speaking. Most people walked around the statue at least once before they headed off to the catered buffet reception, courtesy of the Neskeet Nation, that had been set up over at the Island House.

Carrie had promoted the free gourmet food fest heavily as a way to get people to come to the statue dedication. They had to show up to get a plastic wrist bracelet after the ceremony was over if they wanted to eat and drink for free. She had conscripted Carol Ault, who was wearing a little red dress and Ugg boots, to put the yellow bracelets on people's wrists after the speeches. She had a pocketful of them.

"What did you think?" Carrie asked Bill as they walked across Ocean Park; the wind was still brisk.

"It's all good," he said. "It's a nice gesture by the town for the Indians. For posterity."

"Yeah," Carrie laughed. "Just so you know for posterity, it looks like that Swedish sculptor guy put a sock in your crotch. You got quite a bulge there. Like an incipient hard-on."

Fletcher smiled. "I know, it does. I ended up paying extra for that little enhancement. I had to commission it."

*　　*　　*

Father Peter got back to the rectory after a long day. First the Neskeet statue dedication for that ninny Bill Fletcher, then driving around giving out the sacraments. He put his keys down and glanced at the monthly accounting statement that Margaret had left on his desk that morning.

He had been up-Island all afternoon, giving the sacrament of Holy Communion to shut-ins. It wasn't easy work—in and out of the car, in the hospital, praying and jabbering with sick people, drinking tea, and commiserating.

Plus, he had to be in his full priest uniform the whole time, wearing his black shirt with the uncomfortable dog collar, for the giving of the sacrament. He even had to turn his iPhone to silent, not even vibrate. It wouldn't do to be handing out Communion to an old shut-in and have his iPhone start vibrating in the quiet of the bedroom and everybody hearing it, he knew.

It was a pain in the ass all the way around, Father Peter concluded.

It also meant he didn't get the call from Margaret angling to hook up with him late in the day in the backseat of her tan Volkswagen Beetle behind the cemetery, where he was almost certain to get a quick sexual favor.

It sounded crass when he thought about it that way, like he was some horny teenager. He was irritated that he was a mere mortal. He sometimes fantasized about giving up the priesthood and becoming a real man. It was enticing.

Fumble in the Red Zone

The morning didn't start off well. Fletcher took it as an omen, looking back on it.

He was in Kona Koffee ordering a French roast, dark, and Blinkey was working the counter. He split his time between being a barista at Kona and working the docks.

He saw Fletcher and immediately got animated, talking about the summer and how good things were going. Fletcher thought he had a manic look about him as if he hadn't slept in three nights.

Fletcher asked him how he was doing, chatting him up, and Blinkey told him that he hadn't slept in three nights owing to the fishing boats coming in now that the season was on. Blinkey then proceeded to give him a French vanilla coffee, light, with three sugars.

Fletcher didn't want to cause a scene at the coffee bar about his order. He wanted to get the hell out of there and back to the quietude of his office. So he took the light blond coffee and ran out.

He took the cover off the vanilla coffee, took a sip of the sweet, sugary liquid, frowned, sat back, and tried to take stock of the situation.

Mike Francesca came up the stairs, clomping heavily in his police walking shoes. He wanted to talk, so Fletcher took him into the conference room and closed the glass door. Mike occasionally glanced out at Carol as she worked at her desktop doing new media for the tribe.

She was updating the Neskeet Facebook page with her daily post. She uploaded some pictures of Neskeet "Indians" from the night before at a bar on Main Street, everybody partying and having a good time. There were now over 8,352 friends following the site. She commented on the promotion Carrie was running over at the Equinox—buy two tees and get a Neskeet coffee mug with the new Indian statue embossed on it for free. They were working it hard. She got 157 Likes quickly.

Mike concluded that she was as fine a piece of eye candy as there was on the Island with her slim figure, short suede skirt, and cordless headset on. *Give it to Bill Fletcher to keep himself surrounded with good looking women,* he thought.

Give it to Carol Ault too. She was well aware of her youthful charms on the older guys, really all the men. She would primp and preen and stretch and wiggle at her desk throughout the day. She was a modern-day Hollywood siren plucked straight from Metro Goldwyn Mayer and placed right there in Oak Bluffs, waiting for her casting call. Bill Fletcher was not complaining.

Mike Francesca was a multitasking cop, so while looking at Carol kept things interesting, this wasn't a social visit. He was there in the Neskeet offices for a reason, and that reason was to grind Bill Fletcher a little. He started in easy.

"I like the statue. It's a little abstract for a guy like me, but overall, it's pretty cool. Who has their own statue?" Mike, talking like he's hip to art and statues, nodded his head and pursed his lips to accentuate his coolness.

"What's abstract about it?"

"You in your cowboy boots stepping on the pile of poker chips and broken arrows and that empty bottle of Jack Daniel's. It's a nice touch."

Fletcher nodded. "A couple of eggheads, professor types, told me a few days ago that they thought the whole thing was racist, that the sculpture was playing on old Indian stereotypes. They were calling me out on it, being a white racist and all."

"What'd you say?"

"I agreed with 'em." Fletcher nodded. "That was the point of that heinous shit plus the empty booze bottle at the bottom. That's why I was standing on top of it, overcoming all that crap, that old baggage, and striding forward. The new world order for Indians."

"Is that why you had the BlackBerry up to your ear? Getting a message from the future?" Mike knew how to lay it on too.

"Power to the people," Fletcher said and crossed his arms. He looked out at three Neskeets staffers working the mini phone bank in the office. They were already taking orders that morning. It made him happy.

Mike finally pulled out his notebook and got down to business. He had had enough of the art lesson.

"You're gonna have to scale back on the bingo parties over at the A&P. Everybody in town has their underwear in a knot. The crowds, the parking, the trash, that kid vomiting in the street last week, all of it's too much." He nodded at Bill Fletcher for emphasis. "You can understand, right?"

Fletcher figured it was coming; he had pushed it too far. So he cut right to the chase. "Father Mulcahey and the Catholic Church getting pissed off that we've cut into their business in a big way? Is that it?"

Mike Francesca nodded. "That's one complainer for sure. You got that right. You hit 'em right in the pocketbook too." Mike looked up. "But they're not the only ones. Carl Sunapee and the Fluevogs are pissed that they didn't think of it sooner too. And the selectmen are getting pressure about the trash. People aren't happy."

In the end, Bill Fletcher wasn't a fighter. He was a compromiser and a mediator. It was the only real way to do business.

"Okay, I'll fix it. Simple enough. We'll cut back to two nights a week from four and see how it goes. Make some other changes too. Tighten the drinking up, and I'll have our guys police the street after closing."

Mike Francesca closed his notebook. "That may not be enough. I may have to come at you harder on the liquor sales. Close you down, that kind of thing. We'll see. This is just a heads-up. People aren't happy."

Fletcher knew he had to cut back on the bingo some or the town would revolt. Nobody was getting tax revenues on the money with Fletcher saying it was all exempt under the 501(c)3 rules for the Neskeet Nation. It was all pretty flimsy, but he was in no hurry to change it and start making voluntary tax payments. Nobody in town was looking for a piece of the action, and the tax-free cash flow was immense. He had socked away a lot, but more would be even better.

The meeting ended, and on the way out, Bill Fletcher gave Mike Francesca a check for five thousand dollars for the police chief's retirement fund.

"I'll give it to the treasurer," Mike said as he winked and folded the check, putting it in his chest pocket. "That's my wife."

Bill Fletcher didn't need the wink. He didn't care much where Mike Francesca deposited the check as he had plenty of cash and was going to deduct it as a charitable contribution anyway. He just kept greasing the skids so that everything ran as smoothly as it could.

Blue Skies

It was the best of times and the worst of times, as Charles Dickens liked to say.

Carrie and Bill were sitting around their house on Sunday morning, drinking coffee and talking. They just had good Sunday morning sex. Carrie had on a bandanna and a vintage Lilith Fair T-shirt with a bunch of chunky silver bangles on her arm. Fletcher was in a wrinkled blue Oxford shirt, half-open to the waist, and a pair of rugby shorts. He was drinking coffee in a Crazy Horse mug and checking their bank balances on his laptop.

Carrie was into their relationship. She had decided that Bill Fletcher had moved quickly from being Mr. Right Now to Mr. Right. She was not so surprised. He had a pretty good body and went to the Sweat Lodge every day to work out. He was ten years older than her, but that was okay. He was a lawyer and smart, she was a retailer and smart, and the two of them had a vibe, a thing together. It was definitely working.

As for Bill Fletcher, he was as content as he'd ever been. Carrie was sharp and a looker to boot. She was a bundle of energy and had a great business head. He needed that to straighten out a lot of his cockamamy ideas. The sex was good, and the money was great. He had reached his sweet spot. It wasn't getting any better.

They spent the afternoon on the beach across the street, recharging their batteries under the warm fall sun. Being Indian and running all the businesses they had their fingers in took a lot of energy and time.

Fletcher brought over his mini Weber grill, and he cooked small pieces of striped bass on the glowing coals. Carrie had a bottle of sauvignon blanc that she kept hidden in a plastic cooler. They sipped wine out of Styrofoam cups. They kept it discreet as there was a no-drinking rule on state beach. She relaxed and stretched out on her beach chair in a small tie-dyed bikini.

"How long are we going to do this?" Carrie said, drifting in and out in the sun.

"Until the money runs out," Fletcher said.

"How much do we have?"

"Over thirteen million dollars when I checked this morning."

"Wow! We could retire," Carrie said.

Fletcher didn't say anything. He sipped white wine from his cup and looked out toward the sea. The adventure wasn't over yet as far as he was concerned.

*   *   *

Over at Blessed Sacrament Parish Hall, Father Peter was in a meeting with Margaret and two outside parishioners who were gadfly types. They were active in church and town politics and were usually the kind of people that Father Peter avoided like the plague. He needed their help this time.

They had a pot of coffee brewing behind them in one of those old throwback percolators with the black coffee bubbling up into the glass thing on the top.

They were discussing the parish finances. What had started out as a good summer season had changed dramatically toward the end, like a summer squall rising up on the horizon. Margaret led the discussion, and she was all business.

"Ever since the Neskeet Indians opened their bingo parlor in Vineyard Haven, our parish revenues have declined dramatically. I can definitely trace it back to the week after they opened."

"So why is that?" Father Peter asked innocently, setting it up for her. "Well, Father, it's several things. First, their pots are bigger. One hundred and fifty dollars versus our fifty. That's three times as big. Plus their jackpot each night is three thousand. We're seven fifty. That takes out all the serious bingo players right away."

"Are there many of those people?" one of the parishioners asked. "Serious bingo players, I mean."

"Just about every one of them is all," Margaret said without hesitation. "They're gamblers, pure and simple." You could hear the exasperation in her voice.

"Don't forget to mention the wine, Margaret," Peter Mulcahey said as if she'd forget.

"The wine, Father?"

"The simple fact that they're only charging two dollars and fifty cents for a big plastic glass of wine, and we charge three dollars for a little one. They're killing us on the booze."

"Are they drinking that much?" the other parishioner asked.

"Well, how's this," Father Peter started in. "Mrs. Sanderson backed into a brand-new Land Rover on her way home last week with her husband's pickup truck. Creased the grille and broke both headlights on the vehicle. Never stopped. She basically drove off, not knowing."

"Good Lord."

"It's getting out of control."

They talked some more, and Father Mulcahey finally agreed to apply a little pressure.

"I'll speak to the selectman in camera this week."

"What do you need your camera for?" one of the parishioners asked, the dumb one. "Are you going to take pictures?"

Father Peter shook his head. "In camera. It's Latin. It means privately, by yourself. I don't want to come out and complain in public about the Neskeet Indians. They're fellow Islanders. They may very well get upset. Plus, it's not a Christian thing to do. They're certainly not going to like me trying to close down their bingo hall."

They talked a while longer and then ended it. Everybody wanted to go home, eat dinner early, and clear the decks for *Dancing with the Stars*, which came on at 8:00 p.m. It was the semifinals that night.

Father Peter Mulcahey would take the lead in being the squeaky wheel and addressing the problem of the Neskeet Indians with the selectmen. He was the Irish fixer.

Investigation

Mindy Sanchez came to the Neskeet offices on a Tuesday in late October. It was still Indian summer with warm days and cool nights. Good sleeping weather. There were still boatloads of tourists, but fewer of the families with children as all the kids were back in Malapan, New Jersey, playing soccer and going to grade school. It was a ripe time.

Mindy came off the boat in her Louboutin heels with the red soles and started walking on the long wooden walkway from the ferry to the terminal. She immediately got her right heel caught in the gap between two planks and damn near went ass over tea kettle.

She had to step out of her shoe and reach down to pull it out of the crack. She examined it carefully. It was a little dinged on the heel, but nothing really noticeable.

She was grateful she didn't break the heel off in the gap between the wharf planks. Then she would have had to wear her sneakers that she brought along for running. What a disaster.

She went straight up Main Street in her dark business suit, dress cut above the knee, pearl necklace, pulling her roll-on bag behind her. She was staying overnight. On top of her wheelie, she had a hard-sided audit satchel with a hinged top with all her BIA business papers and laptop inside.

She came clomping up the stairs and into the Neskeet offices. She was immediately befriended by Carol. Mindy, with her cleavage and tight body, found her doppelgänger in the sexy young Indian administrator. They liked each other immediately. She stashed her things in the conference room and then sat down to meet with Bill Fletcher.

He didn't know what to expect from talking to Harold Schumer on the phone before, but one look at Mindy with the heels, the pearls, and the chest, and he knew what to expect. It was going to be a full-on audit colonoscopy, an ass kicking of the worst kind administered by the federal government. He was ready though.

They spent a little while on the preliminaries, but Mindy didn't beat around the bush. She jumped right in. "So we want to look at all your formation documents and incorporation records that you filed with us in the first quarter. Just a routine check, that's all."

"No problem," Fletcher said. He set her up in the conference room where he could bring her the tribe's paperwork to spread out, and he could also keep an eye on her through the glass door as well.

That took all afternoon. After Mindy reviewed all the material, she had Carrie take her for a tour of the Equinox to see the retail side of the Neskeets.

Later in the afternoon, they went up-Island in Carrie's little blue Mini Cooper to see the buffalo and the animal husbandry thing. Carrie knew that the big beasts were a crowd pleaser and that a desk jockey like Mindy would enjoy seeing the gigantic animals. They rode up to the buffalo preserve with the windows open, the warm fall air blowing in.

"Do you like working with the Neskeets?" Mindy figured she'd do a little girl bonding on the ride up-Island. Put Carrie at ease.

"I am a Neskeet," Carrie said and laughed.

"How is that? You don't look like an Indian."

"How do Indians look?" Carrie frowned and put on a fake defensive posture. "That sounds racist."

She knew that going on the attack and always using the word *racist* put white people on the defensive immediately when talking about Indians and the Neskeets. They frequently never recovered. She loved doing it.

Mindy backed off immediately.

"I'm sorry. I didn't mean anything by it. It's just that you don't have any facial features that reflect your Indian heritage, and your name isn't a traditional Indian surname from the area. At least one that I'd expect."

Carrie had got her good. She started laughing. "Mindy, I'm just pulling your leg. I'm no real Indian. I'm just an average Sally. I created the Indian membership thing to drive traffic to our website and to build our retail base. It's worked great. I'll make you a member of the Neskeet Nation too, if you want to be one. You'll get a cool membership card in the mail in a week. Just like the casinos have."

Mindy smiled and thought about it for a while. She then realized that was how the tribe's membership was growing in size so rapidly. She nodded.

"Yeah, I want to be a member. Sign me up." Mindy took out her designer pen and wrote a few notes in her leather notepad as they rode up-Island.

The women turned the conversation to cosmetics and how Carrie was developing a line of Indian light facial moisturizers to sell on a special web page she was designing.

She had seen several top ex-supermodels shilling for moisturizers on late-night TV on the Home Shopping Channel and QVC. She watched Cindy Crawford market herself with a whole package of goodies in tow—face creams, facial exercises, night masks, even a fake German doctor extolling the benefits of the product with some kind of herbal mix-in. It was all very powerful stuff.

So Carrie decided, why not Indian moisturizers? She could sell the cream in the Equinox and establish a whole new product line, a line that responded to the needs of women with a natural Indian theme and local ingredients to go along with it.

She told Mindy how she had met a woman on the Island who was already there making small-batch boutique facial cream in her kitchen and selling it in the upscale salons and hair studios on the Island. She went by the name of Suzie Moonbeam and sold it out of the trunk of her hybrid Highlander. She was a New Age hippie, a modern-day Aquarius, and Carrie was immediately drawn to her.

Suzie was lacing the cream with a key secret ingredient that she called seabuckthornberry. It was some kind of elemental thing, like rose hips or something, Carrie thought. It sounded part hokey and part hip and part hedonistic. Carrie tried to Google it and then tried Wikipedia, but she came up dry every time. She figured that she was probably spelling it wrong as she searched. It might have even been fake for all she knew, something that Suzie made up, but it sounded so essential and romantic.

It didn't matter what it was, really, because it had the key element of mystery, which was what Carrie knew it needed. She had tried the cream and really liked it. Suzie was selling it for $50 for a small container, and it was flying off the shelves in the local salons.

She and Suzie were going to start marketing the cream under Carrie's Natural Indian product line and see what happens. The plan was to cut the price to $19.99, include a facial zit remover, an Indian hair braiding tool, and an elastic scrunchie with little Indian beads on it. Carrie knew it would work.

Carrie planned on doing a photo shoot with sexy Carol from Bill's office, his hot little Indian admin girl. She was going to get a professional photographer to shoot a series of Carol-in-the-beach-grass shots, with her barefoot in an alpaca sweater and tight jeans, black hair touched by the wind. She'd be the natural essence of the product. Carrie figured the cream would fly off the shelves. She just needed some time this fall to put the marketing campaign together. It was fun and totally radical.

"Does it work?" Mindy asked, back now in the conversation, talking about the cream as they rode back down-Island in Carrie's little car. The buffalo tour had been a big success.

"Go in my bag and check it out," Carrie said. She pointed to her shoulder bag with the hemp strap. Mindy rooted around inside for a minute and finally came out with a small container of beige skin cream. "That's it," Carrie said. "It's great stuff!"

Mindy picked up on Carrie's enthusiasm and pocketed the cream. "I'll try it tonight in my hotel room."

There it was. Carrie had made an ally of Mindy just like that. The two women had bonded over face cream. Mindy was becoming Neskeet quicker than she realized.

Later that night after dinner and a bottle of red wine with Carrie and Bill Fletcher recapping the day, Mindy Sanchez was back in her room at the Island Inn. She had her Louboutin high heels kicked off in the corner. She was wearing an XL powder blue Neskeet Nation T-shirt as a nightie with her short bikini bottom underwear. She was lying in bed with three pillows propped up behind her, the flat-screen TV on mute, talking to Harold Schumer.

He had left a message on her voice mail. "Call me tonight. It's urgent."

"It's Mindy. What's up?" she said in a clipped voice after the cell call connected. She hated doing business so late at night. This was her relaxation time.

She had her glasses on and was reading the ingredients on the jar of face cream that Carrie had given her in the afternoon. She was right, there it was—seabuckthornberry as a key ingredient. She had no idea what it was but thought it was cool, just like Carrie had said. She'd get her laptop fired up and Google it to find out. In the meantime, she was half listening to Harold as he spoke.

"Did you find anything good out?" Harold asked. He didn't waste any time, particularly at ten o'clock at night. This was cutting into his own reading time, his Civil War history time, so he got right to the point.

"Find anything good as in what? They're good people, Harold. Bill Fletcher actually seems legit. His paperwork was in great shape. The best I've ever seen. Ever." Mindy had fired a torpedo at Harold.

"How about the money. Any funny stuff? Personal accounts, commingling of funds, all the bullshit things?"

"No, absolutely none of that. But I didn't audit the account either."

Mindy looked down over her glasses at her toes and wiggled them as she talked to Harold. She decided that she had to put on a fresh coat of polish. Her polish was starting to chip. *Shit*, she thought. She wondered if she had brought any toenail polish that matched.

Mindy could tell that Harold was agitated and was looking for something for her to write up. So she tossed him a bone. "There was one thing."

"What's that?"

"Fletcher's signing up new tribal members without doing thorough background checks on their ancestry. It's almost like a casino thing. He gives out membership cards, and they're good for points. They become instant Indians, no checking."

"Points?"

"Yeah, to buy stuff on their website. Like T-shirts and mushrooms and coffee mugs and things."

Harold Schumer got right to the point. "That's not good enough. We need something substantial. Something to take them down. Not little penny-ante stuff. You've gotta get something more substantial than that."

"Well, that's all I've got so far," Mindy said, exasperated.

"Look, Sampson wants to pull the grant from Fletcher and get the money back. All of it. Somebody on top is putting pressure on him."

"Like who, a senator?" Mindy said immediately.

"Could be," Harold said. "I have no idea, really," he lied. "But I'll write a revocation letter tomorrow and send it out FedEx in the afternoon. Fletcher will get it the next day. Finish up your work in the morning and come back to Washington tomorrow night. We need you here to help put this together."

"God. I'll have to change my reservation now. I hope I can. They may charge me a change fee," Mindy said. "This is stressing me out."

Harold couldn't believe what he was hearing. Mindy was worried about a change fee while Rome was burning.

"Don't worry about it. I'll approve it. It'll be fine."

"Okay, but my findings are not going to be earth-shattering, just so you know. These guys are real modern-day Indians. Better than most. It all seems legit."

Harold Schumer frowned and looked at his watch. It was 10:30 p.m. all of a sudden. Christ. He only had a half hour to read before he had to walk the basset hound and then go to bed.

"It doesn't matter. Get back tomorrow. I need you here. We're circling the wagons on the Neskeets."

Red Sky at Night

"Jesus, Mary, and Joseph" was all Father Peter Mulcahey could say when he saw the monstrous fire burning out of control. He couldn't believe it.

He was shocked as he stood at the base of Main Street in Vineyard Haven in the cool night air. He looked out at the scene in front of him. There was a clutch of fire trucks and police cars and official people all running around like chickens with their heads cut off. Hoses were everywhere, and water was running down the street in little rivers.

"What happened?" Father Peter asked the policeman standing at one of the blue wooden barriers they had put up at the bottom of the street.

"It's the A&P, Father. It's bad. It exploded in flames. It went right up," the policeman said as he looked back at the wall of heat and fire. "It started about an hour ago. Two alarms right off the bat. I don't think they'll be able to save it. Just look."

Father Peter was looking at it, wide-eyed. He couldn't believe his good luck. "The Lord provides," he said under his breath to no one in particular.

"Go around by Cottage Street, Father, and you can get a better look if you're interested," the policeman said helpfully. "It's a tinderbox, so be careful though. The sparks are flying everywhere."

He went back to work directing traffic and talking on his Nextel.

"Yeah, I'll be careful," Father Peter said. He walked around the edge of the commercial district to come up Middle Street and then turned right on Cottage to get a better look.

When he turned onto the small feeder street, he finally got the money shot of the A&P burning to the ground in a mass of smoke and flames, just like the policeman had said. He was almost giddy; he was so happy. He went up to one of the firefighters who was adjusting a valve beneath an array of gauges on the side of a big red pumper truck. It was parked on the street, diesel engine idling high, powering the pumps and the machinery.

"Sweet Jesus, what happened to the A&P, can you tell me?" Father Peter asked as he switched into his sympathetic piety mode for a brief conversation.

The fireman looked up at the priest with a soot-covered face. "We don't know, Father. It happened so fast, like spontaneous combustion. It's a shit storm for sure. All we're trying to do now is save the buildings next door, but it's tough."

"Is everybody all right?"

"Well, there's no one inside that we can tell, so far."

"What do you think?"

The fireman checked his control panel for a second before answering. "I think it's arson myself, to be honest. The fire just started too quickly and moved too fast to be natural. But that's just me, Father. I'm a suspicious guy by nature." He looked over at the priest. "We'll know soon enough though, probably tomorrow when the state arson team gets here."

"Now why would anybody want to harm the Indians that run that simple business, will you tell me?"

"I dunno, Father. That's what we'll find out."

Father Peter lingered for a while, talking to the other firebugs and locals, everybody watching the Neskeet bingo emporium burn down. *There was something cleansing and elemental about a big fire*, he thought. He watched the lumber crackle and sparks shoot into the clear night sky.

The firemen were dousing the roofs of the adjacent buildings with big heavy streams of water so the fire wouldn't spread. They were busy beavers. Whoever set the blaze, Father Peter concluded, was a skilled fire starter, like the Indians of yore. *How ironic*, he thought.

Irony aside, Father Peter was happy, as happy as he'd been in a long, long time. His problems with competition from the Neskeets on the bingo front were solved just like that. Instant gratification. But he knew that Bill Fletcher was resourceful and would eventually regroup and find another place to set up shop for his gambling. The guy was unstoppable. Father Peter would make the most of the respite in the meantime.

He got bored looking at the fire after a while and walked slowly down the street toward the shadows on the waterfront. He accepted the miracle. He whipped out his iPhone and called Margaret.

"Do I have a story for you."

"Peter? Why are you calling so late?" Margaret said, sleep in her voice.

"It's me, the Lord's apostle himself," he said. "Do you want to come out for a drink with me and celebrate some good news?" He was almost ecstatic.

"Peter, I'm in bed reading a book," Margaret said. She was curious though as to why he called so late. It was after eleven o'clock at night. That was all the invite Peter Mulcahey needed.

"Good. I'll be right over with a bottle of champagne. We've got a victory," he said into his phone.

Father Peter didn't give Margaret a chance to vacillate and say no to his late-night visit. He pushed the End Call button on his iPhone and quickly put it in his suit coat pocket as he started walking. He remembered that he had a bottle of cheap champagne in the rectory refrigerator for celebrations like this.

He decided that it was going to be a night for celebration of the soul and, in all probability, the flesh too.

*   *   *

Bill Fletcher was at the other end of Commercial Street, standing in the crowd and watching the fire burn out of control. He wasn't shocked by any means. He figured that it was no accident that his Indian bingo parlor was set ablaze.

He didn't store any flammable materials in the bingo space, so he pretty much knew that this was an outside job by someone skilled and talented. He realized that people were starting to intensely dislike the Neskeets and that success ultimately bred jealousy.

He figured that he also needed to start watching his and Carrie's flank more closely. There suddenly seemed to be more detractors than believers outside the tribe. He needed to develop an exit strategy fast in the event of an emergency. He resolved to start the next morning.

Fletcher got into his Vista Cruiser and headed toward the waterfront. The ferry terminal was empty late at night with the big terminal lights casting an eerie glow over the docks and the parking lots. He had a lot on his mind.

Carl Sunapee stood in the shadows of the building nearby, just out of the arc of the terminal lights. He was next to an empty red plastic jerrican of gasoline.

He watched Fletcher drive away. He smiled as he noticed a small dark puddle of transmission fluid on the ground where Fletcher had parked. Carl shook his head. He had told Fletcher to get that fixed or he'd have problems with the engine later on.

They never listen, he thought as he threw the gas can into the bushes and headed down the street.

Deliver the Letter

E-mails, tweets, and countless Facebook posts poured in to Bill Fletcher and Carrie Nation over the course of the next forty-eight hours. The sympathy was raw and intense.

Everybody was sorry that the Neskeet bingo hall was toast. It was a sad thing, a civic and cultural loss for the town—all that cheap $2.50 wine in the big plastic cups and hundred-and-fifty-dollar bingo pots gone. Poof, just like that. The tribe was hurting.

Bill Fletcher, not so much. The various business lines of the Neskeet Nation were still flowing significant amounts of cash. They had over $13 million in total in their bank account at that point. Now Fletcher was focused and thinking practically about who in town was so pissed off at him that they'd torch his bingo emporium so viciously.

Carrie cried in bed most of that first night at the tragedy but then started to come out of it in the morning when she realized that she no longer had to do the scheduling for the bingo hall or manage the bartenders. Now she had her nights free to do other more fun things like hot yoga. At least until they got another bingo parlor up and running.

She and Bill had passionate sex in the morning in the big bed with the six-point deer antlers hanging on the wall directly above them. The sun was rising, and the mallard ducks were landing on Sengekontacket Pond close by. It was all very emotional for Carrie, a watershed of tears and joy all at the same time. The whole Indian thing was an unbelievable roller coaster. She came twice.

Later than morning, Fletcher was riding in the Vista Cruiser on Worcester Avenue to the post office to pick up the Neskeet mail, his daily rite of passage. It was cool out, he had the windows up, and he was listening to WMVY, the NPR station on the Cape, composing his thoughts.

Carrie stayed home to tweet and respond to all the offerings of grief and Indian love for the Neskeets and their lost tribal bingo hall.

Fletcher kept coming back to the thought that it was Carl Sunapee who had taken matters into his own hands at the A&P and set the building on fire. He also knew that the Neskeet bingo had cut deeply into the profits of Blessed Sacrament's own Catholic bingo games in Oak Bluffs, but he figured that Father Mulcahey would never resort to violence to shut the Neskeets down. You never knew though. Maybe he had someone do it for him, a little arson for hire along the way, Fletcher fantasized.

Fletcher parked in the fifteen-minute drop-off zone and went inside to get the mail. He had two pink slips for certified letters in the stack. His stomach immediately tightened. Nothing ever good came in certified letters, he well knew.

He got the letters at the cage in front after he signed both of the pink slips, pushing them across the counter and heightening the sense of drama. He also had a huge stack of regular mail, mostly bills and more T-shirt orders to contend with, all part of the daily paper flow.

He took the whole pile to an empty counter over by the window and examined the certified letters. One was from the Bureau of Indian Affairs and the other was from a law firm that he didn't know. Both were not good signs. His bowels tightened right up. He opened the law firm letter first.

> The offices of Murray, Cohen, and Sullivan hereby represent
> Sara Golding, a recent visitor to the Neskeet Buffalo Petting Zoo
> in Oak Bluffs, who was seriously injured by virtue of a violent
> buffalo bite.

He went on and quickly skimmed the letter. The family of the little girl who got nipped by the buffalo last month at Waban Park had hired themselves a personal injury law firm.

That little bastard child, Fletcher thought. If she hadn't tormented the damn beast, this never would have happened. As it was, the buffalo nip had barely broken the girl's skin. The kid had to toughen up. Fletcher's lawyerly mind immediately jumped to the bottom line. He quickly calculated it as $25,000 for the injury and $25,000 for the girl's pain and suffering. So $50,000. all in, and the problem would be solved. The family's law firm would take one third, so they'd walk away with $35,000 net. Not bad for directing just one letter to the Neskeets written by a PI law firm.

He had a $5,000 deductible on the personal injury and liability policy that he ran for all the Neskeet businesses. So he'd pay the $5K, shut up, and be done with it. The bastards.

It was just a cost of doing business, nothing more. That and no more buffalo petting over at Waban Park. He had learned his lesson. They'd only do the tours in the more controlled environment of the farm up-Island from now on.

He put the lawyer letter aside and opened the Bureau of Indian Affairs letter. It was a two-pager, but it felt heavy for some reason. He skimmed the letter quickly, looking for its essence.

He found it pretty fast. Harold Schumer came on strong in the second paragraph and said that the certification of the Neskeet tribe had been made in error. The US government wanted its money back, all twelve million dollars of it in total, and they wanted it back immediately.

Harold wrote that the Neskeets were either (a) illegitimate or (b) simply a subtribe of the Aquinnah Fluevogs and therefore subject to the tribal authority that currently existed under Carl Sunapee. Bill Fletcher's vision started to blur around the edges for a second, and he flushed red. Carl Sunapee, his nemesis. There was no way, he thought, that he was going to be reporting to Carl. Just no friggin' way.

His hands started shaking, and his heart was palpitating, beating like a jackhammer. He put the letter down and tried to regroup. *This isn't happening*, he thought. He almost expected to see a smiley-faced emoticon at the bottom of the letter under Harold Schumer's flowery government signature saying that it was all a joke, a goof.

But there was no little emoticon at the bottom smiling with one slit eye, no mention of a joke—just a cc to five people at the Justice Department and the FBI. Bill Fletcher knew then that the Neskeets were in trouble.

He grabbed the pile of mail, the bad letters on top, and headed out to the car. He tossed the pile of mail onto the passenger seat, started up the big Olds '88, threw it in Drive, and headed out, trailing a thin ribbon of red transmission fluid behind him.

*   *   *

Jim Barry, the selectman, was sitting with Mike Francesca in Kona Koffee, eating a sugar-rolled doughnut and drinking a regular roast coffee. The sugar granules were big and crystalline and covered the outside of the doughnut. It was beautiful. They stuck to Jim's tongue as he savored a small bite of the artery-clogging confection.

"That's too bad what happened to Bill Fletcher's place over in Vineyard Haven, huh?" Mike asked. He turned his Nextel down low and took a long sip of his coffee, practiced over many years of police work on the Oak Bluffs force. Nobody could savor a cup of joe better than Mike Francesca. He lovingly fingered the cup as he spoke, like he was having sex with the hot liquid.

Jim Barry swallowed. "Yeah, it's a tragedy all right. But on the bright side, it solves a lot of problems for us, you and me. I'm a politician, so I'm always looking to solve problems and trying to keep people happy. It's my job."

"Who you keeping happy?"

"Blessed Sacrament Parish for one. They were sucking hind tit once those renegade Indians started the night bingo at the A&P." Jim nodded to confirm his thought.

"I gotta tell you, my wife liked it over there though," Mike said. "Won two pots at a hundred fifty each. We were able to buy new tires for her Jeep. Not all four, mind you, but a nice pair for the front. Michelin snow lifters."

"Well, my wife liked the bingo there too," Jim replied. "Now she's pissed off about it all. I just turned it off. I couldn't listen."

"At least the Catholics are happy about it. They'll be making more money again with their own lame bingo over in the parish hall. No competition. I hope they ramp it up a bit though."

Mike Francesca pondered that for a moment.

"I think that ole Carl is happy with the outcome too."

"Carl Sunapee?"

"Yeah."

"I know he's happy with it. He hates the fuckers. Fletcher's group is competition for him everywhere. Anything bad happens to the Neskeets, Carl's happy."

Mike Francesca pursed his lips and tapped his coffee cup as he listened. He didn't tell Jim that he wouldn't be surprised to find out that old Carl, enterprising Indian chief that he was, was even the mastermind of the fire at the A&P himself.

*　　*　　*

Over in Aquinnah, Carl Sunapee and the executive council of the Fluevogs were sitting in the tribal council room, meeting and eating again.

Carl had called the noon meeting and then went out and bought everyone steak and cheese subs, complete with sodas, chips, and a jar of hot banana peppers. All the trimmings. He was feeling expansive, and they were celebrating.

The four men unfolded the paper wrappers and tucked in to the steak bombs.

"Man, it's a shame what happened to Bill Fletcher and those Neskeets. I don't wish that shit on anyone."

"Bullshit," Manny Fernandez said between bites. "That fake Indian was getting bigger than the rest of us. And we're the real deal. It serves him right. I ain't sheddin' no tears for that so-called Indian motherfucker."

Carl didn't say a word. He took a big bite of his sandwich loaded with hot peppers and onions. He handled it gingerly for a big man, not wanting to damage the sub roll loaded with the grilled shaved steak.

Finally he spoke. "I can't say as I'm surprised at what happened. Seems like divine intervention if you ask me. Karma, you know? That guy's not on the up and up, so all this bad luck hittin' him is sort of par for the course, if you ask me."

There it was, Carl trying to sound all Zen-like about it, evenhanded. The oracle of Aquinnah, invoking the gods and all. Manny picked up on it quickly. It was easy for Carl to take the high road, be gracious, now that Bill Fletcher had just taken a major kick in the teeth from a cash flow and competition perspective. Not that he was happy, of course. But he sure as shit wasn't sad.

"I don't approve of violence, as you all know," Carl said. He pointed his sub sandwich at the group for emphasis. "I'm hoping that this ends up being an accident in the end and not arson. Give Fletcher something to think on, but nothing serious, just bad luck."

The men nodded. They ate their subs and talked about more upbeat Fluevog topics like the upcoming tribal elder day and whether the Patriots had the mojo to beat the Colts that weekend.

But there was no getting around it. A little dose of schadenfreude was just what the doctor ordered to get the group feeling positive and upbeat about themselves. The Neskeet misery was a balm for the Fluevog soul.

Round the World

Bill Fletcher was in his office in pressed jeans and a casual button-down shirt with yet another large cup of Kona Koffee dark roast on his desktop. He was working the phone with Donna Stevens over at the bank.

"That's right, Donna, I'd like to transfer all of the money to an account in the Dutch West Indies. The thing is, I want to do it this afternoon."

He took a sip of coffee as he let that sink in for a second with the efficient bank vice president whom he now knew on an intimate basis owing to all the deposits and various banking transactions he had done with her since he started the Neskeet Nation account there so many months ago.

The line was quiet. He knew that she was probably peeing through her Spanx underwear at that moment, panicked about what to do. He decided that she was an Island MILF and that under different circumstances, they could be at a bar drinking sea breezes together and flirting. But not now.

"Which island?" Donna Stevens asked into the phone, trying to buy some time. Her heart started palpitating. Fletcher had just called her up out of the blue and immediately started into this crazy conversation about moving all his money out of the bank and around the world. Jack Fraker would have shit a brick if he was there.

Fletcher wanted to say "Does it matter, bitch?" when he heard the question, but he held his tongue and paused. He figured he'd tell her the truth to start. He knew she was just making happy talk, stalling.

"Curaçao."

"Curaçao? Oh, that's a beautiful place."

"I've never been there, actually," Fletcher said. He ignored her inane comment. "Can you get a wire ready for me right now, Donna, and I'll be over in thirty minutes to sign for it? Unfortunately, it needs to go out today."

"Isn't that a money-laundering center?" Donna Stevens said as she pushed on. *What the hell*, she thought. She'd put it out there just to get a laugh from Bill Fletcher, keep it light, while she decided what the hell to do.

"I wasn't aware of that," Fletcher said to her comment. For all he knew, the phone call was being recorded. He needed to get the money moving today so he was going to be straight and businesslike the whole way.

But he made sure to keep the bank vice president engaged so as not to frighten her. It was like he had a big striped bass on the line, and he was slowly reeling her in. He couldn't spook her. He needed to make it all sound plausible.

"No, we're just doing a test of the Neskeet Nation cash management system. Our auditors want us to test our wiring capabilities both inbound and out. Calvin and Smith, the Big Four firm? They want it. For verification, you know." He was making it up as he went.

Donna Stevens, bank vice president, didn't want to appear stupid to Bill Fletcher. She only had an associate degree in business management after all from Cape Cod Community College, and that was nothing to write home about. She had partied most of her time in school and just crammed for her exams. She was good at cramming.

But she knew that Fletcher was customer number one at the bank and, more importantly, in her boss, Jack Fraker's, eyes too. That was plenty enough for her.

And she didn't want to appear stupid because frankly, it seemed dumb to need to move all the Neskeet money out to test the system. Why couldn't he just send a wire for a hundred dollars to see if it worked? It would be the same thing.

"I'm sending you an e-mail with the wiring instructions right now, Donna. We've got to move quickly." Bill Fletcher kept the pressure on and kept it personal with Donna Stevens.

His finger hit the Enter button on his HP desktop keyboard, and the wiring instructions zipped over to the Martha's Vineyard Bank almost instantly via a router in Boston and another back in Falmouth.

It was simple instructions, just a few lines of accounting-speak text. They said

Bank of Boston
Boston, MA
ABA 232 5748 5436
Credit To: Bank of Curacao Corporation, NA
Account: 927-385-187

Those brief lines of code were about to move Bill Fletcher's millions to another part of the world in milliseconds.

"Now how much do you want the wire for?" Donna came back around to the essential question again, like a golden retriever with a duck in her mouth on the marsh at Sengekontacket.

"How much is there in the account?"

"Which one?"

"The main one." Fletcher was patient, almost there.

It was quiet for a moment. Fletcher heard Donna clicking the keyboard at her desk, looking up the account balance.

"$13,237,542.38 is the total in the main account."

"Then make the wire transfer for that amount, the whole thing, like I said before," Fletcher said. He hated repeating himself, and he was getting exasperated, but he didn't want to show it. It was Friday, and he wanted the money moved that day to get a two-day head start in front of the feds.

"We'll have to close your account at that point," Donna said.

The light immediately flashed on for Fletcher. He caught her drift and knew that he couldn't close the account fully; otherwise, panic would set in.

"Oh, shit. I'm sorry. Leave a hundred thousand dollars in the account. That's a small amount, and the auditors won't mind, I'm sure. If they complain, I'll deal with it."

Fletcher knew how to calm Donna down and make it sound real. Leaving a hundred thousand in the account was genius, him saying it was a small amount and her thinking that it was gigantic and too much for him to walk away from.

"And send me the bank's wiring instructions for inbound deposits too, Donna. I'm gonna need them on Monday because all this money needs to be wired back in to the bank. Remember?"

"When are you wiring it back in?"

"Monday morning, as soon as I can," Fletcher said.

That made Donna Stevens much calmer. As soon as she knew it was all coming back in to the bank in two days, she set up the wire quickly and efficiently.

"So how much will it be for?" Fletcher asked again.

He heard the fast click of the keyboard again. Donna Stevens was much more confident that she was doing the right thing this time.

"It's for $13,137,542.38, which is the total less the $100,000 for the account maintenance."

"Perfect. That matches my numbers," Fletcher said, not really having a clue about how much was actually in the account.

Both people were quiet for a second. It was a shitload of money.

"The wire will be ready in twenty minutes," Donna Stevens said. "You'll have to come in to sign it."

"No problem," Fletcher said.

That was one meeting he was not going to miss.

After the call ended, Donna Stevens got up from her desk and went over and closed the door to her office and composed herself for a minute by breathing deeply. Then she picked up her phone again. She knew what she had to do.

She had been trained well. She immediately called up Jack Fraker to get his approval to wire all the Neskeet money out of the bank and find out what the hell was going on.

The bank had reinvested most of Fletcher's money in ninety-day treasury notes after seeing that he didn't use the funds ever for withdrawal. He only deposited money regularly.

If she was going to do the wire, she'd have to use the bank's repo line with their parent company in Boston to fund it. She couldn't redeem the T-notes that afternoon, and there'd be big breakage fees on top anyway if she tried.

Their parent company charged Prime +250 basis points for short-term draws like this. For thirteen million bucks, it would be a big charge to the bank branch, she knew. Jack would definitely shit a brick over this.

He wasn't going to like it. It'd wipe out all their profit from the Treasuries for the quarter. But she hadn't been able to stall Fletcher until Monday. Plus there was the bigger issue of having him just wire all his money out of the bank. That was everything, the whole shooting match. *Christ, what to do!* she thought to herself as she waited for the call to go through.

As luck would have it, Jack Fraker was in an all-day board meeting in the bank's Hyannis branch that Friday. In fact, as Donna Stevens waited on the line to speak with him, he was being grilled by the board on several credits that were going bad in his portfolio in the current economy and what was he doing about them. It wasn't pretty.

An administrative assistant came in to the meeting with a note that she silently handed to Jack Fraker. He paused, read it, and then came out of the room five seconds later. He was frazzled from the grilling and went immediately into an empty office to take Donna Steven's call. *WTF?* he thought. Why would she call him now in the middle of the board meeting?

Jack Fraker already had a migraine at that point and needed a drink badly even though it was only the middle of the afternoon. He was getting the shit kicked out of him in the meeting. But he needed his job like everyone else, and badly. Particularly in this economy. With a wife that didn't work outside the home, he was staring down the barrel of three more years of tuition at Cornell for his son, the sophomore, the gifted English major.

He was having trouble concentrating on what Donna was trying to say about Bill Fletcher on the phone. He couldn't understand the issue.

"Look, if he wants to move some money, let him do it. The account's big enough. He's got millions, for Chrissakes." For the life of him, he didn't understand why she was bothering him about something so trivial and basic as a wire transfer. She was a God damn VP, for Chrissakes. Make a decision and move on, he was about to say.

But at that precise moment when Donna was about to tell him that Bill Fletcher wanted to move all his thirteen million dollars out, William Graves, the chairman of the bank and Jack Fraker's big boss, barged in.

Bill Graves had gone to Harvard, been captain of the football team, and then went on to Harvard Business School. He was a big, imposing guy with a presence, the biggest fish in the small world of Boston regional banking and, in particular, Martha's Vineyard Bank. He always got what he wanted.

And what he wanted right then was Jack Fraker back in the conference room in his seat, taking the shit. Pronto. He pointed his elegant finger in the Brooks Brothers shirt at Jack and then pointed back to the boardroom. Graves then made the cut-across-the-throat sign with his finger and pointed at the phone. "They want you back in there. Now."

That was all Bill Graves had to say as he turned and walked out. He didn't wait for any answer. It was like he had attached a steel cable directly to Jack Fraker's balls and started pulling him back into the boardroom. No time to wait or question.

Jack got up immediately. But before he left the room, he yelled one more sentence into the phone. "Goddamn it, Donna. Just do the bloody wire like he wants!" And then he slammed the handset down hard on the phone and headed back into the conference room to take his licking.

He shook his head as he walked down the corridor. *Why couldn't Donna just take the initiative and keep Fletcher happy?* he wondered. If Fletcher wanted a blow job, then she should give him one, no questions asked. It was that simple. The guy was the biggest customer the bank had in ten years.

Bill Fletcher was Jack Fraker's ace card, his protection, at the bank. It was his relationship with Fletcher that kept all those millions sitting quietly at the bank. Nothing more. He had to protect his big kahuna and keep him happy. He'd talk to Donna when he got back on the Island.

The phone went dead, and Jack Fraker had left the room before Donna had a chance to explain what Fletcher was really trying to do, to explain the whole story. But ultimately, she had got the answer that she was looking for. Do the wire and be quick about it, no more questions asked. That she could do.

So while Donna Fletcher didn't give Bill Fletcher a blow job, she did inadvertently give her old boss, Jack Fraker, a good fucking over, although neither of them realized it at the time.

*   *   *

At the same time, up the street at the Neskeet offices, Bill Fletcher was busy. After he ended his call with Donna Stevens, he checked his e-mail messages. Nothing. He quickly sent one to Harold Schumer and cc'd Mindy Sanchez right then before they sent one to him.

To: Harold.Schumer@bia.gov
Cc: Mindy.Sanchez@ bia.gov
From: W.Fletcher@neskeet.net
Date: 12/1/09 02:11 PM
Subject: RE: BIA Letter

Harold & Mindy,

I received your letter about the return of the funds and am extremely disappointed. I don't understand what is going on, but I am happy to oblige in the interim and return the grant monies until we can sort it all out and provide backup. Please send me the BIA wiring instructions.

Regards, Bill.

Bill Fletcher
Tribal Chief and CEO
The Neskeet Nation

With a quick stroke, he sent it off to Washington, DC. He then immediately opened his Notes Out of Office Assistant and typed in the following:

> Away on personal business thru Monday, 11/25, with very limited access to e-mail and voice mail. Will return Tuesday, 11/26. If this is urgent, please contact Carol Ault at 508 693 1212.

He had the weekend and one business day. That would give him plenty of time as a head start. He logged off his computer and got up to leave.

"I'm out the rest of the afternoon," he said to Carol, who was surfing the Victoria's Secret website for bikini underwear for herself. She always bought it at least one size too small as the men in her life seemed to like it that way, sort of skimpy and tight. "Don't forward any calls, just take messages, and I'll get back to 'em later. If anybody asks, I'm out fishing."

He didn't wait for her to answer. He bounded down the stairs and out the door. When she was sure he wasn't coming back, Carol jumped back on the Victoria's Secret website to continue her underwear shopping. She had all afternoon now. Carol reached down and casually took off her high heels. God, sometimes they hurt her feet so fucking much.

She wrinkled her nose for a second as she scrolled down through pages of underwear models. Bill Fletcher had never told her that he liked fishing, and she hadn't picked up on it around the office. She was a little surprised too. It wasn't like him to leave early in the afternoon when he still had work to do.

Oh well. *Maybe he and Carrie were going home to screw*, she thought. Carrie said they did it a lot. She smiled, thinking.

*   *   *

Bill Fletcher didn't waste any time. He watched his watch, and when it was precisely twenty minutes after his phone call, he strode casually into the bank to do his business.

He hooked up with Donna Stevens in the conference room with all the paperwork. She looked nervous and fidgeted a lot. He was Cool Hand Luke.

"Everything all right?" he asked as he reviewed the wiring instructions with his head down, focused on the details. He couldn't have a fuckup now.

There it was, $13,137,542.38 waiting to go. The number was burned in his brain.

"Yes, no problems. I even spoke with Jack Fraker a few minutes ago. I needed his approval for a wire this size."

Now Fletcher's bowel tightened. He had forgotten that she probably needed to get approval for a thirteen-million-dollar wire from her boss. "No problems?"

"Jack was fine with it."

Fletcher smiled. "Good." He signed the bottom of the wire with a giant flourish. Something to remember him by, an autograph.

"We need to talk about some longer-term investment options next week when all this money is back at the bank," Fletcher said. "This is a long-term relationship after all, and I want to solidify it."

"That would be great, Bill. I'll see when Jack is available."

Fletcher could inspire confidence when he wanted to. Donna's spirits soared knowing that Bill Fletcher was going to meet next week with her and Jack about long-term investment options for his money. This was all going to work out after all.

He stayed and waited for confirmation that the wire went out. It was 2:35 p.m., and he knew that wires usually stopped on Friday at 3:00 p.m. He was cutting it close.

Donna Stevens came back smiling ten minutes later with a paper confirmation. She handed it to him along with a small white box of candy. It was saltwater taffy.

"Here you go, Bill. Everything's all set, the wire just went through, no problem. Also, here's a little gift from us, a present. We're giving it out to all our best customers, a little Cape Cod treat." She smiled warmly. "You qualify."

They both laughed. Bill Fletcher left the bank and walked toward his car with the candy. He was going home to work on his laptop privately.

Before he got into the Vista Cruiser, he threw the box of saltwater taffy into a green trash barrel on Main Street without even looking inside. He hated candy.

Money Management 101

Back home, Fletcher was alone as Carrie was still at the Equinox, working until six. It was nice and quiet. He got on his cell phone with his Bluetooth connection.

He first called his advisor at Horgan Smith, the big securities concern. He had set up an account there about six months ago when all the money started rolling in. Fletcher talked regularly, probably once every two weeks, to Paul Sanders, the young client-account exec assigned to his account.

He wasted no time in talking bluntly to Sanders as the situation deteriorated on the Vineyard. He didn't have time to waste.

He also didn't have to put on a charade when talking to Paul Sanders. Just the truth, the whole truth, and nothing but the truth. Well, most of it anyway, Fletcher figured. He didn't want to alarm Sanders either and have him go to the authorities.

"Bill, good morning." Paul Sanders came on the line, bright and energetic, a real go-getter. He was a young turk building his client base. "I've got some great German spiders that I can get you into today at par. You called at a good time. The euro is taking a pounding too, by the way. Maybe we can short some currency on the DAX. Interested?"

Fletcher didn't have time for the security sales talk or investment bullshit. He cut to the chase.

"Paul, I need to move some money right now, and I need your help."

Paul Sanders was a financial shark, instantly attuned to changes in one of his clients. He sensed it then in Fletcher. So he stopped on a dime, just like his BMW 3 Series car did.

"Sure, Bill. Where to and how much?" the broker said. He got right to the point.

"I've got thirteen million in Curaçao right now, and I need it cleaned up pronto."

"How clean do you need it?"

"Really clean. Like Mr. Clean. Pristine. And I need it to be untraceable. Can you do it?"

Sanders sat back in his Aeron chair, quickly thinking. "Yeah, we can do that pretty quickly and easily."

"Then tell me what the mechanics are." Fletcher was a lawyer by training and needed to understand the details, the granularity.

"Well, Curaçao and the Caymans are a good place to start as the money's out of country already and easier to move around. So we don't have any Treasury filings to do. So the next place we move the money is to Basel, Switzerland, for two days in a secure account."

"Is it still safe in Switzerland now?" Fletcher asked. "I thought I just read about a case with Baby Doc Duvalier from Haiti and how the government was able to pierce the corporate veil and get at his money. It took a few years though."

Sanders was impressed as it was obvious that Bill Fletcher knew his stuff.

"You're right on, Bill. It's called the Duvalier Rule, and for dictators, it's the end of a sweet ride for sure. Switzerland is not bulletproof anymore. It used to be the gold standard for money movement, but it hasn't been for about five years. But it's a great intermediate stop in the process. The Swiss move slowly and methodically, and they respond to court orders even more slowly, so it's a great place for delays. If, for example, a creditor was chasing you, we could hold him off for months in the Swiss court system, and the money would be long gone."

"Creditors or the authorities, huh?" Fletcher asked.

"It's all the same process. They'd have to get a court order. But I'd prefer not to know any more details, Bill, if you know what I mean. Otherwise, Horgan won't be able to help you out if there's possible criminal activity involved."

"I understand, Paul. And there's not. There's nothing illegal about this money that I have. Let me be clear about that."

"Hey, I believe you, Bill. Say no more," Paul said.

Paul Sanders had pulled up a graphic while they were talking that showed how to move money around the world the Horgan Smith way so that it got cleaned up and would be harder to trace at every stop. It was a confidential pdf that the High Net Worth Group used for their client presentations. It was all strictly legal. In fact, Horgan's general counsel had reviewed and signed off it as well as their expensive outside lawyers. They had to. Horgan couldn't take any chances.

Sanders continued the discussion. "Then we send it to Dubai and then back to the Bahamas, and you're set. It's all cleansed and untraceable at that point and ready to invest in any asset classes that we want. Totally safe and sound in a week."

Sanders had set the hook with Bill Fletcher. He could do all the wire transfers for him, and then he'd have Fletcher's funds to invest and get hefty commissions on. Fletcher was fine with that. It was basic business quid pro quo.

"You're the man," Fletcher said, dropping down into frat house-speak for Sanders's benefit.

"So when do we start?"

"How about right now?" Fletcher said.

And with that, Paul Sanders, diligent client-account representative on the make, took the details of Fletcher's Curaçao account and began moving the money for him late that afternoon.

It was near Friday night in Manhattan though, and Paul Sanders had already planned a date with a hot blond stockbroker he met at the deli cart on the street earlier in the week. They were doing dinner and drinks in the meatpacking district that night. Paul had high expectations. He even had a Viagra if things moved along. Not that he needed one.

"Gotta work late. Sorry" was the simple SMS text message he sent her at 5:00 p.m. Bill Fletcher was his biggest client by far in terms of investable dollars, and he wasn't about to fuck it up.

She would understand. She was a money babe too.

Ch-ch-ch-changes

Bill Fletcher and Carrie Nation were having dinner and drinks at Artifact, a boutique restaurant in an old house in Edgartown. Carrie had come home from work, had a glass of wine, and showered. She dressed up in a skirt and heels; no Neskeet Nation T-shirt tackiness tonight. And out they went.

Fletcher was finally a little less edgy by the time they got to the restaurant. He had a beer while waiting for Carrie to finish work and close up the shop.

They ordered dinner, and the bottle of wine came over. It was an expensive bottle of cabernet that Carrie had picked out. She had good taste. She tried the wine when it was opened, and they settled in with two big glasses, talking about the week.

"You like the British Virgin Islands?" Fletcher asked, after the waitress had left. "The Caribbean?" Fletcher swirled the deep-red liquid in his glass, looking down into it, in no rush for Carrie's answer. He already knew it.

Yes, I love it there. You know that." Carrie sipped her wine. "It's my fantasy place. Living on a sailboat, hanging out, watching the world go by. It's my sweet spot. Where I go mentally when I'm stressed out, like my mantra for meditation and yoga." Carrie looked at Bill. "Why? Do you want to go on a vacation there this winter? I'm game. Let's go for a month. We have the money."

Fletcher nodded and drank a little more of his wine. "That's a possibility. You know, we've been together this long, and I didn't even know you liked sailing. We didn't get to sail at all this summer either."

"That's okay," Carrie said. "It's not like we weren't busy."

"Well, I'm thinking that we go on an extended vacation south, really get away soon. Spend some time together."

Carrie brightened. "Cool. When do you want to go? After the holidays? I'll close the Equinox after January first like I usually do."

Fletcher put his wineglass down and paused. He smiled at her before answering. "How about tomorrow morning? I've got the tickets and everything. We'll pack tonight."

*   *   *

Later that evening, Paul Sanders sent Bill Fletcher an e-mail that the initial wire transfer had been made and that Fletcher needed to keep track of the money the rest of the way as Horgan Smith no longer was involved and didn't want to be involved. In the event of problems with police and prosecutors, they needed to show a solid firewall of legitimate activity only.

He sent the wiring confirmation and numbers to Fletcher using an encrypted account so as not to make it too easy for anybody coming along and following the e-mail trail.

Fletcher emailed back "Thx" and that he'd be in touch shortly. He left it loose and a little vague as to when and where from.

Bloody Aftermath

Saturday morning dawned cool and bright in Oak Bluffs. It was late November, and the gulls were swirling in a big pattern around the ferry dock, swooping down on the menhaden in the cold clear water below.

It was a picture-book day on the Vineyard. Except the picture wasn't pretty over at the Martha's Vineyard Bank on Main Street in Oak Bluffs.

The bank was open on Saturday morning, and there was a lot of activity at the carpeted teller cages. All the contractors on the Island were in cashing their paychecks and getting their money. Mothers were making deposits into their Christmas accounts.

In the glass-walled conference room, Jack Fraker and Donna Stevens were conducting an autopsy. They were oblivious to the happy domestic activity going on around them. Jack had taken the gloves off. "How the hell did this happen? Tell me again. From the beginning."

He was beet red and glaring at Donna. He sat across the table from her in his blue L.L.Bean blazer with the three gold buttons on the cuff. He had put on ten pounds over the summer, and the suit coat was tight. He looked like he was in a straitjacket. He felt that way too.

Donna looked at him. His face was flushed and pink. She thought that he could burst a blood vessel in his head at any moment and have an aneurysm right there in front of her in the conference room. She was a little frightened and didn't know what to do.

Jack looked at Donna in the cold hard morning light. He thought she was barely competent. He realized that his VP had let the Indians—one Indian in particular—inside the proverbial fort, and they ransacked everything and then set the powder magazine on fire.

"Jack, I was suspicious at the time. That's why I called you. To get your approval before I made the wire transfer. Remember?"

"I was in a damn board meeting, Donna. I was distracted, for Chrissakes."

"Jack, I called and asked you specifically about that wire transfer," Donna said as she battled back. If she was going to lose her job, she was at least going down with a fight.

Jack Fraker waved her off. "Don't give me that shit. You should have stopped him until Monday at least, when I was back in the office, and we could've strategized together. Think it through, woman."

Donna picked up on the "we" immediately. It meant that she wasn't getting fired yet, that she had a chance to maintain her employment. At least for a little while.

Then Donna quickly realized that Jack needed her as a shield in the developing firestorm. That he at least needed a scapegoat if the shit really hit the fan. He could always fire her later, she figured. She knew that Jack Fraker would do it too; he would throw her under the bus in a New York minute if it at all contributed to saving his own ass and making him look good.

Jack regrouped, thinking. "Let's call him and see if he answers."

"All right," Donna said. She immediately jumped on his suggestion. She'd do anything to diffuse his anger and stabilize the situation.

She quickly pulled the Polycom Starfish over to the center of the table and punched Bill Fletcher's cell number into the speakerphone. She knew the number by heart.

The line connected quickly and rang and rang. It was too loud in the small conference room, the ringing sound reverberating off the glass walls. She fingered the soft rubber volume key with her index finger painted with deep red holiday nail polish. She pushed it repeatedly until the volume went way down to a soft level.

She and Jack Fraker looked at each other over the glass tabletop as the line rang repeatedly.

"He's not answering," Jack said defensively as he frowned.

Fletcher's voice came on the line and said, "I'm not available. Leave a message." Donna left one, a cheery one, asking for Fletcher to call her to confirm some details about the wire transfer. It was bullshit and hopeless, but it was all she could muster under the circumstances. She had to do it to save face with Jack Fraker.

She inhaled and took a deep breath, holding it for a second. Her breasts rose up in her white angora sweater set. She had a nice rack, although she was oblivious to her charms at that moment.

Jack wasn't though. Even in his anger, he watched her breasts swell up in the soft sweater material, a safe harbor in the ensuing storm swirling around them. He shook his head. There was no time to be horny.

Donna let her breath out slowly, staying calm, doing it just the way she read about in the relaxation book. It was working a little. She tried to salvage the situation.

"Bill said that he was going away for the weekend with Carrie. Maybe this is all legit and moving the money is just a test, and we'll be fine on Monday."

Donna brightened as she thought it through. "I'll be at his office first thing Monday morning to follow up and get the money back. It'll be fine."

Jack Fraker smiled, knowing the absurdity of her story. "Bill Graves has already called me this morning. He wants to know why we pulled down the working capital line for thirteen million dollars last night. He was mad as shit on the message."

Donna's bowels instantly tightened up. "What'd you say to him?"

"I haven't called him back yet."

Donna took a second deep breath, holding it, needing more relaxation. Having Bill Graves, the chairman of the bank, involved was not a good thing. "What do you think?" she asked. "What's happening here?" Unfortunately, she already knew the answer.

Jack Fraker didn't look at Donna Stevens's breasts the second time. He looked out the window, far away. His mind was floating. He knew the answer too well.

"Nobody moves thirteen million dollars out of the bank to test the money management system. The system works fine."

He looked back at Donna and sighed. "We're cooked like a goddamn holiday goose."

He frowned as he turned that thought over in his mind. For some reason, the notion of next year's tuition payment to Cornell for his son just popped into his head, $55,000 worth. *Holy shit* was all he could register.

He desperately wanted to believe that something good, something legitimate, was happening here and that it would all be okay come Monday morning. He wanted to believe, just like Donna was doing. But then the cold, hard mind-set of a banker trickled in and laid a pall over everything.

"The only thing Bill Fletcher is testing is our capacity for bullshit. And our patience. That money's not coming back."

And with that, he looked back over at Donna Stevens. "I think we're screwed" was all he could muster.

Miami

Bill Fletcher and Carrie arrived in Miami on Saturday at 1:35 p.m. on American Airlines 352 from Newark. They sat in first class. It was the ultimate aphrodisiac. It was a beautiful day in Florida with the sky full of bright sun and occasional big fluffy cumulus clouds floating across the horizon.

The first thing Fletcher did was cut up their passports into little squares and flush the pieces down the toilet in the men's room at the American Airlines Admiral's Club. He had bought a pair of scissors at a Staples pop-up kiosk in the airport as they walked between gates. He flushed twice to make sure the pieces didn't get stuck halfway down. He washed his hands, ran some water through his hair, and came out, literally a new person. He found Carrie over in the corner.

She was at a small table eating salted nuts and watching CNN on the big flatscreen on the wall. He dropped two new fake passports onto the table and then went to get a drink for the two of them. "Take a look at these," he said as he walked away.

He came back with two Heinekens and put them down on the table.

"What are these for?" Carrie said. She was curious.

"They're for us. They're our new personas."

"Why?" Carrie took a salted peanut and put it in her mouth, chewing deliberately, curious. Bill Fletcher kept it fresh and interesting.

"We only need them for a while to move around."

"What was wrong with our old ones? Our real ones, I mean."

"Well. They're going to be looking for us to return all the federal money."

"Which money?" Carrie asked. "I made a lot of that money selling the T-shirts and coffee mugs. That's our money."

"Yeah, I know it. That's not the money they're coming after though. They're going to want the Indian money back. The cash they gave us to start the Neskeet tribe."

"Why don't you just give it back to them? We have enough on top of that to survive anyway. Plenty to live on for a while."

"I might in the end. But I'm going to file a lawsuit against them in the interim and fight it out. Have some fun with those federal bureaucrats."

Fletcher paused for a mouthful of nuts and a big swallow of cold beer. *Everything tasted better in the warm weather,* he thought.

"They're probably gonna look pretty silly giving a white lawyer money for claiming to be an Indian chief," he finally said.

"You're crazy."

"It's only for a little while until I can get the feds to capitulate. Then we can keep all the money and go back to our real identities and retire. Besides, it's all comingled with our legitimate money we made that you rightly point out. We've got some good defenses here."

Fletcher was already turning lawyerly, thinking through his arguments, drafting his defense brief in his head. He was happy for the stimulation.

Carrie was happy too, but for different reasons. She wanted to tour the islands and explore. Have some fun in the sun and leave the harsh Cape Cod winter behind up north for a while. She thought about it all for no more than a minute.

"So we're kind of a Caribbean version of Bonnie and Clyde, huh?" she said. She nailed it on the first try. "I'm gonna need a new wardrobe for down here then. I've got nothing to wear."

"Now you're talking," Fletcher said. "We've both got to get new clothes. New stuff all the way around for a new way of life. The rejuvenating powers of a wardrobe change."

"How long are we staying in Miami?"

"Just tonight. We're flying down to St. Thomas tomorrow morning to get a jump on it. I'm sure there's going to be a few people looking for us come Monday morning."

"Cool," Carrie said, not asking too many questions.

They drank their beer and ate chicken salad finger sandwiches right there in the business class lounge. They were cut into little triangles with the crust already removed, soft bread all the way around. Fletcher ate four. He was ravenous. The mystique of a new Caribbean life was powerful and had made him hungry as a barracuda.

So they finished lunch and agreed to meet up at their hotel, the Fountainbleau, at five that afternoon. They were each going their own way to shop and get ready for their Caribbean adventure.

*   *   *

The first place Bill Fletcher went was to a hair salon. It was called Mirage and was an upscale place in Miami Beach, just off Brickell, close to their hotel. He found it just walking around the neighborhood. He went in and waited. He was a walk-in.

He finally got his long hair washed by a gorgeous Cuban girl and then towel dried. Next he was seated with an attractive, hip brunette who began running her fingers through his hair in front of a long mirror. Candace had on cargo pants, cork platform sandals, and a red wifebeater T-shirt. She looked like she did 150 sit-ups a day. She smiled as she looked at him in the mirror, fingering and flirting.

"I like your long hair. It looks great for an older man," she said as she ran her fingers through Fletcher's dark thatch. "What are we doing today? Just a trim and thin out?"

"Take it all off," Fletcher said.

"Huh?" the hairstylist said.

"Yeah, cut it off."

Candace smiled and massaged his scalp. She liked him already. "How much do you want off?" she asked, making sure. She loved these kind of radical makeovers. They were sexy.

"You ever watch *Mad Men*?" Fletcher asked. "You know, sixties advertising executives?"

"Are you kidding? I love that show, all the clothes. It's my favorite."

"I'm talking Don Draper here. Give me what any self-respecting creative director at a hip, old-school advertising agency would want."

Candace was happy to oblige. She enjoyed these transformations. "I love Jon Hamm," she said dreamily. "He's incredibly sexy."

And maybe, by extension, so was Bill Fletcher. Or at least that was what Candace would shoot for. Maybe not incredibly sexy, but at least a starter version of Jon Hamm for Miami Beach for that afternoon.

Forty-five minutes later, Fletcher walked out of the Mirage salon a new man. He was sporting a fresh look—a short-haired prepster on the loose. Ralph Lauren style. It fit him well. He had left six inches of long Indian hair on the cutting room floor. It was his old life, and now he was happy to leave it behind.

Next stop was Nordstrom. He bought five Polo shirts and a pair of khaki shorts. And then a canvas belt with little fish on it. Then he went to Johnston & Murphy and got a pair of slip-on kiltie tassel loafers, brown beachy ones, with the basket-weave pattern on the front.

He put the khaki shorts and a blue Polo shirt on right in the dressing room along with the slip-ons with no socks. He didn't tuck the shirt in. He instantly channeled Tommy Hilfiger.

He looked like the guy in all those preppie magazine ads where they had a father and son, both with sweaters wrapped over their shoulders, holding lacrosse sticks along with golden retrievers on a leash.

"Nice look, man." The twenty-year-old who was manning the register in the men's department at Nordstrom watched Fletcher come out of the dressing room in his instant prep. "I didn't see you as a hippy dude anyway."

"You like turquoise?" Fletcher asked as he pulled out his American Express card and paid for all his new clothes.

"My mother does. She and my father went to Taos, New Mexico, one time to ski, and she fell in love with the shit. Why?"

"That seals it then. Here you go." And with that, Fletcher took off his big turquoise bracelet and handed it over to the young salesclerk.

"Wow. This is definitely cool. My mom will like this. How much did it cost?"

"Tell her five thousand. She'll let you smoke weed in the garage for the next month."

"Yeah. I know, right?" the salesboy said. "Thanks a lot for this. You made my day, man."

Fletcher next went to Abercrombie and bought three pairs of madras shorts and two oversize blue cotton button-down shirts. He was done. Same thing, the girl at the checkout gave him her seal of approval. "Cool. All the shorts are on sale. You get an extra 15 percent off."

"Nice," Fletcher said.

He left all his purchases at the last store he went to and paid a personal shopping assistant to take them to the hotel. He had too many packages. He made one more stop before turning around.

He ended up back at the hotel and met Carrie for a drink at the outside bar at five. She couldn't believe the transformation. It was a lot to throw at her all of a sudden. She was cool about it though.

"What happened to my Indian chief?"

She was sipping a glass of white wine. She had bought a skirt, a scoop-neck top, and some mule sandals. She had a set of choker pearls on too. Fletcher's new look caught her a little by surprise.

"Chief Running Dog had to go."

Carrie smiled and took a sip of white wine, looking him over. She finally nodded.

"I like it. Preppy Bill. My island businessman." Carrie did like the new look, but she had to get used to it a bit, she decided.

Fletcher casually put his left hand on the table and was sporting a new $2,000 Rolex Submariner watch where the turquoise bracelet had been. It had a stainless steel band and a big, chunky waterproof bezel.

"What do you think?" Fletcher asked, holding up his wrist.

"Nice," Carrie said. She fingered the watch. "It has a James Bond vibe to it. You really ditched the turquoise jewelry, huh?"

They had drinks and grilled shrimp for dinner at the bar, settling in. After dinner, they headed back to their room to pack. It had been a busy day.

Miami Beach was tropical, and the night was sensuous. They ended up having Miami sex with expensive, brand-name beach clothes scattered all over the floor by the bed.

Afterward, Carrie celebrated their individual transformations and ordered a fruit plate along with a bottle of champagne from room service. She loved ripe papaya.

"We leave tomorrow at nine a.m.," Fletcher said, glancing down at his new Rolex watch.

Cold Light of Day

It was the Monday after Fletcher and Carrie had left for Miami.

The weather along the eastern seaboard had been dark and unsettled. Rain squalls had blown in to Washington, DC, late Sunday night, and the weather had settled to a constant drizzle by Monday morning. Everybody had an umbrella for the morning commute.

Mindy Sanchez was sitting in Harold Schumer's office. Both of them were drinking morning coffees. She had a Starbucks latte, and he was working on a large black straight-up cup from the Coffee Roaster next door. He hated the smoky overroasted coffee at Starbucks.

"They were nice people, Harold, really. Totally honest. I thought the Indian thing was for real. Carrie was a great businesswoman and friend too. She gave me some special facial cream, and it's already done wonders for me."

Harold listened and slowly sipped his coffee, the bitterness suiting his mood perfectly. It was obvious that Fletcher and his lady friend had turned Mindy. He wasn't surprised. It solidified his opinion anyway that she was a bimbo. There was no other explanation. Why she had gone to law school and not a hairdressing academy was still a mystery to him.

He let her finish.

"It doesn't matter," he finally said in response to her explanation after she talked about the face cream and the wonders it performed. He put his coffee down and looked at the folder on his desk. He crossed his arms in a defensive posture unconsciously. "Jim wants to let this thing sink under the waves quickly anyway."

"Huh?"

"Fletcher's already on the lam with the money. I tried to get it over the weekend with the Bureau's help, but he wired it out of the country on Friday to Switzerland."

"Wow. He moved fast."

Harold let that sink in for a second. "The guy's smart, give him that."

"Couldn't you find where it went and get it back?" Mindy at least knew the basics.

"The Bureau tried, but it was too late. He bounced it around the Caribbean before Switzerland and then God knows where. It's going to take us three days to get a court order for the Swiss. It won't matter then because the money's not there now. He just parked it there for a little while. It's gone somewhere else."

Harold Schumer knew in his gut that the cause was lost.

"So what happens now?"

Harold looked up, arms still crossed, and leaned back in his Aeron chair. "We screwed the pooch on this one, all the way around. We'll put out a warrant, quietly, on Fletcher, but I know he's smarter than that. They're going to look for him today in Miami. I don't hold out much hope. The warrant will stay outstanding though. Nothing will ever happen. There's no extradition in the Bahamas."

"I didn't know that," Mindy said, surprised.

"Yeah. I just found that out over the weekend," Harold said. "The thirteen million won't be missed. It's just a drop in the BIA's bucket."

"I never understood why we gave him so much money in the first place," Mindy said.

Howard looked up at her and nodded as he listened. "You should have said something."

*　　*　　*

Over on the Vineyard, the same tropical depression that swept in on Washington was now sitting right smack in the offices of the Martha's Vineyard Bank.

Jack Fraker and Donna Stevens were both in early. Jack had a white shirt and blue rep tie on along with a dark business suit. He had his battle armor on. Donna looked like her firstborn son had died over the weekend in a motorcycle accident.

On the positive side, both Jack and Donna were drinking two fresh cups of Kona Koffee that morning, loading up on caffeine for the disaster sure to come.

"Did you try to retract the wire this morning?" Jack asked. He knew the question was stupid. Donna had showed him the wire confirmation from Friday, but he asked anyway.

"Yes, we did, first thing this morning." Donna was businesslike, precise. "It didn't work. The money had already left."

"Were you able to find out where it went at least after Curaçao?"

"I called the transfer bank and asked immediately."

"They tell you?"

"They did. They had owed us a favor."

"Well?"

"It went to Switzerland, they said."

Donna was nervous just saying that as the words floated out over the room.

"Jesus, Switzerland. Then we're fucked," was all Jack could say.

Donna Stevens didn't respond. She knew Jack was dead right this time.

Her thoughts immediately turned to self-preservation. She hoped she didn't lose her job. Her family had a lot of bills. Her husband was a drywall contractor, and business had been slow owing to the recession. She didn't know how this would end up.

"Well, Graves called me already this morning on it. I can't put it off any longer. I've got to call him now and tell the truth." Jack frowned. "I'm going to call him from my office though."

He got up to walk out.

"Wish me luck," was all he could say with a huge sigh of resignation.

Donna Stevens didn't look up or say anything. She sat at her desk and reached for a Kleenex as a small tear trickled down her cheek. It would be the start of many.

*   *   *

Things were looking decidedly better for Bill Fletcher and Carrie Nation down in Florida. Their money had moved all around the world over the weekend just like efficient, focused Paul Sanders at Horgan Smith had said it would. It was just like the PowerPoint slide he had shown to Fletcher.

Fletcher was a compulsive, nervous type though when it came to the money. He checked on the bank balances three or four times each day to be sure that it was all still there, moving around quickly from place to place, and that the US government hadn't seized it yet. Anybody would have done the same.

It was their entire net worth.

St. John's Bay

The big sailboat swung gently on its anchor line in the secluded cove. A soft breeze pushed the hull around, causing little eddies on the leeward side of the water.

It was big boat, a Tartan 52. It had spacious living quarters belowdecks with a full galley, a dining area, a master bedroom, and a bath suite with a full-size shower. Headroom was six feet six inches belowdecks with plenty of room for Bill Fletcher to walk around and not bang his noggin.

It was majestic. The hull was deep blue, and the big aluminum mast towered above it, running fifty feet into the sky, anchored down with a series of stainless steel stays and cables. The mast itself was over ten inches in diameter.

On the transom of the boat was its name done up in big gold leaf, *HONEST INJUN*, and its homeport, Bermuda, beneath in smaller gold-leaf script. The name stood out and popped on the deep-blue background of the hull paint.

Fletcher thought it was a nice touch and had the work done in a St. Thomas boatyard where they bought the boat and had it outfitted and provisioned. He put the Bermuda location on as a red herring to keep curious onlookers from tying them to the States.

Topsides, the boat was rigged as an island cruiser. It had a big cockpit with cushions along both sides of the deck. The helm had a big ocean racing wheel covered in black nonstick fabric for a good grip for the helmsman when underway. There was a full range of electronics. The boat also had a big radar rig, two actually, with a heads-up display in the cockpit and a second backup unit belowdecks, no screwing around. They could sail around the Cape of Good Hope in a hurricane if they wanted to.

But Bill Fletcher and Carrie Nation didn't need the happy horseshit, sophisticated electronics that they had onboard. All they did was occasionally pull up anchor, cruise to another little protected bay within their sight in the British Virgin Island chain, and then set up shop.

That meant rigging up the big blue cockpit canopy that covered the stern area in shade quickly so they could sit back on the canvas cushions, drink Red Stripe beers, and relax. The Caribbean breezes came off the water and kept the whole deck area cool and comfortable. The cockpit cover was an absolute must in the tropical weather as the sun beat down intensely during the day.

Fletcher became an island Ralph Lauren almost overnight. He wore SPF 50 sunblock all the time, a Polo shirt hanging out, and his big blue cotton Oxford shirt as a coverall in the sun. He still burned to a crisp on his face and neck. He could only take so much sun.

Carrie went the other way and became a total tropical girl. She immersed herself in the climate and the heat. She'd lather up in light sunblock in the morning and then sit out on the bow of the boat, lying on the deck cushions, soaking in the rays in her string bikini every day.

When she'd had enough, she'd put on her Maui Jim sunglasses, a baseball cap, and a Neskeet Nation T-shirt to cover up. She'd row out in the boat's tender near shore and fish for an hour or two, using chunks of cut up fish for bait. She used a small spin-casting rig and became quite proficient at saltwater fishing fast. She'd usually catch a fish for her and Bill to grill for dinner off the stern of the boat. They had a small charcoal Hibachi grill that hung out over the water.

She rowed back to the boat with a grouper in the cooler half-full with seawater to keep it fresh and alive. She tied the tender off the stern and climbed up the side ladder to the shade of the deck.

"Wow! Another perfect day. I've got to pinch myself to make sure I'm not dreaming," Carrie said. "I'm hot."

Fletcher had just come up from belowdecks where he was working on his laptop. Surprisingly, they had good cell coverage in the area with Verizon Wireless. He had bought two air-card hookups for them so that he and Carrie could both use their laptops on the boat. Plus he had a Wi-Fi hot spot with his smartphone. The coverage was good. It was as good as the Vineyard really, like home away from home.

"What'd you catch?"

"A small grouper," Carrie said as she came over and plopped down in the shade next to Fletcher. She smelled like coconut suntan lotion. "It'll be good on the grill. We'll have it later." She put it on ice in a cooler under the seat cushion.

"Want a Red Stripe?"

"Sure."

Carrie and Bill sat in the cockpit and read. They both had Kindles, and each had loaded up on books when they were in port at St. John's Bay the week before.

Fletcher broke out the cheese and crackers, putting them on a small cutting board on top of the beer cooler.

"Not too bad, huh?"

"No, it's beautiful," Carrie said. "I love the Caribbean."

"Are you bored?" Fletcher asked, worried that this would get old quickly for her. She was too frenetic.

"Not yet," Carrie said as she sipped from her cold bottle of beer. "Give me two months down here. Maybe I'll be bored after the winter, but not now. Let's just go with it for a while."

"It's probably snowing back on the Vineyard," Fletcher said.

"I know. Your statue is probably covered in snow." Carrie laughed and spread her legs out on top of Fletcher's.

He nodded.

"Probably more like covered in seagull shit. With a big drop right on my forehead. Like a white bindi dot. I'm sure the Oak Bluffs maintenance crew isn't cleaning it off, though."

"You're probably right," Carrie said.

Fletcher drank his beer and looked over at her. "I checked the accounts this morning. It's all there, all thirteen million and change. Paul Sanders invested it all in money market securities for us for the time being. It's only getting 1 percent, but it's better than nothing." Fletcher smiled.

"You check the accounts every day. I don't think it's going anywhere," Carrie said. "Where is the money now anyway?"

"We moved it again. It's over in Andorra now. Safe and secure."

"Where's that?"

"It's a country next to Spain. It's a tax haven and very secretive. I think we're all set now."

"Oh."

Money wasn't really Carrie's thing. She knew that they had enough to be comfortable for a long, long time, maybe forever to her way of thinking, and that was enough. The details didn't interest her. The Caribbean world did.

Fletcher stretched and rubbed Carrie's brown suntanned legs that were draped over him. He went right up to the edge of her bikini bottom under her T-shirt. He fingered the small triangle of fabric.

"The thing of it is, you know, is that a big money market account balance makes me horny," Fletcher said as he looked serious for a second. "The fullness and ripeness and all."

"Yeah, so?"

"So, you wanna do something about it?" Fletcher, as usual, got right to the heart of the matter.

Carrie thought about it for a brief second then took off her sunglasses, dropping them on the cushion to her right.

"Sure, why not? Take me, my big Indian chief," she said. She took his hand, and they headed belowdecks to the big master bedroom suite.

It was just that simple in the Islands.

Viva Las Vegas

The casino in the Sands was humming for a Friday night. The card tables were full, and the slot machines had a ton of old-timers working the handles. There were busloads of them from as far away as Carson, Henderson, and Pyramid Lake. Vegas was a magnet.

The older retired crowd, the gray hairs, always gravitated to the cheap slot machines where they could push buttons and pull handles all night for twenty dollars. They put their nickels and quarters in big colorful plastic cups or paper buckets that were stacked over by the million-dollar machines at the end of each aisle. It was fairly boring stuff.

Over in the corner were the poker tables where the real action took place. They were full with people as always. Texas Hold 'Em was the game of choice, and the tables drew a lively and boisterous crowd. Most of the players were experienced.

The dealer at the front table had already dealt out three cards, face up, to each of his five players. Everybody was attentive. He was a good-looking guy in his forties with the features of a Black Irishman. He was dressed in a long-sleeve shirt, a vest, and nice slacks, all in black. He looked like he worked out. His nameplate said PETER, and he smiled a lot.

Peter dealt the third card out from the top of the deck to each of the players.

"The flop. Any bets on the flop?" he said quietly as he dealt. He laid down a two of clubs, two jacks, and the queen of hearts to the players.

"The turn," he said next and went around again the table again as he dealt out more cards.

Everybody was nursing a drink and watching quietly. He had their attention. Peter the dealer was working a club soda with a lime twist off to the side. He drank three or four during a night shift.

Finally, the fifth card was shuffled and drawn.

"The river," Peter called out as he slowly went around the table, spinning out the single cards to the players.

There were a lot of sighs and mumbles as the Asian guy with sunglasses and the baseball cap that said NO PRISONERS won the hand. The dealer pushed all the chips, over $700 dollars worth, across the table to him. He smiled and took a sip from his drink.

The game went on for another hour.

Finally at 9:00 p.m., the shift changed, and Peter Mulcahey left the poker game. He lingered at the craps table for a bit where he watched the action, trying to learn the game. It was hard to keep all the different bets in order.

He had gone from Father Peter to Peter Mulcahey to just plain Peter at the poker tables at the Riviera casino in the space of two short months. The change had been easy.

Things had unraveled back on the Island fairly quickly late in the fall. Peter and Margaret continued seeing each other with increasing frequency, and people had noticed. Father Peter noticed too, but he just couldn't stop. Or rather, he didn't want to stop. He figured that he'd be defrocked, excommunicated, or simply caught in a compromised position with Margaret soon enough on the Island. It was an incredibly small and incestuous place.

Even Joanne Proctor saw the change in him. She was a lusty Irish lass herself, and she could smell the scent of sex on Father Peter straight away. Plus the fact that she'd come to the rectory in the morning and start to make beds for the priests, and strangely, Father Peter's wasn't slept in more and more frequently.

"You're sleeping in the church now on a pew, are you, Father?" she'd ask.

"I fell asleep on the couch watching television again, Joanne. The Catholic Channel. I'm doing that a lot lately. I'm just too tired to make it upstairs."

Joanne would nod and say nothing. She ended up being a little bit ticked off as she was herself an attractive divorced woman looking for a little Catholic love and companionship. If she knew that Father Peter was giving it out, she'd have made her move a long time ago. But she hadn't seen it coming with Margaret, the pretty widow.

Margaret Wellington did see Father Peter's passion coming, however, and she rode it like a bucking bronco. It rolled over her like a giant tsunami coming ashore on the beach in Thailand, starting slow, pulling the water out first, then finishing strong and powerful. They fell deeply in love, and that was that.

Peter Mulcahey had the good sense to realize that he enjoyed the pleasures of the flesh a lot more than the passion of Christ.

He met with Bishop Guerin late one afternoon after he had run the bingo class for the area priests in New Bedford. He was good at teaching the priests how to set up gaming programs for their parishes. Bishop Guerin had picked right in that regard.

"Bishop, I'm succumbing to the flesh. I have sinned," Father Peter said.

The thin wiry bishop looked over at him with rheumy eyes. "Tell me it's not one of the altar boys, Father Mulcahey, please."

"No, it's a parishioner, Bishop. A single woman that I've fallen for. I'm in love. Praise the Lord."

The bishop paused. "At least it's not a twelve-year-old altar boy. Thank Christ for that. So yes, praise the Lord indeed."

And that was that. Father Peter Mulcahey left in a week with Margaret Wellington in tow, heading west. They ended up in Las Vegas looking for work. She got a job at Harrah's in the accounting departing at the same time that he made the cut for dealer training at the Riviera. He was handsome and fit the part. It all worked out wonderfully well, as life often does.

*   *   *

"How about a nice steak?" Peter said to Margaret as they sat at the bar at the Bellagio after his shift had ended. She was wearing a sheath dress with a pearl necklace and heels.

She looked fantastic. Margaret had enrolled in an LA Fitness gym the moment they arrived in Las Vegas and even hired her own personal trainer. She had plenty of money from the life insurance trust her husband had set up before he died. Jed had been smart with their money. Now she was determined to spend all her inheritance along the way. Life was fleeting.

Even in a flashy town like Las Vegas, Peter Mulcahey and Margaret Wellington stood out. They were a head-turning couple.

She pulled the dirty olive off the stick in her martini and licked the sweet liquor from its surface. "Sure, why not?" she said. "Where do you want to go?"

Peter Mulcahey sipped his draft beer. It was from a local Nevada microbrewery, an IPA with a lot of hops. He was on his second. He had developed his Irish love of beer since they had moved west and was into trying out as many craft brews as he could find in the area. "How about Hermitage? I made a reservation."

That's what had sold Margaret Wellington on the charms of Peter Mulcahey. He had taken the initiative and made a reservation at one of her favorite restaurants on the Strip. He automatically took care of her, nurtured her without her asking. He was spontaneous too.

She reciprocated by taking care of him. Margaret had made her own personal vow to teach Peter Mulcahey the ways of the secular world as best she could. Particularly as they revolved around the pleasures of the flesh and sex. They purchased a king-size bed with memory foam first thing when they arrived in Las Vegas and rented a town house out by a golf course.

Margaret and Peter got up from the bar, and he paid for their drinks. As they walked toward the door, he put his arm in the small of her back and led her out.

Outside, the Las Vegas night beckoned. The stars exploded in the dry desert sky. It was like a beautiful stage set from Le Cirque du Soleil. Life was good.

Loose Ends

"You miss him?" Manny Fernandez said. He was sitting in the Indian office in Aquinnah, drinking Grey Goose from a shot glass. The tall clear bottle was next to him on the table.

"Huh?" Carl said. "I miss him like I miss a sore tooth."

"I figured as much," Manny said. "I'll tell you one thing, it's a lot quieter here now that Fletcher's gone. Not as much bullshit. And I see a lot fewer T-shirts around on the street."

"You're dreaming," Carl said. He sipped a tall Budweiser beer from a can, true to his roots. "I still see a lot of people wearing the shirts around. Face it, they're nice shirts. That chick of his, whatever her name was, did a nice job on 'em. Artistic and all."

"Artistic, shit," Manny said. He took a sip of his vodka, holding the shot glass gingerly.

Carl watched him.

"Don't spill any of that firewater there, boy. That stuff looks dangerous."

Manny smiled. "You ought to try a little, Carl. This is the true hair of the dog. Prove you're a real Indian chief, a big red man, conqueror of the paleface."

He poured another shot in the glass, not waiting for Carl to answer. This was a time for celebration. The two men sat in the room and talked.

Carl sipped his beer, mellow now that Fletcher was gone. He had been a huge threat to the environment. Now the pressure was off, and he finally had time to think.

"That fucker's not gone, not by any means. He's probably down in Mexico screwing his little girlfriend and thinking up more schemes. He'll be back, and I'll be ready next time. The guy was smart, give him that."

Manny nodded. "I'll say. He made us look like chumps with the gift shop up at Aquinnah and all the key chains and bead bracelets."

"That's right," Carl said. "The Great Spirit sent Fletcher down to teach us a lesson. And we learned from it, didn't we?"

"That we did," Manny said. "Merchandising. That's what we learned."

Manny was a little thoughtful himself, sipping his vodka slowly now, tasting it on his tongue before he let it run down his throat and give him the burn.

Carl put his beer down on the melamine tabletop next to his porkpie hat. He belched loudly and thought for a second.

"What we learned is that we need a vision to run this tribe going forward. A plan with more boots on the ground."

"What the hell's boots on the ground?" Manny asked. "Some kind of Timberland thing?"

Carl shook his head. "I'll tell you one thing I learned," he said. He pointed at Manny for emphasis and paused for a second, teeing it up, the ultimate truth coming.

"Yeah, what's that?"

"We need a marketing person here to help us get our shit together going forward. Someone who can work the Internet and do Facebook and tweeting. That's where it's at. Indian apps for the iPhone and all that shit."

"I expect you're right about that, Carl," Manny said as he nodded and sipped more vodka. It was taking hold; the room was slowly getting warm and soft.

"You just wait," Carl said. "Bill Fletcher was a shot across the bow for us Fluevogs. A learning experience, I'll admit that. But we're coming out of this stronger. We'll be a better tribe in the end. Trust me."

Manny Fernandez folded his hands like he was in prayer. He tapped his thumbs together. He was mellow. "Yeah, I hear you Carl," he said. "It's all good."

*   *   *

Over at the police station, Mike Fernandez and Jim Barry had the same conversation. They were trying to sum it all up and put it in perspective. They were sitting in two chairs in the shift room, relaxed, just talking.

"He left pretty quick, I'll tell you that," Jim said. "Jack Fraker told me that he pulled all his money out of the bank and sent it to the other side of the world, and no one can trace it now. It went straight to Dubai."

Mike Francesca frowned. "Dubai? Once it goes over there, they'll never find it. It's all mixed in with those Arab gun merchants and traders. Shit, al-Qaeda's probably got some of it right now too." He smiled then added, "That guy was a piece of work, wasn't he?"

"Who, Fletcher?" the selectman asked.

"Who else we talking about here? Yeah, of course him," the police chief said.

"I miss the contributions he made to the retirement fund."

"Whose retirement fund? I didn't see much of that."

"My retirement fund," Jim Barry said. "The only retirement fund that counts. There wasn't any paper record for all those donations. I just took care of 'em."

Mike Francesca smiled. "I bet you did."

"I miss him though. I'll tell you that," the selectman added. "He was always doing something creative, keeping it fresh. He knew how to make money like a motherfucker. That guy had more irons in the fire than anybody I knew. The T-shirts and everything."

"Yeah, the T-shirts were good, I'll give him that. My daughter's got about six of them. Wears 'em all the time. They're good quality too."

"Well, it's all good in the end," Jim said. "But he had to go, otherwise Carl and his little band of misfits would have gone to war and killed him straight up. There's just not room for two tribes of Indians on the Island."

"Yeah, old Carl stayed pretty quiet during the whole thing. I'm surprised he didn't do something stupid along the way."

Jim nodded. "You ever find out who set fire to the A&P?" "Unknown origins was how the state fire marshal classified it in the report in the end. It means that they couldn't prove it was arson, but they had a strong suspicion that it was, I can tell you that."

"Doesn't surprise me one bit," Jim said.

They talked some more about the striped bass being in over at Lobsterville and how the clamming was good on the east shore of Sengekontacket. There were piles of littlenecks in the flat at low tide.

"Did I tell you that the FBI sent me a confidential e-mail yesterday?" Mike said. "From that tall guy in Boston, the one that came down after Fletcher left town?"

"No. About what?"

"Turns out, they're not even going to issue an arrest warrant for Fletcher. Said that it was 'under consideration' as to whether they would file any charges against him ever. Said the case wasn't too strong and that he could have been an Indian chief all along based on all the information and that a lot of the money was his anyway. From his business."

Jim Sanders looked over at the police chief. "Under consideration, shit."

"I know. I'm just telling you what they told me, that's all."

"He got away with it, didn't he? Son of a bitch."

Epilogue

It was February on the Vineyard, and deep winter had settled in.

A northeaster pounded the Island with a combination of snow and sleet, the proverbial wintry mix. The wind whipped the flakes across the shoreline and onto the beach in big bursts. Sheets of rain were driving sideways, making it nearly impossible to see beyond a ten-foot radius.

Not a soul was out. It was a night to sit inside in front of a roaring fire, the inside wall stacked high with dry seasoned cordwood, with a dog, a drink, and a good book.

It was fit for neither man nor beast outside.

But one vehicle was out. The maroon Cadillac STS drove slowly and carefully through the night storm. Its high-tech xenon HID headlights cut through into the inky darkness, and the wipers cleared big swatches of rain and snow off the windshield, only to be covered again seconds later.

Carl drove over to Ocean Park through the backstreets of Oak Bluffs. He was driving under the cover of darkness then, the storm erasing his tracks as he went.

He drove with one hand on the steering wheel, sitting back and enjoying the night storm as it exploded around him. He was a native Islander, an Indian tribesman, and no stranger to this kind of weather. Carl had a dark wool watch cap on that night, leaving his porkpie hat at home. This was a night for work and clandestine activity.

He drove around behind Ocean Park, coming in from the rear. Once he got onto the small asphalt ring road around the park, he drove directly over to Wampum Nation, the statue that Bill Fletcher had erected of himself. He approached the statue from the side then swung in a small wide arc, directly in front of it. He pulled up, stopped, and then backed slowly down in front of it, the rear bumper facing the piece of art.

The tires of the car had made beautiful symmetric arcs in the snow as he backed up the Caddy, maneuvering to just where he wanted using two fingers on the wheel.

Carl put it in Park, put his gloves on, and got out. He walked in front of the statue and stopped. He spit on it. He put his hands on his hips and looked up at Bill Fletcher, bigger than life in the swirling storm, illuminated from the cone of light from a single streetlight nearby.

The statue was partially covered in snow and was wet with dark stains all over. Water was dripping down. Fletcher still had his BlackBerry glued to his right ear, Ray-Bans on, blankly gazing out into Vineyard Sound, talking on his cell phone.

Carl looked at the statue, shielding his eyes. "Bill Fletcher. You ever hear of Little Big Horn, you asshole?" He said the words into the storm. They were instantly carried away by the wind. "Well, it's come again."

He didn't wait for Fletcher to answer; he was getting wet.

Carl went over to the trunk of the STS, sitting there idling, with its Lexan taillights glowing red in the inky darkness. He took off his right glove and found the black plastic key fob in his pocket. He pointed it at the car, pushed the Unlock button, and the trunk popped open.

Carl put his gloves back on and pulled a big steel cable from the back then slammed the trunk shut.

He jumped up on the statue and wrapped the cable around Fletcher's torso two times. He climbed down carefully from the slippery pedestal and went back over to the car. He got down on his knees, getting his pants wet now, as he attached both ends of the cable to the rear frame of the Cadillac.

He got back in the car, put it in Drive, and slowly inched forward, taking the slack out of the line. When the cable went taut, he tapped the brake to stop. He dropped the transmission into Low, two notches down. Then Carl pushed down hard on the gas pedal, gripping the wheel with both hands, putting all his energy into it.

The steel cable strained. The rear tires spun, then the car inched forward, the V-8 taking over.

There was a brief bang, and then the big Cadillac surged forward. Carl slammed on the brakes to stop. The eight-foot-high statue of Bill Fletcher was toppled. He looked in the rearview mirror, and there was nothing there. Carl turned around and could see the flat top of the pedestal. It was all that remained.

He got out and looked at his handiwork. Fletcher's statue had been decapitated from the force of the big figure falling over. Carl Sunapee went over to Fletcher's head and picked it up, like a victorious Indian warrior on the Plains.

He immediately noticed that the head was surprisingly light. It was hollow. Carl looked at Fletcher. Fletcher still had his hand, now amputated at the wrist, holding his BlackBerry to his ear. His sunglasses were still on. He looked noble.

Carl held Fletcher's head in both hands. "See what you get fuckin' with me?" he said.

He popped open the trunk and put the head inside for a souvenir. Something to take back to the Fluevog tribal hall and put outside by the door. Head on a post, like the old days.

It was part of the spoils of war. It would be a lesson for all the tribe to see and understand. Don't mess with the chief.

He reached down and unhooked the two cable ends from under the frame of his car. There was no damage to the underside or to the plastic bumper at all. He was pleased. He quietly closed the trunk and got back into the car.

Bill Fletcher's headless statue was facedown in the grass at the side, another banana dictator toppled.

Carl put the Cadillac in Drive and swung left onto Beach Road, heading home. His work was done.

He popped in the Harold Melvin CD that was sitting on the passenger seat. He touched the volume way down low. The mellow Philly Sound came up through the speakers with a deep bass line. He was feeling good, his mission accomplished.

Carl Sunapee was a man in full, a true Indian chief.

Edwards Brothers Malloy
Thorofare, NJ USA
April 19, 2012